Typewriter Pub, an imprint of Blvnp Incorporated
A Nevada Corporation
1887 Whitney Mesa DR #2002
Henderson, NV 89014
www.typewriterpub.com/info@typewriterpub.com

ISBN: **978-1-64434-185-8**

DISCLAIMER
This book is a work of fiction. The characters, incidents, and dialogue are drawn from the author's imagination and are not to be construed as real. While references might be made to actual historical events or existing locations, the names, characters, places, and incidents are either products of the author's imagination or are used fictitiously, and any resemblance to actual persons living or dead, business establishments, events or locales is entirely coincidental.

ALONE

SAMANTHA S. WEBB

To my best friend Elizabeth,
thank you for always being the biggest support someone could ask for.
If it weren't for our middle school days when we first met in seventh grade,
I wouldn't know how my time in grade school would have turned out.
If you hadn't introduced me to Wattpad, I wouldn't have built
the courage to put my writing out there.

CHAPTER ONE
Arrival

CLAIRE JOHNSON

The descent of the plane startled me and my eyes flew open looking around in worry. I turned my head to the passenger sitting next to me finishing up a page of Great Expectations before putting her bookmark in and closing it. I looked down and immediately reached for my seatbelt to ensure it was still fastened. I turned the other way to look towards the window and caught a reflection of myself. My mid-length brunette hair reached just a few inches past my shoulders. My green eyes reflected brightly back at me. They were as green as the view of Coconino National Forest.

There was a sudden surge to go forward as the plane touched down. Being back on the ground gave me relief. Once the plane came to a sudden stop, there was an announcement of our landing and farewell. I unbuckled my seatbelt and remained seated as I waited for the person beside me to retrieve her bag from the top compartment. She sent me a wave before joining her parents in front of her and waited in the aisle to get off the plane. I sighed tiredly as I shut my journal. I reached for the compartment above to reach for my bag. I looked towards my seat once more before I moved along the exit.

As soon as I entered the airport, my eyes scanned over the familiar surroundings and began making my way towards where I'd find my cello, guitar, and luggage. I followed many of the passengers from the plane down an escalator where I found the baggage claim station. I waited patiently to spot my belongings and watched everyone grab their things.

After several moments, my guitar was the first to be spotted before the rest. I grabbed my things and put them down on the floor as I tried to restitute. I wore my backpack in front of me and had my cello on my back since it had straps. I have my guitar in one hand and the luggage handle in the other. I shudder as I realized I'd have to go back upstairs and go through the gates that separated the quietness and the crowd of people waiting to see their loved ones.

A few minutes later, I walked through the gates. I looked for my Aunt Clarisse through the crowd and tried my best to remain calm. Jack's resemblance of blond hair would be easily spotted. Her eyes were brown. I was never the type of person to be in a busy place, not including school of course. You'd always find me in the library doing work, at home locked in my room, or my favorite place in the world—the music rooms. Nothing could ever go wrong when you're in the music room making music.

I now stepped away from the gate and I spotted both my Aunt Clarisse and cousin Jack just a few yards away. I liked to call her Aunt Clarisse. As soon as I was spotted, my aunt smiled and waved to me. She began making her way over and Jack slowly trailed behind with his eyes averted to the ground. When they approached me, Aunt Clarisse gave me a hug and Jack stood there awkwardly as if he did not remember who I was. I decided to focus back on my hug. I've missed my Aunt Clarisse's hugs. Whenever she would give hugs, it would feel very reassuring.

"I've missed you, sweetie," she said, letting go and taking a good look at me. It had been quite a while since I last saw her.

"I've missed you too."

Jack then looked towards me. The frown on his face was present. I could tell his disdain towards me was still there. I don't quite understand why he was being so hard on me when he knew I was only trying to help him. Finding out that he was holding a grudge from that day made me feel uneasy.

"Jack, can you please help Claire with her luggage or maybe her instruments?" Aunt Clarisse said. I focused back on reality. She gave her son a look. He then offered to take my luggage and guitar with a mumble. I timidly thanked him as we began to make our way out. I quietly followed behind as my aunt and cousin led the way. My aunt took a phone call, which left me with my thoughts. Speaking with Jack did not seem to be an option as he stood tall and faced forward.

This was a difficult time for me, but I thought it was best to come here. It was best to leave everything behind for now and take my spring break. Maybe being here could help me to move on and hopefully start the process of healing. That's exactly what I want. I was ready to try and face reality again.

I would soon be hearing back from the schools I had applied to for college. My decision to graduate a year early from high school led me to going to college the following fall. Taking a gap year did not seem like something I wanted to do.

We walked outside and waited for a shuttle. My aunt stood by the pole. I assumed she was talking with her husband while Jack stood near her. I watched as he took his phone out. He scanned over something before he chuckled and started typing. I had a feeling I knew who he was texting.

Finnegan Owens. I wouldn't be surprised if that was who he was texting. The thought of him made my mind race and shut my eyes with fear. I thought of him as someone who intimidated me. I could never figure out why he hated everything about me. I'm not sure what I have done to him in the past, but I do know that he will try to turn everyone against me.

"Shuttle is here!" my Aunt Clarisse called out. I slowly made my way over to them. The three of us boarded the shuttle and sat next to one another. I carefully took my cello from my back and placed it in front of me. Jack shot me a glare and I apologized silently for making him hold some of my things. I turned to face the window as the shuttle started to move. I hoped to avoid Jack's glare since my aunt made Jack sit next to me.

The whole shuttle ride to the parking garage was silent. My aunt must have ended her phone call. Once we reached a certain stop, both Jack and my aunt stood. I slowly stood with them and followed them out.

Quietly, I thanked the driver and she nodded before shutting the door and driving away. I then turned and caught up with everyone as they put my things into the trunk. I opened the door and carefully put my cello in, then I went inside and took a seat. I looked towards Jack, who resumed looking at his phone.

"Are you hungry at all Claire?" My aunt asked as we began making our way out of the airport.

"Yes, but I can wait for dinner."

"We'll stop by somewhere and get you a snack. It may be a few hours until supper is ready."

"Thank you," I said softly. I could tell from Jack's stiffened shoulders that he was clearly annoyed to be here and wanted to be out of the vehicle as soon as possible. It hurt that he was acting this way towards me ever since that day. It confused me and I wish Jack would talk to me. We stopped contacting each other ever since they were caught.

Once we were on the freeway, it took only ten minutes for us to appear on the main road. Shops and restaurants were in every direction. We stopped at a fast food place and I was able to order a milkshake and a dish of fries. I always crave a good milkshake and some fries. I had a small argument with my aunt about who will be paying, but she ignored me handing cash over to her. She gave the cashier her credit card, saying that it wasn't a problem at all.

I thanked her as she drove up to the next window. While we waited for my things to arrive, I noticed everyone on their phones. Looking between the two of them, I felt out of place. They

4

had their iPhone. I . . . don't have that. Long story short, my parents believed in not having cell phones. Why? I don't know their reasoning. I never will.

After waiting for what seemed like five minutes, a worker slid the window open. The worker handed over to my aunt the bag of fries and a long cup with my strawberry milkshake in it. She thanked him then handed over the bag and milkshake to Jack. Jack let out a sigh and handed the bag over to me and I quietly thanked him. He didn't say anything as he continued on with his phone.

Carefully, I placed the milkshake into the car's drink holder and opened the bag of fries. The smell of fries immediately puffed out of the bag and I smiled slightly at the very delicious sight. Soon the car was smelling like my fries as I began to dig into my snack. I'd have a sip of my strawberry milkshake every tenth fry or so. My eyes closed in delight to be having this again.

"Enjoying your snack?" My aunt giggled, looking through the rearview mirror. I nodded and thanked her. The rest of the ride to the house was silent.

She was the very first to talk and to take off her seatbelt as we got to the house. I made sure my hands were not greasy as I did not want to make a mess on anything I touched. Jack stepped out and mumbled something I couldn't hear. He went to the back to open the trunk and took out my luggage and guitar. My aunt took out my backpack and offered to carry it for me. I stepped out of the car and carefully took out my cello. I decided to carry it by hand and closed the trunk before following them into the house.

Once I walked into the house, the familiar scent of cinnamon came rushing to my nose. I immediately knew that this was my second home. The familiar set up and the family portraits still hung on the walls alongside the stairs and the hall leading to the kitchen. I followed Jack up the stairs and could tell he was struggling slightly to get my luggage up the stairs. I followed him into what I realized was the familiar guest room I would sleep in when I would visit. I looked around and noticed that not much had changed. The small changes since I had last been here would be the desk that was by the window and the bedsheets were a mint green sort of color. My aunt had already dropped my bag off as she already left to prepare dinner for tonight. I carefully placed my cello onto the bed and looked towards my cousin, who still stood in the room.

I gave him a small smile hoping he'd acknowledge my presence here, but instead he walked out of the room without saying a word. I sighed in confusion that he was mad? I began to ponder whether Jack knew about my parents or not. If he knew, he wouldn't be acting the way he has been for the past several hours. I hope maybe he would soon realize that there was something wrong.

It felt like moments later, my aunt was calling us down to eat when I knew a few hours had passed. I had sat in the room completely out of it and thought about everything going on. I had to let everything sink in and so those few hours I was staring out the window. I now carefully stood and made my way out of the room bumping into Jack. He sent me a glare and I apologized as we headed down the stairs.

I could easily smell an amazing home cooked meal and my stomach once again grumbled. Jack and I arrived in the dining room and I saw that she had a main dish along with vegetables. Jack took a seat and I slowly took a seat across from him as my aunt came from the kitchen with a pitcher filled with iced tea.

The three of us settled down and began to get food in silence. I waited until both of them had gotten their food and I began reaching for the middle. I carefully made sure to not take too much so it wouldn't go to a waste.

"So, Claire," I heard my Aunt Clarisse start. I looked towards her and continued to eat slowly. "How has school been going?" I heard a sigh from Jack and he made a funny face like he knew what I was going to say. It made me uncomfortable.

"It's going great," my soft voice answered. "I . . . actually have all my credits for school and decided that I'm going to

6

graduate this year." I liked the feeling of my biggest accomplishment. Let's hope the colleges I had applied to would think the same way. A surprised look stretched across her face and she smiled so big that for a moment I thought she would explode.

"That's wonderful! That means you and Jack are graduating this year! Oh! I have to plan your graduation party with Jacks!" she beamed excitedly. "What schools have you applied to?"

Before I could say anything, Jack mumbled something and my aunt caught what he was saying so she nudged him. She frowned at him.

"Jack!" she raised her voice at him.

"Sorry," he mumbled.

"Don't apologize to me, apologize to Claire."

I looked away from my aunt. I could see that Jack did not look apologetic even the slightest bit. I then looked down at my plate. Aunt Clarisse took the hint and tried to change the subject after a few minutes of eating in silence.

"So, Claire, have you heard of the group Krioon?" I shook my head, unfamiliar with the group. What did they do? I was never the person on the internet much unless it had to do with my school work. I've never really given myself time to surf the internet. My aunt explained how Jack and a bunch of other viners and YouTubers were a part of it. Then she said, "You will be going with Jack to the next one in two days."

"What?" Jack asked, getting up annoyed.

CHAPTER TWO
Jack and Finnegan

CLAIRE JOHNSON

I woke up the next morning with the thoughts of what happened last night. Everything started to become clear and I realized I wouldn't be spending the break here. I would be spending it in Florida. My Aunt Clarisse thought it would be great for me to go with Jack and to also, hopefully, enjoy myself.

The idea of going to Florida seemed very exciting to me but at the same time I'm worried how the trip would go. I would be going with Jack and his friends. Maybe I could go to the Disney and Universal parks for a few days while I am down there. I had a feeling Jack would push me away and shoo me to go somewhere.

Last night after I had finished eating my food, I quietly left the dining room unnoticed as the two argued. Jack was clearly not happy about having to take me along with him for Kricon. He was trying to change his mother's mind. I don't think he had won the argument because last night I was not given any update. I also heard Jack's bedroom slammed shut right after the argument died down.

For that time being, I stayed in my room in silence. I put my things on the corner of the room and sat on the bed the whole time. Eventually, I retreated from my room and went downstairs to find my aunt putting away everything. I decided to help her of course. When she noticed I was down here, she smiled faintly. I took all of the dirty dishes as she brought everything into the kitchen and put leftovers away. We worked together and in the matter of ten minutes, we were finished.

My aunt thanked me for helping her and she apologized for Jack's outburst. She then told me that we'd be going to AT&T at the mall tomorrow afternoon, because she wanted to get me an actual phone before I left with Jack for the week. She fussed slightly at my parents for not allowing me to have a cell phone before she realized it was a touchy subject.

That night I went to bed in hopes that I could sleep normally, but instead the nightmare came back to haunt me again. That evening and during the early morning, I had been waking up every so often trying to get the image of my nightmare out of my head. Now, I lay on the soft bed. I have been thinking for a little over an hour. I tend to lose my mind with my thoughts for the past few months. Everything has been difficult and quite traumatizing.

My stomach grumbled and I sighed knowing I'd have to get up and face everything today. Today was another day I had to accept the fact that I can't go back to normal. I wouldn't be waking up to my mother preparing breakfast or my father reading the newspaper. I wouldn't be babysitting or be going to school. I wouldn't be in the familiar suburban town of upstate New York. Nothing would be the same.

I blinked a few times before my sight adjusted to the brightness of the room. I turned my head slightly and saw the curtains were pulled back so the sun came right in. After another minute of pondering, I sat up and looked around the room. I pulled the covers back and shivered to the cold contact of the air to my legs. My feet eventually touched the floor. Food was definitely on my mind now.

I had this strange craving for fries and a good burger this very moment. My stomach grumbled at the thought of it. I should probably eat what was in the house first. Maybe I could get myself

9

some fries and a good burger later. Where exactly would I find a good burger? I'd have to wait until Aunt Clarisse told me. For now, I'm going to figure out what was left from last night. The food was delicious.

In silence, I walked out my bedroom. I stood there for a moment. I immediately headed down the stairs to the kitchen. The lights were off and it felt a bit chilly in here. I walked over to a cabinet to find nothing there. I remembered my aunt had said just last night that she had to go grocery shopping. I'd assume Jack and his friends consumed a lot of food when they were here. I looked around and realized she was right.

I looked in the direction of the fridge and noticed a pale blue piece of paper hanging there. I knew from when I used to visit that if she had gone out, she'd leave a note hanging on the fridge. I walked over to the fridge to take it and quickly checked the fridge to find it quite empty. I guess there weren't any leftovers. I shut the fridge and leaned against the counter as I opened the small note.

> *Hey Claire and Jack,*
> *I had to leave for work early and I was supposed to go grocery shopping, but I did not get the chance. Sorry guys! Hey Claire, if you get to this note first, do not starve yourself. Have Jack take you out to eat. If you guys can, can you guys do the food shopping? Oh and Claire, have Jack drop you off at the AT&T store down at the mall so we can get you your new phone! Meet you there at 2:30*
> *~Love Mom / Aunt Clarisse.*

I placed the note on the counter and shut my eyes for a split-second thinking of the many scenarios going through my mind. I knew this wasn't going to be good for me. I wish she had taken yesterday's reaction as a clue that this wouldn't be the best of ideas. Aunt Clarisse doesn't understand that Jack strongly disliked me. He would not take me anywhere.

Jack was a person you could instantly fall in love with. He loves everyone and many liked him. I may not understand why he was being the way he is now towards me, but I knew when no one is around, he won't hesitate to tear me down and speak his mind. My cousin wasn't the type of person to keep quiet and keep things in. We used to be close my freshman year and before that, but things had changed after that one evening.

I shouldn't starve myself though and I knew Aunt Clarisse wouldn't be home before going to the store. It wouldn't hurt to ask him. He would probably be hungry also. I began to make my way up the stairs and with each step I was getting towards Jack's room, I grew anxious. When I stopped at the door, I heard laughter. Someone else was in there with Jack. I knocked on the door and slowly the laughing died down. I waited for Jack for a moment. The door opened and I saw my cousin glaring already. I peeked to the side to see Finnegan sitting on a beanbag on the floor trying to figure out who was at the door.

"Eww Johnson, What do you want?" Finnegan asked, frowning once he caught sight of me. I then noticed they had the leftovers from last night's dinner sitting on the table. Just about all of it was gone.

"Go away Claire," my cousin groaned, annoyed to see me still standing in front of him. He then looked down to his phone.

"Your mom said to ask if you could take me out to eat. There wasn't anything in—"

"No, I'm not taking you." He frowned, looking up at me again. He looked at me as if I were crazy. I felt betrayal as he kept his act up in front of Finnegan. I assumed the two of them were sitting on the beanbags at the end of the bed, because they had a game going on and they were having breakfast. I felt so left out and they were eating the last of the food. How could he say something like that when I implied to him that I was hungry? Who left their guest, who was a relative, hungry? Did he really not care?

11

This has been the first time in months since I've really talked to anyone around my age. I've shut everyone out of my world for the past few months. I'd thought Jack could at least be caring after everything I've faced. It was so clear he had no idea about my parents or maybe he was a cold hearted person in the first place. I'm going with the first idea.

"Why do you hate me so much?" I blurted out. Finnegan chuckled and my cousin rolled his eyes as he pushed me out of the room and slammed his bedroom door in my face. I faced the shut door for a moment as everything sank in.

Many emotions ran through me at once as I felt a small tug to my heart. I felt the rejection in my chest as I slowly turned around and felt my eyes brimming with tears. I sighed to myself. I moved away from the door and slowly made my way over to my temporary room. It was quite a cool spring morning here in April.

It wasn't exactly a go out and wear only your shorts and T-shirt kind of weather. If I were back in New York right now, there would still be snow on the ground and I'd be wearing my boots, long turtleneck along with my heavy coat and jeans with a scarf to keep me warm. My immune system wasn't the strongest.

Technically if I were back home, I'd probably be in school. It would be towards the end of the third period. I was taking college courses this year, which meant I would be taking AP exams when I get back. I had learned that I no longer had to be there in order for me to take the exam. As long as I prepared for everything on my own, I'd be okay. I had decided last year that I wanted to graduate a year early and so technically I didn't have to attend school at the moment. I was waiting to take my exams in May and for graduation day in June. I mentally shook my head, not wanting to think about that now.

The only place I remember knowing how to get to on my own would be the mall. It has been years since I have taken the bus. Would Jack really make me travel on my own when I don't quite know my way around? I never felt comfortable traveling on my own. I knew I couldn't wait here and starve myself. If Jack wasn't going to do anything, then I'd have to do it on my own.

The thought of contacting Cooper sounded like a good idea. Maybe I could call Cooper Lee to take me to the mall? Realization hit me again. He has always been the nicer one of the three of them after the incident, but I had no way of contacting him. We were never that close, but we always exchanged smiles and a few words whenever Jack and Finnegan weren't around.

Smiling . . . It seemed so long ago since everything seemed normal. I used to smile all the time and people told me I had the best smile for the yearbook. Some told me that I would be voted the best smile. The last time I could remember that I really smiled would be that day before I found out about the news. It was that day I was going to have my full performance. Everything about that time brought shock and pain to me that it had affected my performance since. Since that day, I never found a reason to smile again.

Returning back to reality, I mentally sighed for my antisocial mess. This was something that would happen whenever I kept to myself. My stomach grumbled once again and I quickly changed into a pair of jeans and a sweatshirt. I slid on my flats and looked around the room for my wallet before making my way out. I guess I could take a bus up to the mall. I hope nothing has changed dramatically over the years.

The clock in the living room read ten minutes past ten. I had plenty of time to get to the mall and eat. Maybe once I've found something to eat, I could go to the music store then after, I could meet my Aunt Clarisse at the phone store there. The thought of music made my heart swell as it was the one and only thing I felt that I could still connect to. It was the only thing that was keeping me sane at the moment and the only reason I was ready to face reality again. Making music and playing pieces I love has made an impact to my life. Without it, I wouldn't be so sure now if I would be ready to come back to earth and live out the rest of my life. My cello and music in general have been my rock.

Maybe I could get a few new pieces and learn them. I haven't done that since before my music auditions. It may help me get back into things. I opened the front door of the house and felt the rush of cool air hit my exposed skin. I stepped out to scan the streets. I closed the door behind me and took a deep breath as I began walking in the direction of the bus stop.

There weren't too many times where Jack and I had to catch the bus. When we did, it was only because Aunt Clarisse could not take us or she would be at work and we'd leave the house. I hoped I wouldn't have to wait for the bus too long. I was soon approaching the bus stop at the end of the street and saw it completely empty. Cars drove by and it was quiet out here. I stood at the stop now shivering slightly. I should have put on an extra layer. I should have taken Jack's keys. It would have been a lot better than waiting out here. A part of me also knew that he wouldn't give up his keys. I'm pretty sure he wouldn't let me borrow his car either. I groaned slightly as I looked down the road and to my luck, I saw the bus in view.

CHAPTER THREE
Friends

CLAIRE JOHNSON

"Momma! Can we go to the music shop when we get there?" A boy asked his mother. I awed at the little boy who looked no more than six years old. He sat next to his mother and she looked down at him. He seemed very excited. I wonder why he'd like to go there.

"Of course, we can. Why are we visiting the shop today son?" His mother smiled at him. The boy noticed me staring and I waved awkwardly towards him. He waved back to me.

"I want to get a new piece to play for Dad's birthday!" the boy said.

I flinched my eyes as I felt the sting when he mentioned "dad." I still wish my dad was still here. It has been almost four months now since I lost him and my mother was still not the same. The thought of them pained me and this was the reason I had pushed everything away. I was now trying to fight the pain and push past it all. I also wanted to continue the best I could. It was something I have been trying to cope with.

"Do you know any good cello pieces I could try?" I opened my eyes to see the blond haired boy looking at me with wonder in his big brown eyes. The boy played the cello? This has made my day. His mother was confused as to why he was asking me and apologized for her son.

"Parker, I don't think she knows," his mother told him gently.

"It's alright ma'am," I answered softly and looked towards the boy who I was now very fascinated into, knowing he was a cellist himself. "I actually play the cello myself."

His eyes widened and excitedly looked between me and his mom. "Really? That's so cool! Are you a professional musician?"

I smiled weakly and shook my head. "No, but I hope to be someday. I'm hoping to go to school for music next year." He did not have to know I also applied to the school for sciences.

"That's amazing," Parker beamed with fascination. "So that means you had those big scary auditions? What are they like?"

"Yes, I did have a few auditions to prepare for. I had several of them. They can feel scary, but it's one of the best feelings in the world. You get to play in front of the music department and everything feels very professional. The piece I prepared to play for all of them was something I started preparing for several months. In fact, I think it took me a few weeks to decide what piece I wanted to play at first."

Thinking back to the process brought back many evenings rehearsing and putting everything together. "I practiced a lot and in the end, I thought it was worth it."

"That's amazing! Did you apply to Juilliard?" he beamed. I smiled faintly at his cuteness. I noticed the bus would soon be approaching the mall to let us off. How quickly a trip can be when you're engaged in a conversation.

"I did. Do you have any ideas what you'd like to play for your dad?"

"I want to play something Star Wars for him. My dad is a huge fan." I nodded as we began making conversation even as we were getting off the bus and making our way into the mall. I have learned that he was a level five cellist and it amazed me when his

16

mother told me that he took private lessons. I remembered just several months ago when I was with my private teacher preparing my pieces to play for my music auditions for the schools I applied to. There were some schools I personally went to audition and others I just sent a video audition. For others . . . I never had the chance.

As soon as we stepped into the mall, I realized how cold my face and my fingers were. Instantly, my fingers began to warm up again. Parker now realized that we were probably going different directions and he hoped to see me again. I wished him the best of luck preparing his music for his dad and his future with music. He waved goodbye to me as he took his mother's hand and started walking in the opposite direction I was going. I waved to him. I knew that I was going in the opposite direction unless the food court was moved to a different location. I began walking and looked around for directions for the food court where I hoped there would be a bathroom. The food court was located upstairs and so I took the escalator up. It was midway up that I could instantly smell food.

The sight of the different options for food made my stomach grumble. I rushed towards the other end where I spotted the sign for the restrooms. I went down the halls and into the women's room. Once I was finished, I washed my hands and dried them before making my way out. I went for the water fountain since my throat was a little dry and as soon as I turned, I felt a hard impact to my side from the men's bathroom door hitting me. I lost my balance; sending me to the floor. I fell onto my bottom. I groaned slightly from the impact.

Who created the idea to have the fountain right near the men's room? I'm sure there have been incidents like this. I will be reporting this later. Definitely after I get something to eat. Also, who decided to push the door open with so much force? The doors weren't so heavy.

"Oh sh*t, I'm so sorry," a male voice apologized. I looked up and took a double take to see a really cute guy holding his hand out to me. I sat on the floor and looked up at his gorgeous blue eyes before slowly taking his hand. His short hair was a dark brown color and his cheeks were slightly flushed. He definitely did not seem like any of the guys back in Upstate New York. He helped me up and made sure I was steady. "Are you okay?" he asked, snapping me out of my daze. Wow, he's really cute. I think I could feel my cheeks beginning to heat up. I've never blushed in front of a guy before. I don't think I have before.

"Y—yeah," I said and he chuckled. I could tell, with his kind eyes, that he was a nice person.

"I'm guessing you want a picture?"

"A picture? Isn't that strange for you?" I looked at him in confusion. Why would he ask a question like that? He looked towards me a little confused also. As he was beginning to say something, I heard girls gasping and I turned to see a group of at least twenty girls staring at us with wide eyes. What was going on?

"It's Andy Miller!" One of the girls screamed with excitement. I assumed I was talking to Andy, because of the screams and the girls were staring directly at him with excitement. He immediately squeezed my hand and he started to run in the other direction pulling me along with him. I ran with him really confused and afraid at the same time. Why were those girls screaming for him? He led me outside and towards the parking lot. I had to snap sense into me before he went any further.

"Wait," I said, pulling back. "I don't know you. You can't expect me to run away with you."

"I can see that," he said, glancing back. He looked slightly frantic. "I promise I'll explain everything. Umm, I want to make it up to you for hitting you with the door," he said. I laughed slightly at his statement.

"You can take me somewhere to eat." I found myself trusting him more than I thought. "I haven't eaten yet today." Andy nodded in agreement.

"Okay. We'll go somewhere. Right now though, we need to get out of here." He glanced back at the mall. I agreed with him and followed him into the parking lot until we approached a vehicle. I noticed two others in there. He opened the door for me and I looked towards him unsurely. "I promise we are all nice guys, who don't bite," Andy chuckled.

"O—okay . . ." I slowly got in and Andy quickly followed into the car. The two guys turned around and noticed me. They both smiled once they noticed I wasn't going to say or do anything. Andy had great looking friends. The guy in the driver's seat had light brown hair that shines in the sunlight with brown chocolate eyes. His skin matched close to my usual tanned skin, but had lost over time. The guy in the passenger seat had a darker hair color with brown eyes. So, Andy was the only one with the pretty blue eyes.

"Awe, Andy found a girl while going to the bathroom?" The guy in the driver's seat asked. I turned towards Andy hoping he would answer. I noticed his cheeks were slightly colored. I've never really talked to many males around my age unless it was for a class project where I would be assigned a partner. That person would be some guy or Jack's friends. In this case, Finnegan has never been kind to me and Cooper has only exchanged a few words.

"How did you guys do it?" the other guy in the passenger asked with interest. He had an eyebrow raised at Andy. What were these guy's talking about and what does he mean how did we do it? I frowned slightly in confusion.

"Ken!" Andy's cheeks turned a slightly darker shade of pink.

"What? I'm surprised she's not all over you yet." My face now started to heat up. I thought this was really weird.

19

Do boys tease each other and make each other uncomfortable?

"Actually, I don't think she knows who we are."

"That is new," the guy from the driver's seat said. "Do you have Vine?" I shook my head in confusion. It must be the app that my aunt mentioned to me last night. I also remember my aunt mentioning that Jack is a viner.

"I don't have a smartphone." I look down sort of feeling embarrassed. It shouldn't matter what they thought, but I felt very flushed being in a car full of cute guys.

"Oh?" Andy said in a questioning tone.

"Yeah." The thought of my parents still had an effect on me and I wasn't comfortable about talking about them with people I've just met. It pained me to think about them. I started to tear up slightly, realizing that I miss them so much. I hope to check in with her when I get back to the house. It has been a while since I've last visited her.

"Awe, don't cry," the guy from the passenger seat said with a reassuring tone. He frowned slightly to himself that he had already made me upset.

"Can I please get something to eat?"

"Oh, shoot yeah." Andy half smiled apologetically. "Nate, can we go to a restaurant to eat? I told . . ." He looks towards me realizing that he did not know my name.

"Claire," I said softly.

"That's a pretty name." Andy smiled. "Claire hasn't eaten yet."

"Yeah, no problem. We were going out to eat anyway," Nate said as he backed out of the parking spot. I slowly put my seatbelt on. "Is there a preference of where you'd like to eat?"

"A place where there are good burgers and fries," I said. Nate nods and he started to drive off.

I now leaned my head against the window feeling slightly uncomfortable as I let the thought of me getting into the vehicle. I should have thought this through. Technically I have gotten into a car with complete strangers that I do not know. Andy must have noticed my uneasiness, because he started talking to me as Nate and the other guy Ken started their own conversation about something I wasn't quite sure what they were talking about.

"I'm sorry you had to witness the encounter back there at the mall," Andy apologized. I turned to Andy and he looked towards me. "Are you alright? I want to make sure you're not hurt or anything."

"I'm alright. Um . . . thank you for not leaving me there. Those girls seemed they were going to attack you and never let you go." Andy chuckled and shrugged slightly.

"Well . . . they saw me with you and I was holding your hand. I wasn't going to leave you and have you questioned."

"If . . . they're your fans, why didn't you let them take a picture with you?"

"I've . . . already taken a picture with them earlier and they were sort of stalking me all day. I was only supposed to use the restroom before coming back to the car so the three of us could head over to a friend's house." I nod and began to relax slightly with our conversation.

"So, you have stalker fans who won't leave you alone?" I laughed lightly and he pretended to act offended.

"Hey, everyone needs their space sometimes. I at least didn't leave you to fend for yourself."

"What would they do to me?"

"Well for starters, they'd ask who you are and they'd start interrogating you. I think everyone knows who my friends and family members are. We don't look in any way related. My question is how calm you are right now. Are you sure you're alright? Do you need ice or anything else to ease your fall?"

"I'm alright Andy, really. I can take a fall once in a while."

"You seem pretty cool Claire. I hope maybe we can be friends after today." I looked towards Andy once again to see he actually meant it.

"You've just met me."

"I know," he smiled. "And a girl who isn't going to attack me at first sight is definitely someone I'd like to get to know. Especially since I think you are really pretty and seem like someone who has a great personality."

"You seem like a great guy Andy. Thank you for not leaving me back there alone." He nodded and he then joined in with his friend's conversation. I leaned my head again on the window and looked towards the blue sky. I smiled slightly for the first time knowing that I may have just made a new friend who so happened to also be a viner. I wonder if they knew of my cousin. I'll ask the three of them later once we get to the restaurant.

I looked at the dashboard to read it was twelve thirty in the afternoon, which meant I still had time to eat with them before hopefully going back to the mall. I hope it was alright that they could drop me back off. I wouldn't know how to get back from here unless I called a cab. We soon turned into a restaurant that seemed pretty spacious inside. Nate went to the very front to drop us off.

Andy and I got out of the car. Andy told the guys that he would get us all a table. Nate agreed and drove off to park. Andy led me to the door of the restaurant and held it open for me. One thing I've learned about him so far would be his very good manners. I knew you couldn't find a guy like that back in New York where I went to school. I thanked him as we both went inside.

CHAPTER FOUR
Cousin

CLAIRE JOHNSON

Andy and I were brought to the second level dining area where we had a view of the other buildings. We decided we would sit next to each other while Nate and Ken would sit across. Andy slid into the booth and I followed. A server introduced herself and I noticed she seemed a little frantic to see Andy. She took our drink orders and asked if she could take a picture with Andy. He half smiled towards me and I slid out so he could get out. The girl asked me to take the picture of them. At first, I wasn't sure how to take the picture on the iPhone. I felt afraid that I'd drop the phone. I took several pictures, making sure they all turned out good. The girl thanked me and looked towards me.

"I've never seen you around the guys before," she said curiously. She looked between Andy and I. Her questioning look had me slightly worried after encountering the numerous screaming girls at the mall. I hope we would be able to eat here. "Are you two . . ."

"No," Andy and I said at the same time. Andy's eyes were slightly wide and I felt my cheeks heating up once again. I don't think I've ever blushed so much before. It wasn't until today I've really paid attention to my surroundings again.

"She is a friend of mine," Andy smiled and I nod shyly. As the waiter looked towards me, I lowered my eyes to the table feeling shy. I never was much of a person to socialize.

"Can I take a picture with you?" I looked towards the waiter again and saw she was looking at me with a friendly smile. Nothing in her expression was telling me that she had any bad intentions and I looked towards Andy slightly and he chuckled looking towards me. I then turn back to her, who waited for a response. I pointed to myself questionably.

"You want a picture with me?" I asked softly. I was very confused to why she would want one with me. She doesn't know that I'm Jack's cousin, but I don't think that would matter. She nods and I agreed shyly as I walked over to her. Andy took the servers phone and smiled as he looked onto the screen. The server and I wrap arms around each other posing for the camera. I smile towards the camera the best I could without this feeling strange.

"Thank you so much! I'll be back with your drinks in a moment." She walked away and the both of us slid back into the booth again.

"She seemed nice."

"I think she likes you."

"Does this usually happen when you go out?"

"Yes. Don't worry. Nate, Ken, and I will make sure you're safe and you get to where you need to after this."

"Thank you. I . . . uh have to meet my aunt back at the mall around two thirty," I hesitantly said.

Andy nodded. "Yeah, no problem. We can drop you off then."

Soon we spot Nate and Ken making their way over and they both slide into the booth sitting in front of us.

Once the server came back with the two drinks, the server freaked out all over again. I learned that Nate was her favorite. I could tell by her expression and excitement. They took a few pictures then Nate spoke with her for a little while until she promised them that she would get them their drinks. I picked up the menu and instantly knew exactly what I would be getting. I put the menu down and looked at the guys who were on their phones. I took a glance at Andy and saw he was deciding on what to order. I poked him and his blue eyes found my green ones.

"Do you know what you're getting?" he asked. I nodded, which made him smile and close the menu. "Well, I'm glad you do and if you didn't know, I will be paying for you."

"You don't have to." I frowned slightly. He has been so kind to me. I knew it wasn't necessary for him to. Andy told me that it wasn't a problem and that it was his fault I had to wait even longer to eat. He did have a point there. Eventually I gave up on the idea of paying for my own meal. If I encounter with Andy again, I promise to return the small gesture.

Andy began asking me questions about school and I told him about my plans for graduating a year early. I told him about my passion for music and the many months of practicing for my auditions. I talked about wanting to do a double major in chemistry and music so I'd have a backup plan if pharmacy school didn't fit me. He seemed to be very fascinated in my options for college and the thought I had two completely different things I wanted to do. Then I asked him if he had any siblings. I wanted to keep our small talk going.

He started talking about his family with so much love and pride that I couldn't help but smile. He seemed to really love his family and it was really cool to know he cared very greatly of them. He told me a few stories with each of them and I thought it was amazing that he has spent so much time with his family. The server came back with Nate and Ken's drink and took our orders. After she took our orders, Nate and Ken turned their full attention towards me. It did not seem to bother me. I'm usually someone who didn't like the attention. "I'm Kenji by the way," the other guy smiled introducing himself, "You can call me Ken."

"I'm Nathaniel," Nate waved towards me. "You can just call me Nate." Then Andy turned towards me. He gave me a sheepish smile. I wasn't sure what it was about these guys, but I felt very trusting towards them. It seemed natural to be here.

"I'm Andy Miller, the one who hit you with the door." Nate, Ken and I laughed along with Andy. It was nice to know these guys knew how to make me laugh. It felt great to feel positive. "You never fully introduced yourself to Nate and Ken." Both Ken and Nate sent me a smile and continued to focus their attention on me. I certainty never had the attention I was getting currently. Back at home I was invisible.

"I'm Claire," I finally introduced. They have been nothing but kind to me. I hope to meet more people like them in the future. I'm not uncomfortable or worried about something happening to me. I think these three are amazing people who I was lucky to have met.

"It's nice to meet you," the three of them told me in unison.

"Nice to meet you guys too. So . . ." I tried to think of the name of the app my aunt described to me yesterday. *What was it called? It reminded me of wine for some odd reason. Oh! Vine. That's what the name of the app was.* "Are you guys famous on that app called Vine that you briefly mentioned earlier?" I never had the chance to understand what the app was about, but I'm sure I will soon.

"Yeah," Ken smiled and he pulled out his phone and unlocked it with his passcode before he handed his phone to me. I looked onto the screen to see a video replaying after about six seconds. I started scrolling through the videos trying to figure out what the app is.

I clearly have never seen it before. In the meantime, our food was served to us not too long after our orders were taken and we began eating. Most of them are really cute or I thought they were really funny. I think I've spotted my cousin in one of them also. There's more than the three of them. After watching a good amount of the vines, I hand Ken back his phone. It was definitely entertainment. This seemed nice. "So, are you guys in that Kricon group thing, too?"

Maybe I may be seeing them after all after this brunch session.

"Yes, indeed we are. We love it." Andy smiled. Andy immediately handed his phone over to me and I took it trying to figure what he wanted to show me. I noticed it was a group picture with a banner behind them that said Kricon. I could easily spot Andy, Nate, and Ken. It took me a moment to scan everyone's faces and I noticed Finnegan and my cousin in the group photo. Everyone else I was not familiar with. I then hand Andy his phone. I noticed it was an iPhone. "Then you guys must know my cousin." The three of them froze and look towards me in confusion. Ken's mouth parted slightly. Nate looked very intrigued and interested. Then there was Andy whose eyes were so blue and they were very wide as if he wanted to know. They seem like people who would hang with my cousin. There's a good possibility. "Really? Who's your cousin?" Nate asked curiously.

"Jack Johnson." I watched as their eyes widened at once and they took a closer look at me. Ken leaned forward slightly to take a look at me and I mentally laughed to myself thinking he was pretty funny. Nate nodded slightly and Ken blinked several times before they all verbally reacted. "Wait, you're Jack Johnson's cousin?" they all beamed at once. The three of them looked really surprised. I wouldn't have thought it would have been a great surprise. There was quite a bit of resemblance between Jack and I. If my hair was dyed blonde, you would think we were twins. Our facial structure and our eyes matched completely. When I was younger I'd always ask if Jack was my twin brother. "He has never mentioned you before or that you were here," Ken said. I shouldn't be surprised that I was never mentioned and I had a feeling Jack wasn't going to announce my presence when we were all together. It's pretty clear Jack doesn't stand the sight of me at the moment.

27

"We're not really that close," I answered slowly. "I arrived last night."

"Well, welcome to Omaha," Nate smiled. "Where are you visiting from then?"

"New York. Upstate New York," I pointed out quickly with a shy smile. Many always assumed I am from the city whenever I don't mention the upstate part.

"Huh, interesting. Well, then you're not on spring break then? Last time I remembered, New York has theirs usually in the middle of April."

"I technically don't have to go to school," I smile faintly. I found myself finding it amusing and also nice that they are able get to know a bit about me.

"For real?" Ken asked. "Are you like a genius or something? If you're a genius, can you help me with a physics assignment?" Nate burst into laughter. "What? I really need help. If you haven't taken or currently taking it, of course."

"I can help if you really need it," I smiled faintly. In a way I had no problem of wanting to help Jack's friends. "I'm currently enrolled into AP physics. It should definitely be fresh in my mind."

"Bruh, so you are really smart."

"Smarter than your cousin," Nate raised an eyebrow and I shrugged shyly. I'd say we're the same. The only difference would be the year and a half age difference.

"Speaking of Jack," Andy started. "We're actually here to surprise your cousin and Fin. Are they home?"

"Last time I checked they were," I faintly smiled. "They . . . uh dropped me off at the mall earlier." Nate frowned slightly. Nate seemed like the type of person who can be protective. Like a brother.

"So, they left you? They shouldn't have left you alone. What if you wanted to go back home and you didn't have a way of contacting them?" I looked down at my half eaten food. Speaking of Jack and Finnegan made me feel uneasy about myself as I knew they had no desire of giving any care towards me.

It was my freshman year of high school when everything had gone downhill between my cousin and I. Ever since that day, I had to face being pushed away and was always left out when it came to family gatherings in New York. I always found it difficult especially when Finnegan came around. It was as if him being there made my cousin give me a more difficult time.

At times I felt very intimidated by him. It has been the longest time that I can remember that he used every chance he could to humiliate me and to make me miserable. My cousin used to always stop him and protect me from him, but now it was the other way around and I always had to fend for myself when I am around them. Thinking of them only brought back negative thoughts and I shook my head trying to forget about them for right now.

I am here in Nebraska now to let myself open up again and hopefully find peace in moving on from the tragic incident. My goal is to try and put myself out there a little more and do what I wasn't able to do before. I did not want to limit myself. I wanted to embrace myself by finding my happiness again. It has been a long time. I hoped being around Finnegan and my cousin wouldn't cause anything to change my mind about coming here.

"I'm supposed to meet my Aunt Clarisse at the mall at two thirty." The guys looked down to check the time. Each of them pushed a button on their phone and the screen illuminated all at once.

"Which is . . . in thirty minutes. We can take you back.

In fact, we can surprise mama Johnson." Andy and Ken agreed as they finished up the rest of their food. I still had quite a bit of fries left, but my burger was completely gone. After eating a few more fries, I officially thought I was full to the point that I was a comfortable full. I was very content with the food here and I'd be okay to wait until dinner time to eat again.

Talking with them has made me forget about my constant worries and current problems. I am satisfied that I wasn't back in New York sitting at home in my room trying to face the tragedy of what happened a few months ago. I was now getting fresh air and interacting with others. I began to feel relaxed around them and I knew I could trust them slightly since they knew Jack and my aunt. It was a coincidence to be running into them.

Once everyone was finished with their food, it was the guys who paid for the meal and Andy kept his word for paying for me. The three of them gave the waiter their credit cards and waited for her to bring back their cards and signing before we all stood to prepare to leave. Standing next to all of them suddenly made me feel short. I thanked them for the wonderful brunch as we headed out. Nate held the door open for me as we exit the restaurant. I followed the boys. It was now I think about twenty minutes until I had to meet my aunt at the store. I walked between Nate and Andy as we walked towards their car. Ken ended up driving us and I sat with Andy in the back once again.

CHAPTER FIVE
Surprise

CLAIRE JOHNSON

You'd think when you've met a group of boys for the first time, they would be full of energy and quite intimidating to the point that you weren't sure if you should interact with them. I would have thought on the way back to mall, I would be sitting in the car listening as the guys talked and laughed about things I had no idea would be going on. Surprisingly, that was not the case. Instead, Nate, Andy, and Ken included me in their conversation. Not once did I feel out of place. It was like we were all really good friends.

We were now arriving at the mall and Ken was trying to park near one of the side entrances. While Ken started to back into a parking spot, I checked the time on the dashboard to see I still had about fifteen minutes until I had to be at the store my Aunt Clarisse told me to meet her in. I think I may head over to the music store.

"Thank you, guys, for brunch," I said sheepishly as I looked between the three of them. Ken and Nate turned around to face me. Everyone seemed to be taking their seat belts off.

"It's an honor to be meeting you Claire." Nate smiled and I could feel my cheeks warming up slightly. They sure knew how to make people feel great.

31

"To be meeting you as Jack's cousin, it has been the highlight of my day. Thanks for letting Andy hit you with a door." I playfully glared at him before I began to laugh for the second time, because I couldn't believe Ken would actually say that. Ken's smile widened before he laughed along with me.

"I didn't plan it." I smiled faintly. "I really had a great time with you guys."

"Well of course. The day isn't over and we're coming with you to see mama Johnson." Andy said from beside me. I nodded as the four of us got out of the car. I waited until we were all ready to make our way to the entrance. "We're having a lot of fun with you," Andy added.

"With me?" I asked questionably. "You three are the ones who makes everything seem interesting."

"Well you're the interesting one. In fact, how is it that we've all already bonded so well with you? Many people who don't know us would find us very strange and make sure to ignore us. You're nothing like that."

"You didn't exactly give me choice," I joked. Andy chuckled as he opened the door for me. I thanked him. I looked around trying to figure out which direction the music store was.

"Since we have a bit of time to spare before mama Johnson," Ken said while looking at the time on his watch, "what do you want to do?"

"I was wondering if you guys knew where the music store is? I've been wanting to go there since this morning," I said. The three of them turned to each other for a moment before turning back to me. Each of them had a curious look. Andy of course knew.

"Music?" Nate started.

"Does it run in the family? I had no idea you were into music," Ken said slowly. They began leading me to, which I assumed, where the music store would be. It felt like every time I

32

revealed something new about myself, they were very intrigued to learn more.

"Music has made a huge impact on my life," I said softly. I looked ahead and gasped at the size of the music store. The guys looked at where I was looking to and I started making my way over to the music store once it was in my sight. It looked like a huge one. I am a nerd for music and I wasn't going to lie. As I entered the store, I looked around in excitement. My feet started moving as I looked around and began looking for the section with music pieces for the cello. I had the excitement of wanting to pick up everything. I heard chuckling from behind, but I choose to ignore it as I realized there was a huge section of cello music pieces. My eyes widened as I scanned the piece selection.

"Jacob and Shane are going to love her," I heard Nate somewhere behind me. I spot the piece and immediately picked it up. I opened past the cover and started looking at the piece as I played it in my head. I felt a presence come behind me and I turned around slowly and looked up to see Andy looking at me with amusement. I noticed Nate and Ken walking around. Andy walked closer and I showed him the piece in my hand. He looked down then looked back up at me with a smile. "I'm glad to see you very invested into music."

"Do you play any instruments?" I asked cheerfully. He shook his head then looked at the piece.

"The only thing I understand is the title and the composer. That's about it," Andy shrugged.

"It's alright." I looked down at the piece and saw it was exactly what I was looking for. "I'm going to get this." Andy nodded and he told me that he'd get Nate and Ken. I started to make my way towards the front of the store where I saw a familiar surprising face. He looked up and his eyes widened at first with surprise before he gave me a small smile. His light brown eyes continued to stare as I approached him, he put his phone into his pocket. I noticed he recently had a haircut. It suits him.

33

"Claire . . ." he said breathlessly. "I . . . didn't know you'd be here."

"Hey Cooper," I smiled faintly and hand him the piece in my hand. Cooper to me was a reminder of a young Tyler Posey from the show Teen Wolf. I remember watching a bit of the show last summer.

"How have you been? How has things been?" he asked, concerned as he scanned the piece. My heart swelled at the thought of them and I tried my best to remember I'm trying to face this.

"It has been . . . hard. I wanted to get away." He nodded with understanding. He put the piece in some sort of folder to protect it before putting it into a paper bag. I began to take my wallet out when he shook his head and handed my music over to me.

"No need. It's on me." I looked towards him and could see he was trying to be kind after asking me about my parents. "Are you sure?" He nodded as someone approached behind the cashier. Cooper smiled as he took out cash from his wallet and put it into the register before walking around to me. "Thank you, Cooper," I said lightly.

"Really, it's nothing. Mama J told me you may be coming here. I figured I'd take you to AT&T."

"You're not going to ask where Jack is?" I said softly not wanting anyone to hear me. I suddenly felt that I was back to feeling like my world was going to fall apart. The happiness I had earlier with the guys was slowly fading away. Cooper gave me a knowing look.

"I would, but we both know Jack wouldn't be here after what happened freshman year."

"Don't remind me about that," I sighed. "I don't understand what I did wrong. I was trying to do the right thing."

"Yes, but you also gave Fin the opportunity to turn him against you." I looked down and I sighed not wanting to think about it. Cooper realized what our talk was doing and tried to change the subject. "I'm sorry. This isn't something you wanted to talk about. I'm also really sorry about what happened to your parents." I only nod, because I felt like there was a frog in my throat. Cooper had me sit down on one of the cushioned chairs outside the store. He sat down next to me feeling guilty.

"This is still really hard for me to talk about right now. I really appreciate you caring for me and I wish Jack felt the same way," I sighed. Cooper only nodded and apologized for making me upset. I wasn't planning on being an emotional mess in public. Cooper and I sat here in silence for a few moments until I saw Andy, Ken, and Nate made their way out of the music shop and coming towards us. When Cooper noticed them, he seemed surprised and stood up to exchange some sort of handshake with each of them.

"I didn't know you guys were with Claire?" Cooper questioned them. Nate nodded and told him about the surprise meet up with my Aunt Clarisse in a few minutes. Cooper looked towards me with an interesting look and told me that I was under great hands. I slowly stood and Cooper handed over my music.

"Everything alright Claire?" Andy asked concerned. Ken and Nate had the same look of worry. Cooper got the idea that I haven't told them.

"It has been awhile since I've last seen her and was telling her a sad story from when we were younger," Cooper chuckled trying to cover up everything. I mouthed a thank you to him and he nodded understandingly. The guys nodded and were back to be their happy selves.

"Well, I guess we should be meeting with mama Johnson then," Ken pointed out at the time.

"Right, yeah. It was great seeing you again Claire," Cooper said as we exchanged a small hug. "And since you're getting a phone today, I've already given you my number written down on the receipt."

"It was really nice to see you again," I said softy. "Thank you again for everything." I referred to the last several minutes before he told me he'd see me soon. Cooper said his goodbyes to us before he told us he was going to get back to work.

The four of us were now on our way. It was just down a few shops. Once we walked into the store, I spotted my aunt waiting for us. Once she turned to see me with the boys, she walked over looking stunned. I'm sure she was confused to where Jack would be. I had a feeling she would ask later. "Andy! Nate! Ken! What are you guys doing here?" she asked as she gave each of them a hug. She seemed very thrilled to see them. This was definitely a good sign then. "We actually drove down to surprise Jack and we ran into Claire at the mall," Nate smiled towards me. Andy and Ken agreed with his statement. I'm glad to have met them. "We didn't know Jack had a cousin our age!" Andy said. I laughed at him for his silliness.

"She's actually going to Kricon with you guys." The boys once again looked surprised and very happy to hear the news. I smiled slightly and nodded. They must be really happy that I would be going with them for the trip.

Maybe this trip won't be so bad after all. After spending the last several hours with the three of them, I'd love to be going with them. My aunt and I were making our way over towards a worker who was working behind a desk. The guys followed behind.

"You're so happy today," Aunt Clarisse said to me with a kind smile. She knew how the last few months has been hard for me. She was very happy to see me happy and about.

"These guys are so nice and they're so funny." I smiled sheepishly. They were so kind that it warmed my heart. I wondered if everyone else in the picture I saw earlier were also kind and funny. I could see why they would have many fans supporting what they did.

As I received my new phone, I set everything up and made sure to carefully put in the necessary information. My aunt insisted on me getting an iPhone, because she thought it would be a phone that I would like very much. For the moment, I had no idea how to work it.

My aunt told the four of us to go over to the couch while she did the business part of the purchase. I led the boys over to the couch and sat in the center with Andy. Once my new phone was mostly set up, the guys told me they had to be the first ones to have pictures with me on my phone. We started taking selfies and doing paired pictures so everything wasn't a selfie. After our crazy amount of picture taking, they had me downloading apps like Vine, Instagram, Snapchat and Twitter. The three of them helped me set up all my social accounts, then they showed me some of the features before they personally followed me.

I decided to make my first tweet on Twitter in honor of them. I attached a picture of us and pushed the tweet button. Ken then held up his phone, taking a vine. I felt flustered.

"Hey guys, I'm with Nate, Andy and Jack's cousin, Claire!" Ken said. We were all waving at the camera and I smiled shyly, because it felt strange to me. Andy and Nate wrapped an arm around me before the six seconds were up and a video started to replay over and over. I soon had a notification from Vine about the video. I gave it a like and revined it when I soon noticed I was getting a lot of notifications. Andy and Nate told me I may want to turn off the in app notifications so my phone wouldn't be blowing up. I assumed their fans have now found out about me and started following my account.

We spent about an hour or so socializing and laughing as they tried to show me a few features on some of the accounts. It wasn't until my aunt came up to us that I realized how much time has passed and how much I've learned about the social media apps. It was Instagram and Snapchat I have not really gone into. I was friends with only the guys so far. I had made sure to add their numbers into my phone and also added Cooper's to make sure I could contact him later. "We should get back to the house," my aunt said, walking up to the four of us. We all stood agreeing as the guys talked the excitement of seeing Finnegan and my cousin. I wish I could be feeling the same way. I had told them that I'd ride with my aunt and that I'd see them at the house. As soon as we get into her car I had a feeling she was going to say something.

"Sweetie, where's Jack and why is he not here?" she asked curiously as she backed out of the parking spot and pulled out of the parking lot. I knew she would eventually ask.

"He was sleeping earlier and I didn't really want to wake him," I answered softly. "It's alright. I don't mind." I never liked lying. I'm not really good at it either. I would always get caught when I was younger. I hoped she wouldn't notice.

"But it's freezing out here. How did you get around?" I sighed knowing that Jack may not hear the end of this. "I took the bus." After that she started getting upset and told me that Jack should have taken me and how I could get sick and freeze. She said she'd talk to Jack later this evening before we leave tomorrow to our destination.

CHAPTER SIX
Wonder

CLAIRE JOHNSON

The ride back to the house at first was silent for me. I thought about the many possibilities when Jack finds out about me hanging with his friends. I did not think of when I'd come back to the house and he would be seeing those posts at some point. Would it be okay for me to hang out with some of his friends or would he give me a hard time about it? I really did not think this through. I worried and had this feeling he wouldn't be happy with me being with them.

Neither of them would be happy actually. I thought about how he'd tell me to stay away from them. It pained me that Jack would never tell me to stay. They have been so kind and caring towards me. I never had that back home. Friends. No one knew the tension between my cousin, Finnegan, and I, except for Cooper. Cooper was the only one who knew because he was also good friends with Finnegan and my cousin.

Cooper never liked the way they have treated me and we were friends before everything had happened. We weren't really close but Cooper always kept me company when Finnegan would ask my cousin to do something else that wouldn't involve me. He knew how much Finnegan tried to exclude me when it came to hanging out. He was always friendly and gave me small gestures to let me know that I always had him to talk to when I was here.

Suddenly, a familiar tune came on. I turned towards the radio as the instrumental part of the intro began. It was a song I had not heard in a while. My aunt noticed me looking at the stereo and reached forward to turn the volume up a little. I then let my head lean against the headrest and began to sing softly.

Come up to meet you, tell you I'm sorry
You don't know how lovely you are.

The lyrics came to me. I closed my eyes as I continued to sing the first verse. I have always been the type of person to sing slow, meaningful songs that were sad. I slowly let myself get into it and looked out the window.

I was just guessing. At numbers and figures.
Pulling the puzzles apart.

I've always found this particular song one of my favorites to sing along to. I wasn't sure why, but something in my heart tells me that I could relate in a way. The words flowed through and my heart beat fast whenever I get into the music. I stopped singing and I knew my aunt glanced my way.

"Your voice is so lovely dear. Why did you stop?" my aunt said.

Slowly, I wrapped my arms around myself. "It reminds me of them," I said lightly and let out a sigh. I felt a pat to my shoulder and I looked over to see my aunt giving me a look of sympathy. I haven't performed or sang since that day in music class. My nightmare would occur quite often and it had an effect on me. Thinking back to the time it happened made my heart ache and my throat tight. I have better control now but it didn't mean I didn't miss them. I can still remember everything so vividly.

40

"I know how much you miss them. Your mother is a very strong woman. She'll make it through this."

I knew this wasn't a great topic to talk about with her. We both lost family that day and hoped the other will survive this. "And what if she doesn't wake up? I wish they hadn't gone into work that day."

"Claire . . ." My aunt sighed. "I know this is tough. I am very happy for you when you decided to try and face the world again. It makes me happy that you're here now and that you've decided to continue with school. I lost my younger brother, your father, in the incident. I miss him greatly and I hope your mother will survive this. I am here for the both of you."

"Does Jack know about my mom and dad?" I asked. The car came to a stop at a red light. She then turned towards me with a sad expression. She gave me a look of guilt before shaking her head.

"No, I haven't told him yet and I thought it would have made more sense to tell him on your own time when you're ready."

I nodded. She knew that I wasn't the type of person who wanted to be bombarded. She wanted to let everything happen on my own terms. The song soon came to an end and she turned the volume down once again. "I wasn't sure how you were going to take it when he found out. I hoped to give you two time to catch up," she said.

"I understand." I nodded quietly. We now turned onto the street where the house was. I looked in the rearview mirror and saw Nate driving. Aunt Clarisse parked in her usual spot and the guys parked at the curve. As soon as I stepped out of the car, I instantly grew nervous. The thoughts of my parents slowly faded way and my next worry came into thought. I patiently waited for the guys and they surrounded me as we walked to the front door. My aunt had already opened the door and went inside.

41

I was assuming I heard Jack and Finnegan the moment we were inside. The two came down and looked around in shock to see the guys. We were all crowded by the entryway.

"Surprise!" the guys said in unison as they walked the rest of the way down the stairs. Jack and Finnegan smiled as they hugged their friends. I looked down at my shoes uncomfortably.

"What are you guys doing here?" I heard my cousin ask. He sounded happy and excited to see them. Finnegan seemed the same way as well.

"Came to surprise you guys," Andy chuckled. "You . . . uh forgot to mention you had a cousin our age. I'm so glad she's here. I like her. Not crazy or anything."

I looked up and saw everyone looking towards me. Nate and Ken were agreeing. Aunt Clarisse must have gone into the kitchen to prepare us a snack with the small stash of snacks we had left. She'll probably end up going to the grocery store once she found out Jack may have not went shopping.

"Yeah . . ." Jack said slowly and lightly smiled at me. "She's visiting."

I shouldn't feel hurt that he did not know the actual reason I was here, but I am because he never asked. Aunt Clarisse called the six of us into the kitchen. All of the guys seemed excited to have a snack even though we just ate not so long ago. Everyone started making their way to the kitchen and I was held back.

My cousin and I were the last ones to make our way into the kitchen He blocked the way. I kept my eyes averted away from his eyes as his mouth parted slightly. I knew he was annoyed. He took a step towards me and I took a step back slightly.

"Stay away from my friends Claire. They are not your friends and I don't want you hanging around with them," he said under his breath. My eyes stayed averted to the floor and I sigh. I knew better. He was making everything so difficult. If only he realized how much this affected me and hurt me mentally. It was hard enough having to think about both of my parents possibly being forever gone. Jack wouldn't dare give me a hard time if he knew. Instead, I kept my mouth shut about that.

"They're not going to stop Jack. They'll always find a way unless you make it clear to them," I said softly. Jack rolled his eyes and mumbled before turning away and went towards the kitchen. I took a deep breath before I slowly followed him into the kitchen where everyone was seated. I took a seat by the far corner where I wasn't in the center of attention. Nate sat across from me. I let the guys talk and laugh, letting them catch up.

An hour has passed and I felt really intimidated by Finnegan's cold stare at me. I couldn't be comfortable in my seat. I don't understand what I've done so wrong to have the treatment he was giving me. I went on my phone to pass by time as I felt myself being excluded this time. I did not want to interrupt anything or have Jack give me a hard time about it later.

It was eventually that I found myself on Twitter and noticed the notifications. Many were a mixture of fans of Ken, Nate, Andy, Jack, or Finnegan. I decided to make a tweet. I began typing and mentally sighed to myself as I looked between the boys.

@clairejohnson: They're never going to tell them

As soon as the tweet was posted, there were immediate responses, likes, and retweets. People were asking me what I was talking about and some were asking if I was okay. There were also those few people who asked if I was really Jack Johnson's cousin. I decided to send out another tweet before closing out of my phone and putting it on the table. I wasn't sure if I should respond or to leave it be. I wasn't sure.

@clairejohnson: I don't know what to do

Not even a moment later I looked towards my cousin and saw him glaring at me with his phone in hand. I bit the inside of my

43

lip. I have a feeling he saw the tweets. Maybe it was dumb of me to tweet stuff like that especially if Jack's fans follow me. There were some people who were tagging Jack about it. I did not think this through.

"Claire?" Finnegan asked calmly and I looked up trying to remain calm from the look he was giving me. All attention was now on me. Ken, Nate, and Andy had no clue what was going on. "Don't you have to pack for the trip?"

"Y—yeah," I said softly and tried my best to not show fear. My heart always raced when he talked to me. I slowly stood up and noticed he was also standing. I immediately froze and my thumb started to rub against my other fingers nervously. "You don't have to help," I said. Finnegan smiled towards me which meant a lot of things and it actually frightened me, because I knew Jack wouldn't help me.

"Naw, I want to help." He smiled again. I nodded as I waved a quiet good night to the boys before making my way out. I made my way up the stairs and knew Finnegan was following behind. I shakily reached for the knob of the bedroom door and went inside. As soon as he shut the door to my room, I felt an impact to the left side of my face. I squeezed my eyes shut in pain as I brought my hand to my cheek where it stung the most. I felt the throbbing pain. This would leave a bruise. As I tried to open my eyes, my right eye immediately watered and I let out a small yelp from the aftermath. I stepped away from Finnegan with fright and whimpered slightly. I couldn't believe he just did that. Never in my sixteen years had he ever laid a hand on me. I now looked towards him and I knew he wasn't the least bit happy. I knew it.

"What do you think you're doing?" he asked as he eyed me. He never liked me and he wasn't the nicest person I know. Reminded me of Carla back home. I was unsure of what he meant by his question. I was still focused on the stinging feeling. He knew I was uncomfortable around him and he took advantage of it. He

44

always took advantage when Jack or Cooper weren't around. It was always this way.

"I—I wasn't trying to do anything," I whispered.

"Your tweets, you idiot. Don't think Jack and I are stupid. If word ever gets out, I'll make your life hell."

"I'm sorry. I'll take it down." My voice came out more of a whimper and I held the stinging spot.

"Too late for that moron. People have already seen it. You need to stay away from us and the guys. You understand?" he threatened. I nodded quickly in hopes he'd leave my room. He glared at me for a moment before leaving the room. I let out a sigh realizing I was holding my breath. It was crazy to think I ever had the smallest crush on him.

I looked towards the closet where my suitcase was. I don't really have much to unpack, because I left behind a lot of things back home. I would be going back there in a few weeks to return for my exams and to hopefully do a few senior events that I've already missed out on this year.

The only thing I brought with me were some of my clothes, laptop, guitar, and my cello. I've always been a light packer. As I started to make my way to grab my suitcase, I felt my new phone vibrate a few times in my back pocket. I jumped a little caught off guard. I pulled my phone out slowly.

Nate:
Hey, u ok up there? We miss your presence already!

Andy:
I miss you :(come back down and hang with us

Ken:
We miss you already. Come back soon (':

I stared at the text for a moment and felt my eyes brimming with tears. They were so nice and caring. They honestly warmed my heart and made me feel like I exist. It wasn't until now that I realized that I have been feeling really lonely the last few months. They were the first to really care to check up on me, but I then remembered what Finnegan said. I hope to figure something out.

Being down there for this trip would be lonely and very depressing if I was spending it alone. I didn't like the feeling of being to myself anymore and it would be really nice if Jack could see I'm struggling right now. Today with the guys made me feel happy and I really liked that feeling. I was back to what I felt when I found out my dad died and my mom was no longer able to physically talk to me. It was as if I had no one to talk to. The painful thought brought back the bad vibes. I now made sure I had everything before I decided to get ready for bed.

CHAPTER SEVEN
Flight

CLAIRE JOHNSON

An alarm set for five in the morning went off on my phone. I shivered as I pulled the warm fluffy comforter back and immediately felt the cool air. I sighed, feeling exhausted and a bit shaky since I never went down to eat dinner last night. My stomach grumbled and I brought my hand to the sound.

Slowly my hand reached for my cheek and I pulled away immediately from the sudden pain. There must be a bruise. I stood from the bed and made my way over to the dresser where there was a mirror hanging. I saw my reflection and noticed the purple mark sitting there. My eyes widened. I noticed it was swollen and it was a darker shade of purple in the center which had the most impact. The look of it frightened me as I thought of last night.

I didn't know what to do. If I ever told anyone with my encounter with Finnegan, I do not think they would believe me. I quickly took out the powder that would help cover the bruising for now. For the time being, I couldn't go around looking like this. I quickly changed into something comfy for the plane ride. Once I was ready, I put my cello on my back, my backpack hanging from my arm, guitar in one hand, and the luggage with my other hand.

I made my way over the door and used my foot to open it and went out into the hall knowing I did not want to make a second trip up here. I'm sure the amount of time I had been covering up the bruise, everyone downstairs had started to eat. I wasn't sure if there would be any food left for me.

Quietly, I made my way down the stairs and when I reached the bottom, I put all of my things down close to the door. I walked towards the kitchen. I could hear chatter going on and I averted my eyes to the ground. I hoped to avoid any eye contact from Finnegan and hoped the powder I had put on wouldn't come off. The smell of pancakes made my stomach grumble.

"Mornin' Claire," Andy greeted. I closed my eyes slightly from the slight fear of Finnegan lashing out at me later for talking to his friends.

"Morning Andy," I said quietly. I walked over to the counter to take the last plate before taking two pancakes and some scrambled eggs. Then, I poured myself a glass of apple juice. My aunt kissed my head as I took a seat next to Nate. I greeted everyone and focused on eating my breakfast as I learned that we would be leaving very shortly.

The guys were getting up not long after to begin putting their things into the vehicles. My aunt cleaned up a little before telling me she had to get ready for work and I was left alone in the kitchen. My plate was still half filled with food and I started to eat again. I listened to the boys coming in and out of the house. It wasn't a few minutes later until someone came into the kitchen and I looked up to see Andy with a friendly smile. He was being so kind. I wish Finnegan and Jack didn't make things so hard.

"Hey Claire, I was wondering if you wanted to ride with Nate, Ken and I to the airport?" Andy asked.

My heart told me yes, but my thoughts always return to what "they" would think. "I was sort of hoping to ride with Finnegan and my cousin," I answered apologetically. "I wanted to catch up with them for a little bit before we get to the airport."

"Oh yeah, I understand. I'll see you at the airport then."

I nodded and he smiled once more before turning away. I finished up the last of my food then made my way over the sink to wash the plate, silverware and my cup. I dried my hands with a washcloth before making my way to the front door where I did not find my things.

Outside, the guys were all standing around talking. I tried to look around and Nate noticed my confusion. He waved for me to come over to which I slowly obliged. I looked around to see where my cousin or Finnegan were.

"We already packed your things into the car. Tired?" Nate said. I nodded slightly and Andy chuckled.

"Well, we'll see you at the airport then. Sad you're not riding with us," Ken said.

"I'll ride with you guys next time." I smiled faintly.

"It's fine Claire. See you in a bit!" Ken said.

I nodded and started making my way over to Jack's jeep. I sat in the back and patiently waited for them. Who would have thought I would be getting back on a plane so soon? It felt like having a vacation from a vacation. It has been a long time since I visited the state of Florida. I never went to any of the theme parks then.

Most of the car ride up to the airport consisted with the both of them telling me what I could and couldn't do on this trip. They went into specific topics like where I stayed when they had the event going on and during the free times. I was to stay away from everyone. I looked between the two of them as they made a list of rules for me to follow. I sat in the back, really afraid to answer them.

It had come to a certain point that I was in tears from their words. They were purposely using words to hurt me and it made me uncomfortable. They showed no care and let me cry. I was sniffling and it must have irritated them, because they were groaning. I felt so sensitive and I wanted to crawl up into a ball, because I didn't expect them to treat me like this.

49

"Claire! Shut up!" my cousin exclaimed. He finally turned around and glared at me. I tried my best to stop and so I closed my eyes tightly, hoping to think of happy memories. When we arrived at the airport, everything seemed to pass like a blur to me and I felt really out of it. I tried my best to hide my face from the guys as I was sure they would ask many questions concerning me.

I quickly looked for my seat in the plane and sat down. I kept my head down as I patiently waited for all the passengers to board the plane. After being in that car, I felt panic stricken and really upset. My feelings were hurt, but that didn't matter at all. Moments later, someone sat down next to me and I looked over to see Andy. I was not sure who was supposed to sit next to me.

"Hey Andy," I said softly and forced a smile to appear. Andy smiled and acknowledged me for a moment. I tried to make it seem like I was in a great mood, but in reality, I felt lonely. I've been feeling it for months now. That feeling hasn't gone away yet and I don't think it will go away soon. It has already been a horrible morning with my cousin and Finnegan, so I had to hide everything now. I never liked when they brought me down. I always felt afraid to speak up.

"What?" he chuckled. "I can't sit next to you?" He showed me his ticket and poked my arm. I shrugged. "So, you excited?" he asked.

No, not really, but I really wish I could be. I was, before my conversation with both my cousin and Finnegan. "Yeah." I smiled at him sheepishly. He smiled then frowned slightly once he took a closer look at me.

"You okay?"

My eye contact with Andy broke as I looked away slightly. The pain in my chest was returning again and I could feel my throat clogging up slightly. It was a question I haven't been able to answer truthfully lately. It made me think of my parents so it made me really upset. I couldn't help but feel the need to cry.

"Of course I am. Why wouldn't I?" My face remained calm on the outside, but in reality, I was ready to burst into tears.

"Your face seems a little . . . puffy," he pointed out, concerned.

"Maybe it was something from the airport. I'm actually allergic to some types of peanuts. I usually try to stay away the best I can." I shrugged slightly.

"Oh, I'll try and remember that when I get you food," he said.

I smiled at him for his kindness. I yawned slightly. Being up early and feeling like I haven't rested made my mind very stressed and overworked. I told him I would try to get more sleep before we landed. He nodded, telling me he would wake me up when we land.

SHANE PETERS

"Remember to have fun and don't do anything too crazy," my mom was saying as we walked towards my gate. I was getting ready to get on a flight to the United States and land for the Kricon event. So far, I've really enjoyed going onto stage and singing in front of a crowd. I really liked singing and sometimes the fans would sing along with me. I definitely wanted to get more into songwriting and releasing them.

The thought of me signing with them made me very excited and nervous at the same time. This is something I have always imagined and this was something I wanted to do with my life. First it started with me making covers on YouTube and posting six seconds of covers on Vine. My whole life I've wanted to grow up to be someone who could wake up every day doing what I love to do best; singing and playing in front of a crowd. I want to tour the world and sell out at venues one day.

I was going to Florida without my family for this event and short vacation because they really want me to enjoy myself. Most of the Kricon events, I'd have my mom or dad at least be there with me. There was the one time when the whole family had gone with me. This time they wanted to give me time to myself with some of my friends.

"Of course, Mom," I said. Sarah poked me from my other side which made me look towards her. She seemed sad to see me go. Her light brown eyes matched her hair. "I promise to get something for both you and Dad."

"You don't have to Shane. I hope you have a great time. Maybe you'll meet a girl down there or something," my sister said which made me groan. "What? I think it would be good for you," she added.

"Maybe. I don't know Sarah. I like hanging with my friends."

"Let us know about your time in Universal! Don't forget to call us," my mom said as we were getting closer.

"I won't forget. I'm going to miss you guys."

"I know." My mom smiled and handed me a credit card for emergencies. Once we were in sight of my gate, we came to a slow stop until we were only a few feet away from the end of the line. The both of them turned towards me.

I reached for a hug from Sarah. "I'll miss you," she said softly. "Have fun going to Disney and Universal."

"Thank you. I definitely will. Do well in school and no boys while I'm gone." I knew she was rolling her eyes as we held our hug a little longer. When we pulled away, she punched my arm lightly. I returned the gesture. Next, I looked towards my mom who looked like she was going to tear up at any moment. It was always this way when it would be a while before she next saw me. I went over to hug my mom tightly. "I'll miss you Mom."

"I love you Shane, please be safe."

"Of course, Mom. I promise to be on my best behavior." We pulled away and saw her smiling. The line was almost gone and I sighed knowing this was my time to board my flight. "I'll see you both when I get back." They both nodded as I kissed them on the cheeks.

I then made my way over the gate. I handed over my passport with my ticket. I was welcomed and walked past the lady after they have given me my ticket and passport back to me.

Just before I went through the door, I turned around and looked to see my mom and Sarah standing there with their arms around each other. I smiled sadly while waving at them. I waited for them to wave back before slowly turning away.

Moments later, I took a deep breath and stepped onto the plane, getting the jitters. I am ready for the warmer weather down there and to spend some quality time with some of my friends and maybe do a cover or two while I am down there. I could definitely do one with Jacob or possibly with Jack and Fin. I knew fans have been asking me to do small collaborations with them for a while.

I walked down the aisle and looked for my seat. Most of the seats were filled and I was the last from the line to get on the plane. Once I found it, I placed my bag and guitar up in the compartment and took my seat by the window. I took out my phone quickly and sent a text to my mom, dad and Sarah. After, I went onto Twitter and sent out a tweet about how excited I was to be going to the Florida event. I then put my phone on airplane mode and went to put my seatbelt on. I saw the door shutting and an announcement from the flight attendant came on. After, there was a welcoming message from the chief pilot telling us a few things before we were on our way. Once the plane was in motion, I looked out the window. The plane began accelerating and I smiled to myself.

This is going to be a trip I will remember. The guys, Nora, and I are going to have the greatest time and I knew there were going to be some pranks pulled. There would also be video collaborations and it would hopefully be a stress-free vacation.

CHAPTER EIGHT
Introductions

CLAIRE JOHNSON

The plane ride to Orlando seemed a little lengthy since I had just been on a plane yesterday. These past two days consisted of me doing quite a bit of traveling. I'm glad that I wouldn't be doing anymore lengthy travels for a little while, hopefully. On the way to the hotel, Andy had tried to tell me everyone who would be here. He would show me a few pictures but it was confusing with the names and it seemed like a lot of names to remember.

Over time I hoped to remember each of their names and maybe hangout with them a little when Jack or Finnegan aren't around. It would take time and I hoped everyone was nice. I have never been the type to make friends so easily and I've always kept to myself.

The van that picked us up from the airport was suddenly parking and I looked away from Andy's phone and out the window. I saw the big hotel or resort you could say as we had been brought to the front of the building. On the left side you could see the parking lot filled with cars. The van door opened and everyone started to pile out. I looked around and thought how this resort seemed very nice. The six of us walked into the building that we would be staying at. Once we were inside, I noticed a group of people who I assumed were the Kricon crew. I felt myself being left behind at first as hugs were being exchanged.

While the guys were doing their thing, a girl with red curly hair looked up and noticed me. She sashayed her way over with a friendly smile.

"Hi I'm Nora," she greeted and hugged me. I hugged back with a small smile. She seemed really friendly. Her head full of red natural curls was the most beautiful sight to witness. Her eyes were a pale blue color. "You must be Johnson's cousin!"

"It's nice to meet you too." I smiled at her. She is very pretty and I couldn't begin to describe her hair. "Your hair," I said in awe. She laughed lightly when I noticed two other guys making their way over to us. One was wearing a bandana and the other one was wearing a shirt that had to do with music. I laughed at him as I understood the context of his shirt. and he looked down before looking at me again. I'm guessing he was some sort of musician. I was intrigued that there was another musician here. His short brown hair had curls in them.

"It's a yam session!" I beamed and he chuckled. I really liked his semi curly brown hair and his smile. I noticed his lazy eye being more present when he smiles.

"We have another musician here," he smiled and introduced himself. I noticed his accent wasn't American. It had to be Canadian. I knew it all too well from visiting. "Hi, I'm Shane Peters." He held his hand out and I shyly shook it.

". . . And I'm Aiden Rodriguez," the other guy with the bandana on his head said. A bit of his light hair peaked from it. "I'm the wild and loud one of the groups."

"Hi," I started off shyly realizing I had to introduce myself. Hopefully by the end I'll know how to introduce myself properly. "I'm Claire," I pointed to Jack. "Jack's cousin."

They both giggled. They weren't intimidating to be around so far, but kind and friendly. "We know who you are." Aiden shook my hand, giving me chills that went up my arm. His hands were cold. "We've seen ya on Ken's vine from yesterday. Hey Jacob!" he called out and I saw one of the other guys looking over. The Jacob guy I think made his way over here and he looked at Aiden before looking at me.

"Hey, I'm Jacob." He smiled, introducing himself. "You must be Claire." His dark brown eyes were close to matching his black hair. He was quite tall like Shane.

"I am." I smile lightly. He looked closely at me and his smile widened.

"Two instruments? I'm guessing we have another musician here Shane?" I assumed the two were both pretty close friends.

"Yes, we do," Shane said smiling at me. "Guitar and . . . cello?"

"Yes. Do you guys play any instruments?"

"Guitar and piano," Jacob raised his hand.

"Same," Shane nodded. "I think we must come to your suite and hear you play sometime." I'm sure they were way better at playing the guitar than I am.

"You're welcome to stop by anytime," I said softly. I felt extra shy around them. It could be me talking more and trying to break from the last few months.

"What about me?" Aiden asked pretending to sound hurt. "You invite these two goofs? Making plans with them already?"

Nora laughed lightly and I shrugged. Both Jacob and Shane had smiles on their faces.

"She likes us more," Jacob said, sticking his tongue out.

"She likes my shirt," Shane said proudly.

"Yeah, Yeah." Aiden playfully rolled his eyes. "I was kidding you guys. I bet you'd be talking all this music stuff I wouldn't know anyway." Soon, the rest of the boys started to circle around me and they all introduced themselves.

First, Ian introduced himself. He reminded me of Justin Bieber in a way and he commented that he would get that quite a bit. Second was Aaron, the short dark brown haired guy who had light brown eyes. He told me that he liked to make funny videos.

Ben, short for Benjamin, who I remembered Andy mentioning to me earlier is apparently his brother. Ben was younger, of course. He had the exact piercing blue eyes and hair color, but the style was a lot different. He was also tall like his brother Andy. Not as tall, but I'm sure he would be soon. I could see the resemblance.

Next came Ryder, who had his brown hair styled in a quaff. I couldn't help but laugh, because he seemed quite sassy with his Starbucks drink in his hand. Ryder seemed like a funny guy. They were all so nice and very friendly to me. They melted my heart as I feel welcomed.

Without having to look directly, I knew both Finnegan and my cousin were eyeing me, but I wouldn't quite make direct eye contact with them. I would give away my expression if I looked towards them. I had my cello on my back, my guitar and luggage in my hands. Andy had my backpack. After introductions, it seemed everyone was standing around and I thought it was a good time for me to settle in.

"It was really nice meeting you all. I think I'm going to unpack." They all said their goodbyes as I looked to Nate, who I think now had my room key. Nate handed me a specific key and frowned slightly before handing it over to me. I thanked him quietly. He must have realized that I wasn't going to be with anyone.

I slowly made my way over the elevator. I could get my backpack from Andy later on. I looked between my key number and the map on the wall. I realized everyone would be sharing two suites together and I would have one to myself. I think I may be in a different area from everyone also. I'm pretty sure Jack made it very clear to whoever was in charge of suite arrangements to make sure I did not share with anyone. He wanted me to be isolated. I walked onto the elevator and looked through the door to see everyone standing around and talking. I smiled slightly and saw Shane looking my way and I waved shyly. He smiled and returned the wave before the door closed. He is really cute and attractive.

I let out a sigh as I realize what Jack and Finnegan had told me earlier. All of them seemed like really nice people and they all seemed so cool. Once the elevator opened to the floor, I walked out and looked towards the sign to see which direction I should go.

Getting to my room wasn't too difficult as I was at the end of the hall. I struggled with everything in my hands trying to open the door. I refused to put something down then pick it back up. Once I was able to get the door to open, I used my foot to get the door to fully open. After I was in, I kicked the door shut. I looked around in amazement. It was like a mini condo. I put my cello case and guitar case down in the living room and walked into the bedroom.

Once I entered the bedroom, I gasped at how beautiful it was. There was a queen sized bed with various pillows lined up, two dressers, and a walk in closet. The flat screen TV hung on the wall and the bathroom is huge! I quickly unpacked all my clothes, shoes and my bathroom essentials. It took no more than twenty minutes to organize before I started to make myself comfortable and checked the time. It was now six in the evening.

I heard a knock on the door and stood from the couch to answer it. When I opened the door, I was immediately pushed back as someone closed the door. The person looked so pissed and my eyes widened. My heartbeat escalated in a matter of seconds. What was he doing here?

"I swear Claire, if you say anything . . ." Finnegan started. He tried to grab me, but I blocked him in fear that I would be hit again. I wasn't so lucky when he went for my shin. My eyes shut painfully and I was hoping to only fall onto my butt. I whimpered in pain and tried my best to remain calm. Finnegan gave me one hard look then walked out the door, leaving me here alone.

Jacob and I decided to return to our suite not long after Claire decided to head up. The both of us were in our room and have decided to work a bit on our music before heading out with everyone.

"Jacob?" I asked as I looked away from my phone and saw him looking up from his guitar. He was currently working on a song.

"Yes?"

"Do you know if Claire has a Twitter or Instagram?"

"I'm pretty sure she recently made an Instagram. It's Claire Johnson without any spaces. Same for her Vine and Twitter."

"Thanks," I nodded and typed in her username. I looked closer at the usernames and found her. I saw she had one post so far. I clicked on it and smiled at her cuteness with Nate, Andy, and Ken. I liked the picture and clicked back to her profile to follow her

"Following her?"

"Yeah. She seems really nice, don't you think?"

"Definitely. I like her already. Plays the guitar and the cello? She's so girlfriend material."

I chuckled. "If she sings and plays the piano. I am hands down going to be in love."

Now it was Jacob who was chuckling. "We should maybe go over to her suite later on. Maybe we can all collaborate or something."

"Is it strange that I wish she was here with us right now?"

"You should definitely get to know her Shane. I think you're into her." Jacob smirked slightly and my cheeks felt warm. *Do I really?* "You could talk to her some more when we're all hanging out."

I nodded as I found her on Vine. I could easily find her since Ken tagged her in his recent vine. "I was thinking we'd go over there later. Yeah, that sounds like a plan. She seemed tired and I think she's probably resting."

"Probably. I thought you were working on some music?" Jacob smiled. "Getting carried away?"

"I can't help it," I shrugged. "I think I'm going to take a small break. I could go for something to snack on, want to come?"

"No, I think I'm on a roll right now." I chuckled, nodding. "Take Ben with you. I'm sure he'd go."

"Yeah." I stood and carefully put my guitar back into its case. I placed my song journal on top of the drawer. "I think I'd rather work on some music tonight instead of going out thinking about it."

"Alright. Let's stay in then." I nod in agreement before putting a sweatshirt on.

"I'll be back."

"Maybe you can ask Claire too," Jacob chuckled and I laughed nervously. He wasn't going to let this go.

"Goodbye Jacob," I groaned and started making my way out of the room. As soon as I left the room to go into the living room, I saw Jack, Nate, Andy, and Ben. They were all lounging around.

"Sup Shane?" Jack asked once he looked away from the television with a small smile.

"Hey guys." I half smiled. "Ben, I was going to ask if you wanted to grab a snack?" I scratched the back of my head, feeling awkward about it.

"Of course, sounds good to me." I looked towards Jack, wondering if he knew where Claire was or if they were sharing suites.

"Have a question Peters?" Jack chuckled. Sometimes I forget I'm one of the youngest here. I wonder if Claire and I were the same age.

"I was wondering if Claire can come along maybe?" I asked nervously. "I wasn't sure if she wanted something to eat." The door to the suite opened and I saw Fin coming in. At first it seemed like something was bothering him.

"Fin was just visiting her, right Fin?" Jack asked. Fin looked up towards me.

"Yeah." Fin half smiled. "I invited her to come hang with us, but she's a bit tired from the amount of traveling from the last few days."

"Few days?" I said.

"She arrived from New York yesterday," Jack then clarified.

"Maybe later." Fin shrugged. I nodded and looked towards Ben who put his phone away.

"Well . . . we'll be back," Ben announced and the guys waved us off before the both of us walked out of the suite. It wasn't until we were out the door and walking that he chuckled and shook his head. "You're the first Shane."

"What?" I frowned slightly. We walked down the hall to get to the elevator.

"Do you have any idea how nervous you were when you asked Johnson if Claire could come along with us?"

"It was that noticeable?"

"Everyone in that room probably had an idea. You made it seem pretty obvious. You seemed a bit nervous. Good for you man. I could see you and Claire getting together or somethin'."

"Whoa." We stopped walking and I turned to him. "I just met the girl today. Let's not make anything a big deal yet." The thought of Ben or anyone here having thoughts of Claire and I being together seemed unrealistic.

"Yet"—he emphasized—"dude, I know you seem into her. You didn't think I noticed when you pulled Aiden away so you could be introduced to her? I saw you glancing towards her when she was in the elevator. It was like you were trying to keep yourself from going."

"You don't think she noticed?"

Ben smiled as he pushed the button to the lobby. "Nah. Just be you man. She's into the music stuff like you, right? Start small, maybe go see her later or something. She seems pretty shy," he said.

I nodded. "I was like her with everyone here," I chuckled.

"Yeah. Let her warm up to you. She seemed impressed to see you earlier too with that shirt of yours. I don't think you have to try very hard with your Canadian charm," he said. I nodded again with a smile as the elevator door opened and we walked on.

After a moment of collecting my thoughts, I decided to change the subject to what we were doing now. Ben had a point. My thoughts were mostly on Claire and how pretty her smile was. I could tell earlier she was nervous and shy to meet all of us and her eyes were as green as nature should be. Her hair color was another difference. They could pass as twins if you had taken a quick glance with the two standing next to each other.

We walked into the lobby and looked around before making our way out of the building. Ben and I decided to go to a place that had sushi. We were both sort of in the mood for it and there was a sushi place not too far from the resort.

CHAPTER NINE
Talents

Claire Johnson

The throbbing pain continued as I sat on the floor where he had left me to whimper in pain alone. My eyes continued to squeeze shut from the amount of pain I felt on my shins. I used my palm to wipe away the few tears I had as I tried to wait out the pain.

Two days in a row that he made physical contact. I couldn't believe he was capable of being okay to doing this to me. Does my cousin know about this? Would anyone believe me if I told them what Finnegan has done to me? I had to make sure to tell someone. This couldn't continue to happen throughout the trip with me staying here in fear. I wanted to get away, to try and forget pain.

A part of me always feared him and I'm too afraid to tell someone. What are his intentions?

After what seemed like a long period of time. The pain eased slightly and so I opened my eyes. Blinking, I looked around the living room. I slowly stood with the pain throbbing when I accidentally put pressure on the leg. I bit my cheek from the aching pain that I quickly put all the weight on my other leg leaning one way. I started hopping my way over to the kitchen and went for the freezer.

My hand reached for the door and I opened it to find nothing. I sighed forgetting to start the ice maker. I looked around the kitchen and came to realization that I don't have anything to eat here either. I should eat something soon, knowing I haven't eaten breakfast since earlier this morning. Am I supposed to contact the person in charge of the event or do I ask Jack? I'm sure he'd make me pay for my own food if I went to him. I quickly start the ice maker and closed the door. I hopped onto the counter with my good leg and sat here patiently waiting for some ice to be made. I wonder what I should get to eat or how to contact the guy in charge of this event. I never met the person. To pass a bit of time, I took my phone out wondering what my Instagram and Twitter was like. I went onto Instagram first since I had a better understanding of it. I went onto my profile and clicked on the only picture I had on there so far. My eyes widen at the amount of likes and comments that were now present. The comments showing caught my eye and I smiled faintly.

JacobHolland: Claire's prettier than all of you

ShanePeters: This is beautiful

Shane was the one who waved at me before the elevator closed. I couldn't help but smile at his name. I clicked onto his username and the app took me to his profile. I scrolled through his pictures and started liking them at the same time. I also watched the videos he posted and instantly fell in love with his voice. He sounded amazing and he seemed so talented. My excitement to hear him in person continued to rise.

Some of the pictures I liked would be with his friends and family. It seemed like he really liked spending time with them and he seemed really into music. I wonder if it was something he'd like to do professionally as his career. I knew what it was like to want to do music as a profession.

A part of me wanted to pursue that career while the other part of me wants to do something else that I am really interested in.

I've always wanted to become a pharmacist. I could imagine myself being called Doctor Johnson. The thought of wanting to become a doctor in something had always been an interest aside from music. It was a reason why I've tried so hard in school and had been pushed hard to do well.

It now worried me thinking of the few schools I've already applied to I would be hearing from them soon. Waiting and figuring out where I would be accepted, waitlisted, or declined stresses me out a lot. It worried me a lot since I had not applied to that many. Also, it made sense in a way why I was stressed so much since the schools I applied to are difficult to get into. They were very difficult to get into. The thought of all of this stressed me out. It made me think I am not ready for the professional program quite yet. I may not be the strongest in every science and math course. Music would be either my major if pharmacy wasn't for me or I'd try again later. I came here to get away from that for now. Let's focus on the music.

I spent an hour going through his profile. I felt my face warming up, realizing what I've done. I felt like a stalker. I just spent this whole time liking all of Shane's pictures and watching his videos. He won't notice. He had a little over a hundred thousand followers on here. I clicked the follow button and go back to quickly follow Jacob. Before hopping off the counter, I sent a link of Shane's profile to someone I knew at Briller Records.

I went for the little plastic baggies, that I wouldn't have thought would have been here, and hopped over to the freezer once again. I took a handful putting the cubes into the bag and shut the door. I hopped my way into the living room and carefully eased myself onto the couch. My phone was now buzzing like crazy and I frowned slightly. First, I pulled my leggings up with the leg that had been kicked by Finnegan. It didn't look too bad. It was a bit swollen, but I don't think it's severe enough to get checked out. I put the ice on top as a precaution for now.

I took my phone out of my pocket to see I've been put into a group chat. I began reading through the messages. Everyone already added their contacts into my phone.

> *Aiden: Let's meet in the lobby so we can go to that arcade we saw a few miles from here! It looks pretty big and entertaining!*

> *Jack: I'm in! Sounds like a plan and we could eat there also*

> *Finnegan: Let's go! I'm so in! I've been waiting to go to one!*

> *Nate: Hell yeah! I'm up for it man. Meet you in the lobby*

> *Ken: I'll be right down! Let me just change real quick*

> *Andy: I'm ready! I'm making my way down already!*

> *Jacob: Shane and I are going to stay back to work on some stuff.*

> *Nora: Be right there! I'll be just a few minutes getting down there!*

> *Ian: Sounds good. Meet you guys down there in a few minutes*

> *Aaron: Yeah def! I'll be right down in just a couple of minutes*

The messages continued coming when someone finally asked me through the group chat. I thought they wouldn't notice me not responding, but I guessed wrong.

> *Aiden: Yo Claire, u comin? There will be games and food.*

I quickly sent a reply remembering my cousin and Finnegan were a part of this group chat. I wanted to go and get to know everyone but I couldn't. I wouldn't want to face trouble.

Claire: Sorry guys, I got caught up on working on some music. Maybe next time? Thank you for the offer though! Going to rest up for tomorrow!

That was when the messages stopped. As much as I wanted to go and hangout with all of them, Finnegan and my cousin would be there. After today's and yesterday's encounter with Jack's friends, I knew I would end up facing consequences and I didn't want to face that right now.

Something to keep my mind busy has always been music. I looked towards my cello and reached for the foldable music stand and the sheets. For now, I'd read through some music before deciding to practice. It was two hours later when I was working on a piece from the "Lord of the Rings." I was so frustrated with the piece that my hands started to hurt a little and my fingers were becoming stiff.

Due to the recent incidents right after Christmas, I was not able to make the majority of my auditions. I had applied to all of my schools in the midst of things and so I was given the option to audition once I found out officially that I have been accepted.

I have been working on my scales, perfecting them as it has been a few months since I've really practice. I was always visiting my mom in the hospital or I'd be trying to hide myself from the world.

Coming back to playing the cello was something I found easy to come back to. It took a few days to get back into shape of practicing a few hours a day. As a break from practicing my audition piece, I decided to play around with some of my previous solos I once played. Currently, I decided to play a piece I always loved playing. It helped with my bowing and I worked in the key I really liked. I was about ten minutes into this piece when I heard a knock at the door.

"Come in!" I yelled, not looking up from the music sheet. I trained to stay focus on a piece of work that I am on. I was playing the scene with Gollum saying "my precious." I tried again, but then put my bow down feeling exhausted. I looked up to see Shane and Jacob both with their guitars. They both looked stunned and slowly made their way over.

To my surprise, I waved to them. I had no idea they were going to visit. I wonder how they found me.

"Was that from Lord of the Rings?" Shane asked excitedly.

"Yeah," I smiled at him. Shane and Jacob both had excitement in their eyes that I could immediately tell they were music nerds like me. I liked that. There was this very strong feeling I felt that we would get along with each other.

"I love those movies! That was so good Claire!" Shane said.

"We could hear you as we walked down the hall." Jacob smiled at me. "We were actually looking for you."

"We thought you'd want some company."

"You guys could have texted me!" I laughed at them lightly. They both sat down on the other couch chuckling and looking at each other before turning their attention towards me.

"That's true. So, a cellist huh?" Jacob asked pointing at my cello. I looked down at my cello and smiled towards it. "Yes, I uhh tend to practice a few hours a day when I get the chance."

"You're like us. We approve." Shane looked towards some of the pieces I had spread across the table. "We can start talking about music soundtracks and you'd completely understand."

"Yes!" I beamed. "I love listening to the orchestrated pieces. I uh . . . I also like to play the piano, guitar, and sing for fun." I felt my cheeks warming up. I thought the need to add that in since we were sharing information and interests with each other.

They were giving me the attention I never really had for music. They appreciated this a lot and I found the feeling welcoming.

"Can we hear you sing?" Shane asked. I could feel my cheeks getting warmer by the second.

"Pretty please!" Jacob pouted. "We'll sing for you." It has been a while since I've done a small performance. Every time I tried, I'd breakdown because it only reminded me of that day. I felt a bit uneasy about this.

You can do this Claire. They don't seem like the kind to be very judgmental. I thought for a moment and agreed because I needed to try and sing again in front of others. I put my cello down on its side. "Okay."

Shane came over to the couch I was sitting on and handed me his guitar. He gave me a big smile. I took a deep breath. I felt nervous singing in front of two famous viners, who are amazing I'm sure. Well . . . I did stalk Shane earlier. I started to strum the guitar to "Young and Beautiful" by Lana Del Rey. I always chose a slow paced song.

I started to sing. At first my voice was a little shaky, but then grew accustomed to the room and became comfortable. Both Shane and Jacob were giving me reassuring looks and I could tell they were happy to hear another voice. I began to get lost in the lyrics. My eyes closed and I let myself get into the rest of the song.

Once I ended, I opened my eyes and saw they both looked at me in awe. At first the room was quiet and I tried to read their expressions. They both went back and forth commenting.

"Your voice is beautiful," Jacob said as the very first comment.

"You sang with passion. The emotion and expression felt so real," Shane commented and nodded. They continued to comment, then they sang for me. After they finished, I told them how they were amazing. I think Shane chuckled and I looked towards him with confusion.

"What's so funny?" I asked.

69

"I had a feeling you were going to say something like that," Shane smiled. "Because you were so stalking my Instagram earlier."

It was now Jacob's turn to look surprised and chuckled at the statement. I knew my cheeks were burning, but I couldn't hide it. He caught me. "You stalked Shane?" Jacob smiled to the point that it was contagious.

"She liked just about every photo and video I think. You were so on my profile for a good hour."

"I'm not going to lie," I said lightly and smiled looking down at the guitar shyly. I felt slightly embarrassed, but I also felt okay being around them. "You have some pretty cool pictures and I really like your family pictures. You're . . . from Canada?"

"I am. Love Canada, eh?" he said. I love the way he talks. Is that strange? If he could hear my thoughts at the moment, he would be weirded out.

"Love it there," I answered shyly. Shane smiled showing his perfect white teeth and it took everything in me to remain calm. He was the cutest guy I have ever encountered. I would love to take him out on a date without a second thought. Where are these thoughts coming from? I need to slow down with these thoughts.

"Really? Maybe you should go back with me after this trip for a few days. Have you visited Toronto?" he asked. I shook my head. "Maybe you can visit sometime then. I don't mind having you visit and stay with me and my folks," he then offered.

"I've wanted to visit there and possibly take a look at a school in the Quebec province."

"Right," Jacob said, smiling. "Jack mentioned you are graduating a year early. You've applied to most of your schools already, right?"

"Except for the one in Canada," I answered.

"And which university is that?" Shane asked curiously.

"McGill."

Jacob looked towards Shane as my stomach grumbled. It was like they were having some sort of telepathic conversation for a

70

moment before turning towards me. My stomach grumbled once again and I realized I should probably get myself something to eat at this very moment.

I'd hate having to go searching for a place to eat or figuring out where a market was. Maybe my phone had some sort of maps or search directions for these places.

"You can come back to our room and eat with us," Shane offered after a moment. He must have read my mind. I thought about it and hesitantly accepted the offer.

CHAPTER TEN
Unexpected

SHANE PETERS

I was sure Claire had to be hungry after her flight and resting here for a few hours. Jacob and I were finishing our telepathic conversation about a friend of mine who went there. I'm sure I could talk to someone in the admissions office if Claire still wanted to apply there. Her grumbling stomach caught my attention and I turned back towards her. There definitely wasn't any food here. I knew for a fact there wasn't food put in here, because this room was requested last minute.

After coming into her room and getting to know Claire a little bit, Jacob and I realized how much we liked her. The way she seemed so honest around us was something I really liked. Her personality seemed perfect. She seemed soft spoken and very shy. She reminded me of me a bit.

Claire singing to us was something I found amazing. Once she mentioned that she liked to sing, play the piano, and play the guitar, I wanted to hear her voice. Her voice was the sound of an angel and I loved her choice of song. She hasn't so far failed to amaze me and I could say that she was winning my heart over. Jacob knew how happy I am at the moment. Jacob would take a glance at me often to make sure I am okay. She seems perfect.

"Come back to our place, Claire. We have some food," I offered her. I'm sure she was hungry and even though we didn't have much, I'm sure it would be better than not eating at all. It would also give Jacob and I the chance to talk with her more. We both liked talking to her and spending the time with her. I could see she was thinking. About what though? We were not going to kidnap her. Not until she was more comfortable with us anyway.

"We don't bite," Jacob chuckled. We wanted to hang with her more. We liked having her around and having conversation.

"Okay," she finally answered after what seemed like a few minutes. She loosened her bow before putting it back into the case. She then leaned over to her cello carefully and placed it in the case. Jacob and I both stood and I noticed her having a hard time standing.

"Are you alright?" Jacob asked her. I stepped forward almost instinctively to make sure.

"I may have hit my shin against the metal bar of the bed in the bedroom," she smiled sheepishly. "I wasn't being careful."

I chuckled at her cuteness and she looked towards me. "Well, do we need to get you some ice or any medication for swelling?"

She shook her head and grabbed her phone before slowly walking over to the door. "I'm ready," she said shyly.

Jacob and I nodded before making our way over to the door. She shut the lights off. We walked out the room and waited for her to lock the door. She stood between us as we led her down the halls. "You guys are so tall," she commented softly. We then found the elevator.

"You're so short," Jacob chuckled.

"No, I think I'm average. You're both just pretty tall."

I smiled down at her. I wondered if she is a big Harry Potter fan like I was. Once we were on the elevator, I felt my phone vibrating. I checked the text quickly.

I'm going to shower when we get back. You spend some time with her. Pretty sure she's into you ;) She keeps taking glances at you

I smiled and looked up towards Jacob who was giving me a nod. Claire stood between us and I could tell she still seemed shy. Her one hand was holding her arm. We walked out of the elevator and made our way to the suite Jacob and I shared with Aaron, Ben, and Ryder. The three of them had already left with everyone. Jacob used the key he had and opened the door for us to get in.

"Welcome to our suite," I told Claire from beside me and she smiled. Jacob didn't delay any further and went off to shower as planned. He did not want us to wait for him.

I led Claire towards the kitchen where she took a seat at the stool. I opened the fridge and pulled out the various fruits we had. I know it wasn't much but the guys ate everything we had last night. I began to make a big bowl of fruit salad for the both us. We started eating once I mixed in all of the fruits and handed her a fork. I grabbed one for myself too. I had whip cream in my hand, hiding under the counter, but I wasn't sure if I wanted to spray her some.

"So, you love to sing?" Claire asked, breaking the silence. "Like do you want to go far in your music career?"

I looked down at the bowl. "I've actually never really talked about it with anyone. I actually hope I can go really far, maybe go on tour"—I looked back at her—"but I don't think I'd want to leave Kricon yet. Everyone here is my second family and I know I won't be here forever."

She nodded slowly like she understood, but I don't think she knew the feeling. She seemed interested in knowing my thoughts. I'm not sure how she could relate to leaving something that started everything. I made the friends I had along the way. It felt so strange, but exciting thinking about what has to come in the future.

I felt a hand take mine and I looked to see Claire holding my hand. Her touch was gentle and I held on, feeling slightly nervous because she doesn't make eye contact with me. There was this tingling and funny feeling I felt in the pit of my stomach. How could someone I've only just met today make me feel this way? It hasn't been half a day and she was already taking over my thoughts.

It was like everything I thought about took me back to Claire in some way. I may not know much about her, but I really hope I could on this trip. I wanted to spend every day with her and become close, hopefully. "If you do go big, everyone will support you, because they love you and they would want you to go on. You couldn't miss an opportunity like that." She looked at me with a friendly and genuine smile. I liked how she spoke what was from her heart. Her honesty seemed to calm me when I think of the future.

I smiled at her and thanked her for her advice. She smiled back. I decided to put the whipped cream down and went around to hug her. She immediately hugged back and I felt her bury her face into my chest. It was so perfect and comforting that we stayed in this position for a while. I loved this feeling. I wouldn't admit that out loud, because she may be weirded out, but I never thought I'd enjoy the feeling of hugging someone other than family.

That was until I felt her shaking. Slowly, I pulled back slightly. I noticed her eyes were very glossy and tears were flowing down her cheeks. My heart escalated and my heart ached for her in confusion. I hesitantly reached for her tears with my pointer finger and wiped them away without a thought. Her expression showed pain.

"I'm sorry for y—you to see me like this." She sniffled softly. I knew something was bothering her. I heard the uneasiness in her voice. I continued to wipe her tears with my fingers and held her in my arms. I tried my best to find a way to comfort her. It was an instinctive feeling.

"What's wrong, Claire?" I asked using the same soft tone. I was beginning to worry for her. She looked at me and I noticed fear. I immediately wanted to comfort her and never let go. She looked so fragile state right now. "I won't tell anyone if that's what you want. I'm sorry if I made you upset in any way."

She let out a shaky breath. "You're being really nice to me and no one has ever been so nice towards me before like you have. I've never had anyone to really to talk to when I was back home."

I noticed mentioning home brought a soft spot for her. I continued to listen to her carefully.

"I ummm . . . would always be locked up in my room all the time, because my parents were so strict with me. They never allowed me to hang around guys, go out with friends if I had any, do sports, or extracurricular activities unless it would be helpful to my college application," she explained. I was stunned. I wasn't expecting this. How did I trigger this?

I carefully wiped away more tears. When I brushed her cheek gently, I noticed a bruise. I didn't mention anything about that yet. "How can no one be nice to you? You're one of the nicest girls I've met with amazing talent. I'm sure you have some friends in school," I said. She was probably exaggerating just a bit. I'm sure many likes her for who she is. Jacob and I do.

She looked down. "I lost all of my friends that I had when they realized I could never hang out with them or be around them. I'm sort of invisible to everyone around me usually."

"I would have thought you'd be really popular and everything. You seem like a girl who could have everything in life. You're a really nice girl Claire. I think so."

"Everyone likes to ignore me." She sighed softly to herself. "I've always had a hard time in school. It wasn't perfect."

"Is that why you moved in with Jack?" I asked. She shook her head sadly. "Everything will be alright," I said softly, realizing that I have really upset her. I should be changing the subject. I didn't mean for this to happen.

"You can't tell Finnegan or my cousin that I was here," she suddenly blurted. I frowned slightly.

"Wait, why is that?" I was very confused.

"Please promise me? I'm afraid of what will happen if they found out," she pleaded.

"What's going on Claire? Found out you were with me? You're really having me worried now," I said. Her tone was barely audible now.

"Please Shane?" she repeated. Why did this have an effect on her? She wasn't looking into my eyes now and she had this upsetting slash guilty look. I didn't want her to worry anymore and so I sighed.

"I promise Claire. I wish I understood what's going on."

"I—I have a lot on my plate right now," she sighed. It was clear she wasn't ready to tell me.

"You don't have to tell me," I said softly after a moment of silence. "If you ever want to talk about what is going on, I'll be here to listen."

"Thank you, Shane. That's so thoughtful of you." She made eye contact with me and I felt my heart escalating. She was still in my arms. Slowly she began to pull away and I took her hand, not wanting to let go. She looked at our hands and smiled sadly before looking towards me.

"I should probably get going."

"No." I pouted without thinking and she smiled slightly. "Please stay."

"I'd love to. You and Jacob have been so kind and really fun to be with, but I should go," she said. I only nodded. I'll see her again. "Thank you again for letting me have some fruits."

"I didn't want you to starve," I chuckled lightly. "Promise you'll text or call me if you need anything, alright?"

"I will. Thank you, Shane, really. You have my number from the group chat?"

"Yes. Of course. Let me walk you back to your room."

"I'll be alright," she said lightly now. I knew she was worried. "I'll think about how I stalked your Instagram." A small smile appeared on her face and I smiled.

"Well, I followed you earlier if you didn't know. I was sort of thinking about earlier when I waved to you when you were in the elevator."

Her cheeks slowly turned a light pink. "I'll see you tomorrow Shane." She squeezed my hand slightly before letting go. I followed her to the door and she opened it.

"Good night Claire."

"Night Shane." She slowly turned away. I stood at the doorway for a moment as I watched her walk down the hall. I closed the door and walk back into the suite as I headed towards the kitchen where I noticed a phone sitting on the counter.

I checked the phone having a feeling this was Claire's. Checking the home screen, the phone started vibrating and saw a caller ID. I hesitantly took her phone unsure whether to answer. It was from a hospital. I put the phone on silent and put it into my pocket before making my way out quickly. I made sure the suite was locked before jogging my way down the hall and reached for the elevator.

Tapping my foot nervously, I sent a quick text to Jacob telling him I'd be back in a few minutes before entering the elevator and pressing the button to the floor Claire's suite was on. I found it strange that she was separated from us and was so far.

I exit the elevator and made my way towards the other end of the hall. I wonder if she noticed her phone wasn't with her. I knocked on her door and waited for her to answer. A moment later, I watched as she turned her head and realized it was me.

"Sh—Shane, hey," she said softly. Her eyes seemed happy to see me. "You can come in." She waved me in, which I accepted. I made my way towards the living room.

"I . . . uh hope you don't mind me coming to visit. I know you just left not that long ago, but I wanted to give you your phone back." I reached for her phone in my back pocket. "You left it on the counter and I didn't realize it was yours until after you left."

She gently took her phone out of my hand. "Thank you. I was actually looking for it a moment ago. Also, I like it when you visit. I'm glad you came. I definitely owe you. My aunt would have freaked out if she knew I've already forgotten and misplaced my phone."

"You don't owe me anything." I smiled towards her.

"Oh yes I do."

"Well then . . ." I thought about it for a moment and smiled thinking of something we'd both like. "Call me later tonight."

"You want me . . . to call?"

"Yeah. I like when I get to talk to you." She looked down slightly with a nervous smile before looking up at me.

"I like talking to you too Shane. I'll call you tonight." I nod remembering the call she received.

"Oh . . . before I forget, I'm sure you have a notification, a hospital called your phone." I watched as a worried expression took place. She looked away from me and bit her lip looking sad. "Is . . . everything alright?"

CHAPTER ELEVEN
Claire

SHANE PETERS

I entered the suite thinking about Claire. My mind and heart ached for hers as she told me the news of her mother being in the hospital. She also told me what happened to her dad. She would get calls from the doctor for updates of her mother. She wouldn't delve too much into it as it only really upset her. She said she should call the doctor back. I did not push anything and respected her privacy. I left her room this time.

Realizing that she had lost her dad and that her mother right now was under critical condition made it hard for me to leave her. I want to stay with her to make sure she wasn't left alone. I couldn't imagine wanting to be alone either. Maybe I could talk to Nate about it. I also wondered if Jack knew about this. If Jack knew about this, why was he not looking out for Claire as much and why wasn't he upset for what has happened to his aunt and uncle? It was like he didn't know about it.

Once I entered the living room, I saw Jacob in his sweatpants and t-shirt. He was ready for bed. I would be doing the same, but I was thinking of waiting a bit to see if Claire would want to get something for dinner later. He had a towel wrapped around his neck and he seemed ready to head back into the room pretty soon. He frowned slightly after he looked around.

"Where did Claire go? I thought we'd all maybe go out and do something since everyone went out," Jacob asked curiously. I should definitely make sure that she ate later. I thought it was interesting that Jacob was planning to go out in his sleepwear since he always liked to be a bit dressed up whenever we were going out.

"She said she was really exhausted from her flight and went back to her room," I answered moments later. I never liked lying, but I wasn't sure who she wanted to know about the things going on in her life. I assumed it was private. I'm sure she was tired from her flight also.

"She could have slept over. I'd be fine with that."

"Yeah . . . Maybe next time."

Jacob and I walked into the living room where we both sat on the couch. Everyone hasn't returned from their trip.

"So how was it when you were with Claire?" The mention of her name made me smile slightly. She has made a really good impression on me already. Also, she seemed content being here with all of us, or most of us rather. I wasn't sure what it was between her, Jack and Fin. I had this feeling that something wasn't adding up, but I wasn't sure. I've just met her today.

"It was great really," I answered not as a complete lie, but we did like each other's company. I liked the effect Claire had on me. I wasn't sure how she felt.

"Is she your dream girl?" Jacob chuckled with a smirk. I rolled my eyes playfully, trying to stop myself from smiling. I wonder if I had an effect on her. "Shane, you have this look."

"What look is that?"

"You have nothing to worry about. I'm not going to tell anyone." Jacob chuckled and shook his head trying to hide his smirk. "You know I wouldn't tell a soul if you don't want me too."

"I'm crushing on her man. I don't know what it is about her," I smiled deciding to tell my closest friend here. I trusted Jacob with everything I talked about. We've somehow grown very close with music than from the rest of the guys from the group. Jacob nodded listening to me. "She already has an effect on me."

"Maybe it has to do with her being a musician herself?" I shrugged slightly. "Or the fact that she also sings? You've always said you want to find someone who loves singing as much as you do. Her voice is amazing and I knew you were in love with it the moment she started. I'm guessing you'd like to collab with her."

"Yes, I would love to do a collab with her."

"Of course, you do. I'm not surprised. Are you planning on taking her out sometime or really getting to know her?"

"Yeah, I think I am," I smiled sheepishly. My mind now returned back to Claire as I thought about earlier when Jacob and I first met up with her. What was going on? My mind raced with different scenarios. She seemed terrified and this wasn't okay.

Something was definitely going on. The bruise on her face looked fairly fresh almost as if she had gotten it in the last day. Then there was also Jack and Fin, who she seemed afraid of. I'm not sure if anyone has caught that. I needed to talk to someone about this.

"Do you know when everyone gets back?" I asked after Jacob had turned the TV on and found a show. He looked up from his phone and turned towards me shrugging.

Earlier I had texted Nora, Nate, Andy, and Aiden to meet me down by the pool. I saw them coming from inside the building with confused expressions. They were probably curious.

"Yo, what's up Peters?" Aiden asked as he approached me. We formed a circle. They were all older than me so I trusted them and I knew they could help Claire.

"Everything alright?" Nora asked showing concern. I took a deep breath. I want to help Claire. I had to remember that.

"Have any of you guys noticed anything strange going on with Claire?" I asked curiously. Nora and Aiden shook their heads. Andy and Nate continued to stare towards me.

82

"I've just met her today. She seems pretty quiet like you and Jacob."

"She was acting a bit weird when we were around Jack and Fin," Nate started. "She probably hasn't seen them in a while."

"She was totally fine being with us before that though." Andy frowned. "When I sat next to her on the plane her face was really puffy and I don't think it was peanuts, because she isn't allergic to peanuts. I asked Jack how bad her peanut reaction would be when peanut butter is around her and he told me she wasn't allergic to anything."

Aiden and Nate frowned. That couldn't be it then. Something was strange. "Did something happen while we were out?" Aiden asked. I nod my head slightly. This was to help her and I am concerned.

"Promise you won't tell anyone? Especially Jack or Fin," I said knowing that I promised Claire that I wouldn't tell anyone, but this part seemed really serious. They all agreed. I told them from when Jacob and I first went over to Claire's to how we had to get her to our suite to eat. I emphasized the hesitance in Claire. I also told them what some of our conversations were about, how I hugged her, and how she started shaking and tearing up with fear. I left out what had happened to her parents. That was something personal to her if she wanted to share that particular information with anyone else.

After I finished what I told them, I refocused to the group. They stood there with mixed expressions.

"Oh my God, this is terrible," Nora gasped, covering her mouth.

"She has a bruise and I'm wondering if one of the Jack or Fin hit her . . ." I trailed off looking between all of them unsure.

"Fin and Claire went upstairs to her room and they were gone for a while last night," Nate said. "She looked at her phone almost the whole time instead of talking to us. She felt . . . uncomfortable."

"I'm going to beat the fu—" Aiden started walking towards the building. Nate and Andy had to pull him back into the circle. Aiden would put up with a fight if he had to. "We're not going to do it that way Aiden," Andy said.

"We have to pretend we don't know anything that Shane has told us. She clearly trusts Shane and we want to keep it that way." Andy looked towards me as everyone agreed. "Let her open up to us first," Andy suggested. Everyone agreed and I let out a sigh of relief. I was glad to have them on my side and were understanding of Claire's decision. It made things easier.

"Are you waking her tomorrow morning?" I asked both Nate and Nora.

"Yes, Nate and I will," Nora smiled reassuringly. "We'll get her to breakfast, don't worry Shane." I nodded feeling reassured that I made the right decision to tell them.

"Get some sleep bud." Aiden half smiled. He seemed to calm down slightly for my sake. "You have your performance tomorrow."

"Thank you, guys. I'll see you at breakfast." They nod and I said a goodnight. I started making my way inside when I heard Andy calling my name. I slowly came to a stop to see he was catching up to me. "Hey," I said and I opened the door to the building. We both went in making our way to the lobby. "Hey, I uh . . . wanted to ask you if she's okay?" Andy looked doubtful.

"I think she will be. She's . . . going through a lot right now." I smiled wistfully, thinking of what happened to her mom and dad again. I really couldn't imagine what she must be going through. I felt awful intruding when I asked her.

"You really think everything you said is true?" Andy asked. I turned towards him with a small frown. "Like do you think Jack or Fin could really . . ."

"Yes," I answered without hesitation. "I wouldn't doubt her. She's afraid Andy and so innocent. I don't care if Fin and Jack is my friend. If she says something, I'm going to believe her. I

84

wouldn't think she would lie about this." I thought back to earlier. I witnessed her vulnerable. I'm sure she didn't open to anyone so easily either. "I may not know everything going on her in life, but she trusts me and I want to keep it that way." Andy nodded as we had gone onto the elevator.

"Are you heading back to the room right now?"

"Ye—" My phone vibrated. I pulled it out to see Claire was calling. I wondered how the call with the hospital went. "Hold on a sec," I answered the phone. "Hey Claire," I said smiling into the phone happy that I get to hear from her.

"Hey," she says barely audible. "I . . . was wondering if you wanted to accompany me to get something to eat?" It seemed something was bothering her. I hoped everything was okay with her mother. I'll ask her when I see her in person.

"Of course, I would love to get something as well. Do you want me to come over now?"

"Yeah. That sounds great." I heard a sigh from the other end. I am worried for her.

"Is everything alright?" There was a moment of silence before she responded.

"No . . ." she answered softly. "The doctor told me my mother isn't doing well." I could tell she did not want to be alone.

"I'm so sorry Claire," I said softly and looked at Andy who looked towards me with an eyebrow raised. He was wondering what we were talking about. "I'm on my way. I'll be there in a moment," I said.

"Thank you," Claire replied.

We said our quick goodbyes before I looked towards Andy again. "Should I be concerned?" Andy asked as he now pushed the third floor for me. Andy decided to accompany me down. "I'm going to take her out to eat. She's having a few problems at home, but I don't want to get into it without her permission." Andy nodded understanding as the elevator went back down.

"I hope . . . everything's alright for her. You two have fun tonight."

"It's just getting something to eat Andy," I half smiled. "Sure, it is Peters," Andy chuckled and smiled. "I knew the moment the three of you decided to stay back, there was something bound to happen. I wouldn't be surprised if you three had some sort of music sesh." The elevator to the third floor opened and I stepped out waving Andy off.

"I won't be too late."

"We'll see. Tell Claire I say hey."

"Will do," I said as the door closed again. I turned away and made my way down the hall towards her room. I opened my text message and sent her a message saying I was here. As I was approaching her room, the door opened and she stepped out and was searching for me and once she spotted me, she smiled faintly.

Once she was right in front of me, I noticed her face was flushed and I could tell her eyes were slightly swollen. It did not take any thought as I brought her to my chest and hugged her tightly. Her arms wrapped around me and I let my chin rest on her head.

The both of us stood in the hall in silence for a moment and I gave her time to feel comfortable before talking to her. She really needed this and I thought maybe she really liked hugs. I knew some people, who liked it when someone hugged them. Maybe Claire was one of them. After a moment, she slowly pulled away and I could see her eyes were watery. I still held onto her as I looked down at her. She wasn't making direct eye contact.

"I'm sorry you have to see me like this," she said faintly. I tried to smile, but was not able to. "I—I wasn't sure who to talk to and I didn't want to exactly be alone after the call. I know you just le—"

"It's alright," I said reassuringly. "You're going through a lot right now and I understand if you need company. My question is, why not have your cousin come over?" She seemed hesitant and I knew my theory may be right about them.

"We're not . . . I don't really talk to him," She said slowly. I found that odd since she is here after all. Did she tag along with Fin? I knew asking her these questions wouldn't help.

"It's okay. I'm happy you called me." I smiled at her and she faintly returned one. "How about we get you something to eat? I'm sure you still want to eat?"

She nodded. I unwrapped my arms from her and gently took her hand. "Where should we go?"

"Do you think they have some sort of Chinese food place around here or a buffet? I'm sort of craving Chinese," she said. I chuckled at her and nodded.

"I'm sure there is one around here. I'm pretty sure I saw one on the way here earlier." The two of us then started to make our way out.

CHAPTER TWELVE
Friends

CLAIRE JOHNSON

"Thank you for coming out with me," I said once I sat down from getting my ice cream. Shane and I playfully debated for ten minutes on who would pay for my meal. I argued that I was the one who invited him and that I was the only one eating. Shane refused for me to pay that he reached over the table to take my wallet from me and placed it into his back pocket. He pulled out his own credit card and paid for my meal.

It wasn't so hard to find the restaurant. As soon as we were off the resort premises, we found the main road with plenty of options to choose from. Shane decided it would be a great idea to walk a little farther down the road so we could talk more. Shane chose a restaurant that was based off the ratings on his phone, but also a place that wasn't crowded with many people. He was also thinking he did not want us to be disturbed while I tried to eat and he didn't seem very sure of wanting to leave me out of his sight unless I was going to the bathroom.

Having each other as company was something I really enjoyed. He has been very understanding and I was able to take my mind away from the call. I knew Shane really helped with it. He started talking about himself and he would say a few random facts. I'm sure he only shared this with his friends. He talked a lot about his home in Canada, his friends and family. He also talked about ice hockey and it seemed like something he has always liked to do for fun. He reminded me of Justin Bieber for a split second and he then went into how he started doing covers on YouTube and Vine.

"I liked coming out with you tonight," Shane said. What I really liked for once was the attention on me. I'm usually not the one who liked having too much attention, but he made it seem like he was interested in actually talking to me and hanging out with me. It was nice that he never went on his phone the whole time and he really wanted to engage in a conversation. I liked that he put effort of really being here with me. "I should be thanking you that you invited me. It was really nice to see you again today."

I wasn't sure how he had so much of an effect on me already, but I think he noticed. He did not point anything out and he did not seem like the kind of person to constantly tease someone. I'm sure I was blushing, because my cheeks were heating up and I felt slightly nervous. My mind felt relaxed, but at the same time it was swarming of thoughts about Shane. He seems like a prince charming from a fairytale and I was currently living under a spell.

"And I should be thanking you for everything you've done for me today. You really didn't have to pay for me."

"Just so you know, I rarely ever do this. I really wanted to anyway." He smiled and I felt the heat rising in my cheeks once again. I wonder if he has a girlfriend. Shane now raised an eyebrow amused and I was confused as to what I may have just said. "I used to have a girlfriend. We're not together anymore and haven't been for quite some time."

"Ohh . . ." I said slowly. "I said that out loud?"

"It's okay," he chuckled. "Well since I've answered. I'm wondering if you've . . . had a boyfriend? I know you said a few things earlier."

"No, never," I shook my head feeling embarrassed by the question. Shane nodded and I could tell he was in a way glad to hear I was single? When our waiter had come back with Shane's credit card, she had him sign the receipt before thanking us for coming. Shane stood up and I took that as we were getting ready to leave.

I'm really glad he has accompanied me here tonight. After getting the call from the doctor, Shane was able to keep me company and help keep my mind off the negativity of everything. Being me, at first, I was hesitant of calling Shane. I knew he had just visit for a short few minutes before to give my phone back to me, but my head was telling me that I had a certain trust in him even though I've met him today.

"Ready to go?" I nodded as I followed him out of the restaurant. When we were at the front, he held the door open and I thanked him. Shane Peters is a gentleman and whoever his next girlfriend will be, they'd be very lucky. I've really enjoyed myself tonight and I hoped we could continue to hangout like this during the break. Maybe my cousin or Finnegan wouldn't find out about this. Even the thoughts of them now was only in the back of my head. I wanted to enjoy the time I spent with Shane before I had to go back to my room. "Are you going to be at the event tomorrow?"

"Of course, I am," I smiled. We now walked side by side as I ate my ice cream and we were making our way back to the resort. "I wouldn't miss seeing you perform. From the videos I watched earlier, I think you're very talented."

"Yeah? I think the same for you. You singing for me and Jacob was amazing Claire. We should do a duet sometime."

"You . . . want to do a duet with me?" I was surprised he would bring something like this up. I was sure many people would love to do a duet with him or sing with him. My stomach had this bubbly feeling and I wasn't sure how to really describe how I was currently feeling right now. I wasn't sure how he had this effect on me. I looked towards Shane and he was already looking at me.

"Yes. I've wanted to ask you right after you finished performing, but we all got a bit side tracked. Would you like to be a part of a collab with me for my next YouTube video?"

"I'd be honored Shane. I'd love to."

"Great. I'm glad, because I was a little nervous asking you."

"Nervous?" I laughed lightly thinking it should be the other way around. My mind was racing with many questions of why Shane would want to sing with me of all people. I never thought he'd be asking me and it made me feel jittery.

"Yes," Shane chuckled with a small smile. "I know you're Jacks cousin and well . . . you're amazing Claire. Tonight, was really fun." I'm blushing again. I know I am. I finished my ice cream as we were in sight of the resort. He thinks I'm amazing. This was probably the most amount of time I have ever spent with a guy other than Finnegan or my cousin. I never had the courage to really talk to the guys at my school.

"You're so sweet Shane. You've made my night better honestly. I don't know what I would have done if I stayed back in my room alone for so long."

"I'm sure if you don't want to stay in the suite by yourself, you could stay in any of the other suites with us. You're so far from everyone."

"I'll keep that in mind. Are you ready to sing tomorrow?"

"Yes. I'm excited to be singing again in front of a crowd. It's great to have that nervous feeling."

"Yeah?"

"I get nervous right before I perform, but it's the greatest feeling performing. Someday I hope to be on my own tour and singing the music I make."

"You'll get there," I smiled. "I believe you will have great success in your future."

"I believe the same for you Claire. I could see you as a professional musician and maybe an actress."

"An actress?" I laughed lightly. "I don't think acting is for me." Shane turned towards me and he made this thinking kind of expression and I shrugged at him before a smile appeared on his lips.

"I could see it Claire. Later in the future you're going to be an actress somewhere around the world and you're going to have these amazing kids' named Dean and Grant."

"Dean and Grant, huh?" I couldn't help, but laugh as we tried to predict our futures. "Why would I name one of my kids Dean?"

"Because it's part of my middle name," he smiled widely and I gently used my shoulder to hit his arm. "I'd be honored to be named after one of your children."

The rest of the journey back to my room, Shane and I joked around about our future. Not our future together. That would be strange, but for each other. Shane seemed very happy talking about music being a part of his future and his career. I could definitely see it.

Once we had reached my door, I took my keys out and opened the door. I gave Shane a hug and he told me he'd see me in the morning. He told me that he was always a call away and to never be afraid to call him if I needed anything. I watched as he began making his way down the hall and he'd turn around every few steps to see me watching him.

He let out a laugh and he waved to me as I let my cheeks flush. Once he reached the end of the hall, I waved to him before closing the door. I went to my room feeling relaxed and also tired.

"Claire," I heard all of a sudden. My mind began to wake up. "Claire," the person said softly for a second time. By the third time I heard my name, my full senses came to me and thought it was time to face the world today. I flipped my body around to see Nate and Nora at my bedside. I wiped the sleep out of my eyes. I knew I heard my bedroom door opening, but I thought that was my imagination. I did not realize they had any sort of access. Who had access?

"What are you guys doing here? How did you get in?"

I was a bit confused of who had access to my suite. "We came to get you for breakfast," Nate held up a key. "Wanted to make sure you get something to eat before we all head off to the venue." That was kind of them. "Come get ready!" Nora beamed with excitement taking me out of the bed and began helping me get ready. Nate shook his head and chuckled as he walked out of the room. I went into to my closet to grab my pretty pink dress and black flats with flowers on them. I pulled out a pair of spandex to wear under the dress. It felt like a day to wear it. Nora sat on my bed while I went to take my shower. I wasn't sure how long we had for breakfast, but I couldn't help but stand here as the warm water hit my skin. It felt great.

Today I felt like it would be a good day and after last night with Shane, I went to sleep with a smile for the first time in a long time. After I showered, I slipped my dress on then putting my spandex on before opening the door for Nora to come in. Moments later she walked in and gasps. "Your dress is so pretty! I love it!" I smiled at her and thanked her. I blow dried my hair while she brushed my hair out. She started a conversation to fill the silence. "How was your first night here? Got enough rest?"

"I definitely did. I went out to eat for a bit yesterday and I am loving the weather so far."

"Did someone happen to be with you?" Nora asked. I looked towards the mirror and I could tell Nora had a pretty good idea I was hanging out with a certain someone. I look to myself and saw the blush on my cheeks. I wonder how many times I've actually blushed in the last twenty-four hours.

"Yes."

"I knew he'd try to spend more time with you. I had this feeling he wasn't going to sleep early."

"We came back at a decent time." I now felt shy talking about him when he wasn't here. Shane was very sweet and walked me to my door last night. He made sure I was able to get in before he made his way to his suite.

"Did you and Shane have a great time?" I nodded and Nora smiled. Once we were finished with my hair, we went out of my room to find Nate by the kitchen counter on his phone. I quickly went back into my bathroom to put shaving cream into my hand.

Nora covered her mouth and tried not to laugh once I returned. She took out her phone and indicated that she was recording.

"Smack cam," she whispered and giggled with a smirk on her face. I put a bit more shaving cream into my hand. Quietly, I walked over and once I was a few feet from him everything went fast as I smacked him right in the face.

"Smack cam!" I called out and fell to the ground with fits of laughter. I found myself finding everything funny. It has been a while since I've had a really good laugh. I heard a chuckle from Nate as he came on top of me. He hugged me without trying to get any of the shaving cream on my dress. He chuckled once more then helped me up onto my feet.

"You're good. I'll get you back, Johnson. Be prepared." Nate smiled and I smiled back. Nora laughed while shaking her head at our silliness. We left the suite after Nate took a cloth and cleaned his face.

Without notice, he picks me up and puts me on his shoulders. He started running down the hall as I let out a surprised squeal. Thank goodness I decided to wear the spandex. I could see Nora with her phone and I was sure she was recording this in some way.

"Nate, put me down! I forgot my shoes!" He continued running until we reached the elevator. He was out of breath then.

"We can get them after breakfast." I laughed as he put me down in the elevator. I loved Nate's positivity of everything. We reached the lobby less than a minute later and walked out. I followed both Nate and Nora into the restaurant that was in the front lobby. It seemed that everyone was already there and they all looked up towards me.

"Glad you guys could finally make it!" Aiden shouted as he greeted us.

"I love your dress Claire." A few of the other guys commented also and I thanked them. I sat between Shane and Nate.

Shane smiled once he realized I was sitting next to him. He sent me a simple "hey" before finishing up his breakfast. We all talked mostly about the arcade they went to yesterday. I looked towards Finnegan and he gave me the look.

I started to tense up but Shane took my hand from the right side. I stared at Finnegan. Shane squeezed my hand, trying to calm me down. I took a few deep breaths as we were all waiting for our food.

CHAPTER THIRTEEN
Duet

CLAIRE JOHNSON

Earlier after breakfast, Shane offered to walk me back to my room so I could get my shoes and he helped me clean up the music I had spread around the living room. Shane and I had the same thought of keeping our practice area clean. The both of us then left my room to meet everyone in the lobby. It wasn't long after until the vehicles arrived for us and we piled in.

When we arrived at the venue, there was quite a crowd at the entrance. We were dropped off at the back entrance and I let everyone do what they had to do to get ready for the day. It was Shane and Jacob who had me hang with them. I enjoyed watching them warm up. They didn't seem to mind that I was around and I liked being with them.

Once it was time to let people in, I had decided to leave the room to let Nora and the boys have their space. I did not want to feel as if I was intruding the meet and greet. I wouldn't know what I would have done and said if I was there. I walked around the building for a bit. When I returned, I took a seat from the side view of the stage and remained hidden as I noticed fans were entering the room. There seemed to be a lot of people in the room. I now sat backstage waiting for the show to end. Without paying too much attention, Shane walked over to me and pulled me onto my feet. He pulled me onto stage making me feel anxious. What was he up to?

"I'd like you to officially meet Claire Johnson, Jack Johnson's cousin!" he announced. All of the girls in the crowd were screaming. I nervously looked around the room to see many excited girls. There were only a few guys out there. I felt my cheeks warming up and looked at everyone on stage also. Nora and the guys, besides Jack and Finnegan, did not mind that I was here.

There were so many positive comments. I really liked how the crowd were saying nice things to me even though they did not know me yet. Their positivity gave me this feeling that I've been needing lately. I smiled at them. My eyes scanned through the crowd and you could see many friendly faces. They were being very welcoming.

"I actually would like Claire to sing a song with me. I hope that is okay?" Shane asked into the mic with a smile. My eyes widened at Shane. He did not mention this to me earlier. I haven't warmed up and I haven't sung in front of a large crowd bigger than two since I had found out of the news. This only made me slightly uneasy. I was caught off guard because everyone was cheering for me to sing with him. The thought of my performance right before I found out played through my mind.

My hands were trembling nervously as I held the music sheets in my hand. I had just a few minutes to myself before I start making my way to my last class of the day: music theory. This was the big day I would play one of my audition pieces in front of my classmates. It would also be the first time I would be performing it in front of anyone besides my private teacher.

The searching process of finding the perfect piece took place for a few weeks. I took a week to go over the piece to familiarize myself with the French text and the notes. It was important for me to have a great understanding and connection with the song. Every solo performance had great meaning to me. After a week, I'd work in sections with my private teacher for a few

97

months. This piece was my audition piece to the schools I have applied to for voice. There was a separate piece for cello. A whole other story.

The crazy thought of graduating a year early gave me a shivering thought. I was also very thrilled to know I would be leaving, because I felt there was more out there in the world for me. High school for me was not the experience I had wanted and I wanted to start over fresh. I wanted to do something I love while becoming more social. I didn't have that here.

The first bell rang indicating that seventh period was over and doors flew open as students flooded the halls. I closed my locker and sighed making my way towards the first floor where the music hall would be. I kept my eyes averted to the ground as I tried my best to avoid the cliqued groups, who always gave me a hard time. Shoulders would brush me as I tried to follow the flow of the students to the stairs.

I made it to the music hall with not too much of a hassle. I made my way towards the end of the hall. I passed the big rehearsal rooms and soundproof practice rooms before reaching the classroom. I was one of the first students here. Mrs. Reed was tuning the piano that I would be using for my performance. Quietly, I made my way towards the very end of the row where the windows were to set my things down.

Panic consumed me as I looked down at my sheet music to make sure I didn't crush it or tear it. I somehow tend to always misplace a page or bring the wrong sheet music. Quickly, I scanned the pages to make sure every page was there and in order.

"Claire?"

I looked up towards Mrs. Reed to see her standing from the piano.

"Piano is all set. You can warm up if you'd like," she said. I smiled warmly towards her. She has always been one of my favorite teachers here. I've had her for all of my music classes since my freshman year.

"Thank you," I said. I made sure my things were in place before I took a seat at the piano. I put my piece onto the dashboard of the piano before I let my finger hover slightly on top of the keys. I softly began playing a scale and started to hum along before I really started warming up. At the end of the warm up, the second bell rang and I looked up from the piano to see most of my classmates in their seats. Many of the students in this theory class was a mixture of juniors and seniors.

My eyes wandered to my music and I gently played a few sections I wanted to brush up on before I had to play for the class. Today I was the only person going as the class would take notes and give critiques on things I could still work on before my first audition at Boston University. The weekend after, I would be going to UCLA, Princeton, and Yale to do my audition in person. My private teacher would be accompanying me as my accompanist. I would be out of school for about a week and half to also do overnights and official visits there.

My parents weren't exactly happy to hear at first that I wanted to go to school for music. This was when I had decided I would also apply to the biology programs and do music as my second major to ease my parents that I had my other backup plan just in case music did not work out for me. I was sort of nervous, because I could get into the school, but I may not get into the music program.

My attention was brought to my teacher as I realized she was speaking to the class reminding them of tonight's write-up. She then gave me the cue that the class was ready for my performance. I took a deep breath. I nodded slightly as I counted myself off before starting to play.

The intro was elegant. I closed my eyes, getting into the mood. I trusted myself to feel for the keys as I began to sing. "*Dans un sommeil que charmait ton image . . .*" At this point I had everything memorized. The music was there for reassurance. Every word flowed effortlessly as I pronounced every French word. Every word is translated in my head into English. I wasn't sure how I could relate to the piece from personal experience when I've never felt this way towards someone before.

"*Helas, helas, triste reveil des son*—" The door to the classroom suddenly opened. I lost concentration once I spotted the principal and a police officer. My performance came to a halt, confusion written across my face. I looked towards Mrs. Reed, who walked over to the door. They were murmuring. I noticed Mrs. Reed glancing my way from the hall. I began to feel self-conscious and worried. Have I been caught doing something wrong? Did something else happened? Did they find out about what happened at Jack's school?

Mrs. Reed turned towards me once more and motioned for me to come out of the classroom. Their expressions gave me an unsettling feeling as I stood and made my way out into the hall. The officer then shut the door to the classroom.

"Am . . . I in some sort of trouble?" I asked nervously.

"No." Principal Evans shook his head. He sounded hesitant.

"Miss Johnson," the officer said slowly and I looked towards her. "Your parents were in an accident."

"An accident? Like an accident from the lab? Are they okay?" I found this very distressing. I knew my parents worked with dangerous chemicals in a lab.

"Claire . . ." Mrs. Reed said apologetically. "There was a chemical explosion in the lab your parents were in. Your parents were exposed." I felt myself beginning to panic and backed away until I hit the wall. The officer started going into detail of the incident, but my mind was elsewhere. It became overwhelming to hear what happened. The only thing I understood was my dad dying on site. Nothing else mattered after that statement.

I remember falling onto my knees and bursting into tears after what seemed only a few minutes had passed. Everything in my sight seemed to slow down and everything in my mind raced. I lost

100

my dad. He's gone. What about my mom? I couldn't think straight and I couldn't get the words out of my mouth to speak.

It wasn't for a while until I gained a weak focus and realized Mrs. Reed hugging me from my side. Principal Evans was on his knees, trying to speak to me. I couldn't hear him over the pressure in my ears and my sobs.

I remembered that day as if it was yesterday. It was supposed to be a simple day. I would have gotten my critiques to polish something and try to fix it that night right before I was on a flight to do my auditions. I never went to my auditions and I never sang in front of anyone until last night. I never had my cello auditions. Shane and Jacob were the very first to hear me play a bit since the last time I touched it.

"Shane, I'm not ready to sing in front of a large crowd yet," I said nervously. The only people who could hear us talking would be possibly the few girls in the front row and whoever had good ears on stage. My heart was racing that I could hear it through my ears and I felt as if I was not ready for this. I should have told him what happened last time I was in a middle of a performance. It only brought bad memories and I did not want to panic here. Shane must have sensed my uneasiness and he took my hand not caring what anyone thought at this moment.

I looked down at our hands and I heard small murmurs from the crowd and also from someone on stage. Shane's eyes were trained on mine. I made eye contact with him and it was the most soothing thing. I felt a squeeze to my hand and I felt my shoulders relaxing. I wasn't sure how he had this effect on me.

"It will be okay. Think of it as the small performance you gave to Jacob and I yesterday. Don't be shy. I'll be right here next to you the whole time. I'm not going to leave you." He gave me a reassuring smile. I smiled slightly as he led us to two stools. Slowly, he let go of my hand and made sure I was breathing well. I'm glad he said that, because that was the most reassuring thing I've heard since I've let anyone know about my parent's tragedy.

101

The more time I spent with him, the more comfortable I got. I was slowly letting him into my life. I even told him things I thought I'd never share with anyone but my family. I felt like I could trust him in a way I never did to anyone before. Only since yesterday afternoon have I met the Shane Peters.

The both of us took a seat. I sat on the edge of the seat and let out a shaky breath as I looked out into the crowd. The girls that were standing in the front row seemed to understand how I was feeling. They gave me a thumbs up and a few reassuring words. I looked towards Shane to see his microphone was placed on a stand. Aiden handed the mic over to me. Shane had his guitar in hand and I gave him a nod that I was ready when he was ready to start.

He smiled before he made the first strum. It took a moment to figure out which song he picked. He began signing the first verse and I listened to his voice. My full attention was on him. It felt like I was listening to him for the first time. I started to sing the female verse and Shane looked towards me with a smile as I continued on. I forget where we were and pretended it was a small performance we were doing for each other. For the moment, I felt relaxed and at ease when we harmonized. I've never done a duet before.

When Shane and I finished on our last note, the crowd applauded. We both looked at everyone. Once I realized where I was again, Shane stood up from his stool and came over to hug me.

CHAPTER FOURTEEN
Please

CLAIRE JOHNSON

Today had been one promising and fulfilling day. I had a great time with everyone and had fun for the first time in a while. After Shane and I sang together there was a Q&A session where I'd answer some of the questions with Nora and the boys. The stage was set up where the table was put towards the front of the stage. I had tried to head towards the back to let everyone turn their attention back towards Nora and the guys, but they refused to let me leave. It wasn't for me to decline if they wanted me there.

The thought of them wanting me to stay on stage with them seemed to make me comfortable around them more and they genuinely wanted me there. Well . . . there was Finnegan and my cousin who were hiding the fact that they did not want me here at all. As usual, I mostly kept my attention away from them. I wanted to have a great time with everyone and they wanted me here. It was also the fans who were interested in me having to stay, because they asked quite a lot of questions towards me also. There seemed to be a connection and bond felt between them and it was a feeling I had never experienced before. I learned a lot about everyone on stage as questions were being asked and it seemed like a normal thing to do. The crowd was calm and they were very respectful of everyone.

After the event was over, everyone on the stage were led off to the back as the crowd were told to make their way out of the building. I decided to ride in a van without Jack and Finnegan. I would say it kept me relaxed and I was able to join in on the conversation. When we arrived at our resort, we saw a few fans waiting outside the main building. I assumed they were staying somewhere near the property and that they wanted to get pictures with all of us.

After taking pictures, everyone was making plans to go eat somewhere or head back to the rooms. I told them I'd catch up with them in the morning as I wanted to have a bit of time to myself before going up to my room. I wanted to take in everything that had happened today. Shane and Jacob had offered to come along with me, but I told them it was alright and that I'd be fine.

Currently, I sat on a lounge chair in the pool area because it was the first place I thought about whenever I want to be alone outside. I've always liked the clear view of the water. Sometimes, staring at it somehow soothes me. I also liked the sound of the water making the swooshing sound. It may not be wave sounds and you may not be able to smell the salt water while you sat in the sand, but it was almost the next best thing.

Spending half an hour on my phone seemed to pass by quickly and I was pulled out of my focus when I heard the pool gates creaking, meaning someone or people were coming in. I tore my eyes away from the screen to see both my cousin and Finnegan entering. Immediately, a rush of a million things came rushing to me and I stiffen realizing I was finally alone with them and no one here was able to witness or save me from whatever they may be planning to do or say. I really hoped they wouldn't do anything or put me at some sort of risk or physically hurting me.

Today has been great and I wanted it to stay like that. Slowly, I set my phone onto the small table and stood. I noticed Finnegan with my luggage in hand. I frowned slightly wondering how he was able to get into my room.

I knew from the start that they could sense my fear. I inched my way over to them and tried to take my luggage from him, but my cousin pushed me back with quite force. I lost balance and fell to the ground. My arm got scraped against the pavement but I was able to use my free hand to stop my momentum. A gasp escaped my lips as I lifted my impacted elbow. I could slightly see from an angle that it was bleeding. The hand I used to lean on had little pebbles dug into my skin with a mixture of blood.

What could I possibly do? Screaming wouldn't catch anyone's attention. That would only make them more annoyed and furious with me. No one was here to witness this. Finnegan gave the luggage over to my cousin and with ease, he picked me up and put me over his shoulder. I began to panic as he began walking. He was making his way towards the deep end of the pool. He wouldn't do this. He's insane.

"Please Finnegan!" I pleaded weakly and struggled to get out of his grip. "I'll get sick and you know I can't swim that well under stress." He continued walking with my cousin walking behind us and I saw him looking unsure at first. He should be stopping him! This was going too far and crossing the lines of my safety.

"You should have thought about that before you ignored everything we told you not to do. Hope you enjoy your dip," Finnegan said.

I felt the surge of force as he threw me into the air which made me scream. I could immediately feel the water into my lungs as I sunk to the bottom. I tried my best to float back to the top. My mind raced as I became panicked and I was terrified of everything happening so fast. I pushed from the bottom of the pool and pushed myself up.

Once I was above the water, I coughed and gagged. My lungs burned and I felt like throwing up. I had to do something and my mind was telling me to swim to a ledge, but my legs were refusing me. As I struggled to stay afloat, I noticed my clothes were scattered throughout the pool. Both Finnegan and my cousin were now out of sight.

"H—help!" I managed to get out. I hoped someone was nearby to help. Finnegan Owen knew I wasn't a very strong swimmer and he still threw me in here to drown. There wasn't a chance of me calming down. "Help!" I called out again and I felt myself being pulled underwater as my legs grew tired.

The weight of my legs felt heavy and I went underwater knowing there wasn't much that I could do. I held my breath and closed my eyes for a moment as I thought about the many terrible things that has been going on in my life. Nothing has been easy for me since January. The thought of possibly thinking it would be easiest if I let go would make things easier for me, but so much has already been taken away from me. I couldn't give up, but I did not know how to get out of this situation. It was hard to believe Finnegan would actually use this against me and let me be in fear when I haven't done any harm.

There wasn't an option to be happy when Finnegan and my cousin was an obstacle. Either I choose to seclude myself from everyone or embrace everything like I have done today. My mental and physical health has been put on the line. No matter what I chose to do, I'd get hurt in the process. I had no idea how much time had passed. I began to feel myself beginning to fade away and I was running out of air as I held my breath in. My head began to feel very light and my chest was starting to constrict as I struggled to hold my breath. From a distance, I thought I could hear yelling coming from above, but I felt too weak. My bottom was the first to touch the ground and I tried to raise my arm towards the surface, but instead I was still and began to close my eyes.

The distant yelling continued and I heard two plunges into the water, but I wasn't sure if it was my imagination. My mind was slipping and the water went into my nose as I took the first inhale and felt the painful sensation hit me. I was losing focus and from the struggle of air, I had the instinct of wanting to breathe. A pair of hands grasped my face and waist before I felt an arm being wrapped around my waist and the feeling of floating up seemed to be happening with great force. I was confused and tired that my only sight was blackness, because I must have slipped into something. My mind was faintly there, but I was mostly somewhere else.

"She's having respiratory distress! Aiden, help me get her out." I heard a muffled, but a very worried Nate. Aiden and Nate were here? I felt cold and it was very difficult to breath now. I felt like I was being pulled back from opening my eyes. From a distance Aiden was also panicking and I felt something being put under my head and neck.

"Bro! Do CPR! What are you waiting for?" I heard Aiden say urgently. I then felt my chest being pushed on firmly. My mind seemed to be on and off. It wasn't until the third set of CPR that I felt myself gagging.

A few hands helped put me onto my side and I felt the water up my throat. I was gasping for air. It took me several moments before I felt I could breathe normally again. I slowly tilted so I could lay on my back. I was shivering. It took a while for my hearing to fully come back and to comprehend that I am no longer drowning. Slowly, I blinked open my eyes to see both Aiden and Nate hovering over me with panicked expressions.

"Are you okay?" Nate asked, concerned and unsure. As my emotions came rushing back to me, tears began to well up into my eyes and I shook my head no. In all honesty, I wasn't feeling great and I felt sick of what had just happened. I'm afraid of what Finnegan was capable of and it frightened me that he'd go to the extreme to do this to me. I find it really hard to believe that my cousin let this happen. "Do I need to call an ambulance? Are you hurt anywhere?" Nate asked again. I shook my head. I was emotionally hurt, frightened, and I felt completely drained.

"I can get her clothes out of the pool and dry them," Aiden told Nate softly to which he nodded, thanking him. I slowly started

107

to sit up but I immediately felt nauseous. Nate's eyes widened. His hands immediately close to me to make sure I wouldn't lean one way or fall over.

"Steady Claire," he said gently. I noticed my hands were shaking quite a lot. "You were just unconscious. Let me take you back to your room. I don't feel reassured with you staying alone tonight, alright?" he said. Not being able to find the words, I nodded. My chest continued to feel constricted.

As Aiden began to make his way over to the pool, Nate slowly helped me get onto my feet. It wasn't the greatest idea as I sighed painfully from how nauseous I felt. I wasn't even balancing well. Nate had to quickly react and had me put an arm around him.

"Can you walk?" he asked worriedly. I nodded slightly as I closed my eyes shut, feeling unwell. I was cold and wanted to feel okay again. I wanted things to be okay. "Claire . . ." Nate says softly as he pushed my hair from the front of my face to see him. His eyes were now filled with distress as he noticed I was in tears. "It's okay. You're safe now." No, I was not. I felt far from that.

"N—nothing is okay," I broke into a crying fit. I felt Nate wrapping his arms around me and tried to soothe me as my sobs filled the air. I let every emotion out as I didn't want to hold anything in. My body shook and I let my face bury to Nate's chest. His grip around me tightened. I felt his fingers comb through my hair. "I don't feel safe. I'm trying to forget the painful thoughts of my parents. My parents aren't here because of me," I whimpered.

"Hey, nothing is your fault here. Claire, I know I've just met you a few days ago and I may not know you that well, but know that I am here for you. I'm sorry for what happened with your parents. Whatever happened, I can tell you this is not your fault. You would never put your parents in danger."

"There was a chemical explosion in the lab." I sigh, frustrated. "My dad was in the room and my mother was just outside getting ready to enter." I could have prevented them from going into work that day. It was their day off. "I was told there was

108

a small mistake in the chemical equation and it was too late to stop the reaction."

I finally calmed down after I told Nate everything. I felt sick and uncomfortable. Nate slowly helped me walk as we began making our way towards the main building.

"Does . . . anyone here know about this?" Nate asked hesitantly.

"Sh—Shane knows." My teeth chattered and my heartbeat hasn't returned to normal. Finnegan actually left me in the pool to drown.

"Jack doesn't know?" Nate was confused. I shook my head and closed my eyes painfully. I let him lead me into the building and noticed a burning sensation going through my elbow. I opened my eyes and twisted my arm slightly to see there was a gash. "We'll clean that up." Nate said softly and pushed the button for the elevator.

"Thank you for saving me back there." I looked towards Nate who was also looking at me. He had an arm around me to make sure I would not fall over. He brought me close because he noticed how cold I was. He nodded and kissed the top of my head.

"We'll speak more of this when you're feeling better. You don't look too well and I don't want to push things right now."

"Thank you for understanding." I shivered and closed my eyes, really thankful to have air in my lungs again.

CHAPTER FIFTEEN
Uneasiness

CLAIRE JOHNSON

There was a knock to the bedroom door. I sat in the corner of the room, hugging my knees as tears flowed down my face. The aching pain in my chest remained present. I have lost the thought of using my voice much. It was the morning of my father's funeral. It was difficult to believe that he was really gone. I never expected to have to face losing almost both of my parents at the same time.

I broke down in tears the moment that I had found out about the chemical explosion at the laboratory. Anxiety haunted me ever since. I did not continue with my performance and at the moment I did not care for my upcoming auditions. Many self-conscious thoughts went running through my mind that day and everything went down.

The last several days, I stayed in my room as my Aunt Clarisse had to arrange the funeral. Since my mom was not capable of doing anything at the moment, my aunt flew down here right away. The days passed in a blur and I could never remember when I'd fall asleep or the food that I was forced to eat so I wouldn't starve. Nothing seemed to fully settle with my mind and I couldn't comprehend the talks my Aunt Clarisse would give to my grandmother and grandfather.

I briefly remembered the evening my aunt had arrived in New York and tried her best to take care of me. The only thought that bothered me the most was that my mom may not make it. I've already lost my dad. I did not have a mother who was able to breathe on her own. I wasn't sure if she would ever wake up. What exactly was going to happen now? I heard the bedroom open and I sat still as I heard a small sigh. It was very easy to tell it was my aunt as I knew my grandparents would have made it clear they were here.

"Claire?" I heard my aunt call softly to me and just a moment later, she was kneeling down in front of me and gently massages my shoulder. I sniffled as I was not motivated to stop my depressing thoughts. I didn't have much care for the world anymore. I did not want to face it. "Come on sweetheart. I know this is hard for you. I've lost my brother and have nearly lost my sister in law," my aunt insisted. I shakily looked up and took a tissue from the almost empty box and wiped my eyes. I used the other tissue to blow my nose.

"I . . . I don't know what I'll do after today," I croaked. My aunt's eyes were swelling. She understood what I was going through and she has been the only person to contact me and stay in touch with me these last several days. My Aunt Clarisse and I always had a bond I wish I had with my mother.

"I was going to ask you if maybe you'd like to live with me, your uncle John, and your cousin Jack? You're welcome to stay with us as long as you'd like and we'd love to have you."

"A—are you sure?" I felt a bit hesitant, because of the relationship I had with Jack and his friend Finnegan. "I don't want to intru—"

"You're family, Claire. You are my favorite niece and you're like a daughter to me."

I knew she had only good intentions. I knew she meant well for me and I knew she would take care of me until I was off to college. Even during or after college, she would be there for me. "Can I think about it first?"

"Of course. Take your time. Just know you have family who loves you," she said, which I nod at. At the moment, I sort of wanted to be away from everyone for now. I wanted to shut myself out for a little while and be able to be on my own before having to face people again. I couldn't handle being asked what happened or telling my story of how I ended up where I am now. She looked down towards her wrist to check the time. "We . . . should get going Claire." She sighed knowing we had to get down to the church.

People would be arriving and my Aunt Clarisse wanted to make sure we were there before anyone. Not as many family members from my dad's side would be coming and no one would be coming from my mom's side, except for my grandparents. I never met my mother's siblings or extended family, but she never mentioned them. Many friends and co-workers who did survive or were not in the lab where the explosion happened would be there.

"Of course," I mumbled. Aunt Clarisse stood up and held her hand out for me to take. I stood with her help and felt another wave of emotions. She wrapped her arms around me and we slowly made our way out of my bedroom.

The dream and memory soon began to fade and I felt like I was being brought back to the reality of the present day. I felt my breathing increasing and my conscious telling me to wake up.

The sound of a phone ringing brought me out of my sleep. At first it sounded very distant and I wasn't sure if it would stop ringing anytime soon. I felt movement from the chair somewhere in the room and I slowly flipped my body over before opening my eyes. I found Nate sitting up from the chair he was sitting on and answered the phone.

"Hello?" Nate mumbled. I thought for a moment that he was asleep just a moment ago. What time was it? Shoot . . . my phone. It may still be down by the pool. "Claire fell asleep and I was dozing off here and there. What time is it?" There was silence for a moment as Nate turned his attention towards me and I was now focusing on myself. My stomach felt very uneasy and I felt more nauseous than I had earlier. My head pounded and my body shook from how cold I felt. It wasn't the greatest idea for me to stay in my wet clothes, but I refused to be in only my undergarments with Nate in the room. I was covered in the sheets and with a blanket, but I did not feel the satisfaction of warmth these past few hours. I think we were waiting for Aiden to come back with my clothes.

"All of them? Thanks man. That'd be great if you can . . . Yeah, I'll have her shower first." Nate hung up. Another rush of uneasiness goes throughout my body and I felt like I could puke at any moment. "Are you alright?" he asked gently as he stood from the chair and started to make his way over to me.

"I—I'm not feeling so good," I forced the words out painfully and knew I needed to get up and head for the bathroom. I quickly pushed the covers away and went straight for the bathroom. I flipped the switch on as I fell onto my knees right in front of the toilet. Everything I had eaten from earlier emptied out of my stomach and I painfully groaned from how awful I felt. Nate came from behind and gently pulled my hair away from my face and rubbed my back as I continued to puke. My throat burned and I noticed my eyelids were heavy. I heaved as I tried to control everything and soon I did not have the urge to puke.

"I . . . think I'm good now," I said weakly. I took my face away from the toilet and flushed it before I tried to stand. Nate had to help me stand and led me over to the sink. I brushed my teeth and washed my mouth as I continued to shiver. Nate also had his wet clothes on. He looked towards me as if he knew what I was thinking.

"Aiden's coming here with some clothes. You can stay in a towel after you finish showering" he said as he scratched the back of his neck. I agreed, because I did not trust myself to talk too

113

much at the moment. I handed him a towel since there was another shower he could use in the other bedroom. I waited for him to leave the bathroom, but he continued to stand there waiting.

"Umm . . . Could I do it without you looking?" I said awkwardly. His face turned a slight red.

"Oh, my bad." He walked out of the bathroom and closed the door behind him. I changed out of my dress and took off my undergarments before getting into the shower. I turned the shower on and made sure the water was warm before getting in. I did not spend much time in the shower and when I finished, I wrapped myself in a towel.

I stood in front of the mirror and began brushing my hair. I closed my eyes and inhaled the steam in the bathroom. As much as I wanted to stay in the warm water, I couldn't waste too much time. Getting the tangles out of my hair took no longer than a minute. I made sure my hair was soothing out before putting my brush down and walked over to the door to open it. I walked into the bedroom to find Nate taking the wet sheets and covers off the bed.

He was only wrapped in a towel waist down. My cheeks immediately began heating up and I felt slightly uncomfortable. Why was this happening? I've never actually checked a guy out before and this felt weird to me. He turned around and chuckled. He put the sheets and the covers on the ground.

"You like?" He looked down at himself for a moment. I think he has seen me blush even though it was dark, because he laughed lightly. I coughed slightly and turned my attention away.

"I uhh . . ." We heard a knock from the door in the living room. Nate went to answer it and came back with one of my blouses and some undergarment a moment later. He handed them to me and I quickly went into the bathroom. When I walked into the bathroom, I had to steady myself before slowly putting on my dry clothing. I slowly made my way into the living room where I'd find Aiden and Nate.

Nate changed into a dry set of clothes also. I must have taken quite some time. As I got out. I noticed Aiden had my luggage with my dry clothes I assume. He hands the luggage over to me with a smile. He then reached for something in his sweatshirt and pulled out my cell phone. I left it on the table at the pool. "Thank you so much Aiden," I said softly. My tone and everything else about me felt weak. I realized I continued to feel unwell. "No problem Claire. I'm glad you're okay? You sound sick," he frowned. Nate walked over to me and gently put his hand to my forehead. His hand felt cold to my sweaty forehead.

"Geez . . . You're really warm. I didn't realize you were this warm earlier," he said guiding me over to the couch and had me sit me down. "I mean you did just throw up just not that long ago."

"I'm still not feeling so well." I sighed wishing I wasn't shivering cold, but part of me felt like I was burning up. It was my throat that I now noticed felt very closed up and sore. Aiden walked into the kitchen and turned the lights on. I heard the fridge opening and cabinets opening or closing. It was a few moments later did the kitchen light turned off and he walked back into the living room looking concerned. "We really need to get you some medicine and food."

"I don't think she should get up though. Besides, it's the middle of the night," Nate said towards me. I shrugged not feeling up for going shopping for anything at the moment. I wanted a very fluffy comforter to keep me warm and sleep off whatever I was catching. I began feeling nauseous once more and started feeling like I was feeling off balanced. My head was spinning slightly. I brought my hand to my head. I noticed Aiden moving in front of me and knelt down while Nate rubbed my back.

"I feel so dizzy," I said, trying to control my breathing after a few minutes. Both of them had to make sure I was steady. I didn't like this feeling at all.

"We're going to take you to the hospital now," Nate said. "You're probably running a fever and should take extra precautions

115

since you did just go through a traumatic event not many hours ago." I shuddered at the thought and didn't want to think about that. "Do you think you will be able to walk down to the lobby?"

"Not sure Nate." I squeezed my eyes shut as I felt his arm around my waist. We both stood slowly when I felt myself being lifted off my feet. I opened my eyes to see Nate carrying me. "You're the best," I said weakly and leaned my head against his shoulder as I wrapped my arms around his neck. He smiled weakly and nodded.

"Ready to go?" Aiden asked.

"Let's go," I heard Nate say and we began moving. "Did you not eat dinner Claire?" Nate asked me softly.

"N—no," I said in the same tone. "I never had the chance to."

"Aiden and I promise to get you something to eat as soon as we check you in."

"Thank y—you. It means a lot for you guys to be taking me at this time of night."

"It's my job to make sure that you're alright. Especially after finding you drowning. I'm really concerned and worried. I don't know what is going on between you and Jack, but I'll wait until you're feeling better to talk. I know it must be hard to concentrate."

"My head is really confusing me." I knew I must have been speaking lightly. I closed my eyes from the motion of the elevator going down. "I should have let Shane and Jacob accompany me."

"You didn't know this was going to happen. Jacob and Shane huh? "Don't worry Claire, I'll inform them for you if you want me to." I could tell Nate smirked. I was sure Aiden was looking towards me.

"Yes, please," I said. We reached the main floor. Nate and Aiden stepped into the main lobby and I could hear Aiden taking out keys. I assumed they had a rental car here.

"You'll ride in the back with Claire?" Aiden asked Nate.

116

"Yeah, it's probably the best idea." The cold lobby soon was gone as we left the building for the warm spring evening.

"How 'ya feeling Claire?"

"Really tired and about to puke at any moment," I mumbled.

"You'll be better after we get you a checkup. Don't worry. We'll take care of you." I smiled faintly as I thought about their kindness. I leaned my head against Nate's shoulder once I was in the vehicle and I put my seatbelt on.

After we were settled in, Aiden took off and I slowly started to drift off.

CHAPTER SIXTEEN
We Care

CLAIRE JOHNSON

The one thing I wanted the most was to sleep. Once Nate and Aiden were able to check me in, I was given a room and was immediately evaluated by a nurse. It was during the time period I was being evaluated when Aiden offered to get me something to eat. The evaluation involved questions of anything unusual or something I wouldn't do in the last forty-eight hours.

Quite a few unusual things had happened since I've arrived in Nebraska and now here in Florida but I wasn't comfortable telling the nurse the truth. The nurse also noted my blood pressure and temperature. Turned out my blood pressure was a little on the high side and I did have a fever. It wasn't something to worry about, but she would speak with the doctor about my evaluation before any final decisions are given.

Once the nurse left, Nate and I waited for the doctor to come in with my results. Nate was on his phone for a while and Aiden came back with food. My stomach grumbled and the nurse came back with medication to take with my food. Having some food felt really good as it took away some of the gross taste of the medication. As I was finishing up the last of my soup, there was a knock at the door and the doctor came in.

Speaking with her wasn't as hard as I thought it would be, because I wasn't feeling as nauseous as I had before. She discussed about my fever and how I should be more careful when playing around with the pool. I wasn't ready to speak up about what happened. The thought of pool scene made me panic again. I know that because of this I wouldn't want to be near the deep end of the water for a very long time.

After the discussion, I was told to be monitored overnight to. If the doctor had known what really happened, I was sure there would have been a lot of questioning. The police officers would be involved also. The thought of going through that ordeal made me feel anxious. Once she had walked out, Aiden and Nate looked towards me. Nate had a worried look and Aiden seemed ready to bombard me with many questions and, possibly, accusations. I knew what they were thinking and I had been avoiding it since the incident. I looked towards the wall where the clock hung. It was around four in the morning.

"Please don't tell Jack," I said gently. I was the first to break the silence. Nate sighed. I knew this would be a problem, but I wanted to avoid my cousin at all cost.

"But he's technically your responsibility while you are down here. He has to know. He's your cousin," he told me.

"Please don't, I really don't want him here." I've had enough fear coursing through me for the past several hours. I didn't want to come face to face with Finnegan or my cousin. The awful incident replayed in my mind. I was now feeling unsettled about sleeping again when I had just begun to calm myself from my nightmares. I'm afraid this was not going away anytime soon.

"What happened out there?" Aiden asked. I know I would have to tell them eventually. I looked towards my hands and started to play with them. "Tell us," he pestered.

"I'm not ready to," I said softly.

"Claire . . . you were drowning for Christ's sake. You were put in danger. You should at least tell us what is going on," he urged again. I continued to look towards my hands.

Aiden seemed like the person who wanted straight answers and doesn't give up until he gets an answer. It made him start guessing and assuming people, but I wouldn't say anything.

"Just tell us the damn story Claire!" Aiden snapped at me. I closed my eyes and shivered from his tone. I never wanted to have someone get angry with me. I was tired and unwell.

"Damn it Aiden. Don't force it out of her," Nate seethed towards Aiden, annoyed that he'd snap at me when I just faced a traumatizing event. "She's unwell at the moment Aiden."

"Well I can't sit here not knowing what the hell is going on," he retorted. I opened my eyes and saw Aiden getting up to leave. I flinched when he slammed the door shut.

"I—I didn't mean to frustrate him. I'm sorry," I said, barely whispering. I felt guilty.

Nate shook his head. "You have nothing to be sorry for. Aiden can be very demanding at times, but he'll come around. He just wants to know what happened, because it scared him. Well . . . it scared the both of us."

"Are you . . . mad?"

"No, of course not. Claire, you've been through a lot tonight and you should rest. We should really get you feeling better. Get some rest," he said. I nodded as I took my phone from the table and sent two quick texts. I put my phone back onto the table as I make myself comfortable on the bed. The last text ran through my mind as my head hit the pillow.

SHANE PETERS

There was a vibration against the wooden table next to me and I groaned slightly. My body flipped over and I blindly reached for the table to feel for my phone. It took a moment to find it. I then unplugged it from the charger before bringing my phone close to my face. I squint from the brightness and it took me a moment to see a text.

Claire:

Hey, Shane. I'm really sorry if I woke you. I hope you've slept through this and see this when you wake up. I… wanted to tell you that I'm feeling unwell and is at the Vincent hospital. Nate is with me . . . but I'm scared

I frowned and reread the text as I sat up. Claire is in the hospital? What happened? My mind began to feel slightly panicky. I checked the time to see it was just about to be 5 AM. Something must have been really wrong if she had been up at this time. I looked over to the bed next to mine where Jacob was sound asleep.

In just three hours I would be having breakfast with everyone before making our way over to the convention center. Now that I've received a text from Claire. It concerned me and I wanted to make sure everything was alright. Maybe I could visit her early and still make it for the event. As long as I can see that she's alright, I'll feel better. I now looked towards Jacob again.

"Jacob." I did not get a response and he wasn't budging. I pulled the comforter off and stood from my bed. I walked towards my luggage to grab a T-shirt and jeans to put on then looked for the sweater I was wearing last night.

"Shane? What . . . are you doing?" A confused Jacob said. I turned towards him after pulling my sweatshirt over my head. He was half asleep and was frowning.

"Can you . . . uh cover for me during breakfast and sound check?" I said.

Jacob slowly sat up from his bed confused. "Where are you going?"

"I . . . have to see Claire." I started off slowly. Jacob chuckled softly and shook his head.

"It's 5 AM. You can see her at breakfast," he mused. He had no idea she was at the hospital. I'm not sure if anyone did.

"She's in the hospital." I sighed, feeling worried all over again. Jacob's jaw dropped. I didn't have an explanation. "I just need to see if she's alright. I'll be back in time to perf—"

"Go be with her," he said softly. "You should stay with her until she gets out. Don't worry about the show right now."

"But what about the fa—"

"They'll understand. If they knew you were there with them worried over someone who isn't feeling well . . . they'd want you to be with Claire. Make sure she's alright." Jacob half smiled.

"Thank you." I smiled as I finished putting my shoes on. I took my phone and picked up my guitar case before making my way out the room. As soon as I was out in the hall. I texted Nate.

> *Shane:*
> *Is she alright?*

I began making my way towards the elevator when Nate replied almost immediately.

> *Nate:*
> *She's . . . exhausted and feeling nauseous. Did she text you?*

> *Shane:*
> *Yes. I'm on my way. What room number are you in?*

I put my phone into my back pocket as I exit into the vacant lobby. The only people around was the one receptionist and the door opener. I wonder how early the guy had to be here. I walked over to the front desk to request for a taxi to pick me up before taking a seat on one of the couches.

While waiting, I had used the map to find the exact address of the hospital. I also noticed there was a flower shop close by. Once I exited, the receptionist told me there was a driver out waiting for me and I thanked her before heading out. Heading outside a little past five in the morning was when it was dark, but there was the hint of light that was beginning to show. Sunrise did not start for another twenty minutes. I thanked the doorman as I walked out and went straight for the taxi driver that was already parked.

The cab went straight to the address. It was then I felt a vibration and I took my phone back out of my pocket to see a text from Nate.

> *Nate:*
> *Are you not going to the event today? I'm not sure, but I know you definitely should*

The trip to the hospital was quick and I thanked the driver before getting out. I gave exact change before turning away and quickly went to the flower shop to get her a small bouquet of roses. I hope she likes it.

I quickly made my way over to the hospital that was just across the street. I knew what floor she was on, so I went straight to the elevator. I began to feel more and more jittery with every passing moment. The thought of her only made my mind race. She has that effect on me.

As soon as the door slid open, I slowly stepped out and looked at the sign for directions. She was in the east wing and I knew I was getting closer. I eventually found the wing when I almost bump into a nurse.

"Sir," he said, very confused to see me. "It's not yet time for visiting."

"I know, but my girlfriend told me to come," I said, coming up with the first thing that came to my mind.

123

"Only her pare—"

"We're the only ones who came together on this trip."

His eyes widened. "Right. Sorry sir. You may proceed to her room."

I thanked him before walking into the wing and began looking for the room number. *Three ninety-two, three ninety-three, three ninety-four. Got it.*

I knocked gently before walking in. Past the curtain was Nate, struggling to stay awake. He picked his head up and looked towards me. My eyes then looked to Claire. I immediately walked over to the bed. I set her bouquet down and sat down on the chair. I wanted to take her hand, but I didn't want to wake her. She looked okay to me. She must have been put on some antibiotics to help her.

"What . . . happened?" I asked softly so I wouldn't wake her. I looked towards Nate and he was already looking at her.

"Aiden and I found her drowning in the pool . . ." Nate stated hesitantly. My eyes widened. She was drowning? I don't understand. "At first we heard someone screaming for help. I knew Claire would be by the pool so we immediately thought she was in some sort of danger," he explained further. I opened my mouth to speak, but nothing came out. "I think it had to do something with Fin. There's no other possible reason that I could think. She was afraid and freaking out when we got her out." Nate sighed.

"She hasn't told you?"

"She doesn't have to. It was very evident when Aiden tried to get the answers out of her. He was making her feel worse and I had to stop him."

"I'll stay with her then. I'm not going to leave her alone for so many hours," I said after a moment. That's it. I've made my final decision.

"I don't either. I'm really concerned."

"I'll watch her. Blake wouldn't approve if both of us are not there," I insisted.

Nate sighed and took a glance towards his phone. "Are you sure?"

I nodded. "No problem. Could you uh . . . make sure Claire's room has food?"

"Aiden has already done that a while ago. We weren't sure what she liked, but he decided to get her a variety of stuff from the grocery store."

"That's great. Yeah, I'll make something for her if she's discharged early."

Nate chuckled and nodded. "Clearly you're into her."

"I'm that readable?" I looked at him nervously. Not only does Jacob and Ben think I'm head over heels for Jack's cousin, but now Nate may be thinking the same thing.

"Very. I think she suits you very well."—he slowly stood up from his chair—"I'll check up on you guys. Keep me posted alright?"

"Of course." I felt my cheeks heating. Nate smiled wearily as he began making his way out. I slowly leaned back against the chair and looked towards her sound asleep. She looked peaceful and I thought about how kind she is. I then looked away to read the time on the clock to read a little past 6:30.

I sent a quick text to Jacob telling him that Claire is alright and she'll be okay. I'm sure he'll sleep through the text. A quiet sigh left my mouth and I looked towards the window as I waited for Claire to wake up.

CHAPTER SEVENTEEN
What Everyone Thinks

CLAIRE JOHNSON

The sound of music was the first thing I heard once I felt conscious. The notes made a tune that was unfamiliar to me. It was beautiful and it was something I could wake up to every morning. Once I adjusted, I slowly opened my eyes to see Shane softly playing his guitar. He was so focused on the tune that he didn't notice me at first. My breathing hitched. He's really here.

I moved slightly from the bed to make myself more comfortable which caused Shane to stop playing. He looked up and smiled when he realized that I was awake. He had a mixture of worry and relief on his expression. The curls in his hair were all over. He looked really cute and I was somehow lucky to have a guy like him who was worried for me.

"Hey. How are you feeling?" His tone was soothing that I was beginning to relax. He seemed to know how to make someone feel calm. I took a moment to stare at him.

"I'm feeling a lot better than earlier," I answered softly and rubbed the sleep out of my eyes. I took a quick glance towards the time and frowned. Is Shane not going to the event today? "Did Nate leave for the meet and greet?"

"Yeah. He wanted to stay, but I told him to go so I could stay. He also didn't want to upset his fans. I told him I'd keep an eye on you," he explained.

I was curious about his response. "It's okay. I understand . . . how about you though? You have fans also. Shouldn't you be there too?" I noticed him half smiling and nodding.

"I had to come and see you. I wanted to make sure you were alright. The text you sent me earlier had me really worried and I couldn't go to the event knowing you were here. I've already told my fans I had to do something important today and I've apologized to them," he said earnestly. My heart swelled at how thoughtful Shane has been towards me since we've met just two days ago now.

"You have fans too. I'm sure they are still disappointed to not see you today."

"I have promised myself I'd make it up to them as many times as I can when I go on my tour someday. I'll be sure to come here, Miami and a few other areas here." I nodded, feeling better. He really thinks of everything. "Oh, these are for you." He put his guitar down and reached over to the table where I noticed a bouquet of roses. He handed them to me and I took them gratefully.

"I love them. Thank you." I smiled trying to control how happy this made me. This meant a lot to me. No one has ever given me flowers, let alone a bouquet. It was so beautiful. I brought them close to smell how fresh they were. "This is so thoughtful of you. I can put them in a vase when I get to buy one when we leave here."

"I've already had someone get a vase for it," Shane smiled shyly. He was doing so much already. He is so kind. We heard a knock from the door and I turned towards the curtain to see my nurse coming in with a clipboard. She smiled once she noticed I had new company here with me.

"Hello, Miss Johnson. How are you feeling? Is Mr. Peters here being great company to you?" My cheeks seemed to heat ever so slightly and I wasn't so sure he'd notice. "I'm feeling a lot better. I actually don't feel overheated like I did earlier."

"That's good to hear. You did have a fever, which seems to have gone down for the most part. You are being discharged this morning since your main concerned symptoms have gone away. I recommend you to pick up the antibiotics we will prescribe to you at our pharmacy downstairs then rest for today." She handed the prescription paper to Shane.

"Thank you so much doctor. When would the prescription be ready to be picked up?" I asked.

"It's all set for you to pick up. Your insurance card has covered everything and paper has already been filled out."

"Thank you again."

"Have a good rest, Miss Johnson." The nurse walked out of the room and I looked towards a bag that must be my clothes. Aiden must have come back and brought me a new pair of clothes. Shane saw what I was looking towards and picked up the bag. He handed the bag to me after I sat up and slowly swung my legs over to the side. I thanked him as he nodded and began to put his guitar back into his case. I stood carefully and made sure my legs were stable. I made my way towards the bathroom and shut the door behind me. I put the bag on the table and opened the bag to see a note I took the note and read through it.

> *Yes, I am still frustrated that you wouldn't tell us what had really happened, but I am really worried for you and I just want to make sure you are alright. I can see why you wouldn't want to talk about it yet. I'm not mad at you. You did . . . drown and Nate had to do CPR . . . I'm sorry for giving you a hard time when you weren't feeling so well and you are probably traumatized.*
>
> *Okay, let's forget about that for now. Let's mention that Shane is with you? *smirks* I knew from the day I introduced him to you that he'd be into you. So . . . since Shane will probably be the one with you when you are discharged. I used my fashion senses and*

128

brought you an outfit you can wear when you leave. I'm sure Shane
will be taking you out to eat. Enjoy your mini date -Aiden

I laughed lightly and put the note down as I took out the outfit and my flats. I smiled, thankful that Aiden chose something comfy.

I carefully got out of the hospital gown then put on my outfit. I took my toothbrush and toothpaste out to quickly brush my teeth. I then took my brush from the back and brushed the tangles out of my hair. I decided to put my hair up in a bun. Once I was set, I put all of my necessities back into the bag and left the gown on the table. I opened the door and saw Shane standing.

He looked towards me and smiled. "You look amazing Claire. I mean it Claire. You're beautiful."

I looked down, feeling flustered by his words. "Have I ever told you that your kind words are really appreciated?"

He put on the straps of the guitar so it was on his back then picked up the bouquet, smiling at me.

"I like being honest with you," Shane answered. "I can take your bag and you hold the roses?" he offered. I agreed and handed my bag over to him. He made sure I was steady before nudging me again. "Ready to head to the pharmacy?" he said.

We began making our way out of the room. "Are you sure you're alright not going to the event? I'll be okay until you come back," I said. He looked towards me as we continued to walk out of the wing and I assumed heading towards an elevator. There was one we could walk right into and so I leaned against the wall as Shane pushed for ground floor. He didn't say anything as we went down and left the elevator. We began walking where the pharmacy would be.

"I'm sure. I'd like to make sure you're alright . . . I heard something happened at the pool last night?" He asked softly. I looked away from him and closed my eyes for a moment. I stopped walking. I shivered at the vivid memory and I felt my hands shaking

129

slightly. Fear ran through me again. This was Finnegan's fault. "Claire . . ." I heard him half panicked and he took my hand in his leading me somewhere. He took a sharp turn and I opened my eyes to see a blur.

He leaned me against a wall and put both my bag and bouquet on the ground before taking my hands in his. I tried to look away and I pulled my hands away from him. I brought my hands to my face and sniffled.

"I'm so sorry. I didn't mean to upset you. You're not ready to talk about it. I'm really sorry." His arms went around me then pulled me towards him. I leaned my head against his chest. "We can get your prescription and head back to the hotel."

"Can we get something to eat before heading back?" My voice sounded so distraught. Shane looked so guilty.

"Of course, we can. I should have thought about breakfast. You must be hungry. We can go somewhere to eat after getting your prescriptions." He nodded "Do you want me to go get it, or will you able to come with me to get it?" he asked changing the subject away from the incident. I was grateful for that.

"I'll go with you," I sniffled and he nodded apologetically. He picked up both my bag and bouquet. He hands the bouquet to me and he took my hand intertwining them. I smiled through my tears and he squeezed my hand in return. I wiped my eyes and we walked over to the pharmacy in silence. It was a quick process and I was glad the pharmacist who helped us did not stare at me or say anything. She did tell me to get better soon and hoped I had a great day. "I feel . . . exhausted." Shane looked towards me as he put my medication into my bag. We walked, hand in hand, out of the hospital. The spring air seemed humid for morning.

"You must not have gotten much sleep. Maybe six hours from the time you sent me the text and you waking up. So, are we still up for breakfast?" I nodded. "How about a cafe? We are just down the road from a few of them." I agreed and we began heading over.

We walked up to my suite and stepped inside. Shane followed me in. I walked into the living room and my eyes widen with surprise. I first noticed the flowers and several stuffed animals on the table in the living room. There was also a huge card standing in the middle. I turned towards Shane and he had a smile. He shrugged me towards it.

I placed my roses on the table and went into the kitchen since the lights were on. I noticed several snacks on the counter. I curiously went to the fridge and found it filled with groceries. Everyone must have been here earlier. I walked back into the living room to pick up the giant card. I'd never thought I'd receive something like this. Shane watched me carefully as I headed to my room.

Everything was cleaned up like it hasn't been touched before. I knew Nate must have said something to the others and Aiden must have helped out. This was so sweet of them. I took a seat on the bed and Shane followed. I opened the card and began reading.

Claire, oh my gosh I hope you'll be okay! I heard you weren't feeling well. I hope you'll be alright! I'll see you after the event <3 *- Nora*

Please be okay, Claire! Don't die on me! You're the sweetest girl I've ever met and you're so nice. <3 ~ *Andy*

I'm so sorry that I yelled at you. Sorry, I was really frustrated with Jack and Fin. They have so much explaining to do. Anyway, I hope you get better soon ~ *Aiden*

I really didn't want to leave you this morning, I hope you understand. I feel bad. I know you're going to be okay :) rest up because we have some places to go <3 ~ *Nate*

Beautiful Claire, I want you to be okay. I want to get to know you more on this trip. Please get better soon ~ Ian

You're considered as part of the Kricon family now. I don't care what other people think. I really want you to get better soon and hope Shane is great company <3 ~ Jacob

Claire, we have an amazing trip to get to know each other. Get well soon ~Ryder

I hope you are doing alright! Hope you have a quick recovery! ~Aaron

Claire! I feel awful that you aren't feeling well. I need to spend time with you! ~Ben

Bby girl, I don't want to see you sick. Get better soon. I can't wait 'til we hangout later when we get back <3 ~ Ken

I don't want you to cry and stress yourself out. I really hope you are going to be okay and to get better. Jacob and I love spending time with you and hope we can do a lot together on this trip. ~ Shane

I read through everyone's notes and smiled faintly. I immediately felt like everyone here was being nice, because I was Jack's cousin. Even though I wasn't exactly invited on this trip, I'm glad to meet all of Jack's friends. No one back home ever cared if I was missing or was not around. I closed the card and put it onto the table.

"I don't deserve you guys." I sighed at my pessimism.

"Don't say that," Shane said as he put an arm around me. "Everyone loves you." I looked down unsure about that. I hated how I always thought of the worse.

"That's not true. There are so many people that don't like me."

"We can't always get everyone to like us. Those fans you sang to yesterday definitely loved you. All the guys really like you and Nora loves you too. You don't need the negative people in your life. I don't know what you have with Fin or your cousin or the people at your school, but you're amazing. I think you are so kind and you're . . . well you're you."

He held onto me as he told me how amazing I was to him. My negative thoughts were soon replaced with his soothing one. I was beginning to relax and I knew I had already taken a dosage of my medication. I soon started to drift off at the angelic and kind voice of Shane. I felt myself being lifted somehow, but my mind was starting to slip away as I knew I wanted to sleep. I wanted nothing more, but to get more rest. I was being tucked under the covers and felt a kiss to my head.

"You're perfect in my eyes," he whispered by my ear.

CHAPTER EIGHTEEN
The Story

CLAIRE JOHNSON

It was the smell of food that heightened the interest of my nose and I awoke from the strangest dream. I sniffed slightly to figure out what could be the cause of my grumbling stomach. How long have I been asleep for? I opened my eyes and sat up, looking around my surroundings. The last thing I could remember was Shane holding me in his arms and telling me the things he liked about me. I also remembered him picking me up and putting me under the covers. It may have been my imagination that he kissed my forehead saying one last thing, but I wasn't so sure.

I looked towards the balcony and noticed the sun was starting to set. I reached for my phone to see it was already a little past six thirty. I evaluated myself for a moment. I felt a lot better now with a clear mind, but I continued to feel slightly weak. I'm sure I am due to take another dosage of my prescription.

Slowly, I pulled the comforter back and swung my legs over the bed. I walked over to the door and opened it. Once the door was opened the smell of muffins and lasagna filled my nose. I walked through the living room towards the kitchen. As I was getting closer to the kitchen, I heard humming. I walked into the kitchen to find Shane taking out the lasagna and closed the oven before turning it completely off. He had two plates set already on the counter. I stood by the kitchen opening between the living room stunned. He turned slightly and noticed me standing by the doorway and stopped humming. He smiled towards me.

"Hey, did you have a good rest?" I nodded as he turned quickly to cut the lasagna into pieces. "Feeling better now?"

"Yes. I feel much rested. Did . . . you cook everything on your own?" He must have started cooking for the past hour and a half. I wasn't expecting to wake up to food being cooked.

"Yeah, I thought you'd be hungry when you wake up."

"That's so sweet of you. Thank you so much." He smiled and took both of our plates.

"It was no problem. I didn't mind cooking. Ready to eat?"

"Yes, I'm just going to take my antibiotic really quick."

"I put it on the counter for you." I nodded as he went out of the kitchen with our food and I walked over to the package where my medication sat. I took my medication out and filled the small cup with the right dosage before I drank the whole amount twice. I rinsed the small plastic cup and put it on the counter. Shane walked back into the kitchen to grab the silverware and the plate of muffins. Those muffins looked amazing. I followed him out of the kitchen and went to the table already set in the living room. He had two glasses of water as he set the plates facing each other.

"I really appreciate this Shane. This is amazing."

"Thanks," he said shyly and we both took a seat. Shane would take a glance at me and I continued to have the bubbly feeling I have felt. "I wasn't sure if you'd like lasagna."

"I like a lot of things," I smiled. He smiled back. "Maybe we can ask each other some questions to get to know each other more? I like asking questions."

"Sounds good to me." We began to eat and I enjoyed the taste of the food. I really do like having cooked meals. "So, what do you want to be when you grow up? he asked starting off with the first question. I smiled slightly.

"I want to become a pharmacist and to hopefully play the cello professionally." I then frowned slightly, regretting the decision of not applying to the top school.

When I was a little girl, my parents had to attended separate conferences. I remembered going to Quebec with my father and took that opportunity to visit McGill on a weekend. I fell in love with the campus. Since then, I've always wanted to go there. "I should have applied to McGill even though I probably wouldn't get in." I shrugged at the thought.

"I remember you saying you wanted to apply to McGill. I still think it's amazing you're interested in both the sciences and music." He seemed in awe when we talked about our passions.

"What is something else that you like to do besides singing and playing the guitar?" It was my turn to ask him. I knew how he was introduced to music and how everything started from the stories he shared about his family and friends.

"I love exploring new places," he said. I smiled at the thought of traveling. I've always wanted to travel the world, but that would have to be put on hold until after college. No worries about college right now though. I've just come out of my shell and really take my mind off the stress for a little bit. Shane easily made me forget about my worries.

"If I become really famous, would you visit me while on tour?"

"Of course, I would! You're really fun to be around. I could spend a whole day with you and still want to hang out with you more," he said. That sounded strange. I looked down, my cheeks flushing once again. I knew Shane was looking at me.

"I feel the same way Claire," he said casually. I looked up and he smiled. He wasn't going to point out my heated cheeks. He made the conversation very comforting. I think I've mentioned this a few times already. I was going to ask my next question when my phone went off.

136

"Sorry." I picked up my phone to see who was calling. My heart began to pick up, wondering if there were any good news or if I was being checked up on. "I should really take this." I stood slowly from the table.

"Of course," Shane said, giving me a reassuring smile. I walked towards the doors to the balcony and answered the phone quickly.

"Hi Aunt Clarisse!" I greeted cheerfully. It may have been a few days, but it's great to hear her voice from a distance.

"Hey sweetie! For a moment I thought you weren't going to answer," she said. I heard a giggle from the other end. "I wanted to check up on you. Jack told me you were sick?"

Oh, so Jack told her I wasn't feeling well? "I had a cold, but I'm a lot better now. I'm on some antibiotics and should be a hundred percent better by tomorrow."

"That's good to hear. I really do hope you enjoy your time there. Is Jack there with you right now?"

"No, he actually went out for a little bit with some of his friends. I'm resting for the day," I said.

"Okay. I'll call him later then. It was good to hear from you."

"You too . . . Have you heard any news about my mom?"

"There hasn't been much change from the last news you received hun," she replied weakly. I heard a sigh from my aunt. I looked down at my feet, feeling disappointed and worried.

"Oh . . ."

"I'm really sorry Claire. I really do hope for the best. Only time will tell."

"You're right. Thank you for checking up on me," I answered softly.

"I hope you will be able to enjoy the rest of your time there. Take care Claire."

"I'll talk to you soon." We hung up with each other and I let out a stressful sigh. I feel like I could fall apart again. I really

137

hope everything would be okay for my mom. I know we didn't get along, but she has helped me through a lot. I put my phone into my pocket and massaged my temples.

I slowly fell to my knees and hugged myself. I closed my eyes, taking a deep breath. My heart was aching. Not even a moment later, the door to the balcony opened and I felt Shane rushing towards me. I noticed Shane getting down onto his knees and reached out to my arms.

"What happened Claire? Is it about your mother? Is she alright?" he asked quietly.

"Nothing has changed from yesterday . . . It means she isn't any better either. I—I just wish I . . ." I sighed painfully.

"You wish what?"

I shook my head. I've only told pieces of the story to Shane and Nate.

"Claire?"

I opened my eyes. I could see Shane only wanted to be here and help the best he could. "I should have stopped my parents from going into the lab that day," I said quietly. He looked confused. He was aware that my father was dead and my mother had slipped into a coma, but I never told him how everything happened.

"You didn't know that would happen in the lab. Claire this is not your fault," he said softly. I averted my eyes from him. "Is this the reason why you haven't sung in front of the crowd until now? The accident happened on one of the most important days of your life, didn't it?" he asked and I nodded. He sighed and ran his fingers through his hair. "I shouldn't have made you sing. You must have been traumatized or something!"

"Shane, it's okay. You helped me break out of my shell. I needed that, really. It turned out to be amazing and I enjoyed singing with you." I smiled faintly. He looked so distraught and bothered. "I moved in with my Aunt Clarisse and Jack because my aunt offered me to stay with them until I went off to college. It took time for me to move and when I did, I knew I was ready to open myself up back to the world."

"If I had known before . . ."

"Shane you made a great decision. Don't worry," I insisted. Shane noticed that I was shivering and began taking his sweatshirt off. Before I could protest, he put his sweatshirt over my head. I thanked him.

"Does . . . Jack know about your parents?" he asked hesitantly.

"I don't think so. I've never really had the chance to talk to him." I shrugged, feeling like it was a lost cause with him. "I feel like he hates me and won't forgive me."

"Forgive you? Why would he hate you?" Shane was confused again. He knew about my parents, I may as well tell him the relationship I had between my cousin and Finnegan. "It happened years ago. It was my freshman year when I came to visit for the break and I sort of got him suspended from school. Jack refused to let me get in any trouble and so he took the blame for me."

"I don't see why he would hate you. It looks like he was protecting you."

"He was . . . It has to do with Finnegan. He never liked me and I think he took this opportunity to turn Jack against me since the break in did go into their records."

"What? What did Jack do and why did you break into the school?" Shane's eyes were wide.

"One day when Jack was out with Finnegan, I broke into the school to go into his files. He told me not to do anything. He told me that he'd deal with the problem and turn himself in, but Finnegan was holding him back. So, I went in and Jack went after me." I shook my head, wondering why I did that. I looked towards Shane again to see him with concern in his eyes. He seemed to find what I say intriguing. "The cops found out about the break in and came to the school. Jack told me to run because he did not want me

139

to get caught. I didn't want to leave him, but he insisted that he had to do this and did not want me to get into serious trouble. I ran all the way home. When Aunt Clarisse received the call, she had to talk with the principal and the police officers. Jack was suspended from school and had to do community service . . ." I bit my lip, feeling guilty. Thinking about it now, there probably could have been a better way to solve the problem.

"You did what you thought was right," Shane said softly.

"Yeah, but Finnegan turned him against me. They . . ." I felt afraid of saying things out loud again. Finnegan had that scary effect on me. I don't think he can be questioned after he had attempted to drown me. My breathing quickened and Shane immediately noticed my reaction.

"They what?" I looked at him and he looked right into my eyes. He gently put one hand to the side where my arm was. "Tell me." I lowered my eyes shamefully as I told him.

"They hit me sometimes . . ." I whispered. "They hurt me and scare me . . ."

"Were they the ones who threw you in the pool?" he asked me suddenly. I hesitated but I nodded slowly. "They won't do it again. I won't let them near you alone again on this trip. Everything will be okay. Does anyone know about this?" he asked.

"No," I whispered and closed my eyes. "Please Shane . . . I know you want to tell me this isn't right and I should tell someone. It really hasn't gotten this bad . . . until now."

"We need to tell Na—"

"I'm not ready to tell anyone." I opened my eyes and I saw this was making him mad not towards me, but towards Jack and Finnegan. "I . . . can't, please. I'm scared."

His eyes shut painfully then let out a sigh. My heart was racing. The thought of Jack and Finnegan finding out about this only made me even more scared of what they could do—what Finnegan could do. I wait for Shane to open his eyes, but they remained closed.

After a few moments of silence, I gently reached for one of his hands. I didn't know what he was thinking. I want to solve the problem between me and my cousin. I couldn't care less as long as my cousin sees what Finnegan has been doing to me.

"I—I love my cousin and he was only trying to protect me until yesterday. Finnegan has turned him against me and my cousin Jack has never laid a hand on me. I'm scared of Finnegan. I don't want anything happening to Jack."

"Do you trust me?" Shane asked softly after a moment and opened his eyes.

CHAPTER NINETEEN
The Plan

CLAIRE JOHNSON

"I trust you," I answered after what seemed like a long period of time. For a while, my mind was thinking and doubting everything. Shane has only been here to help me and have been able to pull me out of the darkness of my world I have been in the past several months. These past days with him made me feel like I was living in a dream. I squeezed his hand and he returned the gesture. The wind had started to pick up and the sun was almost down.

"Let's get you inside for a little bit. We don't want you getting worse on top of what you had earlier," Shane said. He slowly stood up. I nodded. He gently helped me up on my feet. He wrapped an arm around my waist and led me inside. "Are you still hungry?" he asked. I shook my head as he led me over the couch. We both sat down and he pulled me closer to him.

"Can we tell Nate tonight?"

"Andy, Jacob, Aiden and Nora also," I said softly. He nodded and I assumed he was sending a text to them. He still had an arm wrapped around my waist and I felt reassured in a way. When he placed his phone on the table, he used his hand to intertwine it with mine. I loved how his hands were bigger than mine. My stomach always felt the butterflies when I held his hand. It also felt like those times right before I would perform.

My head leaned against his and I felt myself relaxing for the moment. Shane's thumb would rub small circles on my hand. I closed my eyes. He understood I needed time in silence and he knew I needed someone here. Shane never questioned or hasn't pushed me to a point where he'd hurt my feelings. He'd try to change the subject or see why something would be so upsetting and be there for comfort.

We heard a knock on the door about ten minutes into our silence. I picked up my head slowly and sighed. I do not know how this could turn out. I let go of Shane's hand so he could get the door. I could hear chatter and I grew nervous each passing second. What if Aiden became frustrated again or Nate doesn't see where I'm coming from? How about the others? What if they thought I was weird or thought that I should be left alone?

I could spot Nora's red hair. Everyone was asking questions to Shane. I slowly stood up and noticed Jacob looking towards me with a friendly smile. Once Nora spotted me, she gasped and came over. The guys stopped talking as well.

"I'm so glad you're feeling better!" Nora said genuinely and attacked me with a hug. I gasped slightly and realized I was not fully recovered yet. I'll definitely have to rest up tonight.

"Let her breathe Nor," Jacob chuckled. The guys, along with Shane, walked over.

"It's great to see you looking well. Nate and Aiden made it seem like it was a lot worse," Andy said, giving me a quick hug. It was definitely worse.

"It's good to know Shane has been taking good care of you." Jacob smiled. "How are you feeling?"

"Better." I tried to smile. "Thank you guys so much for the flowers, stuffed animals and the big card. I loved them."

"And I see you and Shane are enjoying the food." Aiden smirked. The lasagna and muffins were still on the table.

143

"Thank you so much for the food and snacks Aiden," I said shyly. I felt my cheeks warming up from his note earlier. "I can pay you back for the fo—"

"No need. It's fine. I was going to get you food no matter what when I found out you didn't have anything here." He smiled.

"I still owe you," I insisted.

"Well . . . I guess I can think of something. Nothing bad. I promise," he chuckled. Both Nate and Andy chuckled. We all took a seat. Shane and I sat together and Jacob sat on my side. Nate, Andy, Aiden, and Nora took the recliner and pulled chairs from the table.

"So . . . why did you two gather us here to talk?" Jacob said slowly. I felt my heart racing because Shane knew I wasn't ready to tell them what happened on my own.

Shane told them the whole story of me hanging out by the pool. Shane confirmed Aiden and Nate's theory of Finnegan doing something to me. When Shane mentioned how he threw me in the pool, Aiden got angrier. After Shane finished, everyone looked towards me, concerned. Nora looked like she was going to tear up any moment.

"This is so awful. How could he even think of doing that to you?" Nora said softly. I shrugged, unsure of how to answer.

"This . . . is all true?" Andy asked. I nod nervously and was afraid to make direct eye contact with any of them.

"They won't do it again," Nate said. I looked up and saw he was running his fingers through his hair looking very surprised of what really happened. No one expected Finnegan to actually throw me into the pool and leave me there to drown. I told them I wasn't the strongest swimmer when I was put under stress. I struggled with swimming in gym class.

"Damn right they're not," Aiden added as he stood up. Andy and Nate had to hold him back down. "If they lay one more hand on you, I'll . . ."

I bit my lip with slight panic that he would hurt my cousin also. The thought of my cousin getting hurt pained me. I really hope this wouldn't turn into a mess. Jacob noticed my uneasiness and tried to calm me down.

"We're going to fix this," Nora said cutting him off. She could also tell I was uneasy about this. I was glad mostly everyone here wanted to make sure I wasn't going to have some sort of panic attack.

"You're not going to hurt my cousin . . . are you?" I looked over at Aiden. I had a feeling he'd start a fight.

"Do you want me to?" He looked very serious and I shivered.

"Aiden!" Nora raised her voice at him. Aiden sighed in defeat.

"No, I guess I won't, but Finnegan is going to get it," Aiden then said.

I was mostly okay with that, if it's certain that I'd never have to face him again. Sadly, I think I will be stuck with him for several months until I go off to college. That is if I end up going. The thought of my whole college process had been pushed back. It stressed me out.

"I want to talk to him," I said lightly. Shane knew I wanted to talk to Jack. He knew my reasoning, but I wasn't so sure everyone else would understand. I had this feeling Aiden and Nate would see it as a risky idea.

"Why would you want to talk to either of them?" Andy asked. "Your cousin watched you thrown into the pool and did nothing about it. I'm surprised you haven't told your aunt yet."

"My cousin . . . I'd like to talk to him. He'd never do anything to me if Fin wasn't with him."

"Which he usually is," Jacob said from beside me.

"We'll take him somewhere," Shane then proposed. "Nate, Andy, Jacob, Nora, and I could ask Finnegan to go somewhere with us."

"You guys would do that?" I looked around and Andy's jaw seemed clenched. Nate and Andy looked unsure of this.

"I don't know . . ." Nate said slowly.

"He left you to drown Claire. Let's not forget that." Aiden clenched his fists. "I could beat him up a—"

I looked away. I really couldn't stand the thought of violence right now. I don't want any family members hurt.

"If Finnegan knew . . ." I started softly. "I don't think I'd ever feel safe again."

"Exactly my point Claire." Aiden is right. He may be right, but it doesn't help me as I noticed Shane squeezing my hand. I did not like how this was going. He knew I was getting stressed and was fearing the outcome. He knew I've been through a lot and he understood he didn't want to put more on me when I had a lot to deal with already.

"Claire needs time," Shane said, grabbing everyone's attention. Shane looked towards Nate and Aiden. Realization hit Nate so he nudged Aiden as he looked towards me with guilt.

"Right. Claire, I'm sorry again. I shouldn't have pushed this whe—damn I should have realized sooner," Nate said apologetically. Andy, Jacob, and Nora looked towards each other in confusion.

"M—my parents were in an accident," I pointed out softly. Andy's eyes widened. Nora was surprised and Jacob shifted uncomfortably. "My uh mom is in a coma right now and my dad . . ." I let out a sigh and closed my eyes. The aching feeling has already returned. I squeezed Shane's hand.

"Claire," I heard Andy, sounding guilty. I opened my eyes and once again, my eyes felt watery. They burned and I wanted nothing more than to ease the pain. I saw Nora shift in her seat uncomfortably too. I saw the expressions they were giving me. Sympathy. "We didn't mean to upset you," Andy said.

"I'm sorry to hear about your parents. If you ever need anything, you can always text me," Jacob said softly. I nodded slightly before thanking him. I then looked at Nora.

"We're here for you Claire," Nora said softly with a painful look. I look towards my lap, feeling a mixture of fear and sadness.

"We . . . can get Fin away for a little while," Aiden said hesitantly. I nodded as I slowly stood with Shane holding my hand. Everyone started to get up as well.

"Are you sure you want to do this now?" Shane asked quietly. It was obvious everyone was debating whether this was a good idea or not. "We can wait until tomorrow when you're feeling better or when you're ready."

"I'll be okay," I said with a weak smile. Nate seemed to have finished texting someone.

"Fin said he'd meet us down at the lobby in five minutes." Nate then looked towards me. "Jack should still be at the basketball court."

"Jacob and I can walk her," Shane offered. Andy looked between Jacob and Shane.

"We've got her." Jacob smiled and put an arm around my shoulder. "Shane and I will meet you in the lobby after."

"Alright," Nate said as he came over to me. "We'll text you when it's safe. If he does anything to you"—he stared deeply into my eyes—"you scream and get away. I don't care if he is your cousin. Safety first," Nate urged. I nodded, then he hugged me.

Everyone came over to hug me and told me how sorry they were for my loss. I thanked everyone for being understanding and for the card, flowers, and stuffed animals. I promised myself to thank everyone else later. Maybe I could tonight.

We all began to leave my suite. The four waved at me. It seemed like they were seeing me off. Strange feeling. Andy, Nate, Aiden, and Nora were making their way towards the elevator that would lead them straight to the lobby. Jacob, Shane, and I decided to take a different route and took the stairs. We headed towards the back of the building.

"Are you sure you don't want us to come with you?" Jacob asked.

"We could come with you," Shane said softly. I looked up between the two and put my arms around them. I smiled faintly towards them.

"I really appreciate you guys," I said lightly. "I'd really like to do this on my own." They both nod as they have already led me towards the door entrance where the basketball and tennis courts were. My phone vibrated and I looked at the text from the recently made private group chat.

Nate:
It's all clear. You've got this and don't hesitate to call it.

Aiden:
Please be careful. Just say the word and I'll do it

Andy:
Aiden, shut up. You're really not helping. Claire, you can do it. He's at the basketball court outside shooting hoops.

Nora:
I love you and stay safe <3

Shane and Jacob both had looked at the texts. Jacob gave me a hug and told me he would see me soon.

Shane was the last one to hug me. I hugged him tightly. He held me in his arms for what seemed like only a quick second. I wish I could stay in his safe embrace. I had to do this though.

"I'll see you two soon."

"Of course, we will," Jacob chuckled. "I'm sleeping over at your place tonight."

Shane looked towards him and raised an eyebrow. "You are?" Shane asked.

"We both are." Jacob smiled. "Since we didn't have our sleepover the other night, I've decided we'll come to her."

Shane smiled and looked towards me wondering if this was okay. "I'd love for you two to stay with me tonight." I laughed lightly. "Thank you for inviting yourself and Shane."

Both Shane and I laughed together as Jacob fisted the air in excitement. "No problem. We'll have a great time for sure. Text us when you're done?" Jacob said.

"Of course," I replied.

Our phones beeped.

Aiden:
Shane and Jacob. Hurry the hell up and stop flirting with Claire. Fin is already here and we're waiting for you two

My cheeks felt like they were heating up. I noticed both Jacob and Shane rolling their eyes. I laughed at the both of them. They just know how to make me forget about my worries for a short while.

"See ya," Jacob said and pulled Shane's arm. Shane had to let go of my hand. Jacob chuckled and Shane sent him a glare. "You can hold her hand all night when you see her dude. You guys have been holding hands ever since we entered her suite."

It was Shane's turn to have flushed cheeks. It was very evident that he was thinking about our hands and it was the cutest thing.

"See you soon Claire." Shane smiled as he continued walking with Jacob. I waved and watched as the two soon disappeared around the corner and headed towards the lobby.

149

CHAPTER TWENTY
Why

CLAIRE JOHNSON

The basketball court soon came into my sight. It was a humid night and it reminded me that I should shower when I get back. I got more nervous as the sound of dribbling came closer. I could see my cousin dribbling the ball and doing a few layups. It was when I stepped onto the court, I suddenly felt nervous to the point that I could possibly puke. I haven't been alone around Jack for the longest time. It was sort of strange not seeing Finnegan around.

I realized he was very concentrated on shooting. It was like he knew there was someone approaching, but he didn't say a thing. Just about five feet away from him, I stopped and waited for a moment to see if he would say something. He continued to shoot hoops without saying anything. He should know I was standing here.

"Jack?" I said. He stopped dribbling and turned towards me with a frown. I slowly closed the gap and stood in front of him. I waited for him to say something.

"What do you want Claire?" he mumbled then sighed. He had a clenched fist. I remained calm and looked towards him. His bluish green orbs flared into mine and it worried me. But I know he wouldn't punch me

"I wanted to talk to you. I haven't been ab—"

"Exactly. I don't want or need to talk to you. You're my annoying cousin who I've had to bring along. Go away Claire."

"You'd never say that. What happened? I want to know why you're so mad. You told me to run that day, because you wanted to protect me. Please Jack," I pleaded. He looked like he was refraining himself from saying something.

"Go away or else . . ." He gritted his teeth but I stood my ground. I've been through enough already and I think it's time that I'm given a break. Finnegan wasn't around either.

"Jack,"—I looked at him—"I want you to forgive me for whatever I did. I really miss being around you and you were so nice to me before." I felt hurt but I took a step towards him. All of the sudden, he grabbed my wrist tightly.

"I said stay away from me . . ." he warned. I winced from his grip.

"Jack . . . you're hurting me . . ." I said. He twisted my arm so hard that I jerked away and I felt unbalanced. I was going backwards until I turned and felt the crushing impact of my arm hitting the ground. I gasped from the pain. I could feel that something snapped. *Oh no . . .*

My eyes shut tightly as I took in a deep breath. I felt betrayed. It took a moment to gather my thoughts and opened my eyes. I looked up towards Jack.

I quivered from the immense pain but I still told him, "I will never stop." I really hope my arm is okay. The thought of having to return to the hospital was not something I was looking forward to. I hated being in hospitals.

When I was back home, I rarely stepped foot into a hospital. Since my parent's accident, I've been there quite frequently and it only brought negative thoughts. I hated the hospital, because it only reminded me that my mom was still there and there was nothing I could do for her.

"Claire . . ."

"You want to know the reason why I'm living with you?" I beamed. He remained silent. I have to get this out to him. I don't like how he has been giving me a hard time when he could be one of the few family members that I have left. "I'm here because my dad is dead and my mom is in a coma." Tears begun to blur my vision from the ache in my heart and from my arm. "They were in an incident at their lab and I wasn't notified until I was in the middle of doing a music solo in class. I don't know what your problem is. I would have thought you'd at least be nicer or try to be here for me when I actually need you," I said weakly.

I sniffed and closed my eyes for a moment. He definitely did something to my arm. I opened my eyes and looked to my arm to see more than a bruising. Moments later, I looked to my cousin to see him looking shocked of the news. He seemed very unaware and had no clue about my parents. His mouth was parted and the coldness in his eyes were gone.

Jack looked towards me and knelt down. He looked at my arm and tried to reach for it, but I turned my body. I felt very fragile and uncomfortable.

"Sh*t . . ." Jack mumbled and looked towards me apologetically. "Claire . . . I'm really sorry. I didn't mean to hurt you like that."

"I think you broke my arm . . ." I gritted my teeth, keeping myself in control from screaming.

"Let m—"

"Please don't touch me," I said quietly.

"I didn't mean to physically hurt you." He hesitantly reached for my arm gently. "F*ck, I'm so sorry Claire. Crap, I didn't mean to do this. I need to get your arm checked."

"So now you're actually concerned?" I barely managed. I did not want to sound mad towards him, but I was in pain. Guilt was evident in his expression and he sighed.

"I know I've messed up and you don't trust me at the moment, but let me at least get you to the hospital to get your arm checked out."

"Fin could b—"

"I don't care what he thinks," he said firmly and carefully began to find a way to lift me off the ground. "You're still my cousin. I don't care what happens to me at the moment. I need to make sure you're alright first."

"I can stand on my own." I pushed him with my uninjured arm and slowly tried to stand up. Everything was spinning. I closed my eyes for a split second. "Ow," I mumbled. I felt arms immediately wrapping around my waist. My unharmed arm was lifted to Jack's neck. He was looking towards me with concern.

"I'm helping you and taking you to the hospital. You're not okay. I made your arm a completely different color." I looked to my limped arm at my side and noticed the dark color. My eyes widen as Jack began to lead me off the court. "I . . . how long?" he asked.

"Wh—what?" I got confused as the pain continued to throb. It has not eased at all.

"How long were your parents . . . Are they both . . . dead?"

The thought of them brought in more pain to my chest. I could feel a familiar tingling sensation building up. "Jack . . . please not right now. I have so muc—"

"Alright. This is my fault. I shouldn't have gripped you like that. I'm so stupid and should have known better," Jack said softly. I looked towards him again as he walked across the street. I noticed his teary eyes.

"You didn't know about my parents, did you?" I asked quietly. He made eye contact with me before focusing ahead. Cooper knew, so why wouldn't he?

"No. My mom didn't say anything to me. I had no idea. I'm am such an ass and should have realized. You should have told me about this," he said. I frowned slightly, confused with his change of tone.

154

"Are you being serious right now? You've been a complete j—jerk to me since the airport," I beamed. Jack looked towards me again and stopped walking as we approached the recreation center where the parking lot was.

"I'm sorry for putting you through this. I shouldn't have let Fin turn me against you and it's not an excuse." He sighed.

"Why did you let him turn you against me?"

"I didn't want that. It was Fin who saved me and I owed him everything. We've been through a lot together. He's my best friend and we've always had each other's back."

"But your best friend is so mean to me." I sighed and closed my eyes for a moment to try and focus on anything but the pain in my arm. "I don't understand . . ."

"I don't know. That is something I don't know. He did turn me against you and words can't describe how sorry I am. I should have taken responsibility and stood up for you. I also feel awful thinking about all of this, especially about Aunt Mave and Uncle Robert. Claire, I feel so awful not knowing this. You've already been put through a lot." He then made his way towards the parking lot and I looked around in more confusion. I leaned my head against his shoulder.

"Where are you going?"

"I'm taking the rental car we have. I have the keys. You didn't think I was going to walk to the hospital, did you?" he pointed out. I shook my head. We stopped in front of a black Aston Martin V12 Vanquish.

"You rented this?"

"Yeah. I tend to rent a car on my own when I'm somewhere for more than a few days like now. Usually the vans we take to the convention center, we don't have access to in the evenings."

Carefully, I am let down onto my feet then he unlocked the vehicle. I thanked him quietly. I went in and took a seat. I carefully tried to put my seatbelt on, but it was a struggle. I sighed. I don't want to go without a seatbelt. When Jack got into the driver's side, he noticed me struggling then reached over to help fasten the seatbelt.

"Thank you," I said. He nodded before starting the car. We made our way out of resort. I sat quietly and shivered lightly from the cold air blasting through the vents. He reached over and turned the aircon off and I thanked him again.

"Yesterday . . . I . . . hate myself for what Fin and I did."

I did not say anything as I waited for him to continue. I didn't know exactly how to respond.

"You probably don't trust me at the moment and I get that. I could be sent to jail o—"

"I'm not going to say anything. I don't want you getting into serious trouble," I said quietly. Jack glanced at me with hesitance.

"It's unacceptable, what I have let happen to you. There has to be some punishment that I should b—"

"Then don't let Fin hurt me and defend me when I need it. I want the bullying to stop Jack."

"I can't sto—"

"You need to try!" I exploded. "I almost drowned yesterday! Did you think at all what could have happened to me? You're lucky your friends saved me."

"I'm thankful they did. I should have stopped what Fin was doing."

"Why didn't you?" I said. He didn't say anything as he continued driving. "I became sick later last night and you didn't visit me when I went to the hospital. You did not make sure I was going to be okay," I said quietly.

"Sh*t Claire. I'm already feeling awful. I know I messed up. Please don't make me feel sick in the stomach even more. I'm already feeling it and I am trying. From this point on I will try to do everything in my power to protect you."

"You should have been doing that from the beginning." I turned to the window. Jack sighed. I was so upset. He can't just come back into my life and suddenly be nice to me after the stunt he pulled yesterday. I could have drowned and I will keep reminding him of that. Even though I have been trying to talk to Jack for us to get along, it did not mean I was ready to forgive him.

I felt a vibration from my phone and I took it out.

Jacob:
Shane is a bit anxious at the moment and so I told him I'd text you to ask if you're alright

My thumb hovered over the keyboard on my screen as I nervously typed in my response. I wasn't ready to tell anyone what actually happened. I would not want anyone to freak out. I thought it was very sweet of Jacob to text and Shane to worry for me. My phone started vibrating again all the sudden. I panicked slightly as it slipped out of my hand. Jack glanced towards me, concerned. I leaned over to pick my phone up and answered.

"Hey," I answered lightly.

"You . . . sound like you're in pain. Are you alright?" Jacob said uneasily.

"Umm . . . well . . ." I took a glanced towards Jack and knew he was listening.

"What did he do?" he said lowly.

"I was a bit clumsy. It wasn't entirely his fault," I immediately said.

"What happened? The guys are with Fin right now and I am outside making sure you're fine."

"I—I fell and uh . . . possibly broke my arm."

"What?" Jacob exclaimed. I pulled the phone away from my ear for a moment. "Tell me you're joking around."

"No . . . sorry. I really think I broke my arm. I'm getting it checked out right now. Please don't tell anyone yet." There was a big sigh from the other end.

"Alright. Just . . . let me know when you get back to your room or if you're not back yet, I'll text you."

"Okay," I said softly. "I have to go." I looked towards the window and notice we have already arrived at the hospital and were parked in the garage. I remember passing it earlier when I left with Shane. I said my goodbye before I hung up and looked towards my cousin.

"Ready?" Jack asked. I nodded and unfastened my seatbelt.

CHAPTER TWENTY-ONE
The Johnson's

CLAIRE JOHNSON

I winced for what seemed like the tenth time. I opened my eyes as Dr. Shan continued to fit the cast on me. I looked over Dr. Shan's shoulder to see Jack standing with his arms crossed. He looked stressed and guilty. Once my cast was fully on, I was assisted into putting on my sling for support. I've never worn a cast before.

My arm was broken and I would be stuck with it for the next eight to ten weeks. This meant I couldn't write, play my cello, my guitar or do simple things that would require more than using one hand. I would have to go through a lot of struggling and adjusting. It was also terrible that I've been in a hospital within the last twenty-four hours for two different reasons.

"You're all set Miss Johnson. Your cousin has some paperwork to fill out before you go, but other than that you are all set."

"Thank you doctor," Jack said and looked towards me. I thanked the doctor before she left the room. I looked to my red cast that was being supported with my sling. I carefully let myself off from the bed and began making my way out of the room. I walked to the front desk, assuming Jack was following behind. Jack appeared in front of me and asked the guy for my paperwork. Jack received a few pages and began filling out the paperwork. I struggled to get my wallet out of my back pocket so I could hand him my insurance card. I pulled out my insurance card and Jack mumbled a "thank you" before continuing with the paperwork. I turned slightly and saw the waiting area had many open seats. I walked over to an open seat and sat down.

My phone was the first thing I took out. I decided to check social media. I went to Instagram first. I liked the pictures Nora and the boys had posted from earlier today. Currently, I followed Nora and the guys. I paused when I noticed a picture of Shane and I on stage.

It took me a moment to realize it was when we were performing together. The photo must be when I was singing a verse and Shane strummed his guitar as he was looking at me. Our knees were touching and Shane was smiling. It seemed like he was the happiest person in the world.

I looked at the user to see it was Shane himself who posted the picture several hours ago. I was also tagged in the photo and smiled faintly at his caption.

ShanePeters:
I want to thank everyone for letting @ClaireJohnson sing a song with me. I had a great time singing with her and thank you to everyone who came out to the Orlando Show

Shane is amazing and I am truly happy to meet a wonderful guy like him. We've only met just a few days ago and my mind continued to always think of him. He is the only person that I instantly felt flustered with and my heart raced at the thought of him speaking to me.

What was he doing to me? I've never felt this way. This was so new to me. I know I have a crush on Shane Peters. I can't hide from myself. I know that he is the first guy to ever make me feel special. I lied. He's not my first crush, but he's the first guy to ever get to know me. He likes talking to me and hanging out with me.

This was something I wasn't used to. I've never really hung out with a guy, let alone one who has taken any interest in me. Now, I was around many guys and I'm not used to that. The guys back home were so attached to their groups and were never willing to go out of their way to help someone who was outside their clique.

"Claire," Jack called. I looked up. He no longer was filling out the paperwork and he looked slightly bothered. I put my phone away and carefully made my way over to him.

"Everything alright?" I asked. He seemed tensed as we began making our way towards the elevator. "I'm not going to tell your mom the things that yo—"

"But I left after Fin threw you in the pool. I should have stopped that. It shouldn't have happened at all. I take full responsibility," he insisted. We now entered the elevator and I let Jack push for the ground floor.

"It's great to know you've decided to take full responsibility. I'm still not telling your mom," I said. He sighed and he gave me a thank-you look as my phone went off. Jack raised a brow. I took my phone out to see Shane.

I immediately had a mini panic attack and felt very flustered even though he was not here. I answered the phone. I was going to say something, but I heard heavy breathing from the other end.

"Please tell me you're alright," he asked worriedly. I looked towards Jack and noticed he looked towards his shoes with a guilty smile.

"I just talked to Jaco—"

"Jacob told me nothing and I knew something was up. I have been worried and I had to make sure you're okay," he said. I smiled, knowing that he cared for me. It made me feel really bubbly and light.

"I had a bit of an accident, but I'm okay," I said. I heard a sigh of relief which made me skip a beat. I need to calm down.

"You sure? I want to make sure you're alright."

"It's really sweet of you to check up on me. I promise everything is okay, Shane." I smiled into the phone and I think Shane was doing just the same. "I'll be back at the hotel soon."

"Same. I can't wait to see you," he said. My smile widened. Jack completely heard that. I'm pretty sure Jack was trying to hide a smirk.

"I'll see you soon."

"Bye Claire."

"Bye Shane." I laughed lightly and ended the call. I carefully put my phone into my back pocket and looked towards my cousin. "What?"

"No, it's probably nothing . . ." He smiled and shook his head. I used my free hand to punch his arm.

"Hey!"

"Tell me Jack!" I pestered. He glared at me playfully and chuckled.

"You like Shane." His tone made it seem like it was obvious.

"Of course I like Shane. I like all of the guys."

"That's not what I meant," he chuckled. "You like Shane more than that." The statement made my cheeks feel like they were on fire. I could hear my heartbeat ringing in my ears. I really need to learn how to control my emotions.

"How can you tell?" I was looking towards the elevator wall.

"When you talk to him. The way you smile, Claire. Your eyes light up with joy when you see him . . . Should I go on? I could go on for a while."

I do that with him? "Is it really that easy to tell?" I asked, embarrassed.

"Nah, you've only done that when you told me you had a crush on Fin," he said. The idea of Fin sent many negative signals.

"That was a while ago. Before the incident."

"You still had a crush."

"Yes, before he turned you against me. I don't want to be reminded of him at the moment."

"Right," Jack apologized. "So, when are you and Shane going out for a date?"

"What?"

"Oh, I can already see it happening. The question is when will he ask you?"

"We've just met. How can you be so sure he would feel the same way?"

Jack raised a brow as the elevator reached the ground floor. We both walked off and started making our way towards the entrance of the parking garage. "Claire . . . clearly I've noticed the interaction you two have had in the past two days alone. Let's not forget that he didn't go to the second day of Kricon. I heard he was with you at the hospital since this morning and took care of you 'til then. I'm pretty sure the boy has more interest in you than you think."

"He was worried."

"Yes, and he cooked for you. It's more than just a friendship Claire. I'm calling it." I looked towards the floor ahead of me and felt nervous. "Damn, my cousin has a crush on Shane Peters."

"You want me to feel awkward, don't you?" I looked towards him and he shrugged.

"It's in my nature. Do you want to stop through some type of drive through to get something to eat?"

"A shake sounds pretty good right now."

"Milkshake? Umm . . . I'm sure we can find one around here. That sounds pretty good," he said. I nodded as we turned towards the hall that led to a ramp. We then passed a bridge where

163

the garage was. Jack and I walked the rest of the way to his rental car in silence.

Once we were in the car, I carefully put my seatbelt on. Jack looked for directions to the nearest shop that had good reviews on milkshakes. Shake Shack seemed to be a good place to go.

"You okay?" he asked as he began making his way out of the garage. I nodded when my phone vibrated again. I pulled my phone out once again. He is so cute. It really warmed my heart. I put my phone down and Jack glanced towards me.

"Shane texted me," I said shyly. "Are you getting a shake?" I asked. I was hoping to change the subject as I felt strange to be talking about guys with him. He knew I was disappointed and upset with him, but he knew how to make me feel otherwise.

"Thinking of getting strawberry. You?" he said. I mentally sighed with relief that he was going to let it slide.

"I'm thinking cookies and cream if they have it," I said. Jack nodded as he looked forward into the traffic. I wasn't sure what to talk to him about. He seemed a bit distracted in his own thoughts. Maybe it was best if I let him be.

"Claire?" he called out. I hummed and looked towards him again. "When we get back . . . I'm going to talk to Fin."

"He's not going to change over a talk Jack."

"I know. I just . . . I need to tell him that what we've been doing is wrong and I'm going to try to get to his head that he has to stop this."

"I doubt he'll stop." I shuddered. The last several days alone had me feeling afraid and uncomfortable. Jack sighed.

"I'm going to try. I uh . . . I'll try to be more considerate with your parents . . ." He trailed off and I felt the air becoming heavy. "Sorry . . . I didn't mean to bring everything up." I closed my eyes for a split second and thought of a happy memory of them. I opened my eyes and noticed that Jack was watching me carefully.

"If you ever want to talk about them, you can always come talk to me if you'd like."

"Th—thank you," I said softly. "Uh . . . right now isn't a good time."

"Right I understand." He nodded. Up ahead, I noticed a Shake Shack shop. My thoughts melted into having my delicious milkshake. "Ready for your shake?" Jack said. I heard a chuckle from him and I nodded eagerly. "I'm so buying you the largest size they've got here."

"Sounds good to me!" I said.

Jack pulled up to the drive-thru then looked at the menu for the shakes.

"Hi, welcome to Shake Shack. What can I get for you?" a voice asked from the speaker.

"Hi . . . I'd like to get one strawberry shake and one Oreo shake."

"Would that be all?"

"Yes."

"Your total will be $11.42. You can pay at the first window."

"Thank you." Jack then drove the car forward. We approached the first window and saw the worker waiting patiently as Jack handed her a twenty. Jack thanked the lady for his change before moving to the second window. I looked towards the window to see the worker waiting by the window with the sliding door still closed.

"Are we doing anything tomorrow?"

"I'm sure we are. I don't know yet though. You're welcome to hang with us if you'd like. You don't have to if you want to go out on your own and you can take this rental car."

"You'd let me drive it with a broken arm?" I questioned.

"Well yeah . . . I mean if you're not comfortable, I can drop you off someplace and pick you up later. Wait . . . you can drive right?"

"Just got my license about three and a half months ago."

"Do you feel comfortable driving with a broken arm?"

"Not sure," I shrugged. "Never had a broken arm before."

"Wanna try?"

"You . . . want me to drive back to the hotel?"

"Sure, why not?"

"Umm . . . I'm pretty sure I'm not supposed to be driving." I laughed lightly. I remembered some of the rules from when I was studying for my permit and road test.

"I mean you could. It would be difficult though."

"Maybe not. I'm still a new driver. Don't want to risk it." I shook my head. I wouldn't want us getting into any some sort of accident.

"Alright. Make se—" Jack turned his attention towards the window as the worker brought out both of the shakes. "Thank you." Jack smiled towards the worker who slid the door closed.

I took my shake and straw from Jack. I put my shake down to open the straw wrapper and punch the straw into my shake. I crushed the wrapper into a ball and aimed for Jack's head.

"Hey!" he exclaimed. I smiled and laughed at his funny and fake expressions. Jack can be so goofy when he wanted to. "Damn, you still have great aim." He broke into a smile as we made our way back into traffic. "Did you do any sports?"

"I didn't have time for sports. You knew that."

"Right. I'm always thinking you were at least a part of some sort of athletic team."

"If you count running during my free time outside of studying."

"You run? Like distance? How far do you go on a run for?"

"It depends on the day. I tend to run a minimum of four miles a day. I like to go six to seven some days," I shared. It was silent for a moment as he continued to drive.

"I'm guessing you're someone who likes to do those runs?"

"I'd like to. I've never done one before."

"Well . . . Maybe when your arm is fully healed, I can sign us up for a run. Sounds good?"

"You run?" I asked. Jack playfully rolled his eyes and chuckled as he gone into detail about his nonexistent athleticism and weight lifting.

CHAPTER TWENTY-TWO
Thoughts

CLAIRE JOHNSON

The resort buildings soon came into view. The ride back here was silent and strange at the same time. I sat in the passenger seat, hoping everything would be alright. I wondered if Finnegan had realized where Jack had gone off to or if he had told him anything. Jack has been off his phone the whole time that he was with me. I thought so anyway. We passed through some of the main attractions and towards the main building where our rooms were. He turned into the parking lot and found parking close to the front.

Once Jack turned the engine off, he quickly got out and walked around. I carefully unbuckled my seatbelt and tried to avoid hitting or putting any pressure to my cast. It felt weird being in a sling. The door opened on my side and I looked to see Jack holding the door for me. I stepped out and thanked him before he closed the door. He locked the car and we began walking towards the building. We both walked towards the elevator. As I turned around to face the door, I saw Andy coming over. I looked towards Jack nervously. Jack pushed the button to my floor.

Andy realized it was us and his eyes widened once he realized my cast. I looked away from his eyes as he waited for a response. "I thought you said you were okay?" Andy asked. He looked towards Jack and I stepped between them so they wouldn't start anything. I hoped they wouldn't start any type of fight that would lead into a big disaster.

"It's okay. It was an accident. Jack and I are good." I smiled faintly, hoping he would believe me. Andy then looked between Jack and I, trying to process what was happening.

"I'm happy to hear that . . ." Andy decided to hug Jack with me in between them. There wasn't much pressure in the hug, which I was glad for. When the motion of the elevator came to a stop and opened, I walked out first with Jack and Andy right behind me. I began making my way in the direction of my suite and they continued to follow me. I wasn't sure if Andy was following because he did not trust Jack or if he wanted to hangout. The three of us went in my suite and I made my way for the couch. Jack and Andy walked over towards me, but remained standing.

"Sooo . . ." Andy said breaking the silence. Andy looked between Jack and I.

"I'm going to talk to Fin," Jack said, looking down at his fingers. "I have to sort some stuff out."

"You know Nate is ready to attack you. Well, Aiden was."

"Yeah, I know. I mean, I deserve it." Jack sighed. Andy's phone went off and he answered.

"Yo . . . yeah . . . In Claire's suite . . . Yeah, tell everyone. Bring pillows and blankets . . . Of course, bye." Andy hung up and smiled towards me. "Everyone wants to see you. Hope you don't mind having everyone come over and spend the night."

"I don't mind at all." I looked towards my cousin, who looked like he was deep into his thoughts. "Are you spending the night Jack?" I asked. He looked towards me with a sheepish smile.

"Maybe. I'm not sure yet, but don't wait up for me alright? Have fun tonight. I uh . . . I have to go talk to Fin," Jack said. I nod as he gave me a small wave before leaning over to give me a hug. "If I don't see you tonight, I'll see you in the morning," he added. I nodded as he kissed my forehead then made his way out.

Remembering that I wanted to get some snacks ready before everyone arrived, I made my way into the kitchen. Andy followed me into the kitchen while I took a few bowls out for the chips.

"So, you and Shane, huh?" Andy asked, running his hand through his hair. I looked down at the counter, feeling shy. It must be obvious to everyone that there's something going on between Shane and I even though we haven't really gone out. I feel like I can be myself around him, because he has already seen a side of me that he was genuinely into. He has also been really understanding with my mom and stays very sensitive to the topic.

"I'm not really sure," I said. Andy's blue eyes widened and he looked towards me with excitement. He opened a bag of chips for me. Everyone seemed to like the thought of us being together. He hasn't asked me out. The thought of him asking me out makes me happy though.

"It's okay, I won't tell. You guys look cute together," Any teased. I smiled towards him slightly and shrugged. *I wonder if Shane thought I was cute.*

After filling a bowl with some chips, I heard a knock on the door. "I'll get it!" Andy jogged out of the kitchen. I slowly walked over to the window of the kitchen to take a peek. As soon as the door opened, I could hear lots of chatter.

I turned slightly, walking over to the bowls feeling shy again. I've met them already, but I still felt very unsure with everyone. I took a chip and put it into my mouth letting myself taste the barbecue flavor.

"Claire!" Nate exclaimed as he came into the kitchen. I turned to him with a smile. He then saw my arm and carefully hugged me. Maybe Andy told everyone already. He opened the other chips since I struggled with them and poured them into the bowl. He began making his way out into the living room to set it on the table. I followed after him.

As I stepped into the living room, all heads turned towards me. Everyone rushed to me. I felt like I was being crowded by everyone and I felt shy once again. I noticed that the only people who were not here were Finnegan and Jack. I spotted Shane and Jacob giving me a look of relief to see me.

"Can I sign your cast?" Ben asked.

"Same." Ryder smiled. Andy chuckled and rolled his eyes.

"I'd like all of you to sign it. I . . . don't have a sharpie with me though," I said softly.

"We've gotchu." Aaron smiled and held up a black sharpie. I laughed lightly and nod as I carefully took my sling off to put onto the table. I let my casted arm rest on the table and took a seat as they began signing. It was Shane who was the last to sign my cast. I stared at him as he wrote on my cast.

My breath quickened as I looked around to see everyone settling in or bringing snacks into the living room. I looked back to Shane and shifted slightly as he continued to write. I frowned slightly, wondering why it took so long to write his name. I noticed the sharpie in his hand was not the black sharpie Aaron had. It was silver.

"I left a small note for you." He looked away from my arm and towards me. His teeth were perfectly showing and I took a stuttered breath before smiling as he put the cap back on. He stood up and held his hand out. I took it as he pulled me towards everyone who seemed to be getting ready to watch a movie. Shane had me sit between him and Andy. Soon I was cuddling between them.

"Comfy?" Shane asked lightly from beside me. I looked towards him and nodded. Aiden and Nate came back into the living room and placed all of the snacks on the table. The couch Shane, Andy, and I were currently on was pulled out into a bed. Ryder and Ben were on the edge and everyone else were setting up on the floor.

171

"What do you want to watch Claire?" Jacob asked and saw he had the remote in his hand. Ben and Ryder looked up from their phone. I shrugged, unsure.

"No chick movies though," Ben said. Nora rolled her eyes from the chair and hit him in the head, making him glare directly at her. "What?"

"It's Claire's choice. Man up, Ben," Nora said, rolling her eyes again. I laughed lightly as Ben stuck his tongue at her. A few of the guys chuckled and hit Ben's shoulder.

"So, what are you up for watching?" Aaron asked. Most of the attention went back towards me. Slowly, I leaned my head against Shane's shoulder. He immediately wrapped an arm around my waist. Nate raised a brow, but doesn't say anything. I felt very sleepy all of a sudden.

"I'm not sure," I yawned. "Anything is good to me."

"Tired?" Nate smiled. I nodded and carefully shifted as

Shane tightened his grip around me and I snuggled more into him. Andy stood slowly keeping an eye between us.

"I'll get the pillows and covers for us. Claire, is alright if I get the one from your room?"

"No, problem at all," I said sleepily. I closed my eyes, feeling myself drifting to sleep.

After a while, I began to shift from my slumber. I knew immediately that the television was still on. I sat up slowly looking around. I noticed everyone was asleep around the living room, except for Shane, who was no longer next to me. I rubbed my eyes with my one hand and reached for my phone to check the time. It read a little past one in the morning. I yawned and looked towards the balcony door where I saw was slightly opened. I carefully stood up and walked over to the door where the balcony was. I slid the door open to walkout and close it behind me. I turned around to see Shane standing. He was looking out into the view. I walked over to the railing and stood next to him. He turned towards me and smiled.

"Hey," I said softly. Every time I spoke to him, I felt nervous.

"Hey," he said in the same tone.

"Couldn't sleep?" It seemed he has been up for a while.

"Yeah, just been thinking a bit." I frown slightly in wonder.

"About music?" There was a time in the middle of the night that I would think about a piece I was working on.

"No." He paused for a moment before he continued. "I was actually thinking about you." I looked down. I think I may be blushing, because he chuckled a little. The moonlight must be shining on me. I then smiled up at him. He was up at one in the morning thinking about me.

That nervous feeling suddenly returned and it was like that first day we met. He hasn't left my mind since that day. Thinking of it now made my stomach to erupt into butterflies. It felt like the moment right before I go out onto the stage for a performance. He had this effect on me and I think he knew that.

"Is it a good thing that you're thinking about me?" He did not look away from me. In this moment I felt like I was the one who was lost in thought trying to figure him out.

"Yes, of course. When I think about you, it's always positive." We moved closer towards each other 'til our arms brushed each other. He moved closer to me until I was facing him. My breath quickened a little. My heart raced and it seemed I had to hold my breath to hide how much my heart was beating. If he could hear my heart beating out loud, he would be able to tell this was really affecting me. He leaned towards me to kiss my cheek softly and pulled away slowly. His eyes looked directly at me. "I really like you Claire." I smiled at him and looked into his eyes. The words had to sink in for a moment as they left his mouth. I liked the way I felt. "I like you also Shane." He smiled back. He looked down at his hands for a moment before making eye contact again. What was he thinking? What was going through his mind?

173

"I've been waiting to ask you since that first day we talked. I feel like there's a connection between us and I can be myself with you. I also feel that I can tell you anything. What I wanted to ask is if you'd like to go out on a date with me?"

CHAPTER TWENTY-THREE
Realization

Shane Peters

"Yes," she answered after a moment and I let her answer sink in. She said she liked me back and I couldn't have been any happier to hear that. The worry of her not feeling the same way gave me a nervous feeling. I've never been so nervous around someone before. She agreed to let me take her on a date and I felt very relieved. I smiled at the thought, because that meant we had mutual feelings. "You're a really kind guy Shane," she said softly. "I've... never felt like this before." If there were enough lights, I would have been able to tell she was blushing.

"You do realize you're the first girl to say that to me after I've asked to go on a date?" I paused for a moment to take a good at her. "I'm really happy we have mutual feelings." She smiled and I reached for her hand and held it in mine. "Can I show you something?" I said.

She shrugged. "Does it involve leaving the balcony, because I enjoy standing here with you. It's beautiful out here," she said. Not as beautiful as her. I looked towards her more and she had a look of wonder. I smiled towards her, because I had an idea.

"Yes, but it does involve going back to my room. We can go to the balcony there, if you'd like," I said. She smiled and nodded. Quietly, we turned towards the door and went in. I closed the door for her and we carefully went around the guys who were asleep on the floor.

As we passed the table, Claire grabbed her phone and room key. We both decided we wouldn't be needing our shoes and made our way out the door. Once I closed the door to the suite, I turned to see her already looking up at me. I notice her biting the inside of her lip. She deserved happiness and I'm honored to be giving it to her.

"I sort of see this as a date," she said softly.

"Do you want this to be our first date?" I asked her. Her cheeks turned rosy pink. She looked down at her socks.

"I don't mind calling this our first date at all." She looked towards me with a smile and I continued to hold her hand. She nodded. She did not mind me holding her hand at all.

"Welcome to our first date Claire Johnson." I smiled to her and leaned over to kiss her cheek. It was a bold move for me to do, but I didn't mind. I'm pretty sure I would do a lot of things for this girl. She meant a lot to me already. I let our arms swing as we began making our way towards my suite. We continued swinging our arms all the way to the suite and I took out my key to unlock the door.

"Shall I make something for us to snack on while we wait?" she offered.

"No, it's alright. You haven't had dinner, did you?" I asked. She shook her head as I led her towards the room I shared with Jacob. "I can order something for us. What are you in the mood for?"

"Classic wings and fries. I've been wanting to have some really good wings and fries." She smiled eagerly and I chuckled at her cuteness.

"I'm sure there is a place around here that is still open." I opened the door to my room and walked over to the bedside to turn on the lamp. I looked over to see a door that led to the balcony. I forgot that the balcony was connected to our room. I had her sit down on the bed first then I walked over to my guitar case. I turned around to see her with her phone out.

"I found a place," she said with a smile on her face as she continued to look at her phone. She made me feel nervous. It was only a few years ago that I had taught myself to play the guitar. So, I've never performed for a girl I really liked at 1 AM, neither did I ever take a girl out at this time of night. She's the first. I felt my heart racing at the mere thought of her and this first date. We would be having our second date later in the day when we all go out. "The reviews for their wings and fries look pretty great," she said. She looked up and noticed the guitar case in my hand. "Are . . . you going to play?" she asked with a surprised look. I nodded and put the case at the head of the bed and took my guitar out.

"I want to play something for you."

"Okay." She stretched her legs so she was leaning up against the headrest. I placed a pillow on her lap for her cast then she thanked me.

"What was the name of the place you wanted to order from? I can put in an order," I offered. She handed over her phone. I leaned my arm against my guitar as I placed our order. After filling out all the information, I then provided the credit card my mom gave me. I hand her phone back over to her and she smiled as I picked up the guitar.

"What will you be playing Peters?" She asked. I liked it when she called me by my last name. I smiled as I looked down at my guitar. I know she will appreciate this song as I started strumming.

"Every time I think I'm closer to the heart of what it means to know just who I am," I started to sing. I looked up to see her with a meaningful look as she smiled showing her perfect smile. That smile I had never seen until now. She recognized the song. "You're the voice I hear inside my head," I sang to her and continued on with the rest of the song. She carefully crawled over to me on her knees and took a seat next to me. I continued to keep

177

my eye contact with her. Her eyes began to gloss as I went onto the last words of the song. "Yeah, I gotta find you."

"I loved it," she whispered. She leaned forward to hug me, which I returned. "Thank you for playing for me." She pulled away and wiped her tears away. She smiled as I placed the guitar on the table. She took my hand and I can't stop myself from smiling. I placed my other hand on top of hers.

"I'm glad you liked it." I leaned over slightly to kiss her cheek once more, which made her blush.

"You're a prince, Shane."

"I'm glad to hear. It means I'm doing my job right." I pulled her close to me and she leaned her head on my shoulder. I didn't mind.

"I . . . want to tell you something," she started off.

"Okay. Anything you'd like."

"Remember when you, Jacob, and I were hanging out several days ago and we were talking a little bit about me graduating a year early?"

"Of course, I do. Have you heard back from any of the schools since then?" I remembered specifically about McGill.

"I haven't heard anything yet . . . um . . . I wanted to ask you about the senior events that will be going on in June."

"Oh okay." I had a feeling where this may lead to.

"Should I . . . participate in them? I don't know if I should go to the dance, the banquet, doing the senior trip."

"You should go. I think you'd have fun," I said lightly.

"I don't know. I've always felt like the outcast," she said.

"What if . . ." I thought about this for a moment. After this trip and everything, if we worked out, I could ask her to the dance. "You can bring some friends with you. Like Jacob and I." I half smiled. I'd ask her to be my date if we became closer. Before she could respond, her phone went off and she immediately answered.

"Hello . . . ? That's great! I'll be right down . . . Goodbye."
She hung up, looking at me. "Our food is here," she said. I nodded
as we both stood up. I took her hand then we made our way out.

"You seem very eager for our food," I chuckled as she
pulled me along. Without thinking, I twirled her around. She
laughed as I realized she lost her balance. I wrapped my arms
around her and pulled before she could fall.

"Shane, you have to be careful." Her eyes were wide and
they were filled with joy. "We don't need to cause any sort of
accident."

"We don't want that. Just thought I could have a cliché
moment with you." I smiled at her. She took my hand again and
intertwined them as a big smile settled on her face.

"You're amazing."

"Not as amazing as you." I smiled, knowing she'd
appreciate everything I say. She doesn't seem to be a person who
would have any type of judgement towards me. She was so genuine.
I don't know if there were many girls out there like her.

The elevator arrived on our floor and we stepped inside.
Holding onto her hand was something I really liked and I think she
felt the same way. It seemed like a natural thing for us. We have
become close over the past few days. When the elevator came to a
slow stop, the door opened and we both walked into the lobby.

At this time of night, the lobby was completely deserted.
The only living person here would be the receptionist at the main
desk. That was where we saw a paper bag with the logo of the place
where we ordered our food. I walked ahead of Claire. The lady
looked up from the computer and smiled.

"Late night snack?" she asked. I nodded as I took the bag,
which had a bit of weight to it. I thanked the receptionist before
leading Claire towards the elevator.

"Smells amazing," Claire said and my stomach grumbled in
response. She looked towards my stomach and laughed lightly.
"You agree also."

"I guess so," I chuckled. The elevator door opened and we stepped back on. The journey back to the suite was very quick and we decided to sit out on the balcony. I placed our food on the table and pulled the chair out for Claire to sit on. She thanked me as I took the seat next to her. I took our food out of the bag. I then took my phone out to take a picture. Claire laughed and shook her head as she tried to hide behind the bag.

"Shane!"

"What?" I asked innocently. "I just wanted to take a few pictures to remember our first date." Slowly, she put the bag down and nodded. First, I took a picture of her before putting my phone on selfie mode to include myself in the picture.

JACK JOHNSON

There were many things going through my mind as I walked towards my room. I had to talk to Fin about this, because this all has to come to an end with Claire. I shouldn't be tolerating anything that has been happening with my cousin. The way Fin and I have treated her wasn't right. It made me guilty and I knew this wasn't right. I went into the suite and shut the door behind me. I saw Fin on the bed, playing some type of game on his phone. Everyone had left for Claire's for the evening.

"Sup J?" he said, not looking up from his phone. He continued to play the game he was on. He seemed so focused on it. It's always like that with Fin and I.

"We need to talk," I started. I wasn't sure how this was going to go. He continued on with his game.

"Sure, what's up?" He was always chill about our conversations.

"We need to stop." I said lightly as I thought about my cousin.

"Stop what dude?" He continued to focus on the game.

"What we were doing to Claire. It isn't right. What we've been doing. The way we've treated her," I said. He now looked up from his phone and frowned.

"No we're not Jack. Do you remember what she did to you, bro?"

"Yeah and I should have taken care of it myself. It's not her fault. What I did was my bidding. I shouldn't have as—"

"Yes, it is. It was none of her business and she still did it. She shouldn't have gotten into our business. I told you I'd take care of it. You knew I wouldn't let you get into trouble."

"She's my cousin. She was worried about me."

"No. She wanted to get you expelled from school. I got you out remember?" he pestered. I really am thankful for my best friend.

"Yeah but . . ." He wasn't taking this lightly at all.

"No buts," he insisted. I looked towards my best friend who looked furious. He always had something against her. I never could figure out why.

"She's my cousin . . ."

"You're not backing out on me, Johnson. You will not pick her. We've already been through this conversation."

"Watch me," I glared at him now. I was feeling very protective of Claire. I should have always been this way.

"I have proof," he said, holding up his phone.

"What proof? What are you talking about?"

He went onto his phone and pulled up a video. I walked over in confusion. I looked closer and realized this was taken from the school security camera in the office. It made sense why the footage couldn't be found. Fin deleted them from the systems. This was the video from when Claire broke into the school. I watched helplessly as he shut his phone off and put it into his pocket.

"I have more than one copy. With the press of a button, I can anonymously send it to the school and the police. I believe for her it's more than breaking in since she doesn't go to Oakwood.

This could mess up her admissions with colleges. Unless you want her arrested, I'd listen if I were you."

The thought of her college admission decision being screwed over was something I did not want to mess with. No, I couldn't do this. I couldn't do this to her. At a time like this with her mom, my aunt, I can't do this to her. I don't want to risk her future either.

"Understood?" he asked, breaking into my thoughts. I sighed. I looked towards him. He had a hard look.

"Yeah."

CHAPTER TWENTY-FOUR
Feeling Magical

CLAIRE JOHNSON

"You're so adorable Claire," Shane said as he kissed the side of my head. I really liked the cute things he's doing. He continued to show affection and it made my heart beat fast. I felt that there was a new part of me that I was getting to know as I spent time around him. My head was on his lap as we both sat on the swing out on the balcony, looking up at the stars. It was around two thirty in the morning and we have been here since we finished eating.

"You make me feel this way," I said lightly. A yawn escaped my lips. I was beginning to feel tired as if melatonin kicked in.

"You're sleepy. We should head back to your room. We don't want the others getting worried about where we went off to."

"I'm so comfy here with you."

"And I could stay in this position with you all morning, but if we don't go back, we'll never hear the end of it from everyone," Shane insisted while chuckling. He moved a strand of my hair away from my face. Slowly, I began to lift my head then I sat up carefully. I looked towards Shane to see him smiling. His smile is contagious.

"I guess we should get back then," I said lightly. We both stood and immediately, he wrapped an arm around me. I shifted slightly which made him hold tighter.

"Whoa there. Are you okay?"

"Yes, sorry." I smiled sheepishly. We began making our way in. Shane made sure to lock the door before going around to turn off all the lights. I followed him to his bedroom to fix the bed and I shivered slightly. Shane looked up and paused for a moment.

"Here, I have a jacket you can wear." He stepped towards his luggage and took the denim jacket he had worn the other day. He carefully draped the jacket over my shoulders and stood in front of me.

"Thank you for making this our first date," I said quietly. It was almost above a whisper as I felt my stomach flipping in many directions.

"I had a great time with you," he answered in the same tone. His hand reached for the side of my face and his thumb rubbed against my jawline and cheeks. My eyes fluttered. His eyes were staring into mine.

My eyes then looked to his lips. They looked very soft and plump and my mind began thinking about how much I like Shane. I think I want to continue dating and see where it would take us. His hand moved up to my cheek. I skipped a beat.

"Can I kiss you?" he asked me so softly that it made my heart feel as if it could explode at any moment. I looked up to meet his eyes and I could tell by the way he's breathing that he was feeling the same way. I nodded slightly. I reached for his shoulders and continued to look up into his eyes.

He leaned down and my eyes fluttered shut as I felt his nose touch mine. I felt his breath as I felt his other hand reach for my waist and pulled me slightly towards him. He closed the remaining gap between us as I felt soft lips touch mine. My lips immediately moved with his and I suddenly felt as if all of my thoughts washed away. I pulled him closer to me and I felt him smile into our kiss.

When he slowly pulled away, I could hear our heavy breaths. I felt heart beating like a hummingbird. I took a step back slightly and realized my that my hand was against his chest. I bit my lip, feeling slightly heated as I slowly looked up to see Shane's expression. His lips formed a smile and he seemed to enjoy it.

"I think you made our date perfect," I said lightly as he took my hand once more and our fingers intertwined.

"You're the reason why it was perfect." My heart melted at his words. I squeezed his hand as we both headed out of the bedroom and made our way for the door.

There was a gentle shake that woke me from my sleep. "Claire," I heard Shane whisper to me. I turned over with my eyes closed and smiled, thinking about what happened earlier. I thought about my first kiss with him towards the very end of our date.

"Morning Shane," I whispered back. After we shared our kiss, Shane and I went back to the suite to find everyone sound asleep. We both went off to sleep as well. Now here I am being woken up by the one and only Shane Peters himself. I tried to reach for him.

"Someone's very touchy this morning."

I heard a chuckle from someone. I opened my eyes and sat up. Andy and Jacob on the other two couches. My cheeks began to heat up in embarrassment. I completely forgot that we weren't alone. I looked around and noticed everyone else was not here.

"Everyone left to get ready for the day," Andy answered as he saw my confused look. Andy and Jacob seemed very happy to see me. I turned to Shane, who may I add was blushing a deep pink.

"So . . . what were you two up to until 3 AM?" Jacob asked. My eyes widen slightly and Shane shrugged. "I noticed you both weren't here around two this morning when I went to the bathroom," Jacob chuckled. I looked towards Shane, wondering if he'd say something.

"Do you want me to tell them?" he asked me. I nodded shyly. Shane looked to the both of them as I continued to keep my eyes on his hand. His hand reached over for mine. "We went out on a date," Shane said straight. I heard a whistle from Jacob and I had a feeling they were looking at me.

"Was not expecting that answer." Andy's tone sounded surprised. I turned towards them to see that they were both shocked. "So early in the morning . . . What could you guys have possibly done?"

"Won't say," Shane said. I could tell that he was smiling and I knew what he was thinking. He squeezed my hand slightly and I smiled timidly. "It's between Claire and I. If Claire would like to share anything from our date, I'm leaving it up to her."

Jacob raised a brow and I tried to control the heat from my cheeks. "Well, since we're probably not going to get any details, we wanted to make sure you had enough time to get ready," Jacob said.

"Where are we going?" I asked curiously.

"Disney. Hope you're ready to go in about half an hour," Andy answered. My eyes widened and I felt my heart exploding like fireworks. I think the guys noticed it.

"We're going to Disney?" I gushed. This has made my day. I've dreamed of going there my whole life. I wonder what park we're going to. I felt very jittery and excited like any girl would be. The guys looked between each other and I smiled widely.

"I guess today is your lucky day," Shane chuckled. I let go of Shane's hand to pull the covers back and quickly took off towards my room.

"I'm going to get ready! I'm going to shower!" I exclaimed. I heard chuckles from the living room as I closed the door.

"I'm going to use the other bathroom to shower!" Shane said from outside the room. I walked over the closet and looked for the floral top I had recently purchased to go with my shorts. It would go well with my denim jacket. I took a clean pair of my strapless bra and underwear before going into the bathroom.

I placed my clothing on the counter and turned on the shower. I quickly brushed my teeth then stripped off my clothes. I made sure this would be a quick shower. A quick rinse and soak should do the trick. The struggle? I had to avoid my cast getting soaked so it took extra time using one hand. I then went for the soap to scrub a few times before rinsing. I repeated the process before turning the shower off and reached for the towel.

I dried myself the best I could before reaching out for my undergarments and shorts, putting them on. It was quite the challenge getting the strapless bra clipped. Then I reached for my top and put it over my head and tried to get my arms through before pulling the top down. I was able to get my head through and I sighed with content. There was a knock at the door as I picked up my brush and I frowned wondering how I would really brush my tangled hair.

"Come in!" The door opened and I looked through the mirror to see Shane slowly peeking his head in. Once he realized I was fully dressed, he opened the door and came in. Hair dripped with a bit of water indicating he had recently gotten out of the shower himself.

"Hey," He smiled and walked up from behind and looked at our reflection. I took a look at his outfit and realized we were matching quite well. I think he noticed, because he smiled widely. He wore a black tee shirt with a jean jacket over it along with his skinny jeans. "You look amazing," he complimented.

"Thank you." I smiled. He looked towards the brush in my hand then my cast.

"I can brush your hair if you'd like."

"Are you sure?" I turned towards him so I was physically seeing him. He smiled and being unexpected, he put his hands on my hips as he leaned down to gently place his lips to mine. I smiled and let my hand grasp his jacket as I kissed him. Feeling his lips against mine felt like a bliss and it made my heart swoon.

"You're so perfect," he said softly once he slowly pulled away. He was the definition of a gentleman who knew how to say the right things at the right time. He looked down and took the brush from my hand and smiled. He pushed some of the hair from my face. "Turn around," he said softly, which I obliged. I looked to the mirror as he began brushing my hair. After several minutes, he put the brush down on the counter and turned me around so I could face him.

"Thank you, Shane."

"It was no problem. I guess we should get going? Andy and Jacob are waiting for us in the living room. The others will meet us in the lobby."

"Are we going to Magic Kingdom?" I asked curiously.

"No . . . we're all supposed to go to Epcot today."

"Oh okay."

"But . . ."—Shane half smiled—"we could always sneak away from the group at some point for a few hours and maybe head over there then come back. If that's okay with you."

"Are we allowed to do that?" I asked curiously.

"Yeah, we have park hopper passes as a gift to us while we're here. We could go to Epcot for a bit with everyone then hop onto the monorail that would take us straight to Magic Kingdom."

"That would be really cool." I smiled, thinking how today would be filled with magic and much more.

"Yeah, that sounds like a plan. It's a date." Shane smiled. I nodded as we heard someone calling our names. We made our way out of the bathroom. I took my purse with everything I needed inside. I then put my flats on before walking into the living room where Jacob and Andy stared between Shane and I.

"Alright love birds, we have to go," Jacob chuckled. I nodded as the two made their way for the door. I walked over to the table and grabbed my phone. Shane was already at the door, waiting for me.

"So, you're a big Disney fan?" Andy asked curiously as the four of us began making our way to the elevator.

"Yes. I've always wanted to see the castle, meet Disney Princesses and try their Dole Whip ice cream." I was beaming.

"It's good to know you're into rides. So . . . what ride would you say you're most interested going onto? We'll at some point hit all four parks," Andy said.

"Space mountain, Pirates, and Splash Mountain," I said. As we walked onto the elevator, Shane leaned over by my ear.

"I'll take you on those rides then," he whispered then pulled away. I blushed. Both Andy and Jacob were walking onto the elevator. I looked to Jacob and realized he was staring at Shane and I.

"You guys are matching . . . What the hell. Did you guys plan this?" Jacob said after a moment of silence. I shook my head and Shane chuckled.

"We didn't realize, but I'm glad we are though," Shane answered.

"Couple goals," Andy told Jacob softly, which he nodded to. I tried to keep calm as the elevator doors opened and the lobby was filled. As we walked out, I noticed our group was in a general area and we made our way over to them.

"You guys finally made it," Aiden greeted. I looked for my cousin, but everyone was moving around. "We're taking two vehicles. Nate and I are the drivers," Aiden said. Everyone started making their way out and I followed beside Shane. He glanced towards me and took my hand.

"You're definitely riding with Jacob and I." Shane gave a friendly smile to Aiden, who stopped in front of a van and noticed the two of us together. He looked towards us curiously as everyone riding with us got into the van.

"Did I miss somethin'?" he asked, confused, then scratched the back of his head.

"Maybe," Shane answered with a straight face which made me smile. Shane opened the door and I giggled as he helped me into the very back.

"He's suspicious," I said lightly. Shane turned towards me as he buckled his seatbelt on.

"I think everyone is going to realize when we sneak off later." Shane had a friendly smile as he reached over to buckle me in. The van doors closed and I looked towards the front to see my cousin sitting with Finnegan. Soon, the van drove off and Shane began to start a conversation with Jacob and Nora. I waited to see if Jack would look back, but he doesn't. Instead, I noticed Finnegan glaring at me. I closed my eyes and tried to focus my attention somewhere else.

CHAPTER TWENTY-FIVE
Epcot: Part One

SHANE PETERS

It was about a half hour drive to Disney itself and once we arrived, I could see how excited Claire was to be here. This will be her first time and I hope to make this an experience she can remember. She was looking out the window and telling me some of the places she would like to visit sometime. I can't wait to take her to the Wizarding World of Harry Potter. I haven't mentioned it to her yet though.

Everyone was just basically asking Claire questions throughout the journey to get to know her better. I realized, I had spent more time with her than anyone here. She seemed really happy to interact with everyone. The one thing out of place seemed to be Jack and Fin.

Once we were in the Epcot parking lot, we started piling out. I took her hand once I closed the door to the van and she turned towards me with rosy cheeks. I smiled at her cuteness. She was so ready for today. It did not matter that we slept after 3 AM.

The main entrance was close so we all decided to walk. The guys in the other van were a few parking spots away and were following us.

"Date day?" Nate asked from behind. I turned slightly to see him with a small smirk on his face.

"Yes," I answered and squeezed Claire's hand. I heard a stomach growl and turned to her immediately. "You're hungry," I stated, realizing that we haven't eaten breakfast.

"I can wait," she answered, looking towards me.

"You two can go eat somewhere. There's Starbucks and you have restaurants with different cuisines you can eat at. You two can meet up with the group whenever," Nate suggested.

"We have our fastpass for Soarin that starts around 11:30?" I clarified.

"Yes, the other two starts right after that. It would be cool if we all went together for the first one," Nate answered.

"Of course. Claire and I will be there," I assured. We passed the small crossroad and began making our way to have our bags checked. We followed the flow of the crowd.

"Oh my God! It's Shane Peters!" A girl gasped from not too far away. I smiled at the two girls who were probably a year or maybe two years younger than me. Claire smiled, letting go of my hand to fall in line. I began making my way over to the girls.

"Hi," I said warmly. They both engulfed me with a hug. "What are your names?" I liked interacting with my fans.

"I'm Lily and this is my best friend, Sophie," The second girl said excitedly. Sophie reminded me of my sister slightly and Lily remind me of Lily Potter. She had green eyes! *Ah, me and my Harry Potter thoughts.* I hope Claire would be okay with my addiction with the series.

"Can we take a picture with you?" Sophie asked softly.

"Yeah, of course!" I made sure I stood between the two of them then wrapped my arms around them. They hugged me from the side. I smiled at the creativity my fans displayed as we posed for a picture. I looked up to see two guys, who I was guessing, were friends of Lily and Sophie. They both had phones with the camera or video on. After the shoot, they pulled away and gave me another individual hug. Hugging is the best part.

"Thank you so much!" Lily smiled.

"I've always wanted to meet you. I love your voice!" Sophie said right after. I politely smiled at their kindness and thanked them. I have an amazing fan base and it has continued to grow.

"Thank you. Your support means a lot to me." I realized it was their turn to get their bags checked so they waved goodbye. They walked into the park. Claire was talking with Ian, Jacob, Ken, and Aiden.

CLAIRE JOHNSON

I smiled at Shane before making my way towards another line to give him some space with his fans. It was not long getting into a new line when someone snuck up from behind and made me jump. I turned around to see Aiden with a smirk.

"Aiden!" I slapped his arm playfully. Aiden, Ian, Jacob, and Ken started laughing. Nora and the rest of the guys were somewhere else in the line. I wasn't sure where they were or if they had already gone through.

"Awe! Did we scare Claire?" Ian teased. I laughed at the tone he was using. These guys are amazing to be around. I wouldn't think you could ever get bored with the four of them.

"You know,"—Ken eyed me from head to toe—"you're very pretty Claire," he finished. Jacob sent him a look.

"Thanks?" I said, unsure of what to say. Ken began laughing.

"It was just a compliment. I promise I'm not flirting with you, because we ship you and Shane." He smiled.

"I completely agree," Jacob said.

"You're still pretty fine though, but yeah, Shaire all the way," Aiden said, smirking. Did they just give Shane and I a ship name?

"I knew you two would be hitting it off," Ian added. I felt shy once again. These boys are a tease. I looked over to Shane and he was already smiling at me. Things were actually starting to be okay.

Shane began walking over to us. Once he was beside me, he held out his hand for me to take. I gladly accepted. It was now my turn to have my bag checked while the guys waited on the other side. Shane stayed by my side until it was clear for me to go through. Shane zipped my purse before we walk over to our group. We were just outside the ticketing stations to go into the park.

"Where do you guys want to go first?" Nate asked the group.

"Let's go to that test track ride!" Aiden yelled excitedly. Everyone agreed and Nate began leading the way over to the ticketing station. Shane let go of my hand and pulled out his wallet quickly. He handed me a card with a Minnie Mouse on it. I smiled at him as we both went through the ticket process and entered the park.

"Where would you like to eat?" Shane asked and turned towards me. I shrugged, unsure.

"Before you two head off . . ." Aiden called out. Shane and I turned our attention towards the group and everyone seemed to be huddled together. "Come here so we have our group picture."

I noticed a professional photographer. Shane led us over to them and we joined the group. "Claire, next to Nora!" I heard Aaron say. I moved towards the middle where Nora was. She wrapped an arm around my shoulder and Ryder wrapped his around my waist. Shane went somewhere in the group and we all focused on the camera. I smiled at the photographer.

After, Nate walked over to the guy handing him his Disney card to scan. Shane came over to me. Nora smiled, hopping with excitement.

"You two enjoy your date today," she told Shane and I. I thanked her timidly. I looked over my shoulder. Finnegan and my cousin were having a deep conversation about something. Jack hasn't talked to me since last night. I guess we were back to avoiding each other?

"Ready to eat?" Shane asked and nudged me lightly. I turned my full attention towards him and nodded. I waved to Nora and saw Jacob had already walked away from the group. I frowned slightly as Shane led me away from our group who seemed to be discussing where to go first. I don't think Shane noticed Jacob ahead of us.

"Hey Shane?" I asked lightly and he took a glance at me as we walked.

"Yes?"

"Do you think it's alright if we invite Jacob to breakfast?" I pointed to him ahead of us and Shane looked in that direction.

"Yeah, sure. I didn't realize he left the group. I'm pretty sure he was going to get something to eat also. Hey Jacob!" Shane called out. Jacob looked around and stopped walking once he saw us. We walked over to him and I smiled.

"Hey guys. What's up?" Jacob smiled.

"We were going to get something to eat. How about you?" I asked. Jacob smiled towards me.

"I was going to do the same thing."

"You can join us if you'd like," I said.

"You sure? I don't want to intrude," he said, unsure.

"We don't mind. Claire wanted you to join us. It's cool," Shane commented.

"Sure, thanks guys," Jacob said. We began walking. I looked around, feeling happy to be here. "Where were you guys planning to eat?"

"I was thinking of Chefs de France or Monsieur Paul in France. Sorta wanted to hear Claire speak French and she has been craving some pastries since two this morning," Shane said. I knew I was blushing.

"Ah. You're fluent a speaker Claire?"

"*Oui.*" I smiled proudly. "*J'prends le français depuis environ dix ans.*"

"Yeah . . . I have no idea what you said. You also spoke so fast." Jacob was in awe. Shane laughed at Jacob.

"I think she has been taking French for about ten years. I swear if you spoke French to me on the first day I would have thought you were Jack's cousin from France. Your professors have taught you well," Shane chuckled.

"*Merci*, Shane." I smiled and felt my cheeks burning.

Jacob chuckled and looked ahead. "You two are cute."

We approached an area that gave us the view of the countries. I've only seen this view through a screen. Now it was real and it was a really pretty concept. I gasped. Both Shane and Jacob stopped walking.

"What?" I asked. Both Shane and Jacob looked towards each other before turning their attention towards me.

"We thought something was wrong for a moment," Jacob said.

"I can't wait until I take you to Magic Kingdom." Shane broke into a smile. As we walked, I could see the Eiffel tower from a distance. We walked through what I think is United Kingdom before we approached a bridgeway leading into Paris. I saw a professional photographer and I think Shane got the idea.

He led us to the photographer who greeted us. Shane urged me to go forward. I slowly walked over to the railing and turned around to face the photographer. The camera was ready while I saw both Jacob and Shane standing behind him. I smiled for the camera a few times before Jacob and Shane came over to me and stood on both of my sides. We took a normal picture then all of a sudden, they lifted me in the air. I yelped in surprise as I immediately let my arms wrap around their necks. They held me up with their arms under my legs. The photographer had already started taking pictures. I turned to the photographer and smiled.

Once he was done, I was slowly put down onto my feet and Jacob walked over to the photographer to hand him his Disney card. I was about to walk over when I felt a hand gently pulled me back.

"I need a few pictures with just you also." Shane smiled at me. I nodded then went to his side and he put his arm around my waist and we turned to the camera. I smiled again to the camera and he gave a thumbs up that it was taken.

"You guys can do more than that. This can be a romantic picture. It's a Paris view after all, right?" Jacob smirked. My lips pressed into a thin line, trying to hold myself from blushing. Shane and I turned towards each other. He held my hand. The arm with the cast was hidden on the other side.

"Only if you want to," Shane said softly. I nodded. It should be okay. I smiled as he leaned down and placed his lips on mine for the third time today. I felt his free hand reach for my waist. My eyes closed as the thrill of my first experienced returned back to me.

"What the hell guys?" Jacob exclaimed. I pulled away and looked to Jacob who was wide-eyed and jaw dropped. "I didn't realize you guys were going to kiss. When the hell did you become comfortable doing that?" I smiled shyly as I looked towards Shane, who had a small smile.

"Since this morning," Shane answered as he walked over to the photographer. He scanned Jacob's Disney card and handed it back to him. We thanked the guy before we continued on.

"You could have warned me. I didn't even realize how close you two already are. I thought you were going to do some cute sh*t like twirl Claire or maybe make her laugh." I laughed lightly, realizing Jacob was sort of excited about my kiss with Shane. I think he has been a big shipper of Shane and I since day one. "Well, I'm happy for you guys. Assuming you guys are going to leave us later to go to Magic Kingdom later, I hope you guys have a great time later."

"Thank you, Jacob." I smiled at him and Shane glanced towards me and continued to hold my hand as we walked the bridge and enter the bridge area. It may not be the actual Paris, but I was still blown away by the sight in front of me.

One day I'll visit France and see many of the cites there. There were many countries I would like to visit. Maybe during a spring break or summer break I can. There was also the thought of studying abroad sometime. I shook my head slightly at the thought of school. I haven't heard back from my schools yet.

"So . . ." —Shane started—"Monsieur Paul or Chef de France?"

"Chef de France." I smiled and my stomach grumbled.

The boys chuckled as we headed for Chef de France.

CHAPTER TWENTY-SIX
Epcot: Part Two

SHANE PETERS

"We should get going," Jacob said as he took a glance at his phone. Claire sat up so she could look at him. We were currently sitting at a bench in the U.S., facing the waters and relaxing after having our breakfast.

"What time is it?" she asked.

"It's 11:20 now. Soarin is a bit of a walk from here."

"We can take the boat," I suggested and pointed towards the boat that stopped in Morocco and brought you back to the entrance of the showcase. The three of us stood and Claire put her purse on her shoulder.

"Boat sounds good to me," she said. I looked to Jacob to see him also agreeing. We began making our way over to Morocco and smiled. Everything is going great for Claire and I. If everything goes really well with our date tonight at Magic Kingdom, I will ask her on another date. Maybe, if everything went really well between us in the next week and before we return home, I'll ask her if we can officially be together.

The thought of us having to leave each other did not cross my mind until now. We're just a few days into this trip and I'm sure she wasn't thinking about it. She will be having her summer break sometime in June. Right now, I wanted to focus on enjoying my time with her.

"Here we are," Jacob announced. We saw the entrance towards the dock. I looked out into the water to see the boat was just a few meters away. We were finally led onto the boat. Claire decided she wanted us to sit outside so I sat on one side and Jacob sat on her other side. The two of them have gotten along quite well. "Our pictures were uploaded already onto the account." Jacob smiled and look onto his phone.

"Can I see?" Claire asked. Jacob nodded as he handed his phone to her. I leaned over so I could take a look also. The picture started with the group when we had first arrived. There were few pictures where we were all trying to figure things out, funny faces and ones where we were smiling. Then we see some from the group as they were in front of spaceship earth. Then it was the pictures with Claire, Jacob and I on the bridge before entering France. There were the pictures first of just Claire, then the pictures we took with her, then the pictures I did with her. I smiled as she swiped and was on the picture where I was kissing her. We looked like the perfect Disney couple. There were several pictures of us and she smiled. She laughed when she swiped again and a laugh escaped all of us.

"The photographer caught everything," Jacob chuckled as we looked at the expression Jacob made when he saw us kissing. She swiped again and saw a few from breakfast. We looked very happy with our meals and right before we had left, Belle was walking around and Claire was able to get a picture with her. It was a really cute picture. There was more, but we knew it was not of us. "I'll send them to you guys. I just have to save them onto my phone, then I'll send them."

Claire thanked him and we came to a sudden stop. I looked away from them and realized we arrived at the entrance between Canada and Mexico where we first entered to walk around.

"Ladies first," I said to Claire. She took my hand as she stepped onto the dock. I followed her and Jacob smiled as he followed from behind. We walked off the docks and now making our way towards Soarin. From last time I could remember, it was in the building where Living with the Land would be.

"Up ahead," Jacob pointed out as we took a turn. The building was up ahead. Everyone was probably inside waiting for us. "Shane, you have Claire's card?"

"No, she has it," I answered. Claire nodded, confirming my statement as we walked up a small hill to enter the air conditioned building. I decided it would be quickest if we went left that led to the escalators. Jacob and Claire followed as I tried to search for our group. It was when we reached the bottom that I spotted them in front of the fast pass entrance to Soarin. Nate and Andy were the first to see us.

"There you guys are. I was starting to think you three weren't going to show up," Nate said.

"Let's go guys!" Aiden said as everyone began scanning their card before entering. Claire reached for her purse and took out her card before we walked up to scan our cards. The normal line was about a two-hour wait. The normal line always seemed to be long.

Ian and Aaron are suddenly in my view and they linked arms with Claire lightly, pushing me away from her.

"Our turn with Claire. You can spend more time with her after the ride." Ian pouted and Aaron agreed. I smiled as Claire shrugged shyly. I put my hands up in defeat and smiled, feeling nervous. I never really hung out with anyone aside from Jacob.

"Plus, I bet you guys are going to sneak off again anyway." Aaron smiled. They pulled Claire ahead of the group, out of my reach. We went right in and traveled the long hall and straight to where we were assigned a row. Our whole group fit into one row.

Buckling in our seatbelts, we waited until the cast members checked everyone. I let my head rest against the back as the lights were dimming and blue lights came on. The wind feeling occurred as we were being lifted and I smiled getting ready for the great view.

"That was awesome!" Ian yelled as we walked off the ride Soarin. We were all laughing at a joke Aiden was telling when I felt two pairs of hands grab me and pulled me aside from the group. I stopped walking and realized the group had continued on. I turned to see both Fin and Jack.

"Hey, what's up?" I asked, a little confused. I haven't talked to them so far on this trip. I turned to look for our group when I noticed they have now disappeared. I could find Claire after I guess.

"Alright Shane," Fin started. He seemed like he was getting straight to the point. "I need you to break up with Claire."

I frowned as I began to feel anger towards him. What was his problem with Claire? He had no right to tell me anything. "Umm, Excuse me?" I stepped closer towards him. Even though he was taller than me and maybe buffer, it did not mean I would back out of this. Fin has done so much wrong to Claire and that needs to get through his thick skull. She did not deserve anything he had put her through. "First of all, we aren't official yet and second, who are you to tell me what to do?" What were they up to? Why do I have this strange feeling that something was wrong? Why would Jack stand here and let him talk to me like this?

"Doesn't she like you?" He seemed very impatient for some odd reason. I don't know, but it wasn't easing me either.

"Yes, but that doesn't mean I've asked her to be my girlfriend yet." What did her having to like me have anything to—"

"Well I want you to hurt her. I want you to crush her."

My hands were fisting now. "Why the hell would I do that Owen?" I muttered at him.

"Just do it Shane . . ." Johnson said softly. I looked towards him shocked and confused. Weren't they somewhat on good terms yesterday? How could he possibly stand here and let this happen?

"She doesn't know . . ." he said, reading my mind then looked down at his shoes. He looked defeated.

"Jack, how could you do this to Claire? She needs you right now especially at a time like this. She's your cousin for crying out loud!" I said. People were taking glances.

"I'm trying to save her," he croaked and closed his eyes painfully. "To keep her safe. I want her to go to college Shane, I can't risk this."

"What are you talking about?"

Fin pulled out his phone and showed me a video of Claire when she broke into the school. I watched it nervously, because this wouldn't be good at all for any administrator to see. I'm sure he had multiple copies and it made me feel very uneasy.

"Please Shane," Johnson pleaded. I felt myself getting uneasy. There's this unsettling feeling from the pit of my stomach.

"Please, I can't do this to Claire. I can't do this. It will hurt her." I looked at Fin who looked determined. I had to figure this out. This would break her. Maybe I can tell her that I can't hang with her anymore. But I don't want to cause too much pain.

"That's the freakin' point Peters." Fin rolled his eyes. "You either do this or you can see her future be ruined. Her scholarships? Gone."

I looked towards Johnson who had his eyes still averted to the ground. "Okay." I sighed. "I'll talk to her and tell her I can't be around her anymore."

"No, that's not enough," Fin said and I sent him a glare. Fin stood there with his eyebrow raised and I bit my lip knowing I didn't have long.

"What do you want me to do?" I asked, barely a whisper. Fin came back with a girl a few minutes later. She had a smile on her face. She had no clue.

"Break Claire's heart."

CLAIRE JOHNSON

After Soarin, I felt very refreshed. I thought that was very nice to see different views on a screen. It made me more excited to travel the world. Ian, Ken, Aiden, and I somehow separated from the rest of the guys and started making our way towards the countries. I turned around to see if Shane or Jacob was nearby, but they were nowhere in sight. I'm sure Shane will text me soon. He and Jacob went to do something.

"I see Mexico!" Ian pointed out. I laughed lightly and tried to hide myself because there were several parents glaring at him. Suddenly, there were a bunch of teenage girls who came up to the guys and we were now surrounded. I felt a bit uncomfortable being here as the guys talked to their fans. I guess this is what it's like when you are internet famous.

I then stood a distance and waited patiently for them. I felt unsure of what to do. The guys continued to talk and take many pictures. It was after a while that I realized that this wouldn't end soon so I decided to do a little exploring on my own. I sent a text to them telling them I'd go ahead and meet up with them later. I turned away and began walking away. It was a really nice and hot sunny day. It was really nice to finally be here after so many years of wanting to come here. I loved the feeling of being here. I wondered where Shane had gone off to so I texted him. Maybe he thought I went with the guys and wanted me to text him.

Claire:
Hey Shane :) Where are you guys? I didn't see you after.

I waited for a response. I looked around as it was a fairly crowded day here at the park. I wonder how many people enter the parks in a day?

It was not long after my phone vibrated and I opened the text.

Shane:

Hey, I have a surprise for you at United Kingdom. Meet me there around 7:30?

Claire:
Okay, that sounds like a plan. I'll see you then :)

I smiled down at my phone, thinking of how sweet and kind Shane has been to me. I'm really glad to have met a guy like him on this trip. All the guys and Nora has been so kind to me. I put my phone back into my pocket and heard a loud gasp, grabbing my attention. I looked up and saw two girls that were about a year or two younger smiling towards me. They walked over to me nervously. I've never had this encounter before. "Are you Jack's cousin, Claire Johnson?" the first girl asked.

"Indeed I am." I smiled. I saw the sparkle in their eyes as I confirmed their question. I've never really encountered a fan before.

"Y—you sang with Shane during the first day of Kricon. You were amazing."

"Thank you," I answered kindly. "What are your names?"

"I'm Jaz and this is my friend, Sarah."

"It's nice to meet you guys." I felt as shy as they were.

"Can we have a picture with you?" the second girl asked softly. They both seemed very kind.

"Sure." I stood beside the first girl and smiled at her phone while her friend took the picture. Then the second girl walked over to me and posed as the next phone was held up.

"It was really nice meeting you!" Both of the girls said. I gave them both a hug before they began walking away. I took a look of my surrounding. I was now entering China. I realized that I was hungry when I felt my stomach grumble slightly. I wasn't sure if we were eating as a group or if Shane wanted to go somewhere. He did mention that he wanted to sneak off to Magic Kingdom. Maybe we will be going there after I meet him in United Kingdom later. It was currently past 2 PM so we've been here for several hours. I walked into the Chinese restaurant and was seated right away in a booth.

As soon as I ordered, two guys slid into the seat across from me. I realized it was Ryder and Andy's younger brother, Ben. It took me a moment. The heat must be getting to me a bit. "Guuurl, no invite?" Ryder asked in his female voice. I smiled at the both of them. There was never a second of normal when you're around any of them. Except Shane, of course. He and Jacob spoke my language completely.

"I didn't know you guys were here." I laughed and felt a little shy towards them. I haven't actually spent that much time with Ryder or Ben. They seemed nice. "I thought you were with the rest of the guys as a group?"

"Nah,"—Ben smiled—"we left them a while ago. Can we hang with you? You're cooler to be around than the gang."

"Sure. I guess so. You guys won't get surrounded by girls to the point where I have to leave you guys, will you?"

"Nope, don't have to worry." Ben shrugged and smiled.

"Well maybe a little. Plus, we thought we'd keep you company since Shane isn't with you," Ryder pointed out.

"You guys are so sweet. I'm meeting up with Shane in a few hours."

"That's fine. That means we get to hang with you longer." Ben said.

I smiled as a cast member came over to us and asked Ryder and Ben what they wanted to order. I really liked how workers here were called cast members. I really liked my Disney experience so far.

"Yeah . . ." Ryder said. I think he was continuing from our conversation. "I think I saw him with Jack and Fin."

"Oh," I said lightly and took a sip of my Sprite. I wasn't sure how to feel about it. I hope Shane was alright. Jack has been avoiding me today. I wonder if something went wrong.

Ben and Ryder brought me away from my thoughts as we talked about what we would do next.

CHAPTER TWENTY-SEVEN
Fans

CLAIRE JOHNSON

"Ben put me down!" I laughed as I hung from his shoulder. I had to be careful with my casted arm. Ben was only fourteen and he was as tall as me, maybe even a little taller. He definitely gained some energy after the amount of food he consumed. I don't know how he managed to move around after eating so much food. For the past few hours we goofed off so much, took so many pictures in front of the countries with costumes, did a few small rides like Nordstrom, and explored the gift shop and stores. We also tried on different clothing to pass more time.

Jacob sent me the photos we had looked at when we were on the boat earlier. I found out there was this app for Disney that saves all the pictures taken within our group directly on their accounts. Everything is linked together somehow. I showed some of the pictures to Ben and Ryder and they freaked out over the one where Shane and I were kissing. I did not mean for them to see it, but Ben swiped too far. They tried to take my phone to send to themselves. Hence why I am currently on Ben's shoulder holding on to my phone and purse for dear life.

"We'll just have to log onto the account later and get it then," Ryder said as a matter of fact. "Oh, I know everyone is going to get very excited over those photos. No one was sure what exactly was going on between you two. Now we know."

"Don't start posting it though! Shane and I aren't official and people might start assuming things!" I complained. They attracted a lot of attention.

"Nothing to worry about," Ben said with a smile that turned into a smirk. "It will probably be in our group chats. Nothing will be leaked. Anyway, whenever you and Shane do become official, I'm going to need that picture to post anyway." Ben came to a sudden stop. Now we have arrived in Japan. Ben carefully set me down on my feet to make sure he did not bother my casted arm. He held me in his arms and hugged me tightly before letting go. I smiled up at him and asked him what the hug was for. "You seem like an older sister that I wish I could have," he said to answer my question. He gave me a small shrug.

"You have Andy though. You guys are so close!" I said.

"Yeah, but I wish I also had an older sister. You can be like Andy's twin!" he said. I laughed lightly and shrugged. I wasn't sure if Andy and I were the same age. I think Andy was seventeen.

"You're like a younger brother I wish I could have. I'd love to be your older sister!"

He gave me a wide smile. Ryder and I both smiled at his excitement. These two have been so kind to me that it didn't take long for me to warm up to them. Spending these few hours with them so far has been very interesting. I would consider Jacob, Ryder, and Ben as pretty close friends.

"Psssh, she's gonna be my twin Ben," Ryder said, rolling his eyes playfully. I burst out into laughter. The laughter never stopped with them. It felt great to feel carefree and to be under the sun again. We walked towards the shop as I thought there would be some pretty cool things in these shops. I fixed my dress as we approached the store. Ben opened the door for us. I thanked him and walked inside. The first thing I noticed was the amount of people that were in here. I looked around and saw many of the

209

workers wearing kimonos. The workers would wear clothing which represents that country. The coolest thing would be when you look at their name tags for majority of them. They were actually from that country. I thought it was really cool and that fascinated me.

The first thing I went to were the fans. Ryder and Ben followed me as we looked at the different fans and some of the accessories around here. We then went towards the back of the stores where we could try on kimonos. Ben and Ryder took part of it then we took many pictures. It was really fun to try on things and take pictures. Once we were done, I started making my way over to the jewelry section.

"I love looking at these. They're so pretty," I said as I started picking up rings and trying them on.

"Girls and their jewelry," Ben mumbled to Ryder. I turned towards him and frowned playfully before punching him. I smiled when he gasped. I returned to trying on different rings when a particular one stood out to me. I picked it up and stared at it. Ryder half smiled as he took it and slid it on my finger. I smiled at the two of them. It was a dark emerald color. I smiled at the beautiful ring because I loved it and it fit me perfectly.

"It's so pretty," I said in awe. Ben and Ryder looked towards each other. I sighed a little as I slid the ring off and placed it back to where it belonged. I should wait until I have gone to all the parks and see what there is. I have to keep a budget and can't spend too much on this trip. Maybe if this is what I wanted after seeing everything, I'll come back. I really hope it will still be here if I came back. There's hope. I started to walk away, but noticed the two standing there awkwardly and Ryder sent me a half smile.

"We'll be right there," Ben said with a warm smile.

"Yeah," Ryder smiled agreeing. "We'll be right out."

"Okay," I nodded at them. "I'm going to wait outside." They both nodded and I walked out of the store into the warm air. The warm air hit my face. I looked at the horizon and saw the sun was beginning to set. I thought it was really pretty and I couldn't wait to see many more.

I took my phone out to check the time. It was already 6:30 and Shane wanted to meet somewhere in United Kingdom in an hour. I walked over to an empty bench and sat down. I leaned onto the back part of the wooden bench. Taking a deep breath, I let the warm and fuzzy feeling of being here take over. I looked around and saw many children with their parents or groups of teenagers with their friends. Disney seems to be a place for everyone.

It wasn't long when I spotted few girls looking at my way. They came up to me to say hi and asked me if I could take pictures with them. I felt awkward about it, because this was something I am still getting used to. They told me how Jack and I look alike and that we could be siblings. Everyone seemed to know who I was. Not five minutes later, I noticed two guys coming up to me and introduced themselves. I never thought guys would come up to me. I remembered how antisocial I used to be.

"You must be Claire Johnson!" the guy named Zach said with a friendly smile.

"I am," I answered shyly. Really good looking guys coming up to me? I think I could get use to this. Plus, they're being really nice? No harm at all. I wonder how the guys do this when they are home and hanging out somewhere. It made me wonder what school was like for them.

"Don't be shy." The other guy, Dylan, smiled. "We actually think you're really cute on those vines the guys posted. You seem very kind."

"Thanks," I answered, still not knowing what to say. I think they took notice that I am in a cast.

"How did you break your wrist or your arm?"

"I fell. I wasn't being careful the other day," I said softly. The guys nodded.

"Can we . . . uh . . . take a picture with you?" Zach asked scratching the back of his head. I wasn't sure why guys did that.

211

"Sure." I stood up slowly and Zach walked over to one of the workers nearby. When he came back, Zach placed his arm around my waist. Dylan did the same. I was in the middle. I smiled as the worker took the picture. The worker then walked over to us to show us the picture. We all looked at it in awe. Zach's phone took great pictures. It was also an iPhone. I should try with my phone.

"It's perfect, thank you." Dylan smiled. The worker walked away when I spotted Ryder and Ben coming out of the store. I asked what they were doing and shrugged it off.

"It was really nice meeting you." Both the guys had said and smiled at me. I'm not sure if they saw Ben or Ryder.

"You too." I smiled back.

"I'm posting this. You're pretty chill." Dylan smiled, to which Zach agreed with.

"I'll be sure to like it later," I said. Zach and Dylan thanked me and told me they hoped to see me someday perform again, which caught me off. They began to walk away just as Ryder and Ben came up to me. It looks like Ryder has purchased something.

"Who were they? Made new friends?" Ben asked me curiously.

"Fans." I smiled. They both nodded as we decided to walk in the direction of United Kingdom.

"So . . . You and Shane are having a date night I assume?" Ryder asked.

"Yes." My tone was light. Whenever someone brings up my relationship with Shane, I always felt really shy. It felt strange for me to talk about my crush when he wasn't around and the thought of Shane himself made me nervous . . . but thankful. He has been really supportive with my decisions with college and continuing to be involved with music whether it was my major or if it was something I did as a hobby. I knew playing the cello would always stay with me and being with Shane so far has made me realize how much music meant to me.

212

"Anything special planned?" Ben asked curiously.

"He wants to take me to Magic Kingdom tonight I think."

"Awe, does sound like something he would do. So, you like him?"

"Yes. Is it really obvious Shane and I have been around each other a lot?"

"Yes," Ryder said as we were arriving in Italy. "It's quite clear Shane is into you the moment Nate mentioned to him you were a musician and you were his age. I think Shane and Jacob were excited to meet someone who spoke their language."

"Yeah?"

"Shane tweeted about you how many times now?" Ben chuckled. "You also made it to his Instagram page and let's not forget, he didn't go to day two of Kricon to visit you in the hospital. I don't know how that went well with Blake, but somehow he managed to go," Ben said. The thought of that only made me excited for tonight with him.

"Speaking of you and Shane . . ." Ryder smiled as he looked up from his phone. We stopped walking and my eyes widened. Ryder put his phone out for me and I squinted since the brightness on the screen was low. This picture was of Shane, Jacob, and I on the bridge. I read the caption for it.

> *JacobHolland*
> *This is our spot @ShanePeters @clairejohnson*

I noticed some of the comments the guys and Nora posted.

AidenRodriguez: f*cking adorable

AndyMiller: When did you guys take this?

Nora: awe! I love this!

AaronPhillips: friendship goals

JustNate: 3 amazing musicians I know

I smiled and saw some comments from his fans. I briefly looked at them.

THIS IS SO CUTE. I CAN'T EVEN

Awe, Jacob! I love your outfit today You guys should do a cover together!!

Shane and Claire look like a couple. Do you know if they're dating?

I looked away and smiled sheepishly at the amount of attention this was getting. I'm sure my Instagram and Twitter has many notifications.

"Jacob and Shane are treating you pretty well. "They're always hanging with each other talking about music stuff." Ben half smiled. We continued walking until I spotted gelato.

"Ohhh." I smiled. Ryder and Ben's head turned in the direction I was looking.

"You're a gelato fan I'm guessing?" Ryder asked. I nodded as I started making my way over to the shop. Having some gelato sounded really good to me at the moment. I walked into the shop and looked at their selection.

"I think I'm going to buy the chocolate chip one," I smiled as I fell in line and they followed me.

"If I knew you were into gelato, I could have gotten some for you when I was at Target with some of the guys yesterday," Ryder said. I shrugged as we moved up in the line slightly.

"What time did you say you were meeting up with Shane again?" Ben asked curiously.

"Around 7:30."

"Oh okay. You have a bit of time. I was just wondering," Ben said. I nodded as I ordered a medium sized gelato. I moved over so I could be in front of the cashier and she rung me up with my total. I reached for my purse and took my wallet out. I gave the worker exact change.

"Are you two getting—" I stopped when I saw they were smiling from ear to ear. They were looking at something on Ben's phone. They looked up towards me.

"No, we're alright. Thank you though." Ben smiled. I nodded as I turned back to the cashier who had my gelato in their hand. I thanked them before leaving the line and made my way for a table to sit at with Ryder and Ben. I chose a seating outside.

"Picture?" Ryder asked me as we all sat down. I nodded as I held my gelato close to my face and smiled at the gelato itself.

"I wish I could get a girl who would look at me like Claire does her gelato," Ben said. I burst into laughter. I had no idea I had this look and my eyes squeezed shut for a split second before looking at Ben. Ryder seemed to have an amused look. I smiled at Ben and licked my gelato.

"I got all of that," Ryder said and Ben smiled. I rolled my eyes, realizing they probably took a vine instead of pictures. "I promise I took only pictures," Ryder chuckled. "I'll send them to you. They're cute."

"You're the best." I laughed lightly and picked up my spoon to start taking small scoops of my chocolate chip gelato.

CHAPTER TWENTY-EIGHT
Surprised

CLAIRE JOHNSON

"I guess you should get going," Ryder said. I looked away from the view of the water and lights showing around the countries. After sitting around talking and me finishing up my gelato, we decided to get up and move to a bench where we faced Spaceship Earth. It was a distance away and there was also the view of the other countries when you looked around. We wanted a scenic view.

"Enjoy your date with Shane," Ben said, looking up from his phone. I stood carefully and thanked the both of them. I told them I would text them later and to enjoy the rest of their time here at the park. I knew I'd be hanging out with them sometime soon. I wouldn't mind spending a whole day with them the next time we went to a park. I waved at them as I began my way to United Kingdom. I took my phone out of my pocket and took a quick glance at the time. It was now 7:25. I had to pass through U.S., Japan, Morocco and France before getting to United Kingdom. Once I was passing France and onto the bridge, I began to slow down.

Looking around, I could barely see the sunset anymore. It was mostly the shops and the lights that made everything visible. I looked back to see the Eiffel tower was lit up. I smiled, thinking Shane and I could come back here to take a picture. I carried my cup souvenir. I arrived at United Kingdom and I looked around in awe. It was a different view during the evening. Lights were hung around and I could see the pubs were very packed. I saw the red phone booths and the shops.

The view somehow reminded me of Shane instantly. We both have always wanted to go to London. I felt happy knowing that Shane liked me. It felt good and welcoming to know we had the same feelings towards each other. I don't think there has been a guy who had ever cared to really get to know me. I'm really happy to be on this trip. Everything seemed to get better these past few days after leaving New York, minus the few encounters with Finnegan and my broken arm. I don't think I've ever been this happy, given the circumstances.

I looked around trying to figure out where to go. Shane did not say where exactly he wanted to meet. As I took a seat on an empty bench, I took my phone back out and checked the time. It was now five minutes past seven thirty. I sent a quick text to Shane and I decided to go onto Vine to pass some time until he arrived. I laughed at the vines the guys had posted today. I ended up being in a few of them.

So far, I followed Nora and the guys on the app. I found it crazy that there were so many people following, revining, commenting, and liking my first vine that I posted several days ago. I felt the bench shift. Someone else was here.

I looked up from my phone and flinched. Finnegan was looking at me with a small smile. I did not feel comfortable with him here. I looked around and thought it was okay to be out in public with him. "H—hey," I finally said, breaking the awkwardness. He couldn't do anything here in public. He wouldn't try anything with people around. I hope not anyway.

"Hey . . . look I'm sorry about everything," he started. I found it hard to believe he would apologize.

"Oh . . . alright," I said slowly. There must be something behind his actions. I felt intimidated. My pulse continued to increase and I avoided his eye contact.

"I hope maybe we could start over?"

"I'm . . . not really sure."

"I know I did terrible things. It's not an excuse for the things I have done . . ." He sighed.

"I'm sort of waiting for someone."

"Right. Yeah, Jack and I were with him earlier. So, you and Shane are meeting here like a date?" he asked. I looked towards him confused. How did he know about this? Did Shane tell him earlier? Maybe if Shane trusted him now, maybe there was a bit of comfort of knowing Finnegan was trying. I could trust him a little bit.

"I'm not exactly sure," I answered shyly. He raised an eyebrow and seemed curious.

"Well I think it's a date. From his talk earlier, it looked like he really liked you. I saw some of the pictures of you and Shane on the account," Finnegan chuckled lightly. I relaxed slightly as he continued to talk. "He has a surprise for you. Been planning it all day." He smiled. "Peters is so into you. He wanted me to take you to him."

"A—alright." I stood feeling unsure about this. I wasn't sure whether to trust him, but also, I wasn't sure so I sent a quick text to Shane. Finnegan led me over to the closest shop and I walked in being immediately attracted. I walked over to the souvenirs. "This is so cute," I said softly and picked up the stuffed bear that held a flag. It was similar to the one I saw in the shop in Canada earlier. I put the stuffed bear back before moving onto the other souvenirs. My phone vibrated from my purse and I took a look at it.

> *Shane:*
> *Yes, Fin is going to take you to me. I'll see you in a little bit.*

I bit the inside of my cheek feeling nervous. I would have thought he would have given me an explanation why Finnegan was sent to me or maybe had texted me before Finnegan came. It made me wonder why he didn't tell me especially since he knew what Finnegan has done. I continued to feel uneasy as Finnegan followed me around the shop. I turned towards him and held my phone up.

"Shane said you were taking me to him," I said softly as I confirmed his earlier statement. I looked towards his shoes, not wanting to make eye contact.

"I guess we should get going then?"

I nodded as he started making his way to the other end of the store. He led me out of the store into the crowd. I followed him towards the back of the building where the crowd started to thin out. I wasn't sure if there was anything here or if we were allowed to be back here. There wasn't really anything. He led me to a path where there was a beautiful garden and I stared in astonishment for a moment. I saw Finnegan across from the garden and looked towards me before turning the corner. I walked through the garden to catch up to him.

When I turned the corner, I spotted Finnegan, but past him made me stop where I was. I gasped slightly as my souvenir cup slipped from my hands. The cup shattered on the ground. My heart felt like it was being swallowed then shattered. I watch as Shane smiled at the girl in front of him and he had his hands on her waist before leaning in to kiss her. Her arms were wrapped around his waist and I looked away. I felt the swallowing pain and the uneven beat as all of the memories with Shane had been like these past few days came to me.

"S—Shane?" I asked weakly. I don't understand what I had done wrong or why he asked me to be here if he was with her. I was now in front of Finnegan so I had a clear view of Shane. Shane pulled away from her and smiled towards me. How could he lead me on? Why did I trust him? I thought he cared?

"Hey," he said cheerfully like he had just finished having the best kiss he ever had. "I'd like you to meet Stacy."

I stood there in shock and confusion. My mind was racing and my heart was crying out to me. "I—I don't understand, I thought you said this morning out in the balcony that you liked me and you . . ." I felt tears brimming my eyes. He wanted to kiss me. We were enjoying our date as we talked about his family.

He laughed at me and I felt my lips quiver slightly. I should have known a guy like Shane would never be interested in me. There was nothing special about me. "You thought I actually liked you?" He paused. "You thought listening to your story would make me fall for you?" He laughed again.

I felt a tug to my heart. It was disappointment. I felt embarrassed also because I let him in. Finnegan walked over and stood next to Shane with a big smile on his face. I looked towards him knowing he couldn't be trusted. Finnegan rolled his eyes before he laughed.

"Gosh Claire, you're so pathetic," Finnegan said. "No one will ever like you. I don't know why you think that everything will be alright. It never will be!" he said. I took a step back feeling afraid again. "You're just another loser. I'm glad Jack broke your arm. You definitely deserved it," he added. The girl looked down slightly as she held onto Shane's hand.

"I thought you were different," I said quietly as I looked at Shane with sad eyes. Everyone thought we would be great together and they told me how great Shane was. Everyone loved Shane and he seemed amazing. He chuckled as I felt humiliated and there wasn't anything I could do about it.

"You thought wrong. How about you return to your home in New York?" I closed my eyes painfully as the thought of my parents came back to me. I can't believe he would say that after everything I've gone through with my mom recently and having to face the reality of my dad's death. He knew this was a touchy subject and he used it against me. I felt warm tears rolling down my cheeks.

"Y—you know I can't go back to New York." My voice cracked and I opened my eyes. My vision was blurry and the heartache continued to intensify. Shane wanted to hurt me and embarrass me because he wasn't my friend or I wasn't a crush to him. He was Finnegan's friend. "That is so wrong of you to ever bring that up when you know I have been trying to cope."

Shane looked away with a flash of guilt and Finnegan stepped in front of Shane with a bored look. "Really? What lame excuse did you come up with now?" Finnegan asked annoyed.

I sniffled as it all became too much. I no longer wanted to be around them. I felt so disappointed in Shane. I turned away from them and started running. I did not care what I looked like or if security had to come after me. I had to get away from them. I felt crushed and my heart continued to tear apart.

It didn't matter what anyone thought of me, but I slowed down and tried to wipe my face. I wanted to go back to the suite and be alone. I wanted to tell Jack what Finnegan and Shane had done to me. I wanted to get under the covers and crawl up into a ball as I cried my heart out. I left the showcase area. I wasn't so sure where I was going. It wasn't until a few minutes later I heard someone call my name in panic. However, I continued to walk. I felt arms grab mine and I tried to push them away from me. I tried to pull away, but they were . . . very strong? They pulled me close and I began to sob.

"What happened Claire?" I heard a worried Ben. He seemed out of breath from running after me. He pulled me to his chest. "Claire, you're shaking," he said softly and hugged me. "Let's sit down somewhere." He led me to a bench.

"Here are some tissues," I heard Ryder say a few moments later. I thanked him and reached for them to wipe my eyes and blow my nose. It took a few moments to calm down slightly, but the weight of the sadness took over. Both Ben and Ryder were sitting next to me and watched carefully as I tried to take steady breaths. "What happened?" Ryder asked softly after what seemed like a good ten minutes of me trying to calm myself. I looked up and realized we were sitting away from a crowd and we were close by Test Track.

"I—I really don't want to talk about it," I said as I sniffled. I wanted it to be done with and try to move away as quickly as possible. I wanted to return to the happiness I had been feeling not even thirty minutes ago. I also wanted Shane to tell me that it was some twisted thing Finnegan put him to and this was a mistake.

"I'm going to murder Shane," Ryder said getting up. Fear came over me. I know he had done wrong, but he was genuine to his fans. I wouldn't want to be the reason to the problems of the group. I wouldn't want Shane hurt.

"Please don't," I said. I tugged on his arm, but he wouldn't sit.

"Why shouldn't I? You don't deserve this!" he yelled. I know he was angry at Shane, but it felt like he was yelling at me. I jumped slightly from his outburst. Ben wrapped an arm around me from the side and let me lean my head against his shoulder.

"I don't deserve any of you guys," I answered softly as I closed my eyes. I feel insecure. I started my day having the best of times only to have it end feeling like the world was going against me. I hated this. I was starting to close up again.

"Don't say that," Ben said trying to calm me down.

"C—can I talk to my cousin?" I asked after a couple of minutes. It would be nice to talk to him after what just happened. Ben looked towards Ryder and he nodded.

Ryder went onto his phone and after a few moments of silence, the call connected. "Yo Jack, it's an emergency . . . Yeah Claire's not doing so great and wants to talk to you . . ." Ryder's calm expression went from calm to anger. "What the hell . . ." Ryder said. Ben looked up. Finnegan must have gotten to him last night. "How the f*ck do you choose him over your own cousin?"

222

he yelled into the phone. Parents around us covered their children's ears. There was a long pause until he spoke again. "You know what Jack, go to hell, because Claire deserves much better than you," he mumbled and hung up.

He walked back to us with sympathy in his eyes. I understood what was going on. "I'm so sorry," he said softly and I nodded, looking down at my cast.

CHAPTER TWENTY-NINE
It Couldn't Get Worse

CLAIRE JOHNSON

The rest of the night for me had been crushed. I no longer wanted to be at the park any longer. Ben and Ryder accompanied me to the front of the park, but I told them I wanted to go back to the resort on my own. They would not let me as they reminded me that it would have been an expensive cab ride back to the resort. They went on Spaceship Earth with me a few times until Nate sent a text in the group chat to meet back at the vans. I decided I'd ride with Ryder and Ben to avoid seeing Finnegan, my cousin, and Shane.

No one seemed to mind me switching vehicles and everyone in the other van was not there. We left first before they did. I let my head rest against the window and tried to focus my attention outside. Both Ryder and Ben understood right away that I wanted to be left alone.

When we arrived back at the resort, he asked if everyone wanted to eat at the recreation center. Everyone agreed and they all started making their way there. Ryder and Ben watched me get out of the van carefully as I was the last one.

"You guys go ahead," I said softly. They both gave me an unsure look. "I'm fine. I'd like to shower and make myself a snack from the room. I'm not much in a mood to be around anyone right now." I smiled wistfully.

"Okay. We'll text you once we're done eating," Ben nodded.

"We're coming over later," Ryder said. I nodded as I turned away and began making my way towards the main building. The walk towards the main building wasn't too far. I felt a vibration from my phone and took it out from my purse. I closed my eyes and sighed as I opened the long text.

> *Jacob:*
> *I'm really confused why Shane is in the van right now and why you took the other van back when I thought you two were supposed to head over to Magic Kingdom? I've tried to talk to Shane, but he isn't saying a thing. Is everything alright with you two?*

My heart felt heavy and I felt as if this was something I wanted to face alone. I did not want to bring anyone into this after what just happened with Shane.

> *Claire:*
> *Shane wasn't the guy I thought he was. There was a big misunderstanding between us*

I sent the message to him before I said anymore and entered the lobby of the main building. I decided to walk around before heading to the suite. I knew it would be dark and I'd have that feeling of being alone again. Not a moment later, my phone began to ring and I sighed softly thinking Jacob wanted to talk, but I wasn't in the mood to talk. I pulled my phone out again to see an unknown number. I think it was an area code from California, I can't exactly remember which part. I answered the phone.

"Hello?" I said.

"Hi, this is Samantha Prezo from the administration's office from University of California in San Francisco. Can I speak to Miss Claire Johnson?" The woman's tone was soft but also sounded urgent.

"That's me," I confirmed nervously. I had forgotten I updated everything and sent in a new resume with my new cell phone number so I could be contacted directly. I did all of this right before leaving for Florida. I hadn't realized I would be contacted so quickly.

"Claire, how are you doing? It must be getting late for you. I hope I am not disturbing or interrupting your sleep."

"N—no, no, it's okay. I'm doing alright."

"You're wondering why I am calling personally?"

"Yes."

"The school would like to call you on behalf of your early action. Due to your recent change in address, it was best to personally contact you," she said. I thought I would be receiving a letter in the mail or through email.

"Of course, I understand."

"I would like to personally congratulate you for being accepted into the University of California into the six-year pharmacy program and would like to have you in the graduating class of 2021. The pharmacy professors and the admissions thought your application was magnificent and we'd love to have you continue to fulfill your dreams here."

My cast covered my mouth as I let that sink in. I've been accepted into one of my top schools for pharmacy. "Thank you so much." I smiled through the phone and felt my eyes glossing slightly. I felt relieved to be accepted somewhere. "This just made my evening. This is amazing news."

"You will be receiving your official acceptance letter; financial aid packages and the list of scholarships should also be in the package when you open it up. Everything will be mailed to your new address in Nebraska."

"Thank you so much Samantha."

"If you have any questions or need anything, don't be afraid to shoot us an email or call the admissions office. I hope you enjoy your evening Miss. Johnson," she said. I thanked her before ending the call. It left a small smile on my face as I continued to walk through the halls.

Time passed as I found a spot somewhere in the hotel with a big window that had the view of the basketball and tennis court. Checking the time, I'm sure everyone was back at the hotel. I don't think anyone stayed behind. It was almost midnight. I have been looking out the window for several hours now. Yawning, I knew it was time for me to head back to my suite. I carefully stood up and made my way down the hall. It was the hallway everyone's suites were, I spotted my cousin standing there.

A mixture of betrayal, confusion and hurt was how I felt as I looked at him. Before my mind could process what was happening, I was making way towards him and he looked up to see me charging towards him. I built up the little strength I had with my free hand and tried to push him with my emotions. He took a step back before I could hit his chest.

"You told me you wouldn't do this to me. You promised Jack," I said hurtfully. He closed his eyes and sighed before reopening them and looked towards me with cold eyes.

"Promises are always broken, Claire."

"You're not a person to break promises. Jack, I'm your cousin. How could you do this? After what I could have possibly went through, the least you could do is be nicer to me."

"Everything I said yesterday was a lie. Heck, I still do not want you to live with me." I felt so hurt as he ignored what I had just said to him. He seemed really convincing, but a part of me felt as if he was forced to say these things under some sort of pressure. Hearing it in person, did not mean that it didn't hurt me, because it did. It seemed all so real yesterday that we'd be back to the way we were before or at least starting to anyway, because I thought he cared. I thought he would have figured a way to figure this out.

"I—I don't understand."

"Just save it, Claire. Please leave me alone. I don't want you near me."

"You're lying Jack." His words hurt more than Finnegan's because I care more of his words and choices than his. What he happened to do next only hurt me more. He laughed at me and folded his arms.

"I'm pretty sure everyone doesn't want you in their lives. Just like the people at your school. Claire, you don't have friends. Why bother, Claire? At least do me a favor and leave all of my friends alone. Just because you're my cousin doesn't mean that they're your friends too." He took a step towards me and smiled. "You better keep Ben and Ryder from spilling anything to the other guys or I will do much worse to you than breaking your arm. I mean it. Stay away."

"You don't mean all of this," I said softly, sensing fear and devastation from his behavior.

"I'd prefer if you weren't here, but I guess it's too late for that." He backed away. I felt the swollen pain in my heart. It was like I was being swallowed up. It hurt so much that I don't understand how he could be so cold towards me. Even if he didn't mean it, he still went through with this just like Shane. "See you around Claire." He walked away and into one of the suites.

I slowly made my way back to the other side of the building where my suite was secluded from everyone. Once I arrived, I opened the door and quietly went in. The living room was dark and empty. It reminded me of the last several months of my dark times when I was back in New York. I shook my head, trying to push myself away from the thought. I walked over to one of the couches and sat there in the dark as tears began to well up in my eyes again.

Why was this all happening to me? Shane lied about ever caring about me as a person. He hurt me knowing I didn't want to go back to New York. Then there's Jack who turned his back on me when I thought he'd be there for me. The one positive thing I really had at the moment would be my acceptance into the University of California. Is it too much to ask for someone to be a part of my life who really cared?

I wish I could have been happy with Shane and I'd wish Jack would have changed. Maybe I did not deserve them and there was something wrong with me. I felt a vibration on my lap and I shook slightly from being deep in my thoughts.

Ben: Hey Claire, Ryder and I are coming over. We'll be there in five. Don't do anything silly without us. See you soon

I sniffled slightly and tried to use the tissues from the tissue box to clear away anything on my face. I sat here waiting for them to come. I looked around the living room and noticed it had been cleaned up when everyone took their things with them earlier this morning. I sighed thinking about Shane and I only wanted to forget what happened just a few hours ago.

Moments later, I heard a knock on the door and I walked over to open it. I didn't wait until they were in my view or opened the door all the way before I turned around and went back to where I was sitting. Ryder and Aaron slowly came in and I was surprised to see a third person closing the door. It was Jacob who looked towards me with much worry. Would he push me away like Shane did too? The three of them walked over and took a seat facing me.

"I'm really sorry your evening didn't go as planned Claire," Jacob started and I looked down towards my fingers playing with each other. I at the moment did not care if I was sitting unladylike in my dress.

"How you feelin'?" Ben asked, breaking the silence. He figured I wasn't going to respond.

229

"Not really my best," I sighed and closed my eyes painfully remembering the events with Shane, Fin, and Jack.

I was trying to stop the next round of tears because I did not want them to see me like that. "I . . . uh received a call from the University of California about two hours ago. They told me I was accepted." I smiled wistfully to myself before locking up towards them.

"That's amazing Claire. Congratulations!" Jacob smiled and came over to hug me. He then took a seat next to me.

"That means we'll be closer to each other! Congratulations!" Ryder said excitedly. I looked towards Ben and he smiled.

"That's if she decides to go there," Ben pointed out. Ryder rolled his eyes and Jacob chuckled. The three of them somehow made me feel relaxed.

"Is this the first school you heard from so far?" Jacob asked. I nodded.

"How many did you apply to?" Ben asked curiously.

"Well . . ." I had to think about this for a moment. "I applied to the University of California, Berkeley, Stanford, Michigan, St. Lewis, Arizona State, Oregon, St. John Fisher, Buffalo and NYU, Yale . . ."

"That's eleven schools."

"Hard to get into those schools," Ryder added. "Well . . . you are really smart."

"I'm proud," Jacob smiled. "This calls for a celebration."

"That's what Hollywood Studios is for." Ben yawned.

"We can all celebrate tomorrow at the park."

"If you'd like to," Ryder added quickly.

"Sure," I answered lightly. "Sounds like a great plan."

"Sweet."

Our phones went off at the same time and I had a feeling it was from the group chat.

Nora:

*SHANE AND CLAIRE CARE TO EXPLAIN THESE PICTURES OF YOU GUYS KISSING EARLIER?! I SHIP! *Pictures attached**

Aiden:
Damn, it really didn't take you two long.

Nate:
Somehow, I feel like a proud dad. I'm happy for you two

Aaron:
You let Jacob third wheel with you?

Ken:
DATE PLEASE

Andy:
You guys are adorable . . .

I closed my eyes painfully and put my phone down. The next round of tears was about to start as the group had to remind me of the happiness I no longer had. I brought my casted hand and my other hand to my face, wanting to hide the pain.

"Sh*t . . ." Ryder said softly and I felt Jacob putting an arm around me as I began to wallow in the pain. "They must have just gone into the account and saw them."

"Are you going to be alright Claire?" Jacob asked softly. I shook my head. I trusted Shane with a lot. Jacob hugged me as my head rested against his chest. "We should tell Nate or And—" Ryder said before I cut him off. I wanted nothing more than to forget about today. "No, please don't. I don't want everyone involved."

231

"Everyone is going to wonder what's going on in the morning."

"Just please don't tell them . . ." I thought back to what Jack said. I was afraid of an empty threat that I did not want to take a risk of. I let my head turn towards Ben and Ryder who looked worried. "I've been through so much and all I ask for is for you guys to not tell anyone and to not do anything."

They both looked at me and sighed. "Promise me," I said. They both stood up and joined Jacob and I on the couch. I wanted nothing more than this to be a prank.

"We promise," Ryder finally answered after a few minutes.

"Whatever floats your boat," Ben sighed.

"I support whatever you decide," Jacob said softly. *Smile*, I thought.

I'm thankful the three of them were here keeping me company. The thought of the group message made me feel like I have forgotten how to smile.

Both Ryder and Ben stood up. "Are you going to head to bed soon?" Ryder asked Jacob. I turned to Jacob and he nodded.

"I was going to stay here with Claire tonight to keep her company. Is that alright with you?" he asked me. I nodded. Both Ben and Ryder understood that it would be a good idea to keep me company.

"Alright, we'll see you guys in the morning," Ben said.

"Bright and early," Ryder chuckled before I said my goodbyes to them. Jacob stood up and made sure the door was locked before making his way back over to me. He took his bag and looked towards me.

"I'm going to shower and change. You'll be alright until I come back out?" Jacob asked. I nodded as he smiled and made his way to the bathroom down the hall from the guest room. I looked around and decided we could sleep here on the couch. It was a pretty comfy pullout bed. I stood from the couch and took both mine and Jacob's phone, placing them on the table. I took the cushions out and placed them to the side for a moment. I used my one good hand and assembled the pullout bed.

The sheets were still on from yesterday. I put the cushions at the opening towards the head of the bed. I made my way over to my room and decided four pillows would be good for the both of us. I took the pillows from my bed then placed them on the couch. I then noticed my phone was vibrating continuously. It was a New York number with an area code I was familiar with. I bit my lip nervously as I answered. This could be either good or bad.

"Hello?" I said.

"Hello Claire Johnson, this is Dr. Wright from the Roseview Hospital. I was told we were giving you updates on your mother. Is that correct?"

"Yes . . . How is my mother doing?" I heard a sigh from the other end and I knew right away something was wrong. I bit my lip and made my way towards the balcony. I took a seat as a cool breeze came through.

"I wanted to inform you that she has fallen into a more critical condition than she has been in. We're doing everything we can to save her. I'm so sorry miss . . ." Dr. Wright said.

I froze as the words "save her" played on repeat. My phone slid out of my hands before I could hear anything else. My ears felt like they were pounding. It felt like air was being taken away. I couldn't move. My mind went completely blank.

CHAPTER THIRTY
The Pain

CLAIRE JOHNSON

"Claire, please talk to me," Jacob pleaded as he sat next to me and held my hand. "I'm so worried. Talk, Claire."

I blinked, realizing it was already morning and the sun was out. Jacob found me out here on the balcony. He found my phone on the floor and talked to the doctor who I think explained the situation to him before ending the call. He immediately tried to get ahold of my Aunt Clarisse, but she was unable to answer.

Jacob, I think, seemed afraid to let go of my hand or leave at all. We have been sitting out here for several hours and I still felt like I could not move. Everything was in slow motion. My phone died at some point and I wasn't sure what was really going on. I was in shock and I did not have control of it. I continued to look out the view as Jacob held my hand tightly.

"Claire . . . she's going to get better. She's going to be alright and you have the guys and I to support you in any way we can. You also have Nora." Jacob said.

My lips felt like they were glued shut. He had no idea how much I appreciate him being here with me all night and talking to me. I think he knew talking to me helped, because it meant I was able to focus more on him than to my thoughts.

I was afraid to talk or even move, because everything would hit all at once. I didn't want to face it. I had a feeling Jacob knew why I was reacting this way but he was also very concerned.

A distant sound of a door bursting open shook Jacob slightly and made him turn towards the balcony door. I could hear panicking from more than one person. Jacob looked towards me and squeezed my hand. The comfort was very helpful. Andy and Nate came into view with panicked expressions moments later.

"Jacob, why the hell didn't you answer your phone?" Nate said as he kept an eye on me. Both Nate and Andy squatted down in front of me. No one knew what Shane did yesterday or that the hospital called me. I would have talked with Shane about this, but he wasn't here for me. He never was to begin with.

"We texted the both of you also. What is going on and why does Claire look like a ghost?" Andy said. His blue eyes reminded me of the beautiful clear blue skies.

"I'm sorry." Jacob's voice was cracking and I realized he must have been upset or really tired from the lack of sleep. I wanted to turn to him and hug him, but I felt so frozen. "I've been so afraid to even leave her for a second when I found her out here alone and like this. She's so fragile, I couldn't leave her."

"Jacob," Nate said softly. "You have to get some rest. Thank you for staying with her."

"Her mom," Jacob whispered. Both Andy and Nate nodded as I heard a shaky sigh from Jacob. I felt a kiss to my head before Jacob lets go of my hand. I think he went inside. Now it was just Nate and Andy.

"Claire?" Nate asked softly, trying to get me to speak. I took a small breath but ended up choking. To me, being still froze everything. I only felt the pain from a distance. Now that they were bringing me back, my feelings came back to me all at once. My view was now blurred. I felt arms being wrapped around me and my head buried into one of their chests.

"I can't do this," Jack was saying. I was in his room because we were both guilty of what we have done to Claire. I have not been able to think straight or sleep with the thoughts of hurting her.

"Don't you think I feel the same way?" I asked him feeling stressed. The guilt wouldn't leave my gut. I should go and see her. Jack had not been able to sleep either. "She trusted me. She trusted me with her life and she was happy. I was able to give her something she didn't have back in New York, then I just threw it back at her. Do you have any idea how much I'm going to regret this in the future?"

"I don't know how long I can keep this up," I heard Jack say softly to himself. "I have to fix this. I'll figure this out Shane," he said. I closed my song journal then looked towards him. "I have to fix this. You don't understand."

I shook my head and sighed, frustrated. I refuse to have Finnegan taking control of me. He had no right to do this to Claire and I. I could at least tell her what's going on. I should have done that in the first place. I put on a T-shirt and looked at the time on my phone. I frowned slightly.

The faster we could gather, the easier I could maybe try and talk to her. I hoped she'd let me talk to her. I had to let her know it was not my intention to hurt her in any way. I'd never do this to her. It was difficult to act for Finnegan and I wouldn't have done this if I wasn't trying to protect her future career. She would do the same for me and I knew I had to do the same. She may have not applied to her dream school, but I knew I wanted to do something about it. I wanted her to be happy and I'd protect her at all cost.

Jack and I thought it was getting pretty late to start our day. I would have thought Nate would barge in here telling us it was time to go. Jack and I were preparing ourselves to go. We continued waiting for the rest of the guys to call us. It has been an hour since we planned to leave for the parks. We thought we'd get there at opening. It was about a forty-five-minute drive to Universal.

My phone went off indicating I had received an important email. I reached for my phone and held it up to my face. It was from Briller Records. I've heard of the recording label before.

Dear Mr. Shane Peters:

We would like to first introduce our company as Briller Records. Brillers Records is a British-Jamaican record label that operates as a division of Universal Music group. You may know some of your fellow artists like Bob Marley, Demi Lovato, Nick Jonas, Elton John, Queen, Justin Bieber and many more artists you may listen to.

This email is to inform you that one of our colleagues has brought to our attention your platform through YouTube and Vine. After a discussion within the label, we would like to personally invite you to become the next big artist of your generation.

We believe that with your talent, you will become a sensation and we would love to work with you in the future.

If you have any questions or would like to an arrange a discussion with any of our colleagues, you are welcome to email or call XXX-XXX-XXXX.

We are looking forward to hearing from you.

Sincerely,

Amber Daniels
Briller Records Vice President

I read through the email several times before sitting up on the bed and faced Jack. Is this happening? The thought of signing with them was something I have always wanted. This had to be a dream. This would be a start to my career. This was something I have been thinking about for a few years now. Songwriting and performing in front of my fans was something I could only imagine.

How did they find me? They said it's from a colleague? I wonder who the person is. And how was I discovered? I would say there are many people around my age doing similar things as I do. I was interested in meeting the president, vice president and the person who discovered me. I definitely am honored and couldn't wait to tell Mom and Dad.

"You seem to have received some wonderful news," Jack said. I looked away from my phone to see him with a small smile.

"I did. Briller Records is interested in signing me with them." For the first time on this trip, I see him smile and also seemed excited.

"Dude! That's amazing. Wow, that's crazy. I am excited for you man."

"I wish I could tell Claire." The smile on my face disappeared and the guilt returned back to me. Jack seemed to be feeling the same way.

"The group I think is splitting in half today to go to separate sides of the parks. I know Claire will be in the other group Fin and I would be in. Try to go with them and talk to her. I'll cover for you, alright?"

"Thanks Johnson. I owe you."

"Just apologize to her alright?" Jack sighed. "I know she's going through a lot and I wish you didn't have to hurt her yesterday. Just tell her that Fin had put you up to it. I hope she will be alright. I'm worried." The sound of commotion suddenly was heard from the living room.

"Ben, calm down!" We heard Andy yelling in the other room. I looked towards Johnson to see him frowning in confusion. We both got up and I followed him towards the door. He opened it and I had to look past Johnson to see Ben in panic. He was freaking out. All of the guys here must have heard him and they all came into the living room.

"Claire won't answer her door and I'm freaking out! I thought Jacob was with her last night," Ben looked stressed. "Ryder is trying to get the door open." He looked up past Andy and Nate to see Jack and I. He glared towards us before looking away.

"Everything will be alright," Nate said trying to calm him down. I realized Nate had the second key to her room. "Let's go check on her." Ben nodded and the three of them made their way out of the room. Everyone including Jack and I followed them out.

I had a feeling I was part of the problem that Claire was behaving this way. If what Ben said was true, I don't think Jacob would have left her alone. Plus, Jacob did not return to the room after our late snack. He also did not answer my texts. Maybe Claire was okay in her room and Jacob was with her, but his phone is out of reach.

Ben began to sprint towards her room and so did the rest of us. It took no longer than a minute to reach her hall. I saw Ryder looking stressed and panicked as well.

"I—I haven't heard anything," Ryder said as he put his head into his hands. I backed away, feeling overwhelmed for doing what I did last night. I felt a hand on my shoulder. Jack looked worried. I turned slightly to see Fin was here and his jaw was tight. Nate knocked on the door as he fished for the key in his pocket.

"Claire? It's Nate," he called over the commotion from all of us. Nate took out the key and opened the door quickly causing the door to fling back. Everyone piled into the room while Andy and Nate went out to the balcony. I spotted Jacob out there and I think Claire was next to him. I looked towards the table and noticed his phone was there. The sofa was out as a bed and noticed it was fixed to sleep in. Did they not get any sleep?

I looked back out towards the balcony where Jacob was saying something. Claire seemed still and lifeless. Jacob shook his head at something Nate asked then leaned over to kiss her head before coming in. He looked towards me and sent me a glare and shook his head. What caught all of our attention were the sound of her sobs and I looked towards her to see her shaking a moment later. I wanted nothing more than to go to her. I took a step forward and Jacob glared at me for a second time.

"Don't you dare go near her," he said sounding exhausted and angry. I then looked to the balcony to see Nate and Andy trying to comfort her. She then buried her head to Andy's chest and held him pretty tight. My heart raced and it told me to go to her, but this was clearly more than what happened last night. I hoped her mom was alright.

"What the hell happened?" Nora asked, exasperated. She hated it when a friend was in pain and I knew that feeling. I wanted to take her pain away. She was looking between Ben, Jacob, and Ryder. I saw them glancing at each other. They were keeping it a secret. Claire was able to get them to not tell anyone. I don't know how.

"We don't know . . ." Ryder tried to start.

"B*llsh*t," Aiden said, shaking his head. Aiden wasn't buying into any of it. He was more than mad at this point. "I do not believe sh*t! Obviously, something happened!" he yelled, glaring at Fin. He walked over to him and threw a fist at him. Seeing all of this happen so quickly almost made me feel sick to my stomach. Ian and Ken had to pull him away and out of the room before he did something else.

CHAPTER THIRTY-ONE
Talk

NATE

The thing that surprised me the most was to see Claire in the van with me once we all gathered to head back to the resort for the night. I would have thought she and Shane would have stayed and gone to Magic Kingdom. Instead I found a very quiet Claire with both Ryder and Ben. She seemed very out of it. I didn't want to intrude her with so many questions and she seemed tired.

Another thing that should have told me something was wrong would be when we all went to the recreation center to eat without her. She didn't say anything. I should have asked if she was okay. I should have made sure everything was alright when she was quiet. I know she was new here and was trying to adjust. Learning from Shane and Claire together, I learned about why Claire moved in with Jack. It should have been a priority of mine to make sure she was doing okay and to check up on her once in a while.

Claire hanging with Shane and Jacob all the time made me assume she was doing alright and that she had befriended them. The last several days seemed like they had really clicked. They were all about the same age and it seemed that Claire really liked how they were also into the music industry. I knew Shane had a crush the moment they met. I also had a feeling she felt the same way when Shane came forward about Jack and Owen's funny business.

She seemed to have trusted Shane with her secrets and about her personal life more than anyone. I'm sure everyone had an idea there was something going on between them.

I had a feeling they had mutual feelings, because she seemed happier around him and Shane seemed to be a little more out of his shell now that she was here. It seemed like they were both bringing out the best of each other. I let it continue because this was exactly what she needed. I knew Shane was a great guy and he was one of the nicest guys you could possibly meet. I don't think you could meet a nicer Canadian than Shane Peters.

It was terrifying to find out something was going on with Claire when Ben busted into the suite looking flustered and worried. Ben and Ryder had gone to wake Claire up, because she was not answering her phone. We also tried Jacob. There was also the possibility that they had their phones on "do not disturb." They must have been up really late if they couldn't hear Ryder and Ben banging on the door.

I currently feel terrified as I held onto her hand while she sobbed into Andy's chest. I think I've figured out why Jacob didn't want to let go of her hand as she currently squeezed mine. She was saying something that we couldn't quite understand. She was shaking so bad that we had to try our best to calm her. What I did not understand was why Johnson or Shane weren't out here. It confused me because I thought they were all on good terms.

"I'm sorry." She continued to sob and I felt my heart throbbing. I felt awful that she was feeling this way. Where the hell was Shane?

"Shh, everything will be okay," I told her softly. She wanted to have someone there for her but is afraid to ask for it. I began rubbing her back with my other hand. Both Andy and I continued to kneel in front of her for a little while. I needed to get Shane. Maybe it would be better if he was out here. "Do you want me to get . . . Shane?" I asked softly. She continued to sob into Andy and shook her head vigorously. Andy frowned in confusion.

"I don't want him anywhere near me," Her voice cracked and she continued her sobbing.

"What the hell did he do?" Andy mumbled and I glared at him with his choice of words. "He . . . did something obviously. I'm so pissed," he said. I watched as Andy looked towards the inside and wanted to hurt Shane, but I had a feeling that would only hurt Claire. I also had a feeling Andy had some sort of crush on Claire, but he wouldn't admit that to anyone. It was clear something had happened between Shane and Claire.

"H—he pretended to care about me and my feelings. I thought he wanted to get to know me and I opened up to him. It was my mistake!"

"Whoa wait a second. Claire, he cares more than you think. He never pretended for anything," I said softly, but she pulled away from Andy and I saw how puffy her eyes were and tears were everywhere. She was a hot mess and I wanted to get to the bottom of this.

"Explain why he and Finnegan teamed up on me last night. Tell me why my cousin isn't talking to me again and sided with him. Tell me why Shane had to use those words against me," she said weakly. I realized she was frustrated and angry, but she didn't show it. I could only tell by how she was squeezing my hand so tightly.

"Fin was a part of this?" I asked her with a raised eyebrow. She has already warned me what he was capable of. He was the one who also put her life at risk. The anger inside of me started to build. This had to come to an end. Claire did not deserve what he had put her through. "I'll be right back," I mumbled and looked to Andy who nodded. I let go of Claire's hand and stood up making my way inside.

The first thing I noticed was Jacob blocking the way from letting anyone getting through to the balcony. Everyone looked towards me and I searched the room for Fin in anger, because he has now pissed me off. Friend or not, he had no right to treat any girl like this. I spotted him with a bloody nose and Nora in tears. I saw Ben and Ryder with their faces in their hands while Shane and Johnson looked pale with bags under their eyes. I could tell they were guilty about something. As for Aiden, Ian, and Ken, they weren't anywhere to be seen. I sort of figured that would be the case when I returned.

I began walking towards Fin and without any hesitation, I shoved him to the wall in anger. No one stopped me because I was the one in charge around here when Blake wasn't around. I was also the one who took care of things. "What the f*ck did you do this time?" I gritted through my teeth and increased my grip to his shirt. He seemed so unfazed by this.

"Why do you assume it was me?" he asked smirking. I wanted to punch him, but I knew if I did, someone would end up in the hospital. I had to stop everything in me from doing so.

"Because Aiden wouldn't have punched you for no reason." I frowned at him. I forcefully let go of his shirt and walked over to Shane and Johnson continuing to feel angered by the way Claire was feeling at the moment. I grabbed both of them by their shirts and pulled them into Claire's bedroom. When we reached there, I pushed them both in by force. I slammed the door and turned towards them so I was facing them. They both looked guilty and terrified. "You both have five minutes to explain to me what happened," I stated angrily.

"This started with me. This isn't Shane's fault at all," Johnson started. "I told him he had to do what Fin wanted to do, because we were protecting her."

"Protecting her?" I huffed interrupted them. "Please elaborate on that, because uh I don't think she's doing so well out there right now."

"Fin has a video of her," Jack sighed and closed his eyes painfully. "It was a video that put Claire's future in danger and I didn't want that for her. Nate, you don't understand how much it would cost her if that video was to ever get out." I held my hand

244

out before opening the door and walking towards the door and went straight to Fin.

"Phone," I mumbled. He frowned at me.

"Excuse me?" He mumbled. Everyone was still and they watched.

"Unless you want me to go straight to the cops and tell them how you tried to drown Claire and threaten her, I'd hand the phone over buddy." He rolled his eyes.

"What evidence do you have?" He scoffed and the group were in shock of what I just said.

"What the hell?" Ben said in anger.

"When did this happen?" Aaron asked in horror.

"You really want to go there right now Fin?" I challenged him. "If Claire testifies, your life would be ruined. Are you really going to test our limits right now?" He rolled his eyes before reaching for his pocket and took his phone out and slapped his phone into my hand. I glared at him a moment longer before I walked back into the room and shut the door behind me.

"He has more than one copy," Jack said softly. "He wouldn't dare use it," I said.

"Is she going to be okay?" Shane asked softly. I looked towards him and he looked like he was on the verge of tears. "I don't know Shane. She's pretty upset about her mom right now and clearly whatever you did to her."

"Her mom?" he asked worriedly. "I didn't want to go along with anything that happened yesterday evening. I feel awful."

This was unbelievable that Fin was doing this. Johnson and Shane were both terrified of what was going on and I could tell they were truly concerned for Claire.

It was Owen's doing. I felt bad for them, because it really was not their fault. Well, Johnson had some sort of video that was held against both him and Claire. He must have done something wrong. I looked towards them with sympathy, because they were also hurting to all of this. I sighed as they looked at me with wet watery eyes.

I decided to see what the video was a fuss about and went onto Fin's phone by hacking it. I probably could have asked Jack, but I was already in when I realized it. Don't ask me how I did it, I just did. It took me several places for me to find the video and pressed play to watch it.

The video was a bit fuzzy for a moment and I looked at the corner of the screen. This was taken just three years ago. This was maybe when Claire was just a freshman in high school. I watched in pain to see what had caused all this trouble. This was what tore Claire and Jack a few years ago and this is what caused trouble now with Shane, because it was used against him.

It was a video of Claire breaking in to the principal's office. She was scrummaging around looking for something. She looked quite young. She must have grown and matured in these last few years. She then started going through the drawers and I watched as she pulled out a whole bunch of folders.

"She was looking for my file," Jack said softly as the video continued. Shane took a seat and I returned my attention back to the video. Claire held a file in her hand and she opened it taking something out. She read the slip of paper before folding it and putting it in her back pocket. I watch as Jack ran in and it was pretty clear the audio was caught on the video.

"I told you to stay home. I would have dealt with this!" Jack argued with Claire and she shook her head.

"What? You were going to let Fin take care of it?" She asked, hurt. "I'm concerned for you Jack." There was an alarm that went off and they looked around.

"Claire . . . you need to leave."

"I'm not going to le—"

"Claire! I don't want you to get in trouble! Please go. This is my problem and I have to face the actions I have taken. I can't have you getting in trouble for this."

"I'm sorry Jack." She apologized for breaking into the school.

"This isn't your fault. It's my doing. I'll distract them and I'll see you in a few hours." She nodded and put the file on the desk before kissing Jack's cheek before running out. That was the end of the video. I hacked once more of Fin's phone and found every possible file to exist on his phone and deleted them permanently. I didn't know if he had any more copies, but I did not care. This was going to end once and for all. I did not realize where I was until I looked towards Shane and Jack, who had their eyes averted to the ground. "You guys seriously need to make this up to Claire," I started. They both looked to me.

"She probably hates me and will never trust me again," Johnson sighed with a painful look. "What sort of cousin am I to do something like this?

"She won't forgive me," Shane sighed. I could tell how much this pained and upset him. There was sadness in his eyes and he seemed very defeated.

"I didn't say it was going to be easy. It will take some time for her to accept everything and you guys clearly knew what was going on with her mother. You know it's going to be hard for her to accept you both right now, but you guys have to talk to her," I gave them some sort of motherly look that my mom would give me when I was being taught a lesson. They both sighed getting up. What sucked at the moment was that she doesn't want to be anywhere near them and I wanted Claire to have her space. I wished them both the best of luck, because Claire really wasn't doing so well at the moment.

My biggest concern at the moment was for Claire. I really hoped everything would be alright for her mother. For her shake and for her sanity. I don't know what it was like to lose a mother and I didn't want her to go through more misery.

CHAPTER THIRTY-TWO
You're Not Alone

CLAIRE JOHNSON

"I hate this." I hiccupped and tried to calm down but every time I did, I wanted to tear up again. Andy continued to talk me and tried his best to calm me after Nate left. I felt my body shivering and felt sick to my stomach. I wanted more than anything to take my mind away from Shane and my mother. I wanted a distraction or something to lessen the pain.

"Claire, I'm right here," Andy said softly. "I'm here and I'll take care of you. It's going to be alright." He began rubbing my back. I took a deep breath and shook my head. I had a feeling it wouldn't be alright.

"You don't know that for sure. My mom is doing worse than she was before I left."

"I didn't realize . . . I'm so sorry Claire. I wish there was something I could do . . . Is there anything that I can do for you?"

"I—I don't want to be alone anymore." I looked down towards my feet and sighed. I wanted to curl up and hug myself. I felt miserable. Andy's shirt was quite soaked from my tears. I felt embarrassed about it and I think he noticed as he looked down at his shirt. He looked towards me again and there was this sinking feeling inside of me.

"Claire, you're not alone. Nate and I will take care of you. Jacob is here for you too and we'd love to move in here with you for the rest of the week if it's alright with you." I really appreciated what Andy was doing and I was thankful Jacob stayed by my side after receiving that phone call. "How about we go back to my room for a little bit and you can help me pack? You don't have to talk to anyone if you don't want to."

"Can I first shower and change into something fresh?" "Of course, you can," Andy nodded and he stood holding his hand out for me to take. I gently took it and he helped me up. He immediately wrapped his arms around me to give me a hug. I wrapped my arms around him for a moment. I really liked how he gave hugs and seemed to soothe me just slightly. He pulled away and smiled slightly before looking towards the inside. I took a shaky breath as I began making my way in. As I took a step inside I noticed a lot of movement of standing and looking towards me.

I noticed everyone seemed to be worried. I looked around and noticed a few of the guys weren't here and Finnegan seemed to have a bloody nose. He looked away from me and I looked towards Andy to see him giving Finnegan a glare. Ryder, Ben, Jacob were the three who came up to me. Jacob was the first to come up to me and hug me.

"T—thank you for staying with me all night," I said to him. He nodded as he pulled back and gave me a reassuring look.

"I've considered you my best friend since you've first arrived. I'll be here no matter what."

"You're amazing Jacob."

"You're even better." Ben then attacked me with a hug and I carefully moved my cast away before it could be crushed.

"I'm so sorry," Ben apologized for my arm. "You scared me," he said as he tried again with hugging and I returned his gesture.

"I'm sorry for scaring you," I apologized and he gave me a reassuring look that it would be okay. Ryder then gave me a small hug. "I'm going to take a shower and get changed into something fresh." I began to make my room, which seemed to catch everyone off guard. As my hand was on the handle, Nora called out my name. I opened the door.

"Claire wait," Nora said hesitantly and I turned towards the group who looked worried. Finnegan rolled his eyes and I looked towards Jacob for an explanation.

"Nate is in there talking with Shane and your cousin," Aaron said softly since no one spoke up. My head turned towards the bedroom and I saw Shane standing and my cousin looking towards me with wide eyes. Nate looked to me wondering how I was going to react to them here. I looked towards them and I noticed they had a guilty look.

They both hurt me and I couldn't stand the thought of having to talk to them at the moment. Last night's negative memories replayed in my head as I looked between the two. I blinked and let my hand grab hold of the doorframe. I didn't have the heart to listen to anything they had to say at the moment.

"Claire," I heard Shane say softly and the flash of him leaning and getting ready to kiss that girl last night played in my head.

"Don't." I said painfully. I had to stop myself from another round of a sobbing mess. I looked towards my closet. "Get out," I said quietly.

"Claire," Jack sounded concerned. I turned towards him as he tried to take a step towards me. I took a step towards my dresser with the slightest fear running through me. He lost my trust last night and I wasn't looking for any apologies.

"You're the worst cousin ever." My voice was shaky and I felt my emotions ready to spill out. "I needed you yesterday. I needed the both of you." I then turned slightly and took out a pair of undergarments then took an outfit from the closet. I immediately went straight for the bathroom. I slammed the door shut and locked it. I put everything on the counter and turned the shower on. It was supposed to be a quick shower, but I had my cast on, which continued to be a struggle for me.

After finishing my shower, I put on my clothing and decided I'd have my hair up for the day. I used the blow dryer to dry my hair before putting it up in some sort of messy bun. I hung my towel up before making my way to the door. My room was empty. I found my flip flops and slipped them on before I made my way into the living room where I found Nate, Andy and Jacob waiting. They looked up from their phones and stood.

"Hey, you alright?" Jacob said. I nodded as I walked over to where I placed my bag and saw Jacob was also changed from what he had been wearing before.

"Everyone is down in the lobby, except for Aiden, Andy, and Ken," Nate said. "We're uh . . . thinking of going to Universal today. I hope you'd be up for it. You don't have to go if you don't want to."

I nod slightly. "I'll go. I prefer if Finnegan, Shane, and Jack are in the opposite park from me."

"Yeah, we get that. We'll make sure of that," Andy said.

"You'll spend the day with us, if you're really up for it," Jacob half smiled.

"I am. Thank you guys . . . thank you to whoever punched Fin."

Nate smiled and chuckled. "That was all Aiden."

I put my cell phone into my purse before we all began making our way out of the suite and into the hall. "We'll see you two when you get down to the lobby?" Jacob said. I frowned slightly.

"You were going to go with Andy to his room? You forgot?" Jacob smiled.

"Right. Sorry, I'm a bit distraught," I said.

"You have a lot going on," Andy said. "We're not here to give you a hard time."

251

"Plus,"—Jacob smiled and hit my shoulder—"wanna tell them some great news?" I think we've all decided to walk towards the suite on the other side of the building now. I could see Jacob's excitement.

"Shouldn't Claire be the excited one here if it's her news?" Nate chuckled.

"Oh, you have to tell us. Can't leave us hangin'?" Andy asked curiously. I smiled slightly.

"I uh . . . I got into the University of California—" Before I could get anything else out, I was being attacked with arms. I let a small laugh out as I was in between Nate, Andy, and Jacob who seemed to want to be a part of the fiasco.

"Congratulations! That's very exciting!" Andy said.

"Damn girl you're so smart. I'm so proud. Congratulations!" Nate beamed.

"Thank you, guys." I smiled sheepishly as they pulled away. We all started walking again.

"Was this the first school that has contacted you?" Andy asked.

I nodded. "That's really exciting Claire. Today we will definitely celebrate," Nate said.

We approached the suite after taking the stairs and Nate unlocked the door to the room. When I walked in, Andy went to his room. I noticed Ian, Ken, and Aiden sitting on the couch. As soon as they looked up and spotted me, they jumped up and attacked me into a hug; well mostly Aiden did. It was good to know they really cared for me.

"Aiden . . ."—I coughed out—"I can't breathe." He lets go and giggles.

"Sorry Claire. I was really worried for you earlier." He gave me those puppy eyes and bit his lip. I smiled faintly.

"Oh, he was definitely worried when his fist collided with Fin's face," Ken chuckled.

"Oh, he deserved that one," Ian said. I turned to Aiden and gave him a side hug.

"Thank you for doing that," I said. I saw Andy coming out of his room with his wallet.

"I'd do it over and over if I had to. It was very tempting after all the pain he has put you through," Aiden said.

I hummed as a response, not wanting to think of Finnegan so much. "You guys are amazing, thank you," I said.

"So, are we still up for Universal?" Ian asked.

"Of course. I can't wait to have some butterbeer and get my official robe, supplies, and my wand from Ollivanders today." Everyone seemed to shift moods immediately and I frowned in confusion. "Did I say something wrong?"

"I would have thought this would have been a talk with them..." Jacob said softly to Nate.

"You're a Harry Potter fan?" Andy asked.

"Yes, of course I am," I smiled proudly. "Fellow Ravenclaw here."

"They really didn't have that talk then . . ." Jacob said softly.

"What talk?" I asked and looked at the guys.

"Never mind it," Jacob sighed and shook his head. "I had no idea you were a huge fan. You must be really excited."

"Shane's a big fan, isn't he?" I said softly catching on to why Jacob wanted to move away from this. I had a feeling he was referring to him and why they would all suddenly feel hesitant.

"Claire, we didn't mean to bring him up," Jacob said apologetically. I shrugged.

"If you don't mind me asking, what the heck did Shane do to you?" Andy said. The guys were glaring. I did not think it was necessary for them to give him the look.

I know it hurts me, but they deserved to know. Especially since they have been nothing but caring for me. "He was with a girl," I said softly and hugged myself. I don't think the girl realized

253

who I was. She seemed really friendly, but he kissed her. Shane knew he was my first kiss and not long after, he kisses her. Then there was Finnegan. Shane had the decency to smile after he kissed her. "He just . . . said things and told me to go back to New York when he knew that was something not to mention to me. He . . . just used everything against me."

"That sounds like Fin's doing," Aiden mumbled.

"Freaking idiot for thinking he was going to get away with this," Ken said.

"This isn't Shane's fault," Andy said softly. "He looked so gu—"

"It doesn't mean I'm going to forgive him right now Andy," I answered shakily. I realized I was ready to tear up again. I didn't want that. Shane could have told me, texted me or have tried to warn me that Finnegan put him up to that. He could have found a way if he didn't want to hurt me truly. I trusted him and let him in. It was my mistake becoming close with him.

"Andy drop it," Jacob said softly and came over to me. "Shane could have warned her somehow if he was put up to this. Claire was expecting that she was going on a date night with him to Magic Kingdom. This threw her off and she wasn't expecting this. Do you guys really think she can trust him at the moment?"

"I'm really sorry Claire. Let's try to forget about it. I'm sorry for upsetting you," Andy said. I nodded as everyone looked at one another.

"Ready to head to the parks then?" Ken asked and everyone nodded their heads. Both Nate and Andy were at my side. Jacob was close by as we all made our way for the elevator. The trip to the lobby was quick and some of the guys continued to have small talk. It was when we entered the lobby, I averted my eyes to the ground.

"Hey. You guys made it!" I heard Nora call out.

"Let's split up in two groups. I'm taking van one and . . ."—Nate looked around—"Andy, could you drive the other one?"

254

"Sure," he replied.

"Alright! Let's head to them now!" Nate said. Everyone began making their way out. The first person I made eye contact was with Shane. He seemed to be talking to someone on the phone before he looked towards me. I bit my lip and made myself walk with Jacob and Andy before another argument could possibly break loose.

"Hey," Jacob said softly. I looked towards him as I approached the van Andy would be driving.

"Hey," I said softly.

"Will you be okay hanging with Ben and Ryder today?" He had an uncomfortable look. "I know with yesterday and everything, I also want to make sure he's alright. I . . . ." Jacob hesitated. "He's one of my closest friends a—"

"It's alright. Go ahead Jacob. I can see you sometime today or maybe after the parks," I smile faintly. He smiled and nodded.

"I'll text you . . . actually we'll go get breakfast first. We haven't eaten and I have no idea when the last time you have eaten."

"Breakfast sounds good."

"Cool. I'll see you there." I nodded and opened the door to the passenger side and went in.

CHAPTER THIRTY-THREE
Friends?

CLAIRE JOHNSON

"What the hell Claire?" I heard Aiden say from somewhere. I turned around in my Ravenclaw robe with butterbeer in my hand. Yes, I was currently dressed in full Ravenclaw uniform from head to toe. Everything I wore earlier was in a bag. Ben, Ian, and Ryder chuckled. Both Andy and Nora had a smile on their faces. "I didn't realize you were going into full Potterhead mode," Aiden said.

"Hi Aiden," I said with a smile. He looked towards Ben, Ryder and, Andy, who have not left my side. About a few hours ago, Aiden, Nora, and Ken told us they would meet up with us since we were heading towards the Wizarding World of Harry Potter. They knew once we were there, we wouldn't be leaving the area anytime soon so we had gone our own ways. Now they've seen me completely transformed.

"We leave you guys for a few hours and Claire has a complete makeover," Nora smiled. "Claire, you're a true geek."

"Thank you," I smiled. "Want some butterbeer?"

"It's good," Andy said, sipping into his. Both Ryder and Ben agreed.

"That sounds good actually. We haven't eaten, have you guys eaten yet?" Ken said. I shook my head.

"We could eat here?" Aiden asked slowly to wait for my expression. The energetic and excited side of me suddenly gave me this jumpy feeling. I attacked him with a hug and caught him off guard. "Whoa there. I take that as a yes?" Aiden chuckled.

"I'm sure that's a yes. She has been talking about eating here since we walked by the Three Broomsticks," I heard Andy say. I pulled away from Aiden who seemed very amused to see me in my fangirl mode.

"You should have seen her earlier. She and others were casting spells and I don't even know how they all know all the motions." Ryder laughed lightly.

"She's in heaven. So, we've decided to eat at Three Broomsticks? Cool, let go," Ben said excitedly. He has been getting hungry for a while. I took a sip as we all followed Ben out of the shop and into the crowd in Hogsmeade. We began making our way towards the entrance so we could get to the Three Broomsticks.

When we arrived earlier, Jacob and I had breakfast separate from everyone. I enjoyed it. After, the group split up between the parks. Ian, Andy, Ken, Ben, Ryder, Aiden, Nora, and I were in one group going to the Island of Adventure. Shane, Jacob, Finnegan, Aaron, and Jack went to the other park. Nate and Andy thought it would be best if I stayed separated from them for now and I did not have a problem with that. Nate would have been here with us, but he had to make sure the other group would be somewhat under control.

Today was spent going on rides, taking pictures, sightseeing, and shopping. I knew it was a good idea to not spend much when I was at Disney. It was the best decision I've made this whole trip, since I knew I would be spending more here. Everything I bought today was worth it.

We all entered Three Broomsticks and I looked around feeling astonished. I was able to hang with everyone in the group and spend time with each of them individually and get to know them more. Nora and the guys took my mind off of many things and I have been able to enjoy my day.

"What do you want Claire?" Aiden asked me as he handed me a menu. He also gave one to everyone else as we fell into a long line. I smiled knowing I was quite hungry. I saw the dessert section and knew what I'd be getting after.

"Fish and Chips please!" I answered, feeling giddy. "Ohh and a refill on my butterbeer." I held up my empty glass.

"That was your fourth one." Ben eyes widened. "How many are you going to have?"

Ryder rolled his eyes playfully and handed my cup to Aiden. "She can have as many as she wants," Ryder said. "We'll also get you some Gilly water."

"You, Andy, and Ken can find some seats if you'd like. And also take some pictures," Aiden chuckled. I smiled and nodded as the three of us left the line. I took a peek at the cauldron and then walked into the dining area. I gasped slightly as I took it all in. Then I looked around for a spot where eight people could sit. I spotted a bigger sitting area towards the side and made my way there.

"Here we are," I said as I took a seat. Andy decided to sit next to me and Ken sat across from us. Andy handed his glass of butterbeer to me and I felt very happy as I took it. It's one of my new obsessions here.

Ken watched us carefully. "I gotta say Andy, you did a pretty great job amusing Claire the most today. Claire's pretty entertained here," Ken said.

"I think your dance moves did it though," Andy said, smiling at me. I smiled back before taking a sip of butterbeer and savoring it. "Nah it's definitely me," Andy said with a cheesy smile which made me laugh. I handed the cup back to him.

"I think you're both amazing," I said to them and they both awed in unison. "But I think Ben beat you to it," I teased. Their jaws dropped then the three of us burst into laughter.

"My own brother beat me to you," Andy said, pretending to be hurt. I gave him a cheesy smile and he chuckled. I took Andy's glass out of his grip and took a quick sip. "You're addicted Claire. Let's face it, you'll end up having at least six glasses by the time we leave here tonight."

"I have to savor the taste. Who knows how long until I come back here," I said.

"You're cute. I swear you are like perfect for Sh—" Ken stopped himself. I looked towards the table. "It was so natural. I'm sorry Claire."

"It's fine," I said lightly. "Yeah . . . he has been texting me."

"He has? What has he been saying?" Andy asked.

I shrugged, which made the both of them frown. "I haven't read any of his messages."

"So, you're completely ignoring him at the moment?"

"Yes."

"Huh . . ." Ken said. "How long are yo—"

"Bro," Andy glared towards him. "Let's think about this magical place where we're enjoying our time."

"Right, Sorry," Ken apologized and took out his phone. "Say cheese guys." He held his phone up and Andy chuckled before scooting closer to me. I wrapped my arm carefully around his waist since he was sitting to my right. We smiled for the camera.

"Send those," Andy said and I saw everyone coming with our food. I smiled as the food was set on the table and everyone took their seats. Ben sat to my left side and I smiled at him.

"Hungry?" he asked, holding up a piece of fish and chip. I took it and started biting into it. He laughed. "Interesting . . ." He brought the two plates of fish and chips in front of us.

"Claire is interesting, Ben. She's my bestie," Ian said. He gave me a huge grin with his mouth still full of food.

"Well she is my Asian sister, because we're alike and she has that Asian blood," Ken said, smiling at me. I started laughing at

259

the conversation. They really knew how to make me laugh. I guess I could have mentioned I'm part Filipino.

"But she's definitely my older sister," Ben said, giving me a side hug. They really do like their hugs. I don't mind them.

"Ben, we've had this conversation already," Ryder said in his typical white girl voice. We all laughed. "She's mah twin," he added, giving him a pleased look.

"Zayum guys!" Nora laughed at the guys. "You're all fighting over her already. Guys, I feel hurt!" She pretended to pout.

"We love you too Nor. Claire is just so adorable though," Ian said.

"That's true. Forget her being brothers to you guys. She's my sister," Nora said proudly. I felt myself smiling as I took a piece of my fish and chip.

Aiden passed over my glass of butterbeer and I thanked him. I turned slightly towards Andy to see he was already kind of looking at me. He turned his body more so he could face me. I sent him a smile and noticed his cheeks were slightly pink. He looked away quickly then I noticed Aiden watching the two of us as everyone else went on with their conversations. Aiden smirked at us, but doesn't say anything. I continued to eat my food.

"So, Claire . . ." Aiden said, starting a conversation with Andy and I. "Anything I should know about?"

Andy was playing it off. Why do guys automatically think there's something going on? I never understood that.

"No, of course not dude," Andy replied. I felt my cheeks beginning to heat up and I wasn't sure why. When someone pointed out something related to cliché stuff, I tend to get nervous.

Why was I getting nervous though? It's Andy. I thought I liked Shane? Why am I so confused? I thought I'm mad at Shane? There's this connection I don't want to let go between Shane and I, but now I don't trust him. I found it hard to believe he would say what he had said, because I opened up to him. I felt like I could trust him. I was wrong and that trust has vanished. I shook my head. He hurt me like Jack did. My heart felt heavy just thinking about him.

I looked towards Aiden to see him staring at me. I must have drowned in my thoughts before answering his question. I seemed to do that a lot lately. "No, nothing at all," I said with a smile. I took a bite and sipped more of my butterbeer. I knew for a fact I needed to go on a run and do some crunches after the amount of food and butterbeer I've had today.

"Feeling full?" Ben asked from beside me. Ian also looked towards me as he ate his chicken leg. I looked down realizing I finished all of my fish and chips.

"Mostly. I was thinking of a bit of dessert. Can't skip that," I said.

"What kind of dessert?" Ian asked.

"Do you guys want to share a Chocolate Trifle with me?" I said.

"Sure." Ben nodded.

"Sounds good to me. May take me a few more minutes to finish," Ian said, taking a bite into the chicken. I nodded as I stood carefully. Heads turned towards me as I patted my robe for my wallet.

"Getting something for dessert?" Andy asked. I nodded and he also stood up. "I'll come with you." I looked towards Aiden who seemed to have a sudden interest with the development. I playfully rolled my eyes before making my way across the eating area to get into a line.

"How is your arm feeling?" Andy asked me curiously.

"It's okay. I prefer to not wear the sling. It can get annoying," I said with a tight smile. Andy laughed and nodded.

"Relatable. I remember I broke my arm once a few years ago playing lacrosse. Did you ever play any sports?"

"No," I shuddered at the thought. "I was never really into sports. I've always been interested in the arts. Music specifically."

"Right, I remember when we were at the music store the first day we met. You were introduced at a really age I assume?" I nodded as we moved up in the line. "That's pretty neat. So, you sing and play the cello?"

"I also can play the guitar and the piano." I half smiled and thought of the time I was back in my suite the first night. My mind seemed to always return to him. "I . . . I taught myself the guitar and I took private lessons for piano and cello."

"So, you're like the next Yo-Yo Ma?"

I blushed. "I'm not as amazing as him. He is one of my inspirations and the reason why I chose to play the cello. I fell in love with the cello when I was six."

"That's cool. So, being able to sit down in a chair wasn't a reason at all?" Andy mused. I playfully glared towards him and he chuckled as I punched his arm. I noticed I tended to playfully punch the guys often. "I'm kidding! So, I'm guessing you've applied to Julliard?" he asked.

"I did, but it's really hard to get in there. I felt like I messed up during my audition."

"You probably did amazing Claire. Whether you got accepted in there or not, you still have University of California and I'm sure you'll be accepted to the other places you applied to. I heard you applied to several of them?" he said, to which I nodded to. "You're graduating a whole year early and you probably have remarkable grades. I think you stand out and will get into any of the places you applied to."

"You think so?"

"I'm sure you have acceptance letters waiting at your aunt's house waiting for you to open. It's the second week of April. I'm pretty sure decision making is sometime during the first week of May. You should definitely maybe FaceTime your aunt about it or wait until you get back to read everything. Don't sweat it Claire."

"You're very reassuring," I half smiled. "I never was able to talk too much about this process with my parents since . . ." I did not want to go into further explanation.

"I'm sorry Claire. This must be really hard for you. I couldn't imagine . . ." Andy sighed. He shook his head and looked towards me again. "I bet they're very proud of you Claire. Just remember that they left behind a wonderful daughter who will make a big impact to this world."

I turned towards him and let his words process in my mind. I smiled slightly. I leaned to him and gave him a hug. Andy returned the hug then kissed the top of my head. "You also have a group of friends here who also has your back Claire," he added.

"Thank you," I answered and let the moment sink to me.

CHAPTER THIRTY-FOUR
Hurt

SHANE PETERS

"Nate . . . Just let me talk to her," I said privately to Nate as we were finishing up our dinner at Diagon Alley. Jack and Jacob had gone off to get some butterbeer for the four of us. I wasn't sure where Fin had gone to after we split after lunch time. We have been in Diagon Alley for about an hour when we decided to have to dinner at the Leaky Cauldron. Nate and Jack wanted to do everything else here in the park before spending the rest of the evening here. The first thing I purchased was my Gryffindor robe and my elder wand.

Nate sighed as he looked away from his phone and towards me. "She needs space right now Shane. Plus, she's not exactly ready to talk to you right now."

I know I've done her wrong and I wanted to fix this more than anything. I know being here was supposed to be one of my best time, but I couldn't feel excited. I couldn't feel that way with the guilt sitting there.

"Nate . . . I want to apologize. I know I made a mistake and I can't do anything if I can't talk to her. This is really killing me." Pleading seemed to be the only thing I could do. I felt useless being separated from her and forced to go to the opposite park that she went to.

My mind thought of her and the email, but more about her of course. I found it hard to believe that I really went through with the plan and it was eating me to pieces. If something were to really go wrong with her mom, I could or would not forgive myself. I should have thought of something else. I should have figured it out. I should have warned her. I hated myself for this. "Please Nate, I'm begging you." Nate sighed and closed his eyes for a moment, then gave me an apologetic look.

"Not today, Shane. Sorry. Really, I am," Nate said. I buried my face in my hands and leaned my elbows on the table.

"At least tell me she's doing alright today," I said feeling defeated for the moment.

"I've been getting updates on her throughout the day. Andy and Aiden have been telling me she has been doing quite well actually. They think that she's trying to distract herself and I think it's working for the most part. Uh . . . have you guys ever talked about Harry Potter?" I brought my face away from my hands and looked towards him to see him looking down at his phone then to me curiously.

"No . . . I wanted to tell her about it when we were supposed to be on our date." I sighed feeling very upset with myself for not being able to have our date. I was planning a lot for it. "Why?"

"Apparently she's into the series as much as you are." He handed his phone to me and looked at a picture of the most perfect picture you could ever see. It was a picture of Claire in front of the castle. She was dressed in her full Ravenclaw wear while holding a mug butterbeer with her good hand and held her wand with her hand with the cast. I looked towards her face again to see she had the prettiest smile and it seemed to me here when the picture was taken, she seemed stress free at the moment. I was happy to think she was enjoying her time here and having a great time. I hoped she was.

"She looks amazing," I said softly. "I really do hope she is enjoying herself."

"Aiden told me she's currently on her sixth cup of butterbeer." I chuckled and shook my head knowing she was so perfect to me. I handed his phone back to him and took a sip of my butterbeer.

"This would have been one of the best moments of my life if I hadn't screwed up yesterday."

"There is the future Shane. Just know that it will take her some time. I'm sorry you were put in this situation. I wish you would have told me or Aiden or someone about Fin. We could have prevented this."

"I honestly was so worried for Claire that I wasn't thinking straight."

"Andy, Jacob, and I will continue to talk to her, alright?" I nodded as I took another sip of my drink. "Do . . . you want me to send the picture to you?"

"Sure. I really like it." I gave him a wistful smile. It made me happy that she was like me. I was also wearing my full Gryffindor gear. We could have made the cutest Hogwarts duo. My phone began ringing and I looked down to see a New York area code and I had a feeling I knew who it was. I talked to my mom and dad earlier and they were congratulating me. They told me to respond and schedule a quick phone call before a skype session with them. I immediately answered. "Hello?"

"Hello, Can I speak to Mr. Shane Peters?" a male voice asked in a polite tone. He seemed he was no older than twenty-five. He seemed young.

"Hi, that is me." I smiled. Nate looked towards me with a curious look and smiled before looking down at his phone. "Ah, hello Shane. Amber Daniels, the vice president of Briller Records, has just sent me an email saying you had responded and wanted to have a quick phone call. I hope it's not a really bad time," he started.

"No, it's okay," I chuckled lightly. "I . . . uh, am still in the Florida area after doing Kricon. I'm sticking around for a bit before I head back home."

"Ah, yes. A friend of mine pointed that out and that's how I found you."

"You're the one who brought me up to the vice president?" I asked surprisingly. I did not realize I would be speaking to the person who had found me and was scouting me.

"Yes. I'm sorry I haven't introduced myself yet. My name is Andrew Gallen and I'm a talent manager at Briller records."

"Thank you for finding me."

"It was a really good friend of mine who mentioned you. She has been in contact with me these last several days. I'm sure she'd be excited to hear you're interested if you haven't told her already?"

"She?" I frowned confused.

"Yes, Claire sent me the video of you two performing Jason Mraz, 'Lucky' and also told me to check out your Instagram. I do think you have some amazing talent kid. Claire told me how you'd like to become a songwriter with big dreams. I see it." My mouth parts and Nate looked towards me wondering why I'm in shock. Claire is the reason to my career and future dream coming true.

"She didn't . . ."

"Really?"

"This is the first time I'm hearing of this. I had no idea she was the one who told you about me."

"And I'm glad she did. You have a talent that I know is going to take you a long way. I am really happy to hear you are interested in signing with us at Briller Records."

"Yes, I was able to talk to my parents and I was hoping to speak to them more when I get home."

"That is reasonable and if you'd like, maybe sometime in the next few weeks if you decide you do want to sign with us, we can have you and your family fly out to New York and we can meet in person."

"I would really like that. I have to figure out a time with my parents and I have to finish up with school and a few exams."

"I can arrange that anytime you're ready."

"Thank you. I . . . so would I be working a lot with you?" I asked curiously. "Like as in my manager or—"

"Yes, you will be under my management and I will be in charge of booking everything for you and your tours."

"Tours?" I half smiled slightly thinking of the thought of traveling and being able to sing in venues and someday stadiums in front of the people who are supporting me.

"It will be a lot different from Kricon. Traveling would be great of course."

"This really does sound amazing. I should be home to talk more with my parents in person about this then, but yeah I'd love to sign with you."

"Of course, yes, I wanted to have a quick introduction with you and you seem like a great kid. Uh . . . I'll send you an email sometime tomorrow morning with my contact information and you can also keep in contact with Amber also."

"I want to thank you again for this opportunity."

"Anytime, it was great having small talk with you. My flight has been called."

"Alright,"—he was a pretty cool guy—"I'll contact you as soon as I get home and talk to my parents."

Andrew said a few more words before we dropped the call. I turned to my cup of butterbeer and realized it was empty. I'm glad Jacob and Jack were getting more.

"So . . . what was that about?" Nate asked.

"Briller Records wants me to sign with them." I half smiled. Nate smiled and hugged me.

"Bro! That is amazing and so exciting. I'm very happy for you. Congratulations!"

"Thank you." I looked towards the table as we continued to talk.

JACK JOHNSON

The day started out with me getting something to eat around the City Walk and once I finished, I saw Jacob and Claire walking out of a restaurant. My cousin seemed to be smiling and having a good conversation with Jacob. Jacob was saying something towards her when she looked in my direction and looked to him. He kissed the top of her head as she hugged him. She then went off towards a direction which looks like we will be avoiding now.

Shane went missing for a while. We eventually found him seated outside of Ben and Jerry's having ice cream and looking quite miserable actually. When we had all gone up to him, he seemed so out of it. We sat with him for a bit until he finished his ice cream. I was surprised he didn't go straight to Diagon Alley or something because we all knew he liked Harry Potter. Most of us were worried for him because he was upset over Claire. It wasn't until after lunch time and covered most of the park that we decided to take Shane to Diagon Alley to hopefully cheer the guy up.

Now here we are an hour later since we entered Diagon Alley and we thought Shane was feeling more like himself than earlier. The boy had gone excited to try on robes and some gear. It was like his Christmas day or something. We thought for a moment that he had completely forgotten about his thoughts, but that only lasted for a short while. At least he was talking now compared to earlier.

Jacob and I were waiting in a long line to get butterbeer for everyone. "You know if you give her time and continue to show you actually care for her, she'd trust you again."

I turned to Jacob and noticed he was trying to read my mind. "I'm an idiot for even thinking of actually ignoring her after she told me about my aunt, her mom. That was such a sh*tty move and I should have been there for her. For Christ sake, her mother is doing worse now," I sighed, feeling stressed and guilty. "What will happen if it continues to get worse? What do I do then?"

"You be there for her. You're one of the few families she has left. You make sure she knows she isn't alone and you better make sure you stay in contact with her. I can't imagine losing both parents, graduating a whole year early, and also going away for college," Jacob said. We approached the front of the line and ordered for four. While most of us were on our second, Shane was already on his third.

"Thank you," I said. Both Jacob and I took two cups each and made our way back to the table where Nate and Shane were seated. Spotting Shane, I saw him nodding to something Nate was saying. He seemed quite excited about something.

"Hey," Jacob said as we sat down in front of them. I handed Nate a drink and Jacob did the same with Shane. "You seem pretty happy about somethin'."

"Peters here has been invited to sign with Briller Records," Nate said with a smile.

"Dude that's awesome," I said feeling excited for him. "That's freaking amazing man," Jacob said happily.

"Congratulations." Shane's smile increased and I could tell he was really excited for this opportunity given to him. This was really cool and I knew he would continue along his career path.

"We get backstage passes when you go on your first world tour, right?" I chuckled lightly. Shane looked towards me and chuckled also.

"Of course," Shane answers. "Friends will always be welcomed to come to any shows I have." Jacob and Shane began making a conversation I wasn't quite into when Nate decided to make conversation.

"You alright there Johnson?" He asked me.

"Hanging in there. Uhm . . . have you heard from Claire at all today? How is she doing?"

"She's doing better. Coping through it and I think she is having a good time."

"That's good to hear. I bet she's going crazy on the butterbeer like Peters has," I chuckled lightly and Shane looked towards me.

"You mentioned my name?" Shane asked confusingly.

"Yeah," Nate coughed, "Uh . . . how about we get in line for the ride? We should at least ride it once before we go."

"Definitely," Shane said like a little boy and stood up with his mug of butterbeer. He was the only one of the four of us who decided to get a mug. Another funny thing is that before we leave, he planned to take home chocolate frogs to last for a week. "I'm ready when you guys are."

"I bet you are." I smiled and stood up with my bag and cup of butterbeer. Jacob and Nate stood up also and we followed Shane through the crowd as he pretends to cast spells and stop once in a while to look at props. Once we reached the entrance to the ride, I saw the waiting time and whistled.

"Are we about to actually wait four and a half hours?" Jacob asked as he looked down at his phone to check the time.

"I am," Shane said with a huge smile. I looked towards Nate and he shrugged.

"I guess. I'm good with waiting," Nate said. I nodded. We began the wait for the Harry Potter and Escape from Gringotts ride.

CHAPTER THIRTY-FIVE
Luck

CLAIRE JOHNSON

A week has passed by since I last received a phone call from the hospital. I tried my best to push the thought to the back of my head because I wanted to think positive. My mom will be okay and she will wake up.

I spent the whole week hanging with Nora and the guys with the exception of Jack, Shane, and Finnegan. I've been avoiding them every possible moment I could. I haven't really seen them since the day of the incidents. Each day was spent going to the Disney Parks, Downtown Disney, the beach, and the other side of Universal. Andy, Nate, Ben, Ryder, and I grew closer as we spent more time together. Jacob and I have also been doing pretty well but there were days when he would be with Shane. I would never make him choose. They were friends first.

Nate and Andy moved into my suite to keep me company. They never liked the idea of me being so far from everyone. They also offered for me to move to their suite, but then realized Shane was there. They decided it may not be the best idea and moved their things into my suite instead. The company truly made a difference for me and I felt better about it too. When we were not out so late during the evenings, almost everyone would hang out in my suite.

It was currently Monday evening and we just came back from a day at the water park. We have been there all day and just came back about an hour ago. Everyone was showering and I was so ready to rest after a day under the sun. There were just six more days left here until we would all be at the airport and getting ready to go our separate ways. I would be heading back to Omaha with my cousin and Finnegan. I wasn't sure how to feel about going back with them. What would things be like after this trip? I shook my head not wanting to think much about it.

A few days ago, Andy and Ben invited me to stay with them back in North Carolina. They knew I was finishing the rest of my year by submitting the rest of my assignments through computer. They thought it was amazing I was graduating early and they told me they'd love to have me around for a few weeks before I head up to New York for my graduation in June. As much as I would like that, I wasn't sure if my aunt would allow me to go after everything that happened with me. She wasn't very pleased when she heard about me breaking my arm. She had Jack and I FaceTime her and it was awkward, because I was not talking to Jack. I have to ask her about this.

After the two-day Kricon events, it was a two-week vacation for all of us. I thought it was cool that we were able to spend this much time together. They weren't missing too much school as spring break has been cut down to a week. I remember when we would have two full weeks of winter break and a week of spring break in New York. I wasn't sure about other states. Nate had graduated from high school almost two years ago. It was the same for Nora, except she had graduated about three years ago. Ben was going to be finishing up eighth grade then proceed to high school. Shane, Aaron, Ian, and Ryder will be finishing up their junior year. Ken, Jacob, Andy, Jack, and Finnegan were graduating this year. As for Aiden, he graduated last year.

Currently, I was having a snack in the recreation center with Andy and Nate after we had finished showering and changing

273

into fresh clothes. Both Nate and Andy were on their phones watching vines. I looked around the spacious center and thought how wonderful it was to be here when it wasn't crowded. It was around ten in the evening and the recreation center would soon be closing.

I went onto my phone to post one of the photos that was taken today at the water park. We were at Typhoon Lagoon. I went to my Instagram and looked for the picture in my camera roll. It was a photo of Ben, Ryder, and I with the view of the wave pool behind us. Ryder had this basic girl look that he liked to do and both Ben and I were laughing at something he had just said. My arms were wrapped around their waist and they both had their arms around my shoulders. I was short. I added my caption and tagged them before posting it.

ClaireJohnson
A little laugh is needed in your life @BenMiller @RyderEvans

As soon as the picture was posted I received a whole bunch of likes and comments on the posts. I heard Andy and Nate chuckling as they both continued to look at their screens.

"We have our notifications on for you," Nate said.

"Check our comments," Andy replied. I refreshed the page and noticed just about all the guys had replied. The comments of the people I did follow where the at the bottom for me to see.

JacobHolland: This is freakin adorable

AidenRodriguez: Damn ma, you're pretty short compared to these two. Well, you really are

KenRenaldi: You kids are cute

JustNate: I'm in the background being knocked down by the wave!

I giggled as I read their comments. Everyone seemed to be very positive and happy to see pictures like these. I felt a little uneasy at first when I posted it, because I would have thought many of them wouldn't like me for being around them so much out of jealousy. I knew what it was like being a fan, but I never was always a big fan girl or lived through the period of being on social media.

"You two are amazing," I said. I yawned and felt like sleep could take over any moment. I felt very exhausted. I think we're going to have an easy day tomorrow.

"Sleepy?" Nate asked and I nodded, leaning my head against Andy's shoulders.

"We should get you back to the room then," Andy chuckled. I sat up with Andy's help. He wrapped an arm around my waist and had me wrap an arm around him. He smiled down at me. "Hang in there Claire," he said. I nodded as Nate took all our wrappers and put it onto the tray to throw away the trash. "I have your phone," Andy said softly as we began making our way towards the side entrance of the building. Nate caught up to us and held the door open.

"Had a good day?" Nate asked curiously to which I nodded to. I noticed Nate looking towards Andy as we walked out the door. We were just about to go down the steps that led to a pathway back to the main building. We stopped walking and I looked between the both of them.

"I'll carry her," Andy said softly and Nate nodded. "Claire, you can climb on my back if you'd liked.

275

"Are you sure? I might fall asleep on you." I yawned once more and he unwrapped his arms from me and nodded.

"That's alright." Andy smiled and he went down two steps. I looked towards Nate. He made sure I was careful as I went down the first step and leaned over to wrap my arms around Andy's neck. I then jumped up and he caught my legs as he hoisted me up. It did not take long for me to have my head buried to the side of his neck and finding myself cozy. "Claire?" Andy asked.

"I'm here," I answered lightly and closed my eyes.

"She's just about out," I heard Nate.

"Sleep in my room tonight," I said to the both of them before letting my mind slip away.

I was surrounded by the continuation of my dream that has been going on for the past week.

"Claire . . ." I heard him say. I looked away from my music to see Shane standing there with a look of guilt. "Please let me explain to you."

"Explain? You had your chance to tell me before you decided to humiliate me and hurt me in the most painful way you possibly could," I said, hurt and wary of his deception. He had no right to share information I gave to him and use it against me like that, even if it was to protect me from something.

"I know I shouldn't have. Claire, please let me gain your trust again. I wish I could take back everything I said. I wish I never said those things to you." He walked towards me until he was in front of me and squatted down.

"You've already hurt me Shane." I sighed and closed my eyes painfully. "Shane . . . I trusted you," I said, barely audible. My voice became shaky because I felt emotional from that night.

"I know. I'm truly sorry for hurting you Claire," he answered softly and I felt his presence coming closer to me. I felt my eyes squeeze tightly as the tears began to pour through. The emotions for my mom and dad came flooding in. I opened my eyes to see a blurry vision of Shane. My heart raced as I thought about

276

him and how much he made me happy. He used to take my pain away.

I reached forward and wrapped my arms around him. I slowly got off the bench so I was kneeling with him. He held me in his arms. I did not care about my music. I leaned my head on his shoulder and he placed his hand gently on my cheek. He began running small circles with his thumb as his arm held me tightly.

"I never wanted to do this. He had something against you and I completely panicked. I would never intentionally hurt you and you know me Claire. I care about you and I haven't felt so nervous before to be around a girl. You make me nervous and you're the reason I feel so thankful to have you here on this trip. I really like you Claire and I'm not just saying this. I've grown to fall for you since we first met. You treat me like a normal guy. You see me as another musician who understands what I want to do. I understand your stress and emotions when you talk about music."

I sniffled and pulled away and he used his sweatshirt to wipe my eyes. I wasn't sure why he was wearing a sweater, but it was pretty warm out here in the garden. It took a few moments until I could see him clearly and my flowing tears slowed down. He had the most pained look in his eyes and I could tell he meant every word he said.

"You kissed her," I said softly. He shook his head and cupped the side of my face.

"I did not actually kiss her. It was a stage kiss. I've only kissed you Claire."

Then why was my mind telling me no then? Why was a part of me wanting me to push him away? There was also the small part of me that wanted to forgive him.

I spoke before I could process what I was saying. "I'm sorry Shane. I can't do this right now. I just . . . I'm so hurt right now. I . . . I need time." I pulled away from him and slowly stood feeling myself yearn for his touch again. He stood slowly and looked towards me as I saw his eyes glossing slightly. He nodded as he bent down to pick up my music and handed it over to me. I took them. "Goodbye Shane," I said quietly. He closed his eyes painfully before I walked past him and made my way out of the garden. Before I left the garden, I turned around and saw him sitting down on the bench with his face in his hands.

I groaned slightly as if I was being sucked away from a dream. I flipped over while gasping for air. My eyes finally fluttered open and I was welcomed back to my dark room. The dream felt so real. My heart raced and my breathing was rigid. It's as if this just happened but it wasn't real.

I sat up slowly. I noticed my phone plugged in to its charger. My left hand pulled the comforter back as I shivered at the cold air. I slowly stood from the bed and walked over to the closet to take out a sweatshirt. I pulled it over my head and did my best to put both of my arms through the sleeve. I struggled with my right side so I just left it to hang since it would have been a tight fit. My feet made its way to the door. I saw the small lamp on in the living room. Both Nate and Andy were on the couch. They looked away from the TV to see me.

"Hey, everything alright?" Nate said softly. Andy had a worried look as he came over to me.

"Dream woke me up," I answered quietly, remembering how vivid it was.

"It's alright, do you need a glass of warm milk to help you go back to sleep? You still seem very tired," Andy said. I nodded and he gave me a small smile. "I'll prepare it for you. You head back to bed."

"I . . . don't think I want to be in my room alone at the moment," I said. He turned to Nate slightly.

"Head in the room with her? We're just going to bed anyway," Andy said softly. I saw Nate standing from the couch. He turned off the TV. He made his way over to us with a hopeful smile. Andy made his way towards the kitchen while Nate followed me back into the bedroom. It did not take long for me to get comfortable under the comforter. Nate also got in. It took a few moments for Andy to come in with the milk and allowed me to take a few sips before putting the glass on the table. Andy came in on the other side so I would be in the middle. In moments, I was able to close my eyes again.

CHAPTER THIRTY-SIX
Breakfast

CLAIRE JOHNSON

My mind slowly began to wake up. Why did I have that dream with Shane? It has been a while since I last encountered him and it felt strange to be dreaming about him. I continued to have the feeling of hurt and betrayal from him. It felt so real and I noticed my heart racing from it. Shane still had an effect on me even when he was not here. It didn't seem to go away.

My eyes slowly opened and I realized it was morning. My head seemed to be buzzing slightly from the amount of thoughts in my head. The sun was starting to rise. I knew it because I was used to getting up this early to finish a possible school assignment I may have fallen asleep to. There was quite a lot of light coming into the room. I could also hear the birds chirping. I turned my head slightly to the left to see Andy softly snoring. To my right was Nate. I smiled slightly to the both of them and sat up to look at the time. It was 5:30 in the morning. It was so early, but I felt hungry. I always seemed to find myself wanting to eat after waking up from a deep sleep or a heavy nap.

I wanted to let them sleep in because they have been up late. This was the one day they were really given time to really sleep in. I was not sure what we would be doing later on today or if we were really going anywhere, but I knew I wanted to go on a run to shave off all the food I ate. My thought was to get a small snack before going on a morning jog. How do I get out from under the comforter without waking the both of them? I had to keep in mind that I had to be careful of my broken arm.

I honestly could not wait until my arm was fully healed so I could take my cast off. It annoyed me quite a lot that I have not been able to practice my cello or play my guitar. Not being able to practice did throw me off this past week because I would always practice at least two hours a day. It felt strange to not pluck a string or use a bow. I had difficulty holding a bow at the moment and so I had given up on practicing. For the time being, I would listen to pieces and make sure to look at my music as I did.

I slowly pulled myself up against the bed frame before lifting the comforter slightly to get my legs from underneath. I crawled onto my knees and automatically hit Andy's hand. His snoring stopped and I froze for a moment. I looked towards Andy's peaceful face to see a small smile. I took a deep breath and quietly got out of bed. I quickly walked over to the dresser to grab a sports bra, a tank top, and one of my Nike pro shorts. I walked into the bathroom and closed the door behind me. It would be best if I showered after my run and so I quickly changed into my running wear. I folded my sleepwear before placing them on the counter and turning on the faucet.

I struggled to hold my toothbrush using my left hand and used my hand in the cast to carefully squeeze the toothpaste. It felt weird to use my left hand. After quickly cleaning the tooth brush, I used my left hand to rinse my mouth. I could have used a cup, but decided against it. I washed my face and dried it off before looking at the shelf to see my armband on the shelf. Should I leave my phone here during my run? I knew it would be difficult especially with my casted arm, but I wanted to make sure that I'd have a way to contact someone if I were stuck somewhere.

I decided to take the armband with me and walk into the room to see Andy changed into basketball shorts and a black tank.

He looked like he was about to do a workout himself. He turned his head towards me and smiled.

"Mornin' Claire." His bright blue eyes were wide and playful.

"Morning Andy," I whispered back. I felt like we were small children trying to not wake anyone in particular.

"Mind if I join you on your run this morning?" he said. I walked over to him to grabbed my phone off the charger. I looked towards Nate to see him still sound asleep.

"No problem at all. Having company is better. Plus, you know I like having company," I said. He followed me into the closet. I grabbed my running shoes and a pair of socks as I passed the drawers. We both made our way into the living room then sat on the couch, putting our socks and shoes on. It was also a bit difficult to tie my shoes, but I eventually figured it out.

"Do you need help with the armband?" Andy asked after getting his shoes on. I nodded as I put my phone inside and handed the band to him. I held my left arm up as he put it on and I thanked him for securing it.

We both stood and I grabbed a banana from the counter. Andy did the same as he followed me out of the suite. We walked down the hall in silence and threw our peels in the trash before walking onto the elevator. I took a glance towards Andy and smiled. He was looking straight ahead, chewing on his banana.

I took the time to look at his features. I thought all the guys here were cute and they were, of course, good looking. I thought Shane had the look of Prince Charming and he reminded me in a way of one of my favorite characters from the show Vampire Diaries, Stefan Salvatore. I shook my head, catching myself thinking about him again. The dream was really playing with my mind.

When the elevator reached the lobby, I followed him out and into the muggy air. There was also a part of the air that also felt cool, but there was that humid feeling. I looked around, wondering which direction to go. We both had finished our banana and Andy waited for me to start jogging. I chose a random direction and he followed after me.

"So, is three miles good for you?" Andy asked. I looked towards him. I was up for a challenge today. I could always ask.

"Maybe four? Is that alright with you? I feel up for it."

"Really now? Trying to impress me with your broken arm, huh?"

I saw the smile on Andy's face. I laughed at him and shrugged slightly. I haven't worked out in months. Who knew if I was ready to run the pace I used to do when I did this particular distance.

"It does feel weird not moving this arm to be honest. I think I can do it through. I can take a challenge," I said.

"I bet you can. You said you never did a sport in school though? Do you like running during your own time?"

"Yes. I have to keep in shape somehow," I said. It felt strange for me to explain this again, but Andy was a curious guy. Here and there, we would talk. It took us about thirty-five minutes to do our four-mile run. We both decided to take a seat on a bench and I let the muscles in my body relax. We were both out of breath and covered in sweat. The feeling of finishing felt amazing and I think Andy felt the same way.

"You're so dedicated," he said after his breathing returned to normal. I could really go for some water.

"You are too, Miller." I laughed and he looked towards my leg and frowned slightly.

"What happened there?" He asked pointing it out. He gently took my leg and placed it on his lap. I looked at the slight purple bruise that has taken a while to fade away, but it was still noticeable. I honestly did forget about it. Now, it only brought me back to what happened. Andy started to observe it in wonder.

"It's nothing," I said lightly and turned away from the bruise. Finnegan is my bully and I had no idea if it would ever stop with him. He honestly scared me and I wanted nothing to do with him. I was thankful after that day when I received the phone call that he had not been near me at all. It had to do with Nate and Aiden's doing I think. There has always been someone by my side while we were all out. Everyone seemed to make me feel safe. I felt Andy's hand gently take my chin and turned me so I was facing him again. I looked into his baby blue eyes and saw how worried he was.

"This isn't nothing," he said softly and looked towards my leg again with sadness. "This was definitely something Claire." I put my leg down and he continued to look towards me, waiting for an answer. "Tell me," he said softly. I closed my eyes for a moment and took a deep breath.

"It was the day we arrived here," I started and looked down at my lap, feeling embarrassed. I always felt uncomfortable talking about my encounters with Finnegan. "It was when I told everyone I was going to my room to unpack and he came to the suite a while later. He tried to slap me again, but I blocked it and so he kicked my shin." I sighed and shivered from his violence. I was afraid of what he was capable of.

"Claire . . . you should have told someone right away."

"Please don't. I've had this talk before and I . . . I don't want to talk about this right now. Look where it took me when I trusted Shane," I said, feeling betrayed.

"I noticed a bruise on your cheek when we were on the plane. Did . . . Fin give that to you the night before? Is that the reason you were scared to go pack the night before and the reason you declined me when I asked you to ride with Nate and I to the airport?"

I nodded and saw his jaw tightening. We were suddenly a few inches closer. I could feel his breath blowing into my face. I pulled away slightly so I could see his face and avoid feeling too close. "Sorry," he mumbled.

"It's okay," I whispered. We sat here feeling awkward, because I didn't know what to say. I never knew what to say. I found it a little difficult to keep a conversation with Andy and we've never been left alone before. He then spoke a few minutes later.

"So umm . . ." he started nervously, "I know you've been through so much, and I've kinda been waiting to ask you this, but you and Shane were kinda a thing. It's definitely okay if you say no but umm . . . would you like to go out with me sometime?"

It threw me off a little and I turned back towards him. His blue eyes were quite wide and I saw him blushing. This must have been on his mind for a while.

"Andy . . . I don't know, I'm trying to get over everything that happened with Shane and I still have a major crush on him. Well . . . I like him a lot. My feelings for him haven't disappeared nor was it easy to ignore it either. And well . . . I'm not really sure right now," I said softly trying to find the right words. I did not want to let him down but at the same time, I was currently having trust issues. I did not want to give Andy the wrong idea.

"I could take you out on a date. Let me show you how great it will be and we'll have a great time. I could help you forget about Shane, i—if that's what you want."

I looked into his blue eyes and he had this look of hope. I stood from the bench and hugged myself slightly as I closed my eyes painfully.

He did not understand that I wasn't ready to move on yet and there's just too much going on right now. I liked how he was being so sweet and kind, but I was not interested in the possibility of being more than friends. I didn't like the idea of using someone and I wanted Andy to continue to be my friend, but I don't think he saw it that way.

"I appreciate that you want to help," I said quietly. I felt Andy getting up and he moved so he was in front of me.

"Shoot . . . I completely rushed into this. I'm sorry Claire," I heard Andy apologize. I opened my eyes, feeling very emotional. This stressed me out. I did not want to hurt Andy's feelings. "I didn't mean to stress you out," Andy said carefully. He gently

285

placed his hands to my arms holding me and I hesitated to hug him, because he just told me he has a crush on me. "I should have put this in another way. I'm sorry for messing this up. You must think this is weird."

"No, really Andy. I'm sorry for acting this way. It's just—"

"You still like Shane?" He finished for me and I nodded. "If you're not ready I ge—"

"It would be really awkward for us Andy. I would feel as if I was using you and I don't want that."

"Then let's not think of it as a date then. I could take you out for an evening and we'd go out to have fun. Just a normal night out. How does that sound?"

"A—are you sure?" I asked worriedly.

"Yeah," Andy half smiled. "We could go out and get something to eat and just hang out. Nothing formal. Just you know, two friends just hangin' out without everyone. It'll be fun. Plus, I think I have a great idea where we can go. You'd enjoy it. What do you say?"

CHAPTER THIRTY-SEVEN
Forgiveness

CLAIRE JOHNSON

He looked into my eyes, waiting for an answer. It took me a moment to think. Going out and having a fun night sounded great to me. I've gone out with Jacob a few times in the last week and I've spent quality time with Ryder and Ben. I think it was okay say that I would like to hang with Andy. It would be nice to hang with someone my age. I nodded and gave him a small smile.

"Okay," I answered softly. "Let's go out tonight."

"Really?" He smiled and leaned forward to hug me.

"Alright. Does around 6 sound good to you? Today is everyone's free day so I think everyone will be lounging around the resort today."

"Six sounds good." Andy had this excited look and it made me wonder where he was planning on taking me to tonight. I felt my stomach grumbling and Andy's smiled widens. "I guess you're ready for breakfast then?"

"Breakfast sounds amazing." I looked around and noticed an IHOP just down the road. "Can we go there?" I pointed. He turned slightly and nodded. I realized I did not bring any cash with me. Andy started laughing and I looked up towards him as we began making our way over to a crosswalk to cross the street.

"Don't worry Claire. It's on me."

"Thank you so much! I completely forgot to bring any cash with me. I didn't think of it."

"It's no problem, really. Your reaction though was pretty funny though. I had a feeling we would get something to eat after a run."

"You're too kind." I smiled lightly. We reached the other side and began making our way towards IHOP.

"Thank you for thinking this through." He shrugged as we continued to walk alongside each other. Once we reached the building, he held open the door for me. I thanked him before walking inside and we were immediately greeted by one of the workers. Andy did most of the talking. The waitress took two menus before having us follow her to where we would sit. We took a booth by the window. Andy and I decided we'd sit across from each other

"What would you folks like to drink?" The waitress asked us and I thought for a moment.

"I'll have orange juice," I said.

"I'll take a glass of chocolate milk," Andy said, smiling towards her.

"I'll be back with your drinks in a few minutes and give you two some time to look at the menu," the waitress said. Both Andy and I thanked her before she walked away. I looked towards Andy and saw him already looking towards me and chuckled.

"The menu is in your hand Claire," Andy smiled. I smiled feeling the heat rising in my cheeks.

I opened the menu and looked through the choices. Pancakes and some bacon sounded pretty good to me. *Wait a second, but those crepes looked great.* The banana crepes with Nutella looked really good. Yes, I think I'll have that.

"Do you want to share a big bowl of seasonal mixed fruit?"

"That's sounds good, sure," I nodded as I continued to look through the rest of the menu. I think I was pretty set on having crepes. "What are you getting to eat?"

"I think I'm going to have the pancake combo. I've been thinking about it since we've decided to come here."

"Really now?" I asked curiously and he smiled. The waitress came back with our drinks and I thanked.

"Are you both ready to order?" the waitress said. Andy looked towards me and I nodded.

"Ladies first," Andy said. I turned to the waitress who had a pen ready in hand along with her small memo book.

"I'd like to have the banana crepes with Nutella, please."

The woman nodded her head as she jotted down my order before looking towards Andy. "How about you, sir?"

"I would like to get the big bowl of seasonal mixed fruit to share with m'lady here and I'll have the pancake combo."

She jotted that down and looked up. "Would that be all?" Both Andy and I nodded. "I'll be back with your large bowl of seasonal mixed fruit in a few moments and get everything started," the waitress said. We both thanked her before she went away once again. Both Andy and I talked as we waited for our food. When our food did arrive, we did not waste time. We were both pretty hungry from the run. While we ate, he would talk about his home back in North Carolina. It seemed like a place I would like to be. It was towards the end of breakfast when Andy's phone rang.

"It's Nate," he said and answered the phone. I mouthed to him that I was going to the restroom and he nodded. "Hey Nate, what's up?"

I stood up and looked around for a sign for the restroom. I followed the small hallway that led to the ladies' room. I walked into a stall and quickly did my business. Then I made my way over the sink and began washing my hands. I reached for the soap and looked up at my reflection in the mirror. I noticed a bit of Nutella and laughed lightly before wiping the area with my hand. Once I finished, I dried my hands with the hand dryer and made my way out of the bathroom.

As soon as I walked out of the bathroom, I saw someone oddly familiar coming out of the men's bathroom. It wasn't Andy. He also looked like he had just done a workout and when he looked up, he froze. His eyes widened as he spotted me. What was he doing here? Seeing him for the first time in several days made me immediately think about the dream I've recently had and that night in Epcot. My heart began to race and I felt it aching. I've missed him, but I also felt so betrayed. I did not want to be near him after hurting me like that. He looked towards me with guilt, waiting to see what I would do. I also felt panicky with him here.

"What are you doing here Shane?" I asked him softly. This was the first time I've actually talked to him since that evening. He has been keeping his distance. He looked towards me hurt and tried to walk towards me, but I backed away. I did not want to fall under his trap.

"You've been ignoring my calls and texts Claire. I want to apologize," he answered softly.

"I've been avoiding them all week for a reason." He sighed looking stressed and tired all at once.

"I want to thank you for showing Andrew our video and put in a word about me. Claire, you have no idea how happy you've made me and knowing you were the person to let them know about me . . . This means a lot to me."

"I did it, because I believe in you and I know you'd make a great musician in the music industry," I answered softly and folded my arms. I remembered the first night here and I watched him perform for Jacob and I. He had the voice of an angel and I wanted to reach out to Andrew since he was a friend of mine.

Andrew and I had known each other for several years actually. I remember when I was down in the city playing for a festival. My private professor had recommended me to participate as it would expose me a little bit to some of the professors from NYU. It also exposed me to the competition and pressure. I performed one of my favorite Sonatas that I had been working on over the summer. It was the fall semester of my freshman year in high school and I was one of the top musicians in the state.

It was a great honor to be playing there and I was one of the youngest musicians to get in and perform. The evening that I played, I remembered Andrew coming up to me and introduced himself. He was on his last semester in college. He told me how amazing my performance was and how he liked it.

My professor came over, then the three of us spent the rest of the time watching performances. I remembered how he told me he was an American talent manager that represented Briller records. He was interested in having me as an intern at Briller records, but I had to decline due to my age and residence. We stayed in touched and from then on, we would always meet up when he was visiting upstate to visit his parents. From there we became friends and he told me to let him know if I ever needed something music related. Shane was that something.

"I don't deserve this," Shane said softly and I frowned.

"Of course, you do. This is music business. I want you to take that offer."

"But I hurt you. It doesn't feel right if I take it."

"I told you that I believe in you. I believe you'll someday soon be one of the biggest artists out there. This has nothing to do with us."

Shane nodded and made eye contact with me. I still had that nervous feeling around him. "I have to talk to my parents about it first."

I nodded and looked away slightly. I closed my eyes painfully.

"Wh—where does this leave us Claire?" I could tell this was painful for him. "It's really hard not being around you this past week."

"It's hard for me too, Shane." My tone was so soft it felt like my heart was breaking over again. "Apologizing doesn't work after what you did."

"We didn't actually kiss. I'd never do that to you. It was a stage kiss. My lips never touched hers. I can promise you." I felt upset, because it wasn't all about that. It may have been a part of the pain, but that wasn't the major problem. He hurt me and I wasn't going to forgive him easily.

"It's what you said Shane. How could you ever mention the one thing that hurt me the most? Why did you have to make me feel embarrassed and humiliated?" Shane's mouth parted slightly and he moved towards me until I was backed into the wall. His arms wrapped around my waist and my vision blurred from not only the pain, but from his touch. I missed him. He then lifted a hand and gently placed it on my cheek. I noticed his eyes glossing and I bit my lip knowing how much pain this brought us. He shouldn't be here. "You hurt me Shane," I said quietly as the first tear fell and he closed his eyes painfully.

"I . . . wanted to go after you that night. I wanted to warn you before you came. There were so many things I wanted to do, but I was afraid Claire," Shane said quietly. "I should have thought it through."

"You used me," I said hurtfully. He shook his head and looked towards me worriedly.

"No Claire. I would never. Please believe me. Fin had a video of you."

"I know."

"He wanted to use it if Jack and I didn't cooperate with him."

"That isn't the point. I trusted you. I let you in Shane. Do you have any idea how hard it is right now for me? You said things I took very personal from my life hard last week and you just continued. Fin had no idea about my parents nor does he care. I trusted you to be the person that I thought you'd be."

"I'm still that guy Claire." I shook my head.

"You've lost my trust." I pushed him away from me. I wanted to get away from him before we caused a scene that wouldn't end so well. I tried to make my way back to the tables to get Andy, but I closed my eyes. I couldn't see through my tears and I heard murmuring from around me.

"Claire?" I heard a panicked Andy from a distance. I sniffled, wanting to get out of here. "Nate, I'll call you right back."

I immediately felt warm arms wrapping around my waist, guiding me somewhere. I knew it was Andy. I realized we were going through a door and I felt the hot humid air. My face was being wiped off and I could see a very worried Andy. "What happened Claire? Are you alright?"

"Sh—Shane is here," I said shakily and my breath seemed to quicken a bit. It wasn't healthy to feel this way so often.

"Did he hurt you? I swear if he did something to annoy you, I will personally argue with him until he feels awful."

"N—no." I looked up and saw Shane coming out of IHOP. He froze when he found me with Andy. Andy turned towards him and he frowned at him. I had to grip Andy with my left hand to stop him from taking a step towards Shane.

"Shane . . ." Andy said. I could tell he was not happy to see him here. "What are you doing here? Of all possible places to be."

"Andy, I'm sorry, I had to see her," he answered guilty and he looked down. His soft brown eyes looked stressed.

"You should have stayed away." I could hear the anger in Andy's voice. I shivered slightly and looked towards Shane.

"It wasn't on purpose. I saw you guys arrive here when I was eating. I also had gone on a run before you two did and I had no idea you guys would stop here to eat." Shane looked towards me sadly. "Claire, I didn't mean to upset you. I'm truly sorry about everything."

I saw the tears in his eyes. "Leave me alone Shane," I said quietly.

"Is that what you really want Claire?" He tried to take a step forward, but then remembered Andy was here. "If that's what you really want, I want to hear it from you. Not Andy, not Nate, and not from Jacob."

I looked between Andy and Shane to see they were both waiting for my response. "I don't want you to be around me," I said quietly. Those words cut through me painfully, but I wanted him to leave. "Please stay away from me." Getting the words out was the hardest thing to do. I buried my face as I hugged Andy painfully. I needed him to disappear. Andy spoke softly, but I couldn't understand or really hear anything at first.

"Shane, just go," I heard Andy say softly after a moment.

"I'm sorry, Claire," Shane whispered. "I'll leave you alone." It then went silent for a few moments. I felt Andy wrap his arms around my waist and I slowly looked up at him.

His blue eyes looked like a different shade. It could also be my imagination. It took a moment before Andy spoke.

"You should forgive him," he whispered. "And Jack too. They're both a mess right now and won't forgive themselves."

"I'm not ready to."

CHAPTER THIRTY-EIGHT
News: Part One

JACK JOHNSON

"I'm going to head to the pool," I said to everyone who was in the living room. Aiden, Ryder, Ben and looked up from their phones and nodded. I was just in my swimming trunks with a towel wrapped around my shoulder and phone in hand. I wasn't sure where everyone was for the day, but I knew this was our free day. I spent most of the day resting and pondering over my thoughts. I knew Claire was under great care this week and I really wish I could spend time with her.

I heard about the encounter this morning and it only made Shane go silent to the rest of us. It was when he came back from his run that I heard a door slam and I came out of my room just like Ryder and Ben had. Jacob was in the living room with his eyes wide and I was about to walk to his room when Jacob stopped us and shook his head. Jacob explained how Shane busted into the suite.

"The pool was nice," Aiden commented. "Just a warning, Fin is probably still in the pool area."

"Of course, he is," I mumbled. "I'm just going to use the hot tub for a bit. Are we still up for mini golf tonight?"

"Heck yeah," Ryder answered. "We'll see you when you get back."

I nodded as I took a room key off the table and made my way out the room. I locked it before making my way towards the elevators. I took the route to the lobby and looked for the hall that led towards the side of the building where it led to the recreation center. I decided I would go to the main pool area.

Walking out into the humid evening air, I crossed the street into the parking lot. The small walk to the recreation was quick and I went around the building to enter the pool area. Once I opened the gate, the night Fin and I came here and had thrown Claire and her clothing into the pool replayed in my head. My breaths became heavy. I shook my head, regretting that night and all the times before and after that. That night shouldn't have happened and I owe Claire everything.

When I calmed down slightly, I took a step forward and noticed Fin in the pool. He seemed to be deep in thought and did not seem to have notice me entering. I haven't talked to him since the afternoon we were at Epcot. When I found out what really happened to Claire that evening from Shane, I wanted to be as far away as I could from Fin. That was strange for me. He has been my best friend since kindergarten and it felt weird. But it was not as weird as me continuing to hurt my cousin.

As I made my way towards the hot tub, Fin's head turned in my direction and I noticed his bloodshot eyes. I had no idea from what, but I continued walking remembering that I was doing this for Claire. I couldn't be around him if he was going to continue to be the way he was. I wanted nothing more than to be closer with Claire again and be the way we used to be. I wanted to fix what happened between her and Shane. It would take time, but this was something I wanted more than anything at the moment. She deserved to be happy. I walked over to the hot tub and placed my towel and phone on the ground close to where I would get in. I then walked around the hot tub and took the stairs slowly. I made my way to the side with my things and took a seat. I leaned my back against the wall and let myself sink into the water. I closed my eyes as I tried to relax. The problem, I don't think I was able to with the amount of guilt built up. I was disappointed and upset with myself.

Claire trusted me after accidentally breaking her arm. She believed I was changing and I felt that way. I was a coward and turned around to hurt her again when I knew she needed support. I had ruined that chance with her again. The chance to return things back to normal. I felt like the worst cousin in the world. My aunt has the possibility of not making it. She lost her dad. I honestly don't know how I'm going to make this up to her if she doesn't want me near her. She won't forgive me this time and if she does, it won't be for a very long time. I was her only friend and Cooper too before Fin had started all of this bull.

Just earlier this week I remembered when my mom wanted to skype me. She wanted to have Claire there also. That took everything from Andy and Nate to convince her about it and made us stay in one room. She was very uncomfortable around me, but she pretended to be okay when we skyped my mom. She smiled as she told her about Universal and showed her pictures. Not once did Claire talk to me. It was like a one on one conversation and it felt like I did not exist to her. It was when the skype ended, did Claire get up and leave my room without a simple word. I had sat there feeling awful that she was really going to give me the silent treatment.

I wanted to at least be on better terms before we made our flight home. Fin had not tried anything in over a week. I don't think he could have when Claire was always with one of the guys. She surrounded herself with them and if she wasn't with them, she seemed very hard to find until she wanted to be found. I noticed Fin getting out of the pool and grabbed his things before making his way over to me. I frowned slightly as I saw him approaching and he stopped at the foot of the hot tub. He looked down at his feet like he was a lost kid.

"If you're here to plan some evil scheme on Claire, I don't want to hear it," I said.

"I,"—he hesitated and sighed—"I wanted to apologize, J."
His tone was soft and he put his stuff down slowly before putting
his feet into the hot tub and looked towards me guilty. "I've been
stupid and I was a complete ass to her."

"I know."

He sighed and ran his fingers on his hair. "I was jealous,
okay? I was jealous of what you and Claire had."

I frowned. What exactly was he jealous of? "She's my
cousin. What the hell could you possibly be jealous of?"

"I just . . . it's stupid." He paused for a moment before
telling me what was going through his mind. "Claire heard the
rumors when you were being accused of bullying and I had a
feeling she wanted to look into it. I heard from Cooper she was
thinking about snooping into your files and destroying any possible
evidence. Though I never thought she would actually go through
with this, I took this as an opportunity to turn you against her. I
knew she went into the school without a second thought because
she wanted to protect you.

I rolled my eyes wishing he would stop wasting my time. "I
want to apologize for bullying her, turning you against her, and
making her uncomfortable."

"It's not me you should be apologizing to. It's her you
should really be apologizing to."

"And also, you. You're my best friend Jack. I want to make
things right with the both of you. I'd do anything to show the both
of you that I am truly sorry. The guilt, the nightmares this past
week has really shaken me. I can't believe I threw her in a pool
when she begged me not to. F*ck . . . I am beyond sorry I made
you help me. I'm am beyond sorry I was jealous for no reason. I
don't know what is wrong with me."

I watched as Fin started to break down in front of me. I
knew this wasn't something he could fake. I knew him pretty well
and I could tell this was bothering him a lot.

"If you're asking forgiveness, then you need to fix this," I sighed. "It really wasn't fair for you to break Claire and Shane apart either. She was happy and she trusted him. You completely screwed this up."

He nodded, guilty. "I'll fix this. J, I'll apologize to her and I'm going to try to make this right." The sudden change in Fin felt strange. Did this past week really make him see what he was doing? Did he actually have the intention to make things right and fix it? I was shaken out of my thoughts when my phone rang from behind. I shivered slightly as I sat up. Fin looked towards his lap and went on to his phone, staying quiet. I turned around and dried my hands before picking up to see my mom calling. I answered the phone and heard sniffling on the end. I frowned. I was facing Fin and he looked towards me.

"Mom?" It took a few moments before she responded.

"Jack," she said on the other line as she sniffled.

"What's wrong?" I asked again. I had a feeling something really bad happened. She never called being an emotional mess. The last time she was randomly like this in a phone call was a few months ago. I learned just recently it was about her brother's death, Claire's dad. *Oh no* . . . I was now panicking that Claire's worst fear would really come true. She didn't need this kind of news now.

"Honey, she didn't make it." My mom began sobbing on the other end. I closed my eyes painfully and sighed. It was when my eyes opened my vision blurred. My chest began to ache from the loss of my aunt. I looked towards a worried Fin. He did not move from his spot.

"This can't happen. There must have been a misunderstanding."

"Jack, she passed away a few hours ago," she said. The tears began to fall as I let this sink in. "Oh Jack. I can't bear to break this to her. She has started smiling and enjoying herself. The stories she has been telling me about her trip down there. This will crush her. I delayed the phone call the doctor will be making to her this evening," my mom said, upset.

"I'll do it," I whispered. "I'll talk to her." Even though she wanted nothing to do with me, it was the right thing to do. I haven't seen her all day, but I hope she wasn't far. I knew I'd have to find her soon. It was a matter of time.

"Honey, you don't have to . . ."

She shouldn't have to find out through the phone. It would be best if it was in person. "I'll do it. I should break it to her and be there for her. I'll make sure to let her know."

"Alright, honey. I'll be there in a few days and we'll figure this all out. We'll figure everything out when I get there."

"Alright Mom," I answered softly. "I love you."

"I love you too." We said our goodbyes then she hung up. I sighed, feeling slightly overwhelmed. Fin was looking more than concerned.

"What did your mom say?" Fin asked, barely audible. He knew it wasn't good news.

"My aunt didn't make it." I sighed and wiped my face as I decided to get out of the hot tub. Fin's mouth parted slightly in shock.

"Claire . . ."

"I need to find her. She's not going to take this lightly," I said. Fin nodded and stood up. I frowned, wondering what he was doing.

"I'm coming with you."

"This sure is not the time to apologize Fin. She's about to hear heartbreaking news and no offense, but I don't think she wants you around when I tell her."

"I'll wait outside then."

I nodded as I picked up my towel and phone. I slipped on my sliders and Fin did the same.

"I'm not prepared to break this to her. I just . . . I wish there was something good coming her way. I couldn't imagine losing both of my parents around this time. It's terrible . . ."

"What . . . exactly happened?" Fin asked quietly. I completely forgot he had no idea about what happened to Claire's parents. I've only just found out myself just a little over a week ago from Claire.

"Back in January, her parents went into work on their day off. I guess there was this experiment that was going on. According to Claire, they had a miscalculation in the formula . . ."

"Sh*t . . ." Fin said softly. We began making our way out of the pool area.

"There was an explosion. I think it was chemical or something. Her dad was the closest to it and died on the spot and her mom was exposed to it and had knocked her out. Claire has been blaming herself for this and she isn't taking it lightly."

"I didn't realize . . . She can't possibly think this was all her fault? That experiment had nothing to do with her."

"You think we haven't told her that already Fin? She keeps telling us she could have prevented them from going. She continues to tell us that it was their day off and if she had told them to stay home, they would still be alive."

"I thought I felt awful before I found out about this. Now I actually feel like a big jerk. Damn it, that's why Claire's so upset with Shane."

"What?" I asked, confused. I was not a part of the that plan that night at Epcot. I had told Fin I was not going to be a part of it and he did not need me for that. I ended up spending my time with Aaron and Nora at that time. I had no idea what happened.

"Shane mentioned something about going back to New York. I didn't really know how that was supposed to affect her, but it did greatly."

"Way to ruin a possible relationship. Thank you for possibly breaking both of their hearts."

"I'm going to tal—"

"Talking isn't going to do sh*t!" I raised my voice. "You're going to have to do way better than that. She probably doesn't want anything to do with any of us after everything she has been through on this trip. You took the one thing that meant a lot to her and that was Shane." I heard a sigh as he reached for the gate. His head was low. "Fin . . ." I said softly after a moment. We were not walking through the parking lot. He looked up and I saw his eyes bloodshot red like earlier and he had actual tears flowing.

"I get it. I'm going to live with this the rest of my life. I am sorry for causing this much trouble for all of you," he said painfully.

I nodded, unsure what to say. He went on about how he would do everything he could to fix all of this. The only problem was that he couldn't fix Claire's heart once she finds out about her mom.

CHAPTER THIRTY-NINE
News: Part Two

Claire Johnson

"That was really good," I commented as I sat up slowly and looked towards Jacob. He looked away from his guitar. He sat on the chair across. We were practicing for a bit before I would get ready to go out with Andy for the night. It was more like Jacob practicing while I asked a few questions. I looked through a piece I have been working on. Andy offered Jacob to come with us, but he seemed pretty tired for the evening. Nate thought it was a great idea to just hang with someone my age.

"I'm not sure. It's something I have in the works," he said as he looked down at his journal. "It's a long way from where I think I want it at the moment."

"You'll get it to where you want it eventually. Keep working on it." He nodded as he put his guitar down. He closed his journal and also placed it on the table.

"You're not into songwriting, are you?" he asked. I shook my head.

"I love singing and doing covers, but I'm more into the cello and the sciences."

"Right. Sorry, I keep forgetting you're into the medicine and such. I think it's pretty cool that you're into it, because maybe someday I'll be coming to you," he said. I laughed lightly as I heard a door open. I looked up to see Nate coming out of the guest room. "Hey," Jacob greeted as he came over to us.

"Hey . . ." Nate said slowly and checked his phone before looking up towards me. "You're not wearing your pajamas out are you?" he asked me curiously. After I showered from returning from the second part of my run with Andy, I changed into my comfy pajamas to keep cool for the rest of the day.

"No, I uhh . . ." I slowly stood up. "Do either of you want to curl my hair?"

Jacob raised an eyebrow. Nate chuckled. "I can . . . I thought you two were just hangin' out?"

"We are. Can't I feel dressed up a bit for an evening? Plus, Andy and I are going to be taking a lot of pictures," I said.

Someone's phone went off and it was Jacob's. He stood up also. "I'd love to chat and keep you guys company, but I did promise my momma and sister a Skype session. I need to go back to my room to use my laptop. I wish I could help you get ready."

"It's alright. Have a good Skype session with your mom and Sarah."

"Have a good time tonight." Jacob packed his things, but I had a feeling he would be back here to continue our session when I come back sometime later this evening. Jacob let himself out as I led Nate over to my bedroom. My summer dress was out on the bed and my flats were by the chair.

"Change first into the dress?" Nate asked. I nodded. "I'll get everything set up in the bathroom. I'll be in there." He pointed at the bathroom. I smiled as I walked over to the bed. He made his way into the bathroom and closed the door to give me some privacy. I carefully took off my tank top and slipped off my shorts before putting on Nike pros. I then reached for my dress and put it over my head. I sighed knowing I was not able to zip it up on my own with a cast on. I pulled the dress down and made sure it was right before making my way over to the bathroom.

I walked into the bathroom to see him put a stool in front of the mirror. He had my comb, brush, and curling wand set up and ready to use. He smiled, putting his phone down as I made my way towards the stool.

"You look stunning as always Claire," he said as I sat on the stool. I thanked him as he started brushing my hair to make sure the tangles were out. I would look into the mirror once in a while and watch him concentrate on parting my hair to begin the curling process. There was music playing from his phone.

"You must have done this before." I smiled at the mirror and he glanced up for a moment and smiled.

"Of course. I would do my older sisters' hair sometimes. I eventually became a pro."

"Well, I really appreciate you doing my hair." He began taking parts of my hair and curled it.

"It's really no problem Claire. No older siblings that is away at college?"

"No. I'm an only child."

"Ah okay. So . . . you're a huge Harry Potter fan. Anything else you'd like to add to the list I should be aware of? Besides being a cellist and a musician and all."

"Uh . . . I'm a pretty big fan of One Tree Hill and Vampire Diaries? I binged watch both shows last summer."

"Not possible, you've been probably studying all summer and took those ACTs and SATs. You also had your practicing sessions you do. How could you have possibly had that time?"

"I took them the end of my sophomore year. My private lessons and practice sessions took about five hours out of my day. I also had my small job of babysitting."

"You were a babysitter?"

I nodded. "Kids and dogs."

"I did not know that . . . huh."

We continued with our small talk. We talked a bit about what it was like for me back home for a while before he talked

305

about his family and everything in California. I had gone to California for a brief time. I think I've visited San Francisco before going to Vancouver. My parents always had their conferences and they would invite me to travel with them so I could sightsee. It was a great way for me to travel and explore. Nate eventually was just about done when his phone stopped playing music and started ringing. I saw a picture of Andy and Nate on the screen.

"Could you answer that?" he said. I nodded as I reached for his phone. He continued to do the last bit of my hair.

"Hey Andy," I said.

"Hey Claire! I was wondering if you were almost ready?" he asked. I looked up at the mirror to see Nate nodding his head.

"Yes, I'm just about ready! Nate is finishing up with my hair. He curled it for me."

"Ah, I haven't seen you with your hair curled. I'm sure you look amazing as always. I'll be there in a few minutes. I just entered the lobby."

"Okay. See you then. Bye Andy."

"Bye Claire," Andy chuckled and I smiled. We hung up and I looked towards Nate, who was now finished with my hair. I looked at my reflection and continued to smile.

"Thank you, Nate. You're amazing."

He turned the curling wand off and unplugged it from the outlet. "No problem. You look gorgeous by the way," he said. I stood from the stool and gave him a hug. "Ah, you need to zip up your dress," he chuckled as I pulled away and I felt my cheeks warming up. I completely forgot to ask him to do that earlier. He carefully zipped it up and I turned back around to face him. I thanked him once more.

"By any chance, did Andy tell you where he is taking me tonight?"

He shrugged. "No clue. What I do need is to take a mirror picture with you." I giggled and agreed with him. He moved the stool out of the way and he stood behind me with his chin on my shoulder. I looked at the mirror to see our reflection and I smiled as he wrapped an arm around my waist and the other held his phone getting ready to take the picture. I smiled at us as he took the picture. My dress was as blue as Andy's eyes. "Definitely going on Instagram and Twitter," he said. He carefully unwrapped his arm from me and I heard the door opening and closing from the living room.

I walked into my bedroom and Nate made his way to go into the living room. I went over by the chair and slipped my flats on. I then walked out of my bedroom to see Nate facing me and Andy had his back towards me. Nate glanced my way and I put my finger to my lips. I quickly made my way to Andy. I wrapped both of my arms around his neck and he chuckled turning around. His blue eyes looked down at me with amusement and I smiled shyly.

"You look gorgeous," he whispered to me. I shivered slightly.

"And you look stunning, Miller." I smiled up at him

"Why thank you, Johnson. The curls suit you well. I like it."

"Thank you."

"Not to ruin the moment," Nate interjected. Both Andy and I turned towards him. "I would like to take a picture of my favorite, possibly new couple," he said, holding up his phone. I looked towards Andy and he was glaring at Nate.

"This isn't a date Nate. Chill with the couple thing," Andy said. I smiled faintly as he said that. He respected what I said earlier.

"Fine, I would like to get a picture of my two besties, because they look cute," Nate reiterated. Andy chuckled and I nodded as Andy stood beside me and wrapped one arm around my waist. He also hands his phone over to Nate. We both smiled for the phones. It was unexpected after a moment that I was being pulled towards Andy and wrapped his other arm around me. He was being gentle with my arm and I looked up towards him and he was already smiling down at me.

His cologne had a very pleasant scent. He wore beige shorts with a polo shirt along with Sperry's. I continued to look up towards him with a smile. Tonight would be great.

After we took our pictures, Nate went motherly on us and it was the funniest thing. We both laughed at him as we both made our way out the door, taking nothing serious from Nate. He watched us walk off and down the hall until we were in the elevator.

"Sorry about that. Nate can be . . ."

"It's alright. I'm really excited for this evening. Where to tonight?" I asked curiously. The elevator door opened to the lobby and we both walked out and went through the lobby.

"Somewhere where I think you'll love," Andy chuckled.

"No hint?"

"Nah. It's a surprise."

I followed Andy into the parking lot and arrived in a rental car. I frowned slightly wondering how he could rent a car. "This is Aiden's rental car. He's lending it to me for tonight," he said. I nodded as I stepped into the passenger side. "Hope you're alright with me driving. I don't think you've been in a vehicle with me driving before. I know some people tend to feel uncomfortable when they've never been in a car with that person driving."

"It's alright. Do you want me to be a navigator?" I put on my seatbelt as he turned the engine on and made his way out of the parking lot.

"Nice try Claire. I've got it," he mused. I rolled my eyes playfully and he laughed as he turned on the radio. We had the windows opened and we blasted music we could sing along to. It was a nice thirty-minute drive into the suburbs and we were in a neighborhood that seemed really pretty. I looked around at the big houses and wondered where he could possibly be taking me. It was quiet and a lot calmer than the attractive areas. I saw people taking walks and see kids playing. The smell of a barbeque was existent at one point.

"I hope you like being in nature," Andy said once he turned the radio down and we turned into what seemed to be a lakeside. He found parking before shutting off the engine and took off his seatbelt.

I smiled. "I'm all for scenic views. You knew that." I took my seatbelt off and opened the door. I stepped out and a cool breeze blew through my hair. Andy walked around and over to me as I shut the door. He linked his arm with mine and began leading me towards the direction of the lake. It was a breathtaking view. As we were getting closer, I noticed a big blanket on the ground. There was a picnic basket on top and some candles lit. "Did you spend the day setting this up?" I asked and turned towards him. We stopped just before the blanket and he turned towards me.

"Just a few hours."

"You put in a lot of work," I said softly, feeling guilty. I slipped my flats off and he helped me onto the blanket and sat down with him. "Andy "

Andy smiled and faced me. "It's okay. I thought I'd do something really nice for you. With everything going on, I thought it would be nice to have a relaxing evening and to just hang. Plus, we have to celebrate your acceptance into Michigan. Um . . . that's pretty exciting. Second school you've heard from, right?" I nodded and his smile broadens. He seems really excited for me. "Really Claire, that's amazing. I'm sure you are going to get into the other schools you've applied to," he said. I shrugged as I looked out to the view of the lake. "So, you like the place?"

"I love it Andy. Thank you for bringing me here. It's so beautiful out here." I looked around my surroundings. It was a bit more secluded from the rest of the park. You could hear a few kids from a distance where the playground was. The sun was beginning to set and I relaxed at the mere thought of being out here in nature. It was great to be back in the open.

JACK JOHNSON

It was both Fin and I who were jogging over to Claire's room after we showered. It really sunk into me that I needed to talk to Claire really soon. I lost some time and I had no idea what time Claire would be receiving that phone call this evening. What was I thinking when I made her room so far from everyone? It was like its own small run itself. Once we arrived, I knocked on the door repeatedly. We both knew Andy and Nate would be with her. They were always with her and if not, she was with Ryder, Ben, and Jacob. Our number one priority was to get to her.

The door opened and I saw Nate wrapped in just a towel looking between the both of us very confused. I'd be too. "Uhh, hi guys." He waved awkwardly. He waited for me to say something, but before I could, Fin beat me to it. "Is Claire here?" Fin asked, breaking the silence. Nate frowned at him. I wasn't sure if it was because he had asked about Claire or because he had no idea why we'd suddenly show up. "We need to talk to her cause there's some really important stuff we have to talk about here," Fin said. Nate let us into the suite and I walked in, letting Fin close the door. I saw Jacob on the couch with his laptop, looking towards me in confusion.

"What are you doing here? What the hell is he doing here?" Jacob asked. He pointed to Fin in anger. We didn't have time for this. *Where is Claire?*

I sighed. "We don't have time for this. I really would like to speak to Claire for just a moment. She can kick me out after, but it's important."

"Yeah . . . well she isn't here."

"What do you mean she's not here? Then where is she?" I asked exasperated. My mind began to race for every possible scenario that might happen. I should have come straight here after that call.

"Whoa," Nate said with worry. "Calm down. She's fine. She's with Andy right now. They went out for the evening somewhere."

"N—no, no, this is really bad," I mumbled and closed my eyes. I started to talk to myself and paced back and forth. The various scenarios of Claire finding out did not sit well with me at all now.

"What's going on?" I heard Jacob from a distance. I couldn't really hear anything after that, because it seemed like a blur to me. All I remembered was Jacob looking shocked and Nate panicking trying to get ahold of Andy or Claire. To our luck, no one answered.

CHAPTER FORTY
An End

CLAIRE JOHNSON

Andy is one of the most thoughtful and sweetest guy I've ever met. Tonight has been really great for us and it was going so well. It was thoughtful for him to take time out of his day to set everything up and to even prepare the food. I was surprised he spent time to prepare for our meal tonight. He also made desert. I've enjoyed the entire evening with him, but I never doubted that. The one thing that sat in the back of my head which was quite strange was Shane. That bothered me quite a lot. Well, Shane was sweet too, but that was not my point. I shouldn't be thinking about him when I was trying to enjoy my time with Andy.

I really needed to stop with my comparison. This was not a date. This was making our friendship go further and I knew I could trust Andy like I did with most of the guys here. Andy liked to go out of the way to make things easier for me. It was something I really appreciated about him.

They were looking after me and my sanity. I learned they can be crazy, but they were and have been here for me when I really needed it. Nora too of course. I was thankful to have Nora on this trip. We have had some girl time also when we needed to vent about the guys. Nora knew I wouldn't vent to Ryder, Ben, or Jacob. Excluding Shane, my cousin, and Finnegan, everyone has been very supportive and welcoming. I've never been with a group of people who had made me feel great.

Andy just happened to do more. He wasn't a musician like Jacob and he may not be crazy as Aiden, but he seemed like a guy who I would have liked to meet in high school. He seemed like a guy who was always into photography and social media. Somehow our world would have collided. Andy knew how to be more comforting with words when it came to some things. It feels like I had known him my whole life. It really would have been really cool to have known him before.

I felt myself being swept off my feet and I laughed immediately putting my arms around Andy's neck for support. I looked to him to see he had a look that something was planned. He seemed to always be up to something. He could be so random and spontaneous. I looked the other way and saw we were heading straight for the lake. My eyes widened as I looked back at him and gripping him more.

"Andy Miller! Put me down this instant!" I laughed as he carried me towards the lake still in my dress. "The water is going to be cold!" I could hear him chuckle as he entered the water slowly. I was pretty sure I did not have something to change into. Neither did I plan to be in the water. I hoped he wouldn't go too far in. I wasn't ready to go anywhere past the waist level.

"I promise we won't go deep," he said from underneath me.

"But I'll get my dress wet!" I playfully whined.

"You'll be okay. Really, I promise everything will be alright. We're not going any deeper than this. I swear."

I trusted him, because I have been a little anxious with the water since the night I was thrown in. The day when we all went to the water park, I stayed away from the deep ends. I'm glad he said that.

One moment I was on Andy's shoulders and the next I am in the cold water. I shivered slightly as I opened my eyes and stood up feeling drenched, I turned towards Andy, who had a big smile on his face. I began walking over to him. "How's the water?" he asked innocently. He wasn't going to get away with getting me soaked. It was only fair if he was also soaked.

"Don't really know. How about you see for yourself?" I pushed him off balance with my free hand and he went backwards into the lake. He went under and I smiled, feeling satisfied. I crossed my arm thinking he would come back up right away and laugh, but he doesn't. I wait patiently for him to come back up. It was after twenty seconds of no movement did my smile disappear. I instantly started freaking out when he doesn't come back up for another ten seconds. I frowned and began walking around; feeling my way around for him. Just then, I felt a pair of arms wrap around me from behind and I jumped. I turned around to see him. "You scared me for a moment!" I exclaimed. He laughed with an innocent smile and kissed my forehead.

"You're so adorable when you're scared. Did you know that?" he said. I hit his chest and he smiled. "I won't do it again," he said, hugging me tightly.

"Good," I mumbled. I waited for my heart to return to normal. When we pulled away, I looked at my now soaked cast.

"Look what you've done though. My cast isn't waterproof you know."

"Shoot. I'm so sorry Claire. I did not think that through."

"I'm pretty sure I'm supposed to get it replaced if it were ever to get wet."

"Right, this is my fault. After we're finished here, I can take you to the hospital you went to and replace it."

"I don't have my insurance card with me. We'll have to go back to the room to get it." Andy nodded as he took a look at my now squishy cast.

"We can get it then. I'm really sorry about that."

"It's alright. Everything is covered. It's okay."

Andy nodded as I bent down to splash him with water. I wanted to return to being silly. A smile appeared on his face and he chuckled before he started to do the same thing to me. We splashed around in the water for a bit and took a small walk around the park before making our way back to the blanket.

Once we were back and sitting, I shivered. I was quite cold from head to toe. It was a moment later a towel was wrapped around my shoulders, then a blanket. I laughed lightly wondering where this all had come from.

Andy took a seat next to me with a towel wrapped around him.

Andy chuckled. "I had them both in the trunk. They're from the guest bedroom." I looked towards him. He moved a strand of my hair from my face and tucked it behind my ear. I smiled and leaned my head against his shoulder. I then looked up to the sky and relaxed.

"It's beautiful," I whispered as we listened to the rustling of the trees. I also heard a few crickets from the distance. I loved being here and being able to smell the fresh cut grass. I let my mind focus on the wonderful surroundings around me.

"Not as beautiful as you," he said softly and I knew he was smiling at me. "But I think you and Shane are perfect together," he whispered. A part of me felt some sort of stress signal at the mention of his name and his statement. Why would Andy bring this up? I sighed slightly and sat up to look at him. Why do the guys think Shane and I would be so great even after what happened? I don't quite understand. Andy had a look of worriedness and how I would respond to him.

"Why would you mention Shane? I don't understand why you guys continue to get us together when nothing good happened after our second date? He used me Andy."

He shook his head. "Claire, you know he wouldn't use you. You know it was Fin's doing. Shane would never intentionally hurt you." I shook my head, getting slightly worked about this. Did he

315

bring me here to talk about Shane? I stood up and took the blanket off. Andy stood also.

"You weren't there when he said things he shouldn't have. Andy, I know Fin put him up to this, but that doesn't mean it doesn't hurt. I'm the one who was hurt through this."

"You don't think he was hurt through this?" Andy asked throwing up his hands slightly. "You also don't see that Shane has been miserable as much as you are. I swear you're like a drug to him. We wouldn't be pushing it if we all didn't know what kind of person he is. Shane is innocent."

"I don't want to talk about him Andy, why are you bringing him up?"

"Claire, it has been a week." He clearly didn't understand. A week doesn't fix a broken heart and automatically make me trust someone again. "Shane isn't himself and he's distancing himself from the rest of us, because we've been keeping you two at a distance."

"So, this is my fault now?" I took a step away from Andy feeling a mixture of guilt and blame on myself.

"No . . . Claire. Stop don't do this to yourself," Andy said softly. "Shane would do anything to take the mistakes he has done back if he could. Heck, I'm pretty sure you've made him happier than Nora and any of the guys here."

"I don't trust him right now."

"Give him another chance. We all make mistakes here. Shane is human too and really, you should at least talk to him."

"And now you're going to try talking me into forgiving my cousin too? I told you guys that I'm not ready to speak to either of them. I want time away from them."

"You're being unreasonable Claire." Andy sighed and put his hands through his hair. I looked down at my feet, feeling useless.

"I'm so sorry if words don't have meaning to you," I said softly and hugged myself. "You were not there when Shane used

316

words that deeply hurt me. It did not matter to me if he meant it or not. He knew bringing my parents up would hurt me. Finnegan knew nothing about them. He could have used another way to hurt me. He had the choice to say some of the things he said. If you can't understand that, then take me back to the hotel and leave me alone. I am aware he is hurt, but he has been aware since the first day about my mom. He knows so much. I trusted him and opened up to him. It will take time for me to forgive him and if anything happens to my mom, I will think back to that night Shane told me to go home."

Andy had the guiltiest look on his face. He tried to take a step towards me, but I took a step away from him. I noticed my phone alerting me that someone was calling. I walked past Andy and picked up my phone to see it was the number from the hospital.

"Claire, I'm sorry," Andy said. I looked towards him to see him with a look saying how sorry he was.

"I have to take this right now," I said lightly and looked towards the pavilion by the lake. "I'll be over there for a bit."

Andy nodded. "I'll be here when you come back," he said softly. I nodded as I began making my way over to the pavilion. My hand with the arm cast rested against the thick railing. My heart raced and I felt a lump forming in my throat, remembering the last call wasn't a good one. I answered the call.

"Hello?" I answered lightly.

"Hello Miss Johnson," I heard from the other end. It was Dr. Wright from the hospital. He was also the same doctor I had spoken to last week. "I want to apologize for upsetting you last week with the news of your mother."

"Is she okay? Has she been getting better since then?" I asked, getting nervous now. All of the pain that I felt from the day at school returned to me and the doctor still had yet to mention the news. I wanted it to be painless and receive good news about her but I haven't been the luckiest with news lately.

"Miss Johnson . . . I am very sorry for your loss."

I stood there stunned as I let the words sink into my head. *My loss.* His words repeated in my head. My tears were beginning to fill my view as I tried to pull myself back into reality. *She's gone Claire. She didn't make it.* It suddenly became very hot for me and it became hard for me to breathe. "She passed away this morning," I heard the doctor say hesitantly. I covered my mouth, trying to hold back the sobs. She really is gone.

"Why was I not informed earlier?" I croaked. Why wouldn't I have been informed right after she had passed? What took them this long to call me?

"We were told to wait until this evening. We are ver—"

"What time did she pass?" I interrupted.

"10:23 this morning."

I felt very dizzy suddenly. I leaned against the railing as everything seemed like it was beginning to spin around me. I dropped my phone as I brought my free hand to my face. My vision continued to stay blurred and I felt like I couldn't breathe. The burning sensation in my chest returned and I began sobbing to myself. Is this a mental breakdown I was having?

"Claire!" I heard Andy yell from a distance. I tried to take a step forward, but I felt so off. I wanted nothing more than to forget about the pain. I knew I was going into shock and I was shutting down. I felt myself fading away as I felt like gravity took control.

It felt like I was falling, but I couldn't control myself.

When you feel like you're falling into a deep sleep, there is that pull that makes you break out of it. That was how I felt and I didn't want to break through it. I felt the sudden pain and numbness to my head before I collided to the ground. A shooting pain spread through my head. "Claire!" I heard Andy from a distance but I had a feeling he was actually holding me. It was the last thing I heard before I completely faded into the darkness.

Do you like teen fiction?
Here are samples of other stories
you might enjoy!

Caffeine

LIVIA HALTEH

CHAPTER ONE
Café Latte

"Morning, Aspen. Your usual?"

My tired eyes drifted up to the perky bartender, Vivienne. Her black hair was tied into a high ponytail as her pale fingers rested above the cash register. I gave a weary smile in return.

"You know me too well."

She flashed her pearly teeth at me, typing in the order and accepting my money, then returning my exact change. I made my drowsy way towards an empty table. While Café de Fleur was a gorgeous little café that made the best soy lattes in town, it wasn't the most popular, so finding a table was easy for me.

As I took my seat, I couldn't help but let my eyes drift over to the table beside me, hidden in the very furthest corner of the café. Isaac Hensick sat alone at his usual table, his long tanned fingers slid a graphite pencil across a small sketchpad, about the size of his palm, hidden from my sight.

Beside his muscular arm sat an untouched cup. His soft green eyes fluttered across the page, one step ahead of his hand as he marked the paper with his pencil.

Isaac is a classmate of mine, although he was barely seen in class. To be completely honest, my morning visits to the café were the most I had seen of him all day. He was a popular boy, well-liked—if not loved—across the entire school, but he was definitely not the studious type.

Every morning for the past two years he'd sit on that chair, too focused on his drawings to notice me, and too absorbed in his own world to even sip the coffee he always ordered.

Black coffee, three sugars.

"You're staring again, Aspen." Vivienne's booming voice woke me from my thoughts. "Here's your latte."

I looked up to see Vivienne in front of me, her arms extended with a takeout coffee cup in one hand and a small brown bag containing my usual biscotti in the other.

I flashed an embarrassed smile, taking my order from her hand.

"Thanks Viv," I mumbled gratefully, taking a long sip from my coffee. Almost instantly, my pounding headache was relieved. I let out a sigh in relief as the burning coffee slid down my throat and scalded my tongue.

I grinned up at Vivienne and she sent me a knowing smile.

"Have a good day at school," she said before returning to her counter, busying herself by tidying up the cake display.

"You take care," I replied, my eyes subconsciously moving back to Isaac.

He was in my French class, meaning he'd have to leave now to get there before the bell, but he made no effort to move from his seat. Instead, he stayed occupied with whatever he was drawing. His coffee remained untouched beside his scribbling hand, the steam long gone.

Turning away from him, I opened the door to exit the café and make my way to school. He could miss class as much as he wanted to, but I was going to turn up on time.

As I began my walk to school, I watched the people on the street with familiar faces of neighbors and classmates who probably didn't even know of my existence.

I guess I was what you'd call a wallflower. I was never involved with any school dramas or the subject of the grade's daily gossip. It's not like I minded it, though. It was always fun to observe, to not get caught up in all the drama, even if it made my life completely uneventful.

"Aspen, Aspen!"

At least I had my friends.

I turned to see my best friend Riley bounding through the hallway to reach me at my locker, her little blonde ponytail flying around the back of her head. For a such tiny person, she was always filled with nothing but energy, the exact opposite of me.

We've been friends since the fourth grade, when she stabbed Billy Johnson's hand with a pencil after he spent all lunch pestering me. She received a week's suspension and was forced to begrudgingly write an apology letter to Billy and his family. Ever since then, she was my closest and oldest friend.

"Good morning, Riley." I sighed, closing my locker and turning towards her with an exhausted, lopsided grin.

"Aspen, guess what!" she squealed, not even pausing for me to guess. "Arthur Andrews got a haircut!"

My grin turned into a sarcastic smile.

"Great."

"I know right!"

I chuckled at my best friend before turning to the sudden sound of a horde of teenage girls's squeals.

What do you know, Arthur Andrews really did get a haircut. Riley let out a sigh of admiration, leaning against my shoulder with a dreamy grin.

Her eyes followed Arthur Andrews in all his muscular, tanned glory; his cropped brown waves sitting neatly atop his head. He was the soccer team's captain, and Riley had been crushing on him for months.

"He's so cute. I'd love to go out with him."

I snorted at her, shoving her off my shoulder. "You and a hundred other girls."

"I can dream!"

A laugh spurt from my lips when a hand gently tapped my back. Turning, my eyes met with our other best friend, William.

William was a lanky boy with black hair that fell just above his brown eyes. We had become friends in our first year of high school, when Riley had dragged him out of his introverted bubble to sit with us at lunch.

"Aspen." He inhaled hard. He reached a thin arm out to loop around my shoulders.

"Ew, you're sweating!" I exclaimed, shoving his hand away as he panted frantically.

"I had to run for the bus," he explained, leaning against the lockers as he struggled to catch his breath. His face was all red, and a bead of sweat traced its way down from his forehead. He wiped it off, still wheezing.

"Yeesh, how far did you run for it?" Riley joked, nudging me with an amused look.

He gulped air down hungrily, his cheeks still flaming red.

"Well, I missed the bus," he continued, out of breath. "So I had to walk to school."

We stared at him in silence as I took a sip of my coffee. His story itself was tiring me out and I was already on the verge of collapsing from exhaustion. It had been a long week of minimal sleep, as most could probably tell from the purple bags lining my bloodshot eyes.

"But I saw Mitch on the way," William paused to turn to me, "that's my mom's dag of a boyfriend." He faced Riley again to continue, "So I went the long way behind Picasso's and since it's so long I had to run."

I stifled a giggle with a final sip of my coffee. I wrinkled my nose at the taste—it already turned cold from the short walk to school.

"You're an idiot," Riley scoffed, rolling her eyes at William. "You know, you're going to have to speak to him *sometime*."

"Over my dead body!" William spat, causing Riley and I to laugh in unison.

"William," I began, resting a hand on his arm. "It's not so bad. Give him a chance. I refused to talk to Sabrina's boyfriend for half a year, and now they're planning on getting engaged."

William's face contorted into an expression of horror.

"If my mother marries that buffoon . . ." He took a sharp breath through his nose. "I'm moving to Canada."

Riley found this hilarious, evident through her loud, high-pitched laugh. She squealed in short giggles, slapping William on his back. He fell forward, his lanky body no match for Riley's enthusiasm.

William smiled, clearly proud he had been able to make Riley laugh so hard, and I rolled my eyes at the pair. The warning bell soon rang throughout the hallway, alerting us to start making our way to our classes.

"I'm going to go work on that runaway plan," William muttered, turning to follow the trail of students trudging to their classrooms. "See you at lunch?"

I nodded, and Riley started walking with me towards our French class. William had chosen to take Spanish this year, claiming girls loved a Spanish speaking man which earned the silent treatment from Riley for a week for "betraying our friendship."

I took a step in the opposite direction, my shoes squeaking against the floor and causing her to pause in her tracks.

"I'll meet you there," I said to Riley, holding up my empty coffee cup.

She sent me a curt nod, turning to walk towards our class alone as I headed towards a nearby bin.

Before I knew it, the hallways were cleared, with me being the only person left as I made my way towards the closest rubbish bin. I quickly tossed the empty cardboard cup into the trash can before making my way back to Riley before Mrs. Dubois arrived.

My legs felt heavy as I dragged myself across the hallway. The sound of my shoes squeaking against the linoleum rang through my ears, contributing to the throbbing headache that had returned just behind my eyes.

I pressed my eyes shut, wishing I had gotten a second coffee to get me through first period. My body ached with fatigue, and my arms felt heavy by my side.

Six hours to go.

The sound of running footsteps snapped me out of my self-pitying daze. I peeled my eyes open a second too late when I collided with a sudden well-clothed wall, causing me to shout and trip backwards. Before I could fall, an arm snaked around my back to hold me back from the impact.

I squinted my eyes open, blinking through the confusion the collision caused, only to see the dazzling green eyes of none other than Isaac Hensick, who was studying my face with concern.

His hand gripped my waist tightly, his hair falling in messy locks over his forehead as he leaned forward to hold me. His brow furrowed as he watched me.

"Are you okay?" he asked, his voice raspy.

I nodded, speechless, stumbling out of his arms and on to my own two feet. His eyes sent shivers down my spine, preventing me from looking away. I felt locked, frozen in place, and quickly forgot about my fatigue and the pain coursing through my head.

How did he get to school so fast?

His perfectly pink lips parted once more, letting out that gorgeously raspy voice that I had only heard from a distance in Café de Fleur. His cheeks imprinted with those famous dimples as he spoke.

"Do I know you?"

My heart fluttered from nervousness. I never thought I'd see him this close before. I watched with fear as he narrowed his eyes, scanning my face, a hint of familiarity and confusion lingering behind them.

He was even more gorgeous up close.

Up close, I could see the brown lining in his eyes, blending with the green as it glittered beneath the fluorescents. I could also see the grooves of his dimples in the corners of his grin.

Silence settled between us. I swallowed thickly, my chest swelling with anxiety as I realised I had left an awkwardly long pause since he asked the question.

My throat felt tight and, unable to speak, I shook my head wildly, causing him to frown and wrinkle his brow at me. It felt so strange seeing him up close rather than our usual encounters at the café, if they could even be called that.

"Are you sure? I swear I've seen you before. Are you new here?"

I chewed on my bottom lip anxiously, shaking my head once more and clearing my throat.

How could he not recognise me? Despite being a wallflower, I expected him to at least be aware of my existence from the English class we share. Or the French class; or the art class; or literally from just walking around the same school for the past four years.

"No, I'm sure," I squeaked out, desperate for this awkward encounter to end and my heart to stop pounding so hard.

I clenched my fists, my nails biting into the skin of my palms.

He opened his mouth, ready to speak, when the final bell sounded. My heart began to race as I took the chance to escape.

"Well, that's the bell, better get going!" I rushed, stepping around him as I began to power walk towards my class. "Don't want to be late!"

Mrs. Dubois was way past retirement age, meaning she often turned up to class a little late, but I didn't want to be with Isaac for a moment longer.

I sent a thin-lipped smile and began taking long strides, sliding down the hallway as fast as possible.

His brows rose, and his mouth fell open—ready to speak, but with no words to voice. I kept walking, feeling incredibly awkward and watched as I moved through the halls, rushing to get to my French class nearby.

Nevertheless, I could feel his eyes on my back, tempting me to turn back.

Sending one last glance behind me, I noticed him still staring at me as I sped away from him just as I had suspected.

But I didn't expect his wide eyes to be swimming with one emotion.

Recognition.

If you enjoyed this sample, look for
Caffeine
on Amazon.

Tyler's Gem

Rua Hasan

PROLOGUE

I looked at my reflection with dull eyes while drops of water were dripping from my hair. The steam from the shower was fogging the mirror, but I could still see myself through it. I sometimes thought that maybe, just maybe, one day I would see a different person with happiness and confidence.

I looked in the mirror to see my flaws that I have grown to accept. The flaws everyone used against me, but why should I care?

Yes, I could be a better person. I could walk to school every day with so much confidence that would bring everyone to their knees.

But why haven't I done that yet? Why did I keep on staring at myself every morning as if it would make things better or make a difference for everyone to like me?

My chubby cheeks and fat belly were one of the reasons why nobody liked me. I was the chipmunk of the whole middle school. I would walk around while everyone called me names, emphasizing why I stood out so much.

It had been like this since elementary school. Probably because I was not much of an active person. I would usually stay home all day and watch TV. I didn't like most things except eating. I mean, who wouldn't? It helped ease the stress. My dad owned a pizza shop that was quite known in our little town of Strawberry Forest in California.

Yes, I knew it was a weird name. Our town was known for growing strawberries in the old days that covered our land like a forest.

I used to go to his pizza place every Friday just to have a bite of heaven, which was probably another reason why I became chubby.

I wrapped the towel tighter around my body as I let my short, straight hair fall down to my shoulders.

I really needed to let it grow.

Walking out of the bathroom, I then headed to my closet. I grabbed a pair of baggy jeans and my favorite sweatshirt that my mom bought me on my twelfth birthday. My fashion sense was another thing I needed to fix.

But should I really care about what everyone would think of how I dress?

I put the clothes on, let my wet hair fall down naturally, and climbed down the stairs to smell the scent of my mom's amazing pancakes. I inhaled it happily and skipped towards the kitchen to see my dad sitting down, reading a book while my mom works at the stove.

My dad was the first to notice me and gave me a smile as he put his book down. He then motioned me to come over.

"Good morning, pumpkin," my dad said, catching my mom's attention. She put the pancake she had on the pan into a plate and turned the stove off. She wiped her hands on the towel next to her and turned to look at me.

"Good morning, mom and dad," I said as I kissed each of them on the cheek. I then grabbed the chair next to my dad and sat down, licking my lips as I stared at the plate in front of me with hungry eyes.

"Is my little girl excited to finish school today?" my mom asked.

Who wouldn't be? School was a living hell because of the constant bullying from none other than Tyl—

No! I promised myself I would never bring up his name as long as I'm alive!

Okay, maybe I was exaggerating a bit. Could you blame me when everyone constantly picked on me just because of how I looked, especially if it was only because one person started it?

"Mom, I'm not a little girl anymore." I groaned playfully as I cut a little piece of my pancake and shoved it in my mouth. The delicious taste in my mouth made me want to moan.

My mom took a seat in front of me and smiled as she pinched my cheek.

"Oh, but you'll always be my little girl," she said, attracting my father's attention. He put his book down again and glared at my mom.

"Hey, that's my line," he said.

I rolled my eyes at them, knowing what they were about to start.

My mom leaned against the table as she put her fist under her chin and smiled teasingly.

"Well, I stole it. *Whatcha* going to do about it?" She teased.

"Why, you!" my dad said.

That was my cue to look away. I ate my breakfast quickly before it got cold. It was obvious that I preferred to watch the pancakes over my parents smooching.

I ignored my parents' little playful argument which would lead to a make out season right here in front of me because trust me, it would always make me want to gag. I finished my plate and placed it in the sink. I turned around and found my parents eating each other's faces.

Ew, couldn't they get a room?

"Mom." I whined.

"Dad!" I said a bit louder and heard a knock at the front door.

"I'll get it," I muttered and headed to the door. I looked through the peephole and smiled when I saw who it was. I opened it and jumped into my best friend's arms as I ruffled his hair and messed it up.

I pulled away and smiled seeing Matt's annoyed face. He was probably the only reason I wake up every morning to go to school. He was practically my rock who was always there for me when I needed a shoulder to cry on, and defended me from all the bullying.

It wasn't like he could stop it in general, but his presence would help me cope with it.

We met somewhere in elementary school and clicked instantly. Matt was like the big brother I never had, supporting me through both the ups and the downs.

"What?" I asked with a smirk. He glared at me and pointed at his hair.

"Really? It takes me forever to fix this." He whined as he tried to fix his hair. Sometimes, I thought he cared about his looks more than I cared about mine.

I grinned and shrugged my shoulders.

"Oh, don't be such a grouch! It's the last day of school, lighten up," I said, punching his shoulder. He gave me a small smile and nodded his head.

"Are you ready?" he asked.

"Yeah, just give me a second," I said and ran back into the kitchen. "Mom, dad, I'm leaving." They smiled and engulfed me a big hug and wished me good luck.

My parents knew that I was being picked on, but they didn't really know that I was being bullied every single day by Ty—

No! Not again.

As I was saying, I thought it was best that they didn't know for them not to worry. Besides, they have already reported it to the principal countless times, but nothing happened. It just wouldn't stop.

I went to the front door where Matt was waiting and closed it behind me. The chill of the morning hit my face as the breeze quickened. It was still early, about seven something, but classes wouldn't start until eight.

I was actually excited to finish this day without problems. Matt and I walked to the school which wasn't too far away and talked about summer. Time went by quickly and the next thing I knew, I was in front of the place I hated the most. I started walking down the hall with Matt at my side as I tried to ignore everyone including the snickers made by some girls hanging by their lockers. As long as I wouldn't bump into him today, I would be fine.

When the bell rang, I sprinted out of my seventh period class and down the hall to head to the school gates at the edge of the school's parking lot. I would usually head towards that direction to meet Matt and walk home together afterwards. Surprisingly, this day just went by simply. I mean, I got called with names a few times, but there was nothing new. I guess everyone was too busy to go home from school and begin their summer vacation, so I wasn't their priority today.

Matt and I usually took our lunch together, and as I went between my classes, I would hide in the mass of children who were bumping into each other to avoid being spotted by my enemy.

Luck was on my side for not seeing him today. I stepped out of the door at the end of the hallway, walked to the parking lot, and looked around for Matt but couldn't see him. I assumed that I was early so I waited under a tree that was planted on the side of the gate. After all, it wasn't the first time he was late.

Suddenly, my vision blurred as something cold hit my head. I squealed in surprise and wrapped my arms around me. When I opened my eyes, I heard laughter echoing through the air and found myself soaking wet.

I wiped the water blurring my vision and looked up in the branches to see two boys, holding empty buckets and laughing their butts off. I was embarrassed, and I felt tears run through my cheeks, but I held them back.

Why would they do this to me? All I wanted was to go home and forget about the worst seven hours of my life that I had to repeat five times a week. All I wanted was to have a normal life like everyone else.

I pushed those thoughts away and was about to shout at the boys when someone else called my name. Shivers ran down my spine as I feared what I was about to face.

Taking a deep breath, I looked upon the face that I hated the most—the one who made my life a living hell.

Tyler Grey was holding something in his hand which I thought a water balloon.

"Just a little reminder of me throughout your summer," he said with a smirk, and threw the balloon at me before I could even move.

Paint. It was paint.

The boys up in the tree climbed down and walked over to Tyler. They were barely able to contain themselves from laughing and gave him a pat on the back. It was then that I could no longer control the tears in my eyes from running down my cheeks. I saw Tyler's eyes glaring at me, and clenched my fists as I watched them walk away with taunting smiles as if they had just won the lottery.

I took a shaky breath as the tears blurred my vision. My day spiraled from ten all the way to a zero because of him. I was freaking wet and my favorite grey sweatshirt now turned pink. I fell to the ground as I sobbed with my knees on my chest and hid my head.

I heard Matt call out from a distance, but I didn't pay attention. My mind was clogged and overflowing with hateful thoughts toward Tyler Grey.

My eyes were blinded from any light that I could have seen. My ears were plugged with his words. He got what he wanted; I was never going to forget him this summer. His face would forever haunt my mind.

CHAPTER 1

I stepped out of the taxi and paid the driver his tip. My long, tan legs resembled like hotdogs that were being heated under the bright, shining sun. I pulled the sunglasses away from my eyes and rested them on my head, looking around the place I used to call home where I lived many years ago.

Once I was completely alone in the quiet, familiar streets, I made my way to the house, and could instantly tell that not much had changed. The grass was as green as ever, and the birds were flying from branch to branch. It was as if I had never left. Although, it did look like it needed some dusting and a few plants in the front yard. But other than that, everything was fine.

I had argued with myself countless times about whether to buy a new house or just come back to this place. My childhood wasn't quite the best, but I would always choose my heart's desire. It wanted to go back home—to the place where I was raised.

I decided to come back to this small town everyone called Strawberry Forest. Was going back to the same house that hold good yet disturbing memories a good idea? Would I enjoy my life here? Or would I just end up regretting my decision?

I walked to the front door and stared at it for what seemed to be hours but were only seconds. Was I ready to face the past? Coming back here after so many years could be a good thing. I may had been away for so long, but it wasn't enough to help me erase and forget the dreadful memories of what this house and town gave me. Nevertheless, I couldn't exactly stop now. I was here for a reason, and that was to stop running away. I had to face reality.

I looked around to see that the house next to us was a bit different than I remembered. Its paint was in a different color and had a different vibe radiating from it. The decorations were of a different taste than that of the previous owner.

New neighbors perhaps?

I finally gathered all the courage that I had and grabbed the keys in my pocket. I opened the door and it creaked as I opened it slowly. Dust flew in the air as the house had not been touched for years. I took a step into the house, and looked around to see memories of the past flood my mind.

The interior and furniture were untouched. I didn't want anything removed when I moved away. I didn't even let my grandma sell it, knowing that I would be back one day.

I closed the door and realized that I would need help in cleaning this place; I didn't think I could do it alone. I grabbed my phone from my bag to send my best friend a text message on my arrival, telling him that I would be expecting his presence in a couple of minutes. I rubbed my eyes to prevent the tears from falling. I was done running away and was going to start a new life now that I had returned. A life that would make my parents proud.

*   *   *

Three years ago

I walked up to the front door as I wiped the water off my face with the napkin Matt gave me. Matt had been furious throughout the entire walk. He was ranting about how people could be so cruel, especially on the last day of school. Well, we were talking about Tyler Grey so I wasn't surprised.

He also blamed himself for being late. In his mind, if he was there sooner then maybe he could have prevented it. I disagreed and told him that it was fine. My life had been like this for years so I was pretty used to it.

After saying our 'goodbyes' a couple of blocks away, I stood right outside the front door, too afraid to face my parents. What would they say if they saw me like this? They would definitely freak out.

What would I tell them?

I could just lie and say that it was a goodbye prank from a couple of friends. Or, that there was this activity in school where we fought with water balloons. But of course, that would be such a lame lie, and they would not believe me. They knew me too well, and would be suspicious of the pink paint that stained all over my sweatshirt.

I decided to just tell them the truth and get it over with.

I rang the doorbell, waiting for the door to open. Moments passed as I stared at the door and rang the doorbell again, assuming they may have just not heard the first attempt. I waited another minute or two until I figured out no one was going to open the door. I rolled my eyes and guessed that my parents were probably up in their room making out because this wasn't the first time they've been getting it on while I waited outside.

Sighing, I grabbed the pot that had a plant in it and dug for the emergency key to open the door. I walked in to see no one. I took the risk of going upstairs to my parents' room and was surprised to hear nothing and thought that maybe they have fallen asleep.

Pft, come on. Who sleeps at this time?

I knocked on the door and waited for an answer, but nothing happened. I knocked again but this time, I opened the door to stare at nothing. There was no one in the room. It was completely empty as if it haven't been touched since I had left for school.

I ran down stairs to the kitchen and saw that my mom haven't made dinner at all. Well, that was strange. My parents used to leave something for me to eat before going somewhere else. It wasn't that I was always hungry; I just found it strange.

I walked into the living room and grabbed the house phone. I dialed my mom's number, but no one answered. I dialed dad's number, but he didn't answer either.

I was just about to go upstairs to my room when the doorbell rang. I skipped toward the front door thinking it might be them. When I peeped through the peephole, it wasn't my parents standing outside but two men wearing police uniforms.

I opened the door and stared up at the strangers who were standing in front of me, both of whom gave me sympathetic looks for some unknown reason. I lifted an eyebrow in confusion.

"Can I help you officers?"

They both glanced at each other then looked at me.

"You must be Crystal Clare," one of them said.

I nodded my head slowly, wondering why and how they knew my name.

"Yes, that's me. Is there something wrong?" I asked nervously.

"Yes. Unfortunately, your parents were in an accident, and we need to take you to the police station for some information."

My eyes widened, and my heart started to beat so fast that I could feel it hitting my chest. I felt a lump form in my throat as his words sunk into my brain and my world started to spin.

"An accident?" I gasped softly.

I felt tears form in my eyes, and my palms began to sweat.

"Are they okay?" I asked.

I couldn't imagine living without my parents. They were one of the reasons I stayed positive in life. They were amazingly supportive and always gave me warm hugs when I needed them.

If something were to happen to them, then I would be in this life all on my own. I didn't have anyone else here in this small town to take care of me. My life would become way worse than it already was.

One of the policemen took off the cap he was wearing and looked down at me with tender eyes, shaking his head.

"I'm sorry for your loss," he said.

After hearing those words, I couldn't stop the tears from flowing. My parents were dead.

*   *   *

I snapped out of my thoughts when I heard the doorbell rang. I took the sunglasses off my head, placed them on the counter, walked over to the front door, and took my shoes off. I looked through the peephole and smiled.

I quickly yanked the door open only to face the sight of Matt holding a broom.

"Matt!"

I jumped into his arms, causing him to drop the broom as he wrapped his arms around my waist. He picked me up off the ground, and our laughter filled the air.

He put me down on my feet and smiled, showing me his straight white teeth. He then looked at me from head to toe and whistled as he gave me a wolf grin.

I laughed as I punched his shoulder playfully.

"Oh my god! It's been ages," I said, letting him in before closing the door behind me.

"Yeah, I know, right? How have you been?" he asked.

"I've been good. What about you?"

It's been a very long time since I've seen Matt. But ever since I've moved to my grandparents' house in New York four years ago, we have been keeping in touch by using *Facebook* and *FaceTime*. Later on, I bought my own phone, and we called each other every day.

"Better now that you're here," he answered, as we walked toward the living room.

"You look the same like I never left," I said.

He still looked and felt like the Matt I knew many years ago, except that he had grown much taller and broader with facial hair.

"You...well, you look—"

"Different?" I asked.

He shook his head and gave me a smile wrapping his arm around my shoulders.

"Beautifuler," he said.

"That's not even a word, idiot." I chuckled, punching his shoulder again.

"It is for me," he said.

I smiled at his compliment.

Now, don't get me wrong. It wasn't like in the past four years I've been trying to change myself and get skinnier so that everyone would like me. No, that's not what happened.

I got depressed when my parents died and lived in a place I'm not familiar with. I had to meet new people which I wasn't a big fan of, but I found a solution to deal with it.

No, it wasn't drugs or alcohol. It was exercise. I would go out for a run and feel free. I wouldn't stop until I was panting for air and soaked all my clothes with my own sweat.

Doing the same routine every day, running became a hobby and made me into how I looked today.

"I hope you're ready because this place needs some cleaning," I said, as I grabbed his broom and threw it at him.

"Some?" he asked, as he grabbed the broom. "You mean, a lot. This place hasn't been touched in ages."

I cleaned the kitchen while Matt got to work in the living room. My house didn't seem huge when I lived here with my parents. We had two bedrooms upstairs and a bathroom. But now that I was going to live here all alone, it seemed so big and lonely.

I thought about it a lot and came to a conclusion that I wouldn't be moving out anytime soon. This place was sentimental, and I couldn't just let it go. I was pretty sure this was what my parents would have wanted, and I booked the nearest flight ticket to return home, the minute I turned eighteen. I've been planning that ever since I've left.

I was never close to my grandparents. I appreciated them for taking me in though, but I knew that once I turn eighteen, I'd be on my own.

After an hour and a half later, Matt and I were done cleaning the first floor. I walked out of the bathroom after cleaning myself up and saw Matt in the kitchen drinking some water.

"Let's take a break and have something to eat. I'm pretty sure you're hungry," he said.

I watched as Matt took his phone out and ordered pizza. I took two cups and a bottle of *Pepsi* to the living room and placed them on the coffee table in front of the couch. I sat down and grabbed my phone out since the TV wasn't working, and it needed some fixing with the wires and stuff.

Matt walked into the room and sat next to me. We spent time talking about everything that happened in the past four years and how the people at school were sorry for me and my loss. I wasn't planning on holding grudges against anyone, but I could never forget what they have done to me.

I told him about New York and how awesome it was. But I guess I was just a Californian girl who could never trade California for any city. I was born here after all.

Twenty minutes later, a knock was heard on the door. Matt got up to open it while I sipped on the Pepsi I had in my hand. I wasn't such a big fan of soda and preferred juice more, but there wasn't any in the fridge at the moment. I needed to buy groceries.

Matt came back with a box of pizza in his hand. I licked my lips as my stomach grumbled in hunger. When the box was opened, we dug in and ate until we were full. We pretty much finished the box, but you can't blame us. It's been a long day.

We sat in silence, gathering our thoughts until Matt spoke.

"You ready for school on Monday?" he asked.

I sighed. I knew this topic was going to be brought up. Besides, I still had to go to school.

I wished I could delay the time of me having to go to school sooner.

"Yeah," I said, nodding my head. Let's just hope that some things have changed while I was gone.

If you enjoyed this sample, look for
Tyler's Gem
on Amazon.

ACKNOWLEDGEMENTS

To my family, friends, and peers on Wattpad for the many years of encouragement and memories made bonding.

AUTHOR'S NOTE

Thank you so much for reading *Alone*! I can't express how grateful I am for reading something that was once just a thought inside my head.

I'd love to hear your thoughts on the book. Please leave a review on Amazon or Goodreads because I just love reading your comments and getting to know you!

Can't wait to hear from you!

Samantha S. Webb

ABOUT THE AUTHOR

Samantha Webb is a student athlete studying biology at a university. She is part of the Track & Field team and her main event is pole vaulting. Samantha had come from a strong background of gymnastics before she had picked up a pole. Music has always been a part of Samantha's life. The idea of creation and imagination within an instrument fascinated her. She played the violin for twelve years and sang in choir for fourteen years. Music and the sciences has always been a passion for Samantha. She hopes to continue her future in creating music and exploring within the science field.

Made in United States
North Haven, CT
08 November 2021

10957865R00197